T0162442

Mysterious and Horrific Stories

Mysterious and Horrific Stories

Joseph Sheridan Le Fanu

MINT EDITIONS

Mysterious and Horrific Stories features stories first published between 1838–1872.

This edition published by Mint Editions 2021.

ISBN 9781513211855 | E-ISBN 9781513210650

Published by Mint Editions®

MINT
EDITIONS

minteditionbooks.com

Publishing Director: Jennifer Newens
Design & Production: Rachel Lopez Metzger
Project Manager: Micaela Clark
Typesetting: Westchester Publishing Services

More in This Series
Weird and Horrific Stories
Fantastic and Horrific Stories
Romantic and Horrific Stories
Scientific and Horrific Stories

Contents

An Account of Some Strange Disturbances
in Aungier Street   7

A Chapter in the History of a Tyrone Family   26

An Authentic Narrative of a Haunted House   60

The Child That Went with the Fairies   71

The Drunkard's Dream   80

The Fortunes of Sir Robert Ardagh   91

The Murdered Cousin   113

The Mysterious Lodger   142

The Phantom Fourth   191

Sir Dominick's Bargain: A Legend of Dunoran   203

The Spectre Lovers   216

Squire Toby's Will: A Ghost Story   227

Stories of Lough Guir   255

Schalken the Painter   265

The Vision of Tom Chuff   283

An Account of Some Strange
Disturbances in Aungier Street

It is not worth telling, this story of mine—at least, not worth writing. Told, indeed, as I have sometimes been called upon to tell it, to a circle of intelligent and eager faces, lighted up by a good after-dinner fire on a winter's evening, with a cold wind rising and wailing outside, and all snug and cosy within, it has gone off—though I say it, who should not—indifferent well. But it is a venture to do as you would have me. Pen, ink, and paper are cold vehicles for the marvellous, and a "reader" decidedly a more critical animal than a "listener." If, however, you can induce your friends to read it after nightfall, and when the fireside talk has run for a while on thrilling tales of shapeless terror; in short, if you will secure me the *mollia tempora fandi*, I will go to my work, and say my say, with better heart. Well, then, these conditions presupposed, I shall waste no more words, but tell you simply how it all happened.

My cousin (Tom Ludlow) and I studied medicine together. I think he would have succeeded, had he stuck to the profession; but he preferred the Church, poor fellow, and died early, a sacrifice to contagion, contracted in the noble discharge of his duties. For my present purpose, I say enough of his character when I mention that he was of a sedate but frank and cheerful nature; very exact in his observance of truth, and not by any means like myself—of an excitable or nervous temperament.

My Uncle Ludlow—Tom's father—while we were attending lectures, purchased three or four old houses in Aungier Street, one of which was unoccupied. *He* resided in the country, and Tom proposed that we should take up our abode in the untenanted house, so long as it should continue unlet; a move which would accomplish the double end of settling us nearer alike to our lecture-rooms and to our amusements, and of relieving us from the weekly charge of rent for our lodgings.

Our furniture was very scant—our whole equipage remarkably modest and primitive; and, in short, our arrangements pretty nearly as simple as those of a bivouac. Our new plan was, therefore, executed almost as soon as conceived. The front drawing-room was our sitting-room. I had the bedroom over it, and Tom the back bedroom on the same floor, which nothing could have induced me to occupy.

The house, to begin with, was a very old one. It had been, I believe, newly fronted about fifty years before; but with this exception, it had nothing modern about it. The agent who bought it and looked into the titles for my uncle, told me that it was sold, along with much other forfeited property, at Chichester House, I think, in 1702; and had belonged to Sir Thomas Hacket, who was Lord Mayor of Dublin in James II's time. How old it was *then*, I can't say; but, at all events, it had seen years and changes enough to have contracted all that mysterious and saddened air, at once exciting and depressing, which belongs to most old mansions.

There had been very little done in the way of modernising details; and, perhaps, it was better so; for there was something queer and by-gone in the very walls and ceilings—in the shape of doors and windows—in the odd diagonal site of the chimney-pieces—in the beams and ponderous cornices—not to mention the singular solidity of all the woodwork, from the banisters to the window-frames, which hopelessly defied disguise, and would have emphatically proclaimed their antiquity through any conceivable amount of modern finery and varnish.

An effort had, indeed, been made, to the extent of papering the drawing-rooms; but somehow, the paper looked raw and out of keeping; and the old woman, who kept a little dirt-pie of a shop in the lane, and whose daughter—a girl of two and fifty—was our solitary handmaid, coming in at sunrise, and chastely receding again as soon as she had made all ready for tea in our state apartment;—this woman, I say, remembered it, when old Judge Horrocks (who, having earned the reputation of a particularly "hanging judge," ended by hanging himself, as the coroner's jury found, under an impulse of "temporary insanity," with a child's skipping-rope, over the massive old bannisters) resided there, entertaining good company, with fine venison and rare old port. In those halcyon days, the drawing-rooms were hung with gilded leather, and, I dare say, cut a good figure, for they were really spacious rooms.

The bedrooms were wainscoted, but the front one was not gloomy; and in it the cosiness of antiquity quite overcame its sombre associations. But the back bedroom, with its two queerly-placed melancholy windows, staring vacantly at the foot of the bed, and with the shadowy recess to be found in most old houses in Dublin, like a large ghostly closet, which, from congeniality of temperament, had amalgamated with the bedchamber, and dissolved the partition. At night-time, this "alcove"— as our "maid" was wont to call it—had, in my eyes, a specially sinister and suggestive character. Tom's distant and solitary candle glimmered vainly into its darkness. *There* it was always overlooking him—always itself impenetrable. But this was only part of the effect. The whole room was, I can't tell how, repulsive to me. There was, I suppose, in its proportions and features, a latent discord—a certain mysterious and indescribable relation, which jarred indistinctly upon some secret sense of the fitting and the safe, and raised indefinable suspicions and apprehensions of the imagination. On the whole, as I began by saying, nothing could have induced me to pass a night alone in it.

I had never pretended to conceal from poor Tom my superstitious weakness; and he, on the other hand, most unaffectedly ridiculed my tremors. The sceptic was, however, destined to receive a lesson, as you shall hear.

We had not been very long in occupation of our respective dormitories, when I began to complain of uneasy nights and disturbed sleep. I was, I suppose, the more impatient under this annoyance, as I was usually a sound sleeper, and by no means prone to nightmares. It was now, however, my destiny, instead of enjoying my customary repose, every night to "sup full of horrors." After a preliminary course of disagreeable and frightful dreams, my troubles took a definite form, and the same vision, without an appreciable variation in a single detail, visited me at least (on an average) every second night in the week.

Now, this dream, nightmare, or infernal illusion—which you please—of which I was the miserable sport, was on this wise:—

I saw, or thought I saw, with the most abominable distinctness, although at the time in profound darkness, every article of furniture and accidental arrangement of the chamber in which I lay. This, as you know, is incidental to ordinary nightmare. Well, while in this clairvoyant condition, which seemed but the lighting up of the theatre in which was to be exhibited the monotonous tableau of horror, which made my nights insupportable, my attention invariably became, I know not why, fixed upon the windows opposite the foot of my bed; and, uniformly with the same effect, a sense of dreadful anticipation always took slow but sure possession of me. I became somehow conscious of a sort of horrid but undefined preparation going forward in some unknown quarter, and by some unknown agency, for my torment; and, after an interval, which always seemed to me of the same length, a picture suddenly flew up to the window, where it remained fixed, as if by an electrical attraction, and my discipline of horror then commenced, to last perhaps for hours. The picture thus mysteriously glued to the window-panes, was the portrait of an old man, in a crimson flowered silk dressing-gown, the folds of which I could now describe, with a countenance embodying a strange mixture of intellect, sensuality, and power, but withal sinister and full of malignant omen. His nose was hooked, like the beak of a vulture; his eyes large, grey, and prominent, and lighted up with a more than mortal cruelty and coldness. These features were surmounted by a crimson velvet cap, the hair that peeped from under which was white with age, while the eyebrows retained their original blackness. Well I remember every line, hue, and shadow of that stony countenance, and well I may! The gaze of this hellish visage was fixed upon me, and mine returned it with the inexplicable fascination of nightmare, for what appeared to me to be hours of agony. At last—

The cock he crew, away then flew

the fiend who had enslaved me through the awful watches of the night; and, harassed and nervous, I rose to the duties of the day.

I had—I can't say exactly why, but it may have been from the exquisite anguish and profound impressions of unearthly horror, with which this strange phantasmagoria was associated—an insurmountable antipathy to describing the exact nature of my nightly troubles to my friend and comrade. Generally, however, I told him that I was haunted by abominable dreams; and, true to the imputed materialism of medicine, we put our heads together to dispel my horrors, not by exorcism, but by a tonic.

I will do this tonic justice, and frankly admit that the accursed portrait began to intermit its visits under its influence. What of that? Was this singular apparition—as full of character as of terror—therefore the creature of my fancy, or the invention of my poor stomach? Was it, in short, *subjective* (to borrow the technical slang of the day) and not the palpable aggression and intrusion of an external agent? That, good friend, as we will both admit, by no means follows. The evil spirit, who enthralled my senses in the shape of that portrait, may have been just as near me, just as energetic, just as malignant, though I saw him not. What means the whole moral code of revealed religion regarding the due keeping of our own bodies, soberness, temperance, etc.? here is an obvious connexion between the material and the invisible; the healthy tone of the system, and its unimpaired energy, may, for aught we can tell, guard us against influences which would otherwise render life itself terrific. The mesmerist and the electro-biologist will fail upon

JOSEPH SHERIDAN LE FANU

an average with nine patients out of ten—so may the evil spirit. Special conditions of the corporeal system are indispensable to the production of certain spiritual phenomena. The operation succeeds sometimes—sometimes fails—that is all.

I found afterwards that my would-be sceptical companion had his troubles too. But of these I knew nothing yet. One night, for a wonder, I was sleeping soundly, when I was roused by a step on the lobby outside my room, followed by the loud clang of what turned out to be a large brass candlestick, flung with all his force by poor Tom Ludlow over the banisters, and rattling with a rebound down the second flight of stairs; and almost concurrently with this, Tom burst open my door, and bounced into my room backwards, in a state of extraordinary agitation.

I had jumped out of bed and clutched him by the arm before I had any distinct idea of my own whereabouts. There we were—in our shirts—standing before the open door—staring through the great old banister opposite, at the lobby window, through which the sickly light of a clouded moon was gleaming.

"What's the matter, Tom? What's the matter with you? What the devil's the matter with you, Tom?" I demanded shaking him with nervous impatience.

He took a long breath before he answered me, and then it was not very coherently.

"It's nothing, nothing at all—did I speak?—what did I say?—where's the candle, Richard? It's dark; I—I had a candle!"

"Yes, dark enough," I said; "but what's the matter?—what *is* it?—why don't you speak, Tom?—have you lost your wits?—what is the matter?"

"The matter?—oh, it is all over. It must have been a dream—nothing at all but a dream—don't you think so? It could not be anything more than a dream."

"Of *course*" said I, feeling uncommonly nervous, "it *was* a dream."

"I thought," he said, "there was a man in my room, and—and I jumped out of bed; and—and—where's the candle?"

"In your room, most likely," I said, "shall I go and bring it?"

"No; stay here—don't go; it's no matter—don't, I tell you; it was all a dream. Bolt the door, Dick; I'll stay here with you—I feel nervous. So, Dick, like a good fellow, light your candle and open the window—I am in a *shocking state*."

I did as he asked me, and robing himself like Granuaile in one of my blankets, he seated himself close beside my bed.

Everybody knows how contagious is fear of all sorts, but more especially that particular kind of fear under which poor Tom was at that moment labouring. I would not have heard, nor I believe would he have recapitulated, just at that moment, for half the world, the details of the hideous vision which had so unmanned him.

"Don't mind telling me anything about your nonsensical dream, Tom," said I, affecting contempt, really in a panic; "let us talk about something else; but it is quite plain that this dirty old house disagrees with us both, and hang me if I stay here any longer, to be pestered with indigestion and—and—bad nights, so we may as well look out for lodgings—don't you think so?—at once."

Tom agreed, and, after an interval, said—

"I have been thinking, Richard, that it is a long time since I saw my father, and I have made up my mind to go down tomorrow and return in a day or two, and you can take rooms for us in the meantime."

I fancied that this resolution, obviously the result of the vision which had so profoundly scared him, would probably vanish next morning with the damps and shadows of night. But I was mistaken. Off went Tom at peep of day to the country, having agreed that so soon as I had secured suitable lodgings, I was to recall him by letter from his visit to my Uncle Ludlow.

Now, anxious as I was to change my quarters, it so happened, owing to a series of petty procrastinations and accidents, that nearly a week elapsed before my bargain was made and my letter of recall on the wing to Tom; and, in the meantime, a trifling adventure or two had occurred to your humble servant, which, absurd as they now appear, diminished by distance, did certainly at the time serve to whet my appetite for change considerably.

A night or two after the departure of my comrade, I was sitting by my bedroom fire, the door locked, and the ingredients of a tumbler of hot whisky-punch upon the crazy spider-table; for, as the best mode of keeping the

Black spirits and white,
Blue spirits and grey,

with which I was environed, at bay, I had adopted the practice recommended by the wisdom of my ancestors, and "kept my spirits up by pouring spirits down." I had thrown aside my volume of Anatomy, and was treating myself by way of a tonic, preparatory to my punch and bed, to half-a-dozen pages of the *Spectator*, when I heard a step on the flight of stairs descending from the attics. It was two o'clock, and the streets were as silent as a churchyard—the sounds were, therefore, perfectly distinct. There was a slow, heavy tread, characterised by the emphasis and deliberation of age, descending by the narrow staircase from above; and, what made the sound more singular, it was plain that the feet which produced it were perfectly bare, measuring the descent with something between a pound and a flop, very ugly to hear.

I knew quite well that my attendant had gone away many hours before, and that nobody but myself had any business in the house. It was quite plain also that the person who was coming down stairs had no intention whatever of concealing his movements; but, on the contrary, appeared disposed to make even more noise, and proceed more deliberately, than was at all necessary. When the step reached the foot of the stairs outside my room, it seemed to stop; and I expected every moment to see my door open spontaneously, and give admission to the original of my detested portrait. I was, however, relieved in a few seconds by hearing the descent renewed, just in the same manner, upon the staircase leading down to the drawing-rooms, and thence, after another pause, down the next flight, and so on to the hall, whence I heard no more.

Now, by the time the sound had ceased, I was wound up, as they say, to a very unpleasant pitch of excitement. I listened, but there was not a stir. I screwed up my courage to a decisive experiment—opened my door, and in a stentorian voice bawled over the banisters, "Who's there?" There was no answer but the ringing of my own voice through the empty old house,—no renewal of the movement; nothing, in short, to give my unpleasant sensations a definite direction. There is, I think, something most disagreeably disenchanting in the sound of one's own voice under such circumstances, exerted in solitude, and in vain. It redoubled my sense of isolation, and my misgivings increased on perceiving that the door, which I certainly thought I had left open, was closed behind me; in a vague alarm, lest my retreat should be cut off, I got again into my room as quickly as I could, where I remained in a state of imaginary blockade, and very uncomfortable indeed, till morning.

Next night brought no return of my barefooted fellow-lodger; but the night following, being in my bed, and in the dark—somewhere, I suppose, about the same hour as before, I distinctly heard the old fellow again descending from the garrets.

This time I had had my punch, and the *morale* of the garrison was consequently excellent. I jumped out of bed, clutched the poker as I passed the expiring fire, and in a moment was upon the lobby. The sound had ceased by this time—the dark and chill were discouraging; and, guess my horror, when I saw, or thought I saw, a black monster, whether in the shape of a man or a bear I could not say, standing, with its back to the wall, on the lobby, facing me, with a pair of great greenish eyes shining dimly out. Now, I must be frank, and confess that the cupboard which displayed our plates and cups stood just there, though at the moment I did not recollect it. At the same time I must honestly say, that making every allowance for an excited imagination, I never could satisfy myself that I was made the dupe of my own fancy in this matter; for this apparition, after one or two shiftings of shape, as if in the act of incipient transformation, began, as it seemed on second thoughts, to advance upon me in its original form. From an instinct of terror rather than of courage, I hurled the poker, with all my force, at its head; and to the music of a horrid crash made my way into my room, and double-locked the door. Then, in a minute more, I heard the horrid bare feet walk down the stairs, till the sound ceased in the hall, as on the former occasion.

If the apparition of the night before was an ocular delusion of my fancy sporting with the dark outlines of our cupboard, and if its horrid eyes were nothing but a pair of inverted teacups, I had, at all events, the satisfaction of having launched the poker with admirable effect, and in true "fancy" phrase, "knocked its two daylights into one," as the commingled fragments of my tea-service testified. I did my best to gather comfort and courage from these evidences; but it would not do. And then what could I say of those horrid bare feet, and the regular tramp, tramp, tramp, which measured the distance of the entire staircase through the solitude of my haunted dwelling, and at an hour when no good influence was stirring? Confound it!—the whole affair was abominable. I was out of spirits, and dreaded the approach of night.

It came, ushered ominously in with a thunder-storm and dull torrents of depressing rain. Earlier than usual the streets grew silent; and by twelve o'clock nothing but the comfortless pattering of the rain was to be heard.

I made myself as snug as I could. I lighted *two* candles instead of one. I forswore bed, and held myself in readiness for a sally, candle in hand; for, *coûte qui coûte*, I was resolved to *see* the being, if visible at all, who troubled the nightly stillness of my mansion. I was fidgetty and nervous and tried in vain to interest myself with my books. I walked up and down my room, whistling in turn martial and hilarious music, and listening ever and anon for the dreaded noise. I sate down and stared at the square label on the solemn and reserved-looking black bottle, until "FLANAGAN & Co's BEST OLD MALT WHISKY" grew into a sort of subdued accompaniment to all the fantastic and horrible speculations which chased one another through my brain.

Silence, meanwhile, grew more silent, and darkness darker. I listened in vain for the rumble of a vehicle, or the dull clamour of a distant row. There was nothing but the sound of a rising wind, which had succeeded the thunder-storm that had travelled over the Dublin mountains quite out of hearing. In the middle of this great city I began to feel myself alone with nature, and Heaven knows what beside. My courage was ebbing. Punch, however, which makes beasts of so many, made a man of me again—just in time to hear with tolerable nerve and firmness the lumpy, flabby, naked feet deliberately descending the stairs again.

I took a candle, not without a tremour. As I crossed the floor I tried to extemporise a prayer, but stopped short to listen, and never finished it. The steps continued. I confess I hesitated for some seconds at the door before I took heart of grace and opened it. When I peeped out the lobby was perfectly empty—there was no monster standing on the staircase; and as the detested sound ceased, I was reassured enough to venture forward nearly to the banisters. Horror of horrors! within a stair or two beneath the spot where I stood the unearthly tread smote the floor. My eye caught something in motion; it was about the size of Goliah's foot—it was grey, heavy, and flapped with a dead weight from one step to another. As I am alive, it was the most monstrous grey rat I ever beheld or imagined.

Shakespeare says—"Some men there are cannot abide a gaping pig, and some that are mad if they behold a cat." I went well-nigh out of my wits when I beheld this *rat*; for, laugh at me as you may, it fixed upon me, I thought, a perfectly human expression of malice; and, as it shuffled about and looked up into my face almost from between my feet, I saw, I could swear it—I felt it then, and know it now, the infernal gaze and the accursed countenance of my old friend in the portrait, transfused into the visage of the bloated vermin before me.

I bounced into my room again with a feeling of loathing and horror I cannot describe, and locked and bolted my door as if a lion had been at the other side. D—n him or *it*; curse the portrait and its original! I felt in my soul that the rat—yes, the *rat*, the RAT I had just seen, was that evil being in masquerade, and rambling through the house upon some infernal night lark.

Next morning I was early trudging through the miry streets; and, among other transactions, posted a peremptory note recalling Tom. On my return, however, I found a note from my absent "chum," announcing his intended return next day. I was doubly rejoiced at this, because I had succeeded in getting rooms; and because the change of scene and return of my comrade were rendered specially pleasant by the last night's half ridiculous half horrible adventure.

I slept extemporaneously in my new quarters in Digges' Street that night, and next morning returned for breakfast to the haunted mansion, where I was certain Tom would call immediately on his arrival.

I was quite right—he came; and almost his first question referred to the primary object of our change of residence.

"Thank God," he said with genuine fervour, on hearing that all was arranged. "On *your* account I am delighted. As to myself, I assure you that no earthly consideration could have induced me ever again to pass a night in this disastrous old house."

"Confound the house!" I exclaimed, with a genuine mixture of fear and detestation, "we have not had a pleasant hour since we came to live here"; and so I went on, and related incidentally my adventure with the plethoric old rat.

"Well, if that were *all*," said my cousin, affecting to make light of the matter, "I don't think I should have minded it very much."

"Ay, but its eye—its countenance, my dear Tom," urged I; "if you had seen *that*, you would have felt it might be *anything* but what it seemed."

"I inclined to think the best conjurer in such a case would be an able-bodied cat," he said, with a provoking chuckle.

"But let us hear your own adventure," I said tartly.

At this challenge he looked uneasily round him. I had poked up a very unpleasant recollection.

"You shall hear it, Dick; I'll tell it to you," he said. "Begad, sir, I should feel quite queer, though, telling it *here*, though we are too strong a body for ghosts to meddle with just now."

Though he spoke this like a joke, I think it was serious calculation. Our Hebe was in a corner of the room, packing our cracked delft tea and dinner-services in a basket. She soon suspended operations, and with mouth and eyes wide open became an absorbed listener. Tom's experiences were told nearly in these words:—

"I saw it three times, Dick—three distinct times; and I am perfectly certain it meant me some infernal harm. I was, I say, in danger—in *extreme* danger; for, if nothing else had happened, my reason would most certainly have failed me, unless I had escaped so soon. Thank God. I *did* escape.

"The first night of this hateful disturbance, I was lying in the attitude of sleep, in that lumbering old bed. I hate to think of it. I was really wide awake, though I had put out my candle, and was lying as quietly as if I had been asleep; and although accidentally restless, my thoughts were running in a cheerful and agreeable channel.

"I think it must have been two o'clock at least when I thought I heard a sound in that—that odious dark recess at the far end of the bedroom. It was as if someone was drawing a piece of cord slowly along the floor, lifting it up, and dropping it softly down again in coils. I sate up once or twice in my bed, but could see nothing, so I concluded it must be mice in the wainscot. I felt no emotion graver than curiosity, and after a few minutes ceased to observe it.

"While lying in this state, strange to say; without at first a suspicion of anything supernatural, on a sudden I saw an old man, rather stout and square, in a sort of roan-red dressing-gown, and with a black cap on his head, moving stiffly and slowly in a diagonal direction, from the recess, across the floor of the bedroom, passing my bed at the foot, and entering the lumber-closet at the left. He had something under his arm; his head hung a little at one side; and, merciful God! when I saw his face."

Tom stopped for a while, and then said—

"That awful countenance, which living or dying I never can forget, disclosed what he was. Without turning to the right or left, he passed beside me, and entered the closet by the bed's head.

"While this fearful and indescribable type of death and guilt was passing, I felt that I had no more power to speak or stir than if I had been myself a corpse. For hours after it had disappeared, I was too terrified and weak to move. As soon as daylight came, I took courage, and examined the room, and especially the course which the frightful intruder had seemed to take, but there was not a vestige to indicate anybody's having passed there; no sign of any disturbing agency visible among the lumber that strewed the floor of the closet.

"I now began to recover a little. I was fagged and exhausted, and at last, overpowered by a feverish sleep. I came down late; and finding you out of spirits, on account of your dreams about the portrait, whose *original* I am now certain disclosed himself to me, I did not care to talk about the infernal vision. In fact, I was trying to persuade myself that the whole thing was an illusion, and I did not like to revive in their intensity the hated impressions of the past night—or to risk the constancy of my scepticism, by recounting the tale of my sufferings.

"It required some nerve, I can tell you, to go to my haunted chamber next night, and lie down quietly in the same bed," continued Tom. "I did so with a degree of trepidation, which, I am not ashamed to say, a very little matter would have sufficed to stimulate to downright panic. This night, however, passed off quietly enough, as also the next; and so too did two or three more. I grew more confident, and began to fancy that I believed in the theories of spectral illusions, with which I had at first vainly tried to impose upon my convictions.

"The apparition had been, indeed, altogether anomalous. It had crossed the room without any recognition of my presence: I had not disturbed *it*, and *it* had no mission to *me*. What, then, was the imaginable use of its crossing the room in a visible shape at all? Of course it might have *been* in the closet instead of *going* there, as easily as it introduced itself into the recess without entering the chamber in a shape discernible by the senses. Besides, how the deuce *had* I seen it? It was a dark night; I had no candle; there was no fire; and yet I saw it as distinctly, in colouring and outline, as ever I beheld human form! A cataleptic dream would explain it all; and I was determined that a dream it should be.

"One of the most remarkable phenomena connected with the practice of mendacity is the vast number of deliberate lies we tell ourselves, whom, of all persons, we can least expect to deceive. In all this, I need hardly tell you, Dick, I was simply lying to myself, and did not believe one word of the wretched humbug. Yet I went on, as men will do, like persevering charlatans and impostors, who tire people into credulity by the mere force of reiteration; so I hoped to win myself over at last to a comfortable scepticism about the ghost.

"He had not appeared a second time—that certainly was a comfort; and what, after all, did I care for him, and his queer old toggery and strange looks? Not a fig! I was nothing the worse for having seen him, and a good story the better. So I tumbled into bed, put out my candle, and, cheered by a loud drunken quarrel in the back lane, went fast asleep.

"From this deep slumber I awoke with a start. I knew I had had a horrible dream; but what it was I could not remember. My heart was thumping furiously; I felt bewildered and feverish; I sate up in the bed and looked about the room. A broad flood of moonlight came in through the curtainless window; everything was as I had last seen it; and though the domestic squabble in the back lane was, unhappily for me, allayed, I yet could hear a pleasant fellow singing, on his way home, the then popular comic ditty called, 'Murphy Delany.' Taking advantage of this diversion I lay down again, with my face towards the fireplace, and closing my eyes, did my best to think of nothing else but the song, which was every moment growing fainter in the distance:—

> *"'Twas Murphy Delany, so funny and frisky,*
> *Stept into a shebeen shop to get his skin full;*
> *He reeled out again pretty well lined with whiskey,*
> *As fresh as a shamrock, as blind as a bull.*

"The singer, whose condition I dare say resembled that of his hero, was soon too far off to regale my ears anymore; and as his music died away, I myself sank into a doze, neither sound nor refreshing. Somehow the song had got into my head, and I went meandering on through the adventures of my respectable fellow-countryman, who, on emerging from the 'shebeen shop,' fell into a river, from which he was fished up to be 'sat upon' by a coroner's jury, who having learned from a 'horse-doctor' that he was 'dead as a door-nail, so there was an end,' returned their verdict accordingly, just as he returned to his senses, when an angry altercation and a pitched battle between the body and the coroner winds up the lay with due spirit and pleasantry.

"Through this ballad I continued with a weary monotony to plod, down to the very last line, and then *da capo*, and so on, in my uncomfortable half-sleep, for how long, I can't conjecture. I found myself at last, however, muttering, '*dead* as a door-nail, so there was an end'; and something like another voice within me, seemed to say, very faintly, but sharply, 'dead! dead! *dead*! and may the Lord have mercy on your soul!' and instantaneously I was wide awake, and staring right before me from the pillow.

"Now—will you believe it, Dick?—I saw the same accursed figure standing full front, and gazing at me with its stony and fiendish countenance, not two yards from the bedside."

Tom stopped here, and wiped the perspiration from his face. I felt very queer. The girl was as pale as Tom; and, assembled as we were in the very scene of these adventures, we were all, I dare say, equally grateful for the clear daylight and the resuming bustle out of doors.

"For about three seconds only I saw it plainly; then it grew indistinct; but, for a long time, there was something like a column of dark vapour where it had been standing, between me and the wall; and I felt sure that he was still there. After a good while, this appearance went too. I took my clothes downstairs to the hall, and dressed there, with the door half open; then went out into the street, and walked about the town till morning, when I came back, in a miserable state of nervousness and exhaustion. I was such a fool, Dick, as to be ashamed to tell you how I came to be so upset. I thought you would laugh at me; especially as I had always talked philosophy, and treated *your* ghosts with contempt. I concluded you would give me no quarter; and so kept my tale of horror to myself.

"Now, Dick, you will hardly believe me, when I assure you, that for many nights after this last experience, I did not go to my room at all. I used to sit up for a while in the drawing-room after you had gone up to your bed; and then steal down softly to the hall-door, let myself out, and sit in the 'Robin Hood' tavern until the last guest went off; and then I got through the night like a sentry, pacing the streets till morning.

"For more than a week I never slept in bed. I sometimes had a snooze on a form in the 'Robin Hood,' and sometimes a nap in a chair during the day; but regular sleep I had absolutely none.

"I was quite resolved that we should get into another house; but I could not bring myself to tell you the reason, and I somehow put it off from day to day, although my life was, during every hour of this procrastination, rendered as miserable as that of a felon with the constables on his track. I was growing absolutely ill from this wretched mode of life.

"One afternoon I determined to enjoy an hour's sleep upon your bed. I hated mine; so that I had never, except in a stealthy visit everyday to unmake it, lest Martha should discover the secret of my nightly absence, entered the ill-omened chamber.

"As ill-luck would have it, you had locked your bedroom, and taken away the key. I went into my own to unsettle the bedclothes, as usual, and give the bed the appearance of having been slept in. Now, a

JOSEPH SHERIDAN LE FANU

variety of circumstances concurred to bring about the dreadful scene through which I was that night to pass. In the first place, I was literally overpowered with fatigue, and longing for sleep; in the next place, the effect of this extreme exhaustion upon my nerves resembled that of a narcotic, and rendered me less susceptible than, perhaps, I should in any other condition have been, of the exciting fears which had become habitual to me. Then again, a little bit of the window was open, a pleasant freshness pervaded the room, and, to crown all, the cheerful sun of day was making the room quite pleasant. What was to prevent my enjoying an hour's nap *here*? The whole air was resonant with the cheerful hum of life, and the broad matter-of-fact light of day filled every corner of the room.

"I yielded—stifling my qualms—to the almost overpowering temptation; and merely throwing off my coat, and loosening my cravat, I lay down, limiting myself to *half*-an-hour's doze in the unwonted enjoyment of a feather bed, a coverlet, and a bolster.

"It was horribly insidious; and the demon, no doubt, marked my infatuated preparations. Dolt that I was, I fancied, with mind and body worn out for want of sleep, and an arrear of a full week's rest to my credit, that such measure as *half*-an-hour's sleep, in such a situation, was possible. My sleep was death-like, long, and dreamless.

"Without a start or fearful sensation of any kind, I waked gently, but completely. It was, as you have good reason to remember, long past midnight—I believe, about two o'clock. When sleep has been deep and long enough to satisfy nature thoroughly, one often wakens in this way, suddenly, tranquilly, and completely.

"There was a figure seated in that lumbering, old sofa-chair, near the fireplace. Its back was rather towards me, but I could not be mistaken; it turned slowly round, and, merciful heavens! there was the stony face, with its infernal lineaments of malignity and despair, gloating on me. There was now no doubt as to its consciousness of my presence, and the hellish malice with which it was animated, for it arose, and drew close to the bedside. There was a rope about its neck, and the other end, coiled up, it held stiffly in its hand.

"My good angel nerved me for this horrible crisis. I remained for some seconds transfixed by the gaze of this tremendous phantom. He came close to the bed, and appeared on the point of mounting upon it. The next instant I was upon the floor at the far side, and in a moment more was, I don't know how, upon the lobby.

"But the spell was not yet broken; the valley of the shadow of death was not yet traversed. The abhorred phantom was before me there; it was standing near the banisters, stooping a little, and with one end of the rope round its own neck, was poising a noose at the other, as if to throw over mine; and while engaged in this baleful pantomime, it wore a smile so sensual, so unspeakably dreadful, that my senses were nearly overpowered. I saw and remember nothing more, until I found myself in your room.

"I had a wonderful escape, Dick—there is no disputing *that*—an escape for which, while I live, I shall bless the mercy of heaven. No one can conceive or imagine what it is for flesh and blood to stand in the presence of such a thing, but one who has had the terrific experience. Dick, Dick, a shadow has passed over me—a chill has crossed my blood and marrow, and I will never be the same again—never, Dick—never!"

Our handmaid, a mature girl of two-and-fifty, as I have said, stayed her hand, as Tom's story proceeded, and by little and little drew near to us, with open mouth, and her brows contracted over her little, beady black eyes, till stealing a glance over her shoulder now and then, she established herself close behind us. During the relation, she had made various earnest comments, in an undertone; but these and her exclamations, for the sake of brevity and simplicity, I have omitted in my narration.

"It's often I heard tell of it," she now said, "but I never believed it rightly till now—though, indeed, why should not I? Does not my mother, down there in the lane, know quare stories, God bless us, beyant telling about it? But you ought not to have slept in the back bedroom. She was loath to let me be going in and out of that room even in the day time, let alone for any Christian to spend the night in it; for sure she says it was his own bedroom."

"*Whose* own bedroom?" we asked, in a breath.

"Why, *his*—the ould Judge's—Judge Horrock's, to be sure, God rest his sowl"; and she looked fearfully round.

"Amen!" I muttered. "But did he die there?"

"Die there! No, not quite *there*," she said. "Shure, was not it over the banisters he hung himself, the ould sinner, God be merciful to us all? and was not it in the alcove they found the handles of the skipping-rope cut off, and the knife where he was settling the cord, God bless us, to hang himself with? It was his housekeeper's daughter owned the rope, my mother often told me, and the child never throve after, and used to be starting up out of her sleep, and screeching in the night time, wid dhrames and frights that cum an her; and they said how it was the speerit of the ould Judge that was tormentin' her; and she used to be roaring and yelling out to hould back the big ould fellow with the crooked neck; and then she'd screech 'Oh, the master! the master! he's stampin' at me, and beckoning to me! Mother, darling, don't let me go!' And so the poor crathure died at last, and the docthers said it was wather on the brain, for it was all they could say."

"How long ago was all this?" I asked.

"Oh, then, how would I know?" she answered. "But it must be a wondherful long time ago, for the housekeeper was an ould woman, with a pipe in her mouth, and not a tooth left, and better nor eighty years ould when my mother was first married; and they said she was a rale buxom, fine-dressed woman when the ould Judge come to his end; an', indeed, my mother's not far from eighty years ould herself this day; and what made it worse for the unnatural ould villain, God rest his soul, to frighten the little girl out of the world the way he did, was what was mostly thought and believed by everyone. My mother says how the poor little crathure was his own child; for he was by all accounts an ould villain every way, an' the hangin'est judge that ever was known in Ireland's ground."

"From what you said about the danger of sleeping in that bedroom," said I, "I suppose there were stories about the ghost having appeared there to others."

"Well, there was things said—quare things, surely," she answered, as it seemed, with some reluctance. "And why would not there? Sure was it not up in that same room he slept for more than twenty years? and was it not in the *alcove* he got the rope ready that done his own business at last, the way he done many a betther man's in his lifetime?—and was not the body lying in the same bed after death, and put in the coffin there, too, and carried out to his grave from it in Pether's churchyard, after the coroner was done? But there was quare stories—my mother has them all—about how one Nicholas Spaight got into trouble on the head of it."

"And what did they say of this Nicholas Spaight?" I asked.

"Oh, for that matther, it's soon told," she answered.

And she certainly did relate a very strange story, which so piqued my curiosity, that I took occasion to visit the ancient lady, her mother, from whom I learned many very curious particulars. Indeed, I am tempted to tell the tale, but my fingers are weary, and I must defer it. But if you wish to hear it another time, I shall do my best.

When we had heard the strange tale I have *not* told you, we put one or two further questions to her about the alleged spectral visitations, to which the house had, ever since the death of the wicked old Judge, been subjected.

"No one ever had luck in it," she told us. "There was always cross accidents, sudden deaths, and short times in it. The first that tuck, it was a family—I forget their name—but at any rate there was two young ladies and their papa. He was about sixty, and a stout healthy gentleman as you'd wish to see at that age. Well, he slept in that unlucky back bedroom; and, God between us an' harm! sure enough he was found dead one morning, half out of the bed, with his head as black as a sloe, and swelled like a puddin', hanging down near the floor. It was a fit, they said. He was as dead as a mackerel, and so *he* could not say what it was; but the ould people was all sure that it was nothing at all but the ould Judge, God bless us! that frightened him out of his senses and his life together.

"Sometime after there was a rich old maiden lady took the house. I don't know which room *she* slept in, but she lived alone; and at any rate, one morning, the servants going down early to their work, found her sitting on the passage-stairs, shivering and talkin' to herself, quite mad; and never a word more could any of *them* or her friends get from her ever afterwards but, 'Don't ask me to go, for I promised to wait for him.' They never made out from her who it was she meant by *him*, but of course those that knew all about the ould house were at no loss for the meaning of all that happened to her.

"Then afterwards, when the house was let out in lodgings, there was Micky Byrne that took the same room, with his wife and three little children; and sure I heard Mrs. Byrne myself telling how the children used to be lifted up in the bed at night, she could not see by what mains; and how they were starting and screeching every hour, just all as one as the housekeeper's little girl that died, till at last one night poor Micky had a dhrop in him, the way he used now and again; and what do you think in the middle of the night he thought he heard a noise on the stairs, and being in liquor, nothing less id do him but out he must go himself to see what was wrong. Well, after that, all she ever heard of him was himself sayin', 'Oh, God!' and a tumble that shook the very house; and there, sure enough, he was lying on the lower stairs, under the lobby, with his neck smashed double undher him, where he was flung over the banisters."

Then the handmaiden added—

"I'll go down to the lane, and send up Joe Gavvey to pack up the rest of the taythings, and bring all the things across to your new lodgings."

And so we all sallied out together, each of us breathing more freely, I have no doubt, as we crossed that ill-omened threshold for the last time.

Now, I may add thus much, in compliance with the immemorial usage of the realm of fiction, which sees the hero not only through his adventures, but fairly out of the world. You must have perceived that what the flesh, blood, and bone hero of romance proper is to the regular compounder of fiction, this old house of brick, wood, and mortar is to the humble recorder of this true tale. I, therefore, relate, as in duty bound, the catastrophe which ultimately befell it, which was simply this—that about two years subsequently to my story it was taken by a quack doctor, who called himself Baron Duhlstoerf, and filled the parlour windows with bottles of indescribable horrors preserved in brandy, and the newspapers with the usual grandiloquent and mendacious advertisements. This gentleman among his virtues did not reckon sobriety, and one night, being overcome with much wine, he set fire to his bed curtains, partially burned himself, and totally consumed the house. It was afterwards rebuilt, and for a time an undertaker established himself in the premises.

I have now told you my own and Tom's adventures, together with some valuable collateral particulars; and having acquitted myself of my engagement, I wish you a very goodnight, and pleasant dreams.

A Chapter in the History of a Tyrone Family

Introduction

In the following narrative, I have endeavoured to give as nearly as possible the ipsissima verba of the valued friend from whom I received it, conscious that any aberration from Her mode of telling the tale of her own life would at once impair its accuracy and its effect.

Would that, with her words, I could also bring before you her animated gesture, her expressive countenance, the solemn and thrilling air and accent with which she related the dark passages in her strange story; and, above all, that I could communicate the impressive consciousness that the narrator had seen with her own eyes, and personally acted in the scenes which she described; these accompaniments, taken with the additional circumstance that she who told the tale was one far too deeply and sadly impressed with religious principle to misrepresent or fabricate what she repeated as fact, gave to the tale a depth of interest which the events recorded could hardly, themselves, have produced.

I became acquainted with the lady from whose lips I heard this narrative nearly twenty years since, and the story struck my fancy so much that I committed it to paper while it was still fresh in my mind; and should its perusal afford you entertainment for a listless half hour, my labour shall not have been bestowed in vain.

I find that I have taken the story down as she told it, in the first person, and perhaps this is as it should be.

She began as follows:

My maiden name was Richardson,[1] the designation of a family of some distinction in the county of Tyrone. I was the younger of two daughters, and we were the only children. There was a difference in our ages of nearly six years, so that I did not, in my childhood, enjoy that close companionship which sisterhood, in other circumstances, necessarily involves; and while I was still a child, my sister was married.

---

1. I have carefully altered the names as they appear in the original manuscript, for the reader will see that some of the circumstances recorded are not of a kind to reflect honour upon those involved in them; and as many are still living, in every way honoured and honourable, who stand in close relation to the principal actors in this drama, the reader will see the necessity of the course which we have adopted.

The person upon whom she bestowed her hand was a Mr. Carew, a gentleman of property and consideration in the north of England.

I remember well the eventful day of the wedding; the thronging carriages, the noisy menials, the loud laughter, the merry faces, and the gay dresses. Such sights were then new to me, and harmonised ill with the sorrowful feelings with which I regarded the event which was to separate me, as it turned out, forever from a sister whose tenderness alone had hitherto more than supplied all that I wanted in my mother's affection.

The day soon arrived which was to remove the happy couple from Ashtown House. The carriage stood at the hall-door, and my poor sister kissed me again and again, telling me that I should see her soon.

The carriage drove away, and I gazed after it until my eyes filled with tears, and, returning slowly to my chamber, I wept more bitterly and, so to speak, more desolately, than ever I had done before.

My father had never seemed to love or to take an interest in me. He had desired a son, and I think he never thoroughly forgave me my unfortunate sex.

My having come into the world at all as his child he regarded as a kind of fraudulent intrusion, and as his antipathy to me had its origin in an imperfection of mine, too radical for removal, I never even hoped to stand high in his good graces.

My mother was, I dare say, as fond of me as she was of anyone; but she was a woman of a masculine and a worldly cast of mind. She had no tenderness or sympathy for the weaknesses, or even for the affections, of woman's nature and her demeanour towards me was peremptory, and often even harsh.

It is not to be supposed, then, that I found in the society of my parents much to supply the loss of my sister. About a year after her marriage, we received letters from Mr. Carew, containing accounts of my sister's health, which, though not actually alarming, were calculated to make us seriously uneasy. The symptoms most dwelt upon were loss of appetite and cough.

The letters concluded by intimating that he would avail himself of my father and mother's repeated invitation to spend sometime at Ashtown, particularly as the physician who had been consulted as to my sister's health had strongly advised a removal to her native air.

There were added repeated assurances that nothing serious was apprehended, as it was supposed that a deranged state of the liver was the only source of the symptoms which at first had seemed to intimate consumption.

In accordance with this announcement, my sister and Mr. Carew arrived in Dublin, where one of my father's carriages awaited them, in readiness to start upon whatever day or hour they might choose for their departure.

It was arranged that Mr. Carew was, as soon as the day upon which they were to leave Dublin was definitely fixed, to write to my father, who intended that the two last stages should be performed by his own horses, upon whose speed and safety far more reliance might be placed than upon those of the ordinary post-horses, which were at that time, almost without exception, of the very worst order. The journey, one of about ninety miles, was to be divided; the larger portion being reserved for the second day.

On Sunday a letter reached us, stating that the party would leave Dublin on Monday, and, in due course, reach Ashtown upon Tuesday evening.

Tuesday came the evening closed in, and yet no carriage; darkness came on, and still no sign of our expected visitors.

Hour after hour passed away, and it was now past twelve; the night was remarkably calm, scarce a breath stirring, so that any sound, such as that produced by the rapid movement of a vehicle, would have been audible at a considerable distance. For some such sound I was feverishly listening.

It was, however, my father's rule to close the house at nightfall, and the window-shutters being fastened, I was unable to reconnoitre the avenue as I would have wished. It was nearly one o'clock, and we began almost to despair of seeing them upon that night, when I thought I distinguished the sound of wheels, but so remote and faint as to make me at first very uncertain. The noise approached; it became louder and clearer; it stopped for a moment.

I now heard the shrill screaming of the rusty iron, as the avenue-gate revolved on its hinges; again came the sound of wheels in rapid motion.

"It is they," said I, starting up; "the carriage is in the avenue."

We all stood for a few moments breathlessly listening. On thundered the vehicle with the speed of a whirlwind; crack went the whip, and clatter went the wheels, as it rattled over the uneven pavement of the court. A general and furious barking from all the dogs about the house, hailed its arrival.

We hurried to the hall in time to hear the steps let down with the sharp clanging noise peculiar to the operation, and the hum of voices exerted in the bustle of arrival. The hall-door was now thrown open, and we all stepped forth to greet our visitors.

The court was perfectly empty; the moon was shining broadly and brightly upon all around; nothing was to be seen but the tall trees with their long spectral shadows, now wet with the dews of midnight.

We stood gazing from right to left, as if suddenly awakened from a dream; the dogs walked suspiciously, growling and snuffing about the court, and by totally and suddenly ceasing their former loud barking, expressing the predominance of fear.

We stared one upon another in perplexity and dismay, and I think I never beheld more pale faces assembled. By my father's direction, we looked about to find anything which might indicate or account for the noise which we had heard; but no such thing was to be seen—even the mire which lay upon the avenue was undisturbed. We returned to the house, more panic-struck than I can describe.

On the next day, we learned by a messenger, who had ridden hard the greater part of the night, that my sister was dead. On Sunday evening, she had retired to bed rather unwell, and, on Monday, her indisposition declared itself unequivocally to be malignant fever. She became hourly worse and, on Tuesday night, a little after midnight, she expired.[2]

---

2. The residuary legatee of the late Frances Purcell, who has the honour of selecting such of his lamented old friend's manuscripts as may appear fit for publication, in order that the lore which they contain may reach the world before scepticism and utility have robbed our species of the precious gift of credulity, and scornfully kicked before them, or trampled into annihilation those harmless fragments of picturesque superstition which it is our object to preserve, has been subjected to the charge of dealing too largely in the marvellous; and it has been half insinuated that such is his love for diablerie, that he is content to wander a mile out of his way, in order to meet a fiend or a goblin, and thus to sacrifice all regard for truth and accuracy to the idle hope of affrighting the imagination, and thus pandering to the bad taste of his reader. He begs leave, then, to take this opportunity of asserting his perfect innocence of all the crimes laid to his charge, and to assure his reader that he never PANDERED TO HIS BAD TASTE, nor went one inch out of his way to introduce witch, fairy, devil, ghost, or any other of the grim fraternity of the redoubted Raw-head-and-bloody-bones. His province, touching these tales, has been attended with no difficulty and little responsibility; indeed, he is accountable for nothing more than an alteration in the names of persons mentioned therein, when such a step seemed necessary, and for an occasional note, whenever he conceived it possible, innocently, to edge in a word. These tales have been WRITTEN DOWN, as the heading of each announces, by the Rev. Francis Purcell, P.P., of Drumcoolagh; and in all the instances, which are many, in which the present writer has had an opportunity of comparing the manuscript of his departed

I mention this circumstance, because it was one upon which a thousand wild and fantastical reports were founded, though one would have thought that the truth scarcely required to be improved upon; and again, because it produced a strong and lasting effect upon my spirits, and indeed, I am inclined to think, upon my character.

I was, for several years after this occurrence, long after the violence of my grief subsided, so wretchedly low-spirited and nervous, that I could scarcely be said to live; and during this time, habits of indecision, arising out of a listless acquiescence in the will of others, a fear of encountering even the slightest opposition, and a disposition to shrink from what are commonly called amusements, grew upon me so strongly, that I have scarcely even yet altogether overcome them.

We saw nothing more of Mr. Carew. He returned to England as soon as the melancholy rites attendant upon the event which I have just mentioned were performed; and not being altogether inconsolable, he married again within two years; after which, owing to the remoteness of our relative situations, and other circumstances, we gradually lost sight of him.

I was now an only child; and, as my elder sister had died without issue, it was evident that, in the ordinary course of things, my father's property, which was altogether in his power, would go to me; and the consequence was, that before I was fourteen, Ashtown House was besieged by a host of suitors. However, whether it was that I was too young, or that none of the aspirants to my hand stood sufficiently high in rank or wealth, I was suffered by both parents to do exactly as I pleased; and well was it for me, as I afterwards found, that fortune, or rather Providence, had so ordained it, that I had not suffered my affections to become in any degree engaged, for my mother would never have suffered any SILLY FANCY of mine, as she was in the habit of styling an attachment, to stand in the way of her ambitious views—views which she was determined to carry into effect, in defiance of every obstacle, and in order to accomplish which she would not have hesitated to sacrifice anything so unreasonable and contemptible as a girlish passion.

When I reached the age of sixteen, my mother's plans began to develop themselves; and, at her suggestion, we moved to Dublin to

---

friend with the actual traditions which are current amongst the families whose fortunes they pretend to illustrate, he has uniformly found that whatever of supernatural occurred in the story, so far from having been exaggerated by him, had been rather softened down, and, wherever it could be attempted, accounted for.

JOSEPH SHERIDAN LE FANU

sojourn for the winter, in order that no time might be lost in disposing of me to the best advantage.

I had been too long accustomed to consider myself as of no importance whatever, to believe for a moment that I was in reality the cause of all the bustle and preparation which surrounded me, and being thus relieved from the pain which a consciousness of my real situation would have inflicted, I journeyed towards the capital with a feeling of total indifference.

My father's wealth and connection had established him in the best society, and, consequently, upon our arrival in the metropolis we commanded whatever enjoyment or advantages its gaieties afforded.

The tumult and novelty of the scenes in which I was involved did not fail considerably to amuse me, and my mind gradually recovered its tone, which was naturally cheerful.

It was almost immediately known and reported that I was an heiress, and of course my attractions were pretty generally acknowledged.

Among the many gentlemen whom it was my fortune to please, one, ere long, established himself in my mother's good graces, to the exclusion of all less important aspirants. However, I had not understood or even remarked his attentions, nor in the slightest degree suspected his or my mother's plans respecting me, when I was made aware of them rather abruptly by my mother herself.

We had attended a splendid ball, given by Lord M——, at his residence in Stephen's Green, and I was, with the assistance of my waiting-maid, employed in rapidly divesting myself of the rich ornaments which, in profuseness and value, could scarcely have found their equals in any private family in Ireland.

I had thrown myself into a lounging-chair beside the fire, listless and exhausted, after the fatigues of the evening, when I was aroused from the reverie into which I had fallen by the sound of footsteps approaching my chamber, and my mother entered.

"Fanny, my dear," said she, in her softest tone, "I wish to say a word or two with you before I go to rest. You are not fatigued, love, I hope?"

"No, no, madam, I thank you," said I, rising at the same time from my seat, with the formal respect so little practised now.

"Sit down, my dear," said she, placing herself upon a chair beside me; "I must chat with you for a quarter of an hour or so. Saunders" (to the maid) "you may leave the room; do not close the room-door, but shut that of the lobby."

This precaution against curious ears having been taken as directed, my mother proceeded.

"You have observed, I should suppose, my dearest Fanny—indeed, you MUST have observed Lord Glenfallen's marked attentions to you?"

"I assure you, madam—" I began.

"Well, well, that is all right," interrupted my mother; "of course you must be modest upon the matter; but listen to me for a few moments, my love, and I will prove to your satisfaction that your modesty is quite unnecessary in this case. You have done better than we could have hoped, at least so very soon. Lord Glenfallen is in love with you. I give you joy of your conquest"; and saying this, my mother kissed my forehead.

"In love with me!" I exclaimed, in unfeigned astonishment.

"Yes, in love with you," repeated my mother; "devotedly, distractedly in love with you. Why, my dear, what is there wonderful in it? Look in the glass, and look at these," she continued, pointing with a smile to the jewels which I had just removed from my person, and which now lay a glittering heap upon the table.

"May there not," said I, hesitating between confusion and real alarm—"is it not possible that some mistake may be at the bottom of all this?"

"Mistake, dearest! none," said my mother. "None; none in the world. Judge for yourself; read this, my love." And she placed in my hand a letter, addressed to herself, the seal of which was broken. I read it through with no small surprise. After some very fine complimentary flourishes upon my beauty and perfections, as also upon the antiquity and high reputation of our family, it went on to make a formal proposal of marriage, to be communicated or not to me at present, as my mother should deem expedient; and the letter wound up by a request that the writer might be permitted, upon our return to Ashtown House, which was soon to take place, as the spring was now tolerably advanced, to visit us for a few days, in case his suit was approved.

"Well, well, my dear," said my mother, impatiently; "do you know who Lord Glenfallen is?"

"I do, madam," said I rather timidly, for I dreaded an altercation with my mother.

"Well, dear, and what frightens you?" continued she. "Are you afraid of a title? What has he done to alarm you? he is neither old nor ugly."

I was silent, though I might have said, "He is neither young nor handsome."

"My dear Fanny," continued my mother, "in sober seriousness you have been most fortunate in engaging the affections of a nobleman such as Lord Glenfallen, young and wealthy, with first-rate—yes, acknowledged FIRST-RATE abilities, and of a family whose influence is not exceeded by that of any in Ireland. Of course you see the offer in the same light that I do—indeed I think you MUST."

This was uttered in no very dubious tone. I was so much astonished by the suddenness of the whole communication that I literally did not know what to say.

"You are not in love?" said my mother, turning sharply, and fixing her dark eyes upon me with severe scrutiny.

"No, madam," said I, promptly; horrified, as what young lady would not have been, at such a query.

"I'm glad to hear it," said my mother, drily. "Once, nearly twenty years ago, a friend of mine consulted me as to how he should deal with a daughter who had made what they call a love-match—beggared herself, and disgraced her family; and I said, without hesitation, take no care for her, but cast her off. Such punishment I awarded for an offence committed against the reputation of a family not my own; and what I advised respecting the child of another, with full as small compunction I would Do with mine. I cannot conceive anything more unreasonable or intolerable than that the fortune and the character of a family should be marred by the idle caprices of a girl."

She spoke this with great severity, and paused as if she expected some observation from me.

I, however, said nothing.

"But I need not explain to you, my dear Fanny," she continued, "my views upon this subject; you have always known them well, and I have never yet had reason to believe you likely, voluntarily, to offend me, or to abuse or neglect any of those advantages which reason and duty tell you should be improved. Come hither, my dear; kiss me, and do not look so frightened. Well, now, about this letter, you need not answer it yet; of course you must be allowed time to make up your mind. In the meantime I will write to his lordship to give him my permission to visit us at Ashtown. Goodnight, my love."

And thus ended one of the most disagreeable, not to say astounding, conversations I had ever had. It would not be easy to describe exactly what were my feelings towards Lord Glenfallen;—whatever might have been my mother's suspicions, my heart was perfectly disengaged—and hitherto, although I had not been made in the slightest degree acquainted with his real views, I had liked him very much, as an agreeable, well-informed man, whom I was always glad to meet in society. He had served in the navy in early life, and the polish which his manners received in his after intercourse with courts and cities had not served to obliterate that frankness of manner which belongs proverbially to the sailor.

Whether this apparent candour went deeper than the outward bearing, I was yet to learn. However, there was no doubt that, as far as I had seen of Lord Glenfallen, he was, though perhaps not so young as might have been desired in a lover, a singularly pleasing man; and whatever feeling unfavourable to him had found its way into my mind, arose altogether from the dread, not an unreasonable one, that constraint might be practised upon my inclinations. I reflected, however, that Lord Glenfallen was a wealthy man, and one highly thought of; and although I could never expect to love him in the romantic sense of the term, yet I had no doubt but that, all things considered, I might be more happy with him than I could hope to be at home.

When next I met him it was with no small embarrassment, his tact and good breeding, however, soon reassured me, and effectually prevented my awkwardness being remarked upon. And I had the satisfaction of leaving Dublin for the country with the full conviction that nobody, not even those most intimate with me, even suspected the fact of Lord Glenfallen's having made me a formal proposal.

This was to me a very serious subject of self-gratulation, for, besides my instinctive dread of becoming the topic of the speculations of gossip, I felt that if the situation which I occupied in relation to him were made publicly known, I should stand committed in a manner which would scarcely leave me the power of retraction.

The period at which Lord Glenfallen had arranged to visit Ashtown House was now fast approaching, and it became my mother's wish to form me thoroughly to her will, and to obtain my consent to the proposed marriage before his arrival, so that all things might proceed smoothly, without apparent opposition or objection upon my part. Whatever objections, therefore, I had entertained were to be subdued; whatever disposition to resistance I had exhibited or had been supposed to feel, were to be completely eradicated before he made his appearance; and my mother addressed herself to the task with a decision and energy against which even the barriers, which her imagination had created, could hardly have stood.

If she had, however, expected any determined opposition from me, she was agreeably disappointed. My heart was perfectly free, and all my feelings of liking and preference were in favour of Lord Glenfallen; and I well knew that in case I refused to dispose of myself as I was desired, my mother had alike the power and the will to render my existence as utterly miserable as even the most ill-assorted marriage could possibly have done.

You will remember, my good friend, that I was very young and very completely under the control of my parents, both of whom, my mother particularly, were unscrupulously determined in matters of this kind, and willing, when voluntary obedience on the part of those within their power was withheld, to compel a forced acquiescence by an unsparing use of all the engines of the most stern and rigorous domestic discipline.

All these combined, not unnaturally, induced me to resolve upon yielding at once, and without useless opposition, to what appeared almost to be my fate.

The appointed time was come, and my now accepted suitor arrived; he was in high spirits, and, if possible, more entertaining than ever.

I was not, however, quite in the mood to enjoy his sprightliness; but whatever I wanted in gaiety was amply made up in the triumphant and gracious good-humour of my mother, whose smiles of benevolence and exultation were showered around as bountifully as the summer sunshine.

I will not weary you with unnecessary prolixity. Let it suffice to say, that I was married to Lord Glenfallen with all the attendant pomp and circumstance of wealth, rank, and grandeur. According to the usage of the times, now humanely reformed, the ceremony was made, until long past midnight, the season of wild, uproarious, and promiscuous feasting and revelry.

Of all this I have a painfully vivid recollection, and particularly of the little annoyances inflicted upon me by the dull and coarse jokes of the wits and wags who abound in all such places, and upon all such occasions.

I was not sorry when, after a few days, Lord Glenfallen's carriage appeared at the door to convey us both from Ashtown; for any change would have been a relief from the irksomeness of ceremonial and formality which the visits received in honour of my newly-acquired titles hourly entailed upon me.

It was arranged that we were to proceed to Cahergillagh, one of the Glenfallen estates, lying, however, in a southern county, so that, owing to the difficulty of the roads at the time, a tedious journey of three days intervened.

I set forth with my noble companion, followed by the regrets of some, and by the envy of many; though God knows I little deserved the latter. The three days of travel were now almost spent, when, passing the brow of a wild heathy hill, the domain of Cahergillagh opened suddenly upon our view.

It formed a striking and a beautiful scene. A lake of considerable extent stretching away towards the west, and reflecting from its broad, smooth waters, the rich glow of the setting sun, was overhung by steep hills, covered by a rich mantle of velvet sward, broken here and there by the grey front of some old rock, and exhibiting on their shelving sides, their slopes and hollows, every variety of light and shade; a thick wood of dwarf oak, birch, and hazel skirted these hills, and clothed the shores of the lake, running out in rich luxuriance upon every promontory, and spreading upward considerably upon the side of the hills.

"There lies the enchanted castle," said Lord Glenfallen, pointing towards a considerable level space intervening between two of the picturesque hills, which rose dimly around the lake.

This little plain was chiefly occupied by the same low, wild wood which covered the other parts of the domain; but towards the centre a mass of taller and statelier forest trees stood darkly grouped together, and among them stood an ancient square tower, with many buildings of a humbler character, forming together the manorhouse, or, as it was more usually called, the Court of Cahergillagh.

As we approached the level upon which the mansion stood, the winding road gave us many glimpses of the time-worn castle and its surrounding buildings; and seen as it was through the long vistas of the fine old trees, and with the rich glow of evening upon it, I have seldom beheld an object more picturesquely striking.

I was glad to perceive, too, that here and there the blue curling smoke ascended from stacks of chimneys now hidden by the rich, dark ivy which, in a great measure, covered the building. Other indications of comfort made themselves manifest as we approached; and indeed, though the place was evidently one of considerable antiquity, it had nothing whatever of the gloom of decay about it.

"You must not, my love," said Lord Glenfallen, "imagine this place worse than it is. I have no taste for antiquity—at least I should not choose a house to reside in because it is old. Indeed I do not recollect that I was even so romantic as to overcome my aversion to rats and rheumatism, those faithful attendants upon your noble relics of feudalism; and I much prefer a snug, modern, unmysterious bedroom, with well-aired sheets, to the waving tapestry, mildewed cushions, and all the other interesting appliances of romance. However, though I cannot promise you all the discomfort generally belonging to an old castle, you will find legends and ghostly lore enough to claim your respect; and if old Martha be still to the fore, as I trust she is, you will soon have a supernatural and appropriate anecdote for every closet and corner of the mansion; but here we are—so, without more ado, welcome to Cahergillagh!"

We now entered the hall of the castle, and while the domestics were employed in conveying our trunks and other luggage which we had brought with us for immediate use to the apartments which Lord Glenfallen had selected for himself and me, I went with him into a spacious sitting-room, wainscoted with finely polished black oak, and hung round with the portraits of various worthies of the Glenfallen family.

This room looked out upon an extensive level covered with the softest green sward, and irregularly bounded by the wild wood I have before mentioned, through the leafy arcade formed by whose boughs and trunks the level beams of the setting sun were pouring. In the distance a group of dairymaids were plying their task, which they accompanied throughout with snatches of Irish songs which, mellowed by the distance, floated not unpleasingly to the ear; and beside them sat or lay, with all the grave importance of conscious protection, six or seven large dogs of various kinds. Farther in the distance, and through the cloisters of the arching wood, two or three ragged urchins were employed in driving such stray kine as had wandered farther than the rest to join their fellows.

As I looked upon this scene which I have described, a feeling of tranquillity and happiness came upon me, which I have never experienced in so strong a degree; and so strange to me was the sensation that my eyes filled with tears.

Lord Glenfallen mistook the cause of my emotion, and taking me kindly and tenderly by the hand, he said:

"Do not suppose, my love, that it is my intention to SETTLE here. Whenever you desire to leave this, you have only to let me know your wish, and it shall be complied with; so I must entreat of you not to suffer any circumstances which I can control to give you one moment's uneasiness. But here is old Martha; you must be introduced to her, one of the heirlooms of our family."

A hale, good-humoured, erect old woman was Martha, and an agreeable contrast to the grim, decrepid hag which my fancy had conjured up, as the depository of all the horrible tales in which I doubted not this old place was most fruitful.

She welcomed me and her master with a profusion of gratulations, alternately kissing our hands and apologising for the liberty, until at length Lord Glenfallen put an end to this somewhat fatiguing ceremonial by requesting her to conduct me to my chamber if it were prepared for my reception.

I followed Martha up an old-fashioned oak staircase into a long, dim passage, at the end of which lay the door which communicated with the apartments which had been selected for our use; here the old woman stopped, and respectfully requested me to proceed.

I accordingly opened the door, and was about to enter, when something like a mass of black tapestry, as it appeared, disturbed by my sudden approach, fell from above the door, so as completely to screen the aperture; the startling unexpectedness of the occurrence, and the rustling noise which the drapery made in its descent, caused me involuntarily to step two or three paces backwards. I turned, smiling and half-ashamed, to the old servant, and said:

"You see what a coward I am."

The woman looked puzzled, and, without saying anymore, I was about to draw aside the curtain and enter the room, when, upon turning to do so, I was surprised to find that nothing whatever interposed to obstruct the passage.

I went into the room, followed by the servant-woman, and was amazed to find that it, like the one below, was wainscoted, and that nothing like drapery was to be found near the door.

"Where is it?" said I; "what has become of it?"

"What does your ladyship wish to know?" said the old woman.

"Where is the black curtain that fell across the door, when I attempted first to come to my chamber?" answered I.

"The cross of Christ about us!" said the old woman, turning suddenly pale.

"What is the matter, my good friend?" said I; "you seem frightened."

"Oh no, no, your ladyship," said the old woman, endeavouring to conceal her agitation; but in vain, for tottering towards a chair, she sank into it, looking so deadly pale and horror-struck that I thought every moment she would faint.

"Merciful God, keep us from harm and danger!" muttered she at length.

"What can have terrified you so?" said I, beginning to fear that she had seen something more than had met my eye. "You appear ill, my poor woman!"

"Nothing, nothing, my lady," said she, rising. "I beg your ladyship's pardon for making so bold. May the great God defend us from misfortune!"

"Martha," said I, "something HAS frightened you very much, and I insist on knowing what it is; your keeping me in the dark upon the subject will make me much more uneasy than anything you could tell me. I desire you, therefore, to let me know what agitates you; I command you to tell me."

"Your ladyship said you saw a black curtain falling across the door when you were coming into the room," said the old woman.

"I did," said I; "but though the whole thing appears somewhat strange, I cannot see anything in the matter to agitate you so excessively."

"It's for no good you saw that, my lady," said the crone; "something terrible is coming. It's a sign, my lady—a sign that never fails."

"Explain, explain what you mean, my good woman," said I, in spite of myself, catching more than I could account for, of her superstitious terror.

"Whenever something—something BAD is going to happen to the Glenfallen family, someone that belongs to them sees a black handkerchief or curtain just waved or falling before their faces. I saw it myself," continued she, lowering her voice, "when I was only a little girl, and I'll never forget it. I often heard of it before, though I never saw it till then, nor since, praised be God. But I was going into Lady Jane's room to waken her in the morning; and sure enough when I got first to the bed and began to draw the curtain, something dark was waved across the division, but only for a moment; and when I saw rightly into the bed, there was she lying cold and dead, God be merciful to me! So, my lady, there is small blame to me to be daunted when anyone of the family sees it; for it's many's the story I heard of it, though I saw it but once."

I was not of a superstitious turn of mind, yet I could not resist a feeling of awe very nearly allied to the fear which my companion had so unreservedly expressed; and when you consider my situation, the loneliness, antiquity, and gloom of the place, you will allow that the weakness was not without excuse.

In spite of old Martha's boding predictions, however, time flowed on in an unruffled course. One little incident however, though trifling in itself, I must relate, as it serves to make what follows more intelligible.

Upon the day after my arrival, Lord Glenfallen of course desired to make me acquainted with the house and domain; and accordingly we set forth upon our ramble. When returning, he became for sometime silent and moody, a state so unusual with him as considerably to excite my surprise.

I endeavoured by observations and questions to arouse him—but in vain. At length, as we approached the house, he said, as if speaking to himself:

"'Twere madness—madness—madness," repeating the words bitterly—"sure and speedy ruin."

There was here a long pause; and at length, turning sharply towards me, in a tone very unlike that in which he had hitherto addressed me, he said:

"Do you think it possible that a woman can keep a secret?"

"I am sure," said I, "that women are very much belied upon the score of talkativeness, and that I may answer your question with the same directness with which you put it—I reply that I Do think a woman can keep a secret."

"But I do not," said he, drily.

We walked on in silence for a time. I was much astonished at his unwonted abruptness—I had almost said rudeness.

After a considerable pause he seemed to recollect himself, and with an effort resuming his sprightly manner, he said:

"Well, well, the next thing to keeping a secret well is, not to desire to possess one—talkativeness and curiosity generally go together. Now I shall make test of you, in the first place, respecting the latter of these qualities. I shall be your BLUEBEARD—tush, why do I trifle thus? Listen to me, my dear Fanny; I speak now in solemn earnest. What I desire is intimately, inseparably, connected with your happiness and honour as well as my own; and your compliance with my request will not be difficult. It will impose upon you a very trifling restraint during your sojourn here, which certain events which have occurred since our arrival have determined me shall not be a long one. You must promise me, upon your sacred honour, that you will visit Only that part of the castle which can be reached from the front entrance, leaving the back entrance and the part of the building commanded immediately by it to the menials, as also the small garden whose high wall you see yonder; and never at anytime seek to pry or peep into them, nor to open the door which communicates from the front part of the house through the corridor with the back. I do not urge this in jest or in caprice, but from a solemn conviction that danger and misery will be the certain consequences of your not observing what I prescribe. I cannot explain myself further at present. Promise me, then, these things, as you hope for peace here, and for mercy hereafter."

I did make the promise as desired, and he appeared relieved; his manner recovered all its gaiety and elasticity: but the recollection of the strange scene which I have just described dwelt painfully upon my mind.

More than a month passed away without any occurrence worth recording; but I was not destined to leave Cahergillagh without further adventure. One day, intending to enjoy the pleasant sunshine in a ramble through the woods, I ran up to my room to procure my bonnet and shawl. Upon entering the chamber, I was surprised and somewhat startled to find it occupied. Beside the fireplace, and nearly opposite the door, seated in a large, old-fashioned elbow-chair, was placed the figure of a lady. She appeared to be nearer fifty than forty, and was dressed suitably to her age, in a handsome suit of flowered silk; she had a profusion of trinkets and jewellery about her person, and many rings upon her fingers. But although very rich, her dress was not gaudy or in ill taste. But what was remarkable in the lady was, that although her features were handsome, and upon the whole pleasing, the pupil of each eye was dimmed with the whiteness of cataract, and she was evidently stone-blind. I was for some seconds so surprised at this unaccountable apparition, that I could not find words to address her.

"Madam," said I, "there must be some mistake here—this is my bed-chamber."

"Marry come up," said the lady, sharply; "Your chamber! Where is Lord Glenfallen?"

"He is below, madam," replied I; "and I am convinced he will be not a little surprised to find you here."

"I do not think he will," said she; "with your good leave, talk of what you know something about. Tell him I want him. Why does the minx dilly-dally so?"

In spite of the awe which this grim lady inspired, there was something in her air of confident superiority which, when I considered our relative situations, was not a little irritating.

"Do you know, madam, to whom you speak?" said I.

"I neither know nor care," said she; "but I presume that you are someone about the house, so again I desire you, if you wish to continue here, to bring your master hither forthwith."

"I must tell you, madam," said I, "that I am Lady Glenfallen."

"What's that?" said the stranger, rapidly.

"I say, madam," I repeated, approaching her that I might be more distinctly heard, "that I am Lady Glenfallen."

"It's a lie, you trull!" cried she, in an accent which made me start, and at the same time, springing forward, she seized me in her grasp, and shook me violently, repeating, "It's a lie—it's a lie!" with a rapidity and vehemence which swelled every vein of her face. The violence of her action, and the fury which convulsed her face, effectually terrified me, and disengaging myself from her grasp, I screamed as loud as I could for help. The blind woman continued to pour out a torrent of abuse upon me, foaming at the mouth with rage, and impotently shaking her clenched fists towards me.

I heard Lord Glenfallen's step upon the stairs, and I instantly ran out; as I passed him I perceived that he was deadly pale, and just caught the words: "I hope that demon has not hurt you?"

I made some answer, I forget what, and he entered the chamber, the door of which he locked upon the inside. What passed within I know not; but I heard the voices of the two speakers raised in loud and angry altercation.

I thought I heard the shrill accents of the woman repeat the words, "Let her look to herself"; but I could not be quite sure. This short sentence, however, was, to my alarmed imagination, pregnant with fearful meaning.

The storm at length subsided, though not until after a conference of more than two long hours. Lord Glenfallen then returned, pale and agitated.

"That unfortunate woman," said he, "is out of her mind. I daresay she treated you to some of her ravings; but you need not dread any further interruption from her: I have brought her so far to reason. She did not hurt you, I trust."

"No, no," said I; "but she terrified me beyond measure."

JOSEPH SHERIDAN LE FANU

"Well," said he, "she is likely to behave better for the future; and I dare swear that neither you nor she would desire, after what has passed, to meet again."

This occurrence, so startling and unpleasant, so involved in mystery, and giving rise to so many painful surmises, afforded me no very agreeable food for rumination.

All attempts on my part to arrive at the truth were baffled; Lord Glenfallen evaded all my inquiries, and at length peremptorily forbid any further allusion to the matter. I was thus obliged to rest satisfied with what I had actually seen, and to trust to time to resolve the perplexities in which the whole transaction had involved me.

Lord Glenfallen's temper and spirits gradually underwent a complete and most painful change; he became silent and abstracted, his manner to me was abrupt and often harsh, some grievous anxiety seemed ever present to his mind; and under its influence his spirits sunk and his temper became soured.

I soon perceived that his gaiety was rather that which the stir and excitement of society produce, than the result of a healthy habit of mind; everyday confirmed me in the opinion, that the considerate good-nature which I had so much admired in him was little more than a mere manner; and to my infinite grief and surprise, the gay, kind, open-hearted nobleman who had for months followed and flattered me, was rapidly assuming the form of a gloomy, morose, and singularly selfish man. This was a bitter discovery, and I strove to conceal it from myself as long as I could; but the truth was not to be denied, and I was forced to believe that Lord Glenfallen no longer loved me, and that he was at little pains to conceal the alteration in his sentiments.

One morning after breakfast, Lord Glenfallen had been for sometime walking silently up and down the room, buried in his moody reflections, when pausing suddenly, and turning towards me, he exclaimed:

"I have it—I have it! We must go abroad, and stay there too; and if that does not answer, why—why, we must try some more effectual expedient. Lady Glenfallen, I have become involved in heavy embarrassments. A wife, you know, must share the fortunes of her husband, for better for worse; but I will waive my right if you prefer remaining here—here at Cahergillagh. For I would not have you seen elsewhere without the state to which your rank entitles you; besides, it would break your poor mother's heart," he added, with sneering gravity. "So make up your mind—Cahergillagh or France. I will start if possible in a week, so determine between this and then."

He left the room, and in a few moments I saw him ride past the window, followed by a mounted servant. He had directed a domestic to inform me that he should not be back until the next day.

I was in very great doubt as to what course of conduct I should pursue, as to accompanying him in the continental tour so suddenly determined upon. I felt that it would be a hazard too great to encounter; for at Cahergillagh I had always the consciousness to sustain me, that if his temper at anytime led him into violent or unwarrantable treatment of me, I had a remedy within reach, in the protection and support of my own family, from all useful and effective communication with whom, if once in France, I should be entirely debarred.

As to remaining at Cahergillagh in solitude, and, for aught I knew, exposed to hidden dangers, it appeared to me scarcely less objectionable than the former proposition; and yet I feared that with one or other I must comply, unless I was prepared to come to an actual breach with Lord Glenfallen. Full of these unpleasing doubts and perplexities, I retired to rest.

I was wakened, after having slept uneasily for some hours, by some person shaking me rudely by the shoulder; a small lamp burned in my room, and by its light, to my horror and amazement, I discovered that my visitant was the self-same blind old lady who had so terrified me a few weeks before.

I started up in the bed, with a view to ring the bell, and alarm the domestics; but she instantly anticipated me by saying:

"Do not be frightened, silly girl! If I had wished to harm you I could have done it while you were sleeping; I need not have wakened you. Listen to me, now, attentively and fearlessly, for what I have to say interests you to the full as much as it does me. Tell me here, in the presence of God, did Lord Glenfallen marry you—ACTUALLY MARRY you? Speak the truth, woman."

"As surely as I live and speak," I replied, "did Lord Glenfallen marry me, in presence of more than a hundred witnesses."

"Well," continued she, "he should have told you THEN, before you married him, that he had a wife living, which wife I am. I feel you tremble—tush! do not be frightened. I do not mean to harm you. Mark me now—you are NOT his wife. When I make my story known you will be so neither in the eye of God nor of man. You must leave this house upon tomorrow. Let the world know that your husband has another wife living; go you into retirement, and leave him to justice, which will surely overtake him. If you remain in this house after tomorrow you will reap the bitter fruits of your sin."

So saying, she quitted the room, leaving me very little disposed to sleep.

Here was food for my very worst and most terrible suspicions; still there was not enough to remove all doubt. I had no proof of the truth of this woman's statement.

Taken by itself, there was nothing to induce me to attach weight to it; but when I viewed it in connection with the extraordinary mystery of some of Lord Glenfallen's proceedings, his strange anxiety to exclude me from certain portions of the mansion, doubtless lest I should encounter this person—the strong influence, nay, command which she possessed over him, a circumstance clearly established by the very fact of her residing in the very place where, of all others, he should least have desired to find her—her thus acting, and continuing to act in direct contradiction to his wishes; when, I say, I viewed her disclosure in connection with all these circumstances, I could not help feeling that there was at least a fearful verisimilitude in the allegations which she had made.

Still I was not satisfied, nor nearly so. Young minds have a reluctance almost insurmountable to believing, upon anything short of unquestionable proof, the existence of premeditated guilt in anyone whom they have ever trusted; and in support of this feeling I was assured that if the assertion of Lord Glenfallen, which nothing in this woman's manner had led me to disbelieve, were true, namely that her mind was unsound, the whole fabric of my doubts and fears must fall to the ground.

I determined to state to Lord Glenfallen freely and accurately the substance of the communication which I had just heard, and in his words and looks to seek for its proof or refutation. Full of these thoughts, I remained wakeful and excited all night, every moment fancying that I heard the step or saw the figure of my recent visitor, towards whom I felt a species of horror and dread which I can hardly describe.

There was something in her face, though her features had evidently been handsome, and were not, at first sight, unpleasing, which, upon a nearer inspection, seemed to indicate the habitual prevalence and indulgence of evil passions, and a power of expressing mere animal anger, with an intenseness that I have seldom seen equalled, and to which an almost unearthly effect was given by the convulsive quivering of the sightless eyes.

You may easily suppose that it was no very pleasing reflection to me to consider that, whenever caprice might induce her to return, I was within the reach of this violent and, for aught I knew, insane woman, who had, upon that very night, spoken to me in a tone of menace, of which her mere words, divested of the manner and look with which she uttered them, can convey but a faint idea.

Will you believe me when I tell you that I was actually afraid to leave my bed in order to secure the door, lest I should again encounter the dreadful object lurking in some corner or peeping from behind the window-curtains, so very a child was I in my fears.

The morning came, and with it Lord Glenfallen. I knew not, and indeed I cared not, where he might have been; my thoughts were wholly engrossed by the terrible fears and suspicions which my last night's conference had suggested to me. He was, as usual, gloomy and abstracted, and I feared in no very fitting mood to hear what I had to say with patience, whether the charges were true or false.

I was, however, determined not to suffer the opportunity to pass, or Lord Glenfallen to leave the room, until, at all hazards, I had unburdened my mind.

"My lord," said I, after a long silence, summoning up all my firmness—"my lord, I wish to say a few words to you upon a matter of very great importance, of very deep concernment to you and to me."

I fixed my eyes upon him to discern, if possible, whether the announcement caused him any uneasiness; but no symptom of any such feeling was perceptible.

"Well, my dear," said he, "this is no doubt a very grave preface, and portends, I have no doubt, something extraordinary. Pray let us have it without more ado."

He took a chair, and seated himself nearly opposite to me.

"My lord," said I, "I have seen the person who alarmed me so much a short time since, the blind lady, again, upon last night." His face, upon which my eyes were fixed, turned pale; he hesitated for a moment, and then said:

"And did you, pray, madam, so totally forget or spurn my express command, as to enter that portion of the house from which your promise, I might say your oath, excluded you?—answer me that!" he added fiercely.

"My lord," said I, "I have neither forgotten your COMMANDS, since such they were, nor disobeyed them. I was, last night, wakened from my sleep, as I lay in my own chamber, and accosted by the person whom I have mentioned. How she found access to the room I cannot pretend to say."

"Ha! this must be looked to," said he, half reflectively; "and pray," added he, quickly, while in turn he fixed his eyes upon me, "what did this person say? since some comment upon her communication forms, no doubt, the sequel to your preface."

"Your lordship is not mistaken," said I; "her statement was so extraordinary that I could not think of withholding it from you. She told me, my lord, that you had a wife living at the time you married me, and that she was that wife."

Lord Glenfallen became ashy pale, almost livid; he made two or three efforts to clear his voice to speak, but in vain, and turning suddenly from me, he walked to the window. The horror and dismay which, in the olden time, overwhelmed the woman of Endor when her spells unexpectedly conjured the dead into her presence, were but types of what I felt when thus presented with what appeared to be almost unequivocal evidence of the guilt whose existence I had before so strongly doubted.

There was a silence of some moments, during which it were hard to conjecture whether I or my companion suffered most.

Lord Glenfallen soon recovered his self-command; he returned to the table, again sat down and said:

"What you have told me has so astonished me, has unfolded such a tissue of motiveless guilt, and in a quarter from which I had so little reason to look for ingratitude or treachery, that your announcement almost deprived me of speech; the person in question, however, has one excuse, her mind is, as I told you before, unsettled. You should have remembered that, and hesitated to receive as unexceptionable evidence against the honour of your husband, the ravings of a lunatic. I now tell you that this is the last time I shall speak to you upon this subject, and, in the presence of the God who is to judge me, and as I hope for mercy in the day of judgment, I swear that the charge thus brought against me is utterly false, unfounded, and ridiculous; I defy the world in any point to taint my honour; and, as I have never taken the opinion of madmen touching your character or morals, I think it but fair to require that you will evince a like tenderness for me; and now, once for all, never again dare to repeat to me your insulting suspicions, or the clumsy and infamous calumnies of fools. I shall instantly let the worthy lady who contrived this somewhat original device, understand fully my opinion upon the matter. Good morning"; and with these words he left me again in doubt, and involved in all horrors of the most agonising suspense.

I had reason to think that Lord Glenfallen wreaked his vengeance upon the author of the strange story which I had heard, with a violence which was not satisfied with mere words, for old Martha, with whom I was a great favourite, while attending me in my room, told me that she feared her master had ill-used the poor blind Dutch woman, for that she had heard her scream as if the very life were leaving her, but added a request that I should not speak of what she had told me to anyone, particularly to the master.

"How do you know that she is a Dutch woman?" inquired I, anxious to learn anything whatever that might throw a light upon the history of this person, who seemed to have resolved to mix herself up in my fortunes.

"Why, my lady," answered Martha, "the master often calls her the Dutch hag, and other names you would not like to hear, and I am sure she is neither English nor Irish; for, whenever they talk together, they speak some queer foreign lingo, and fast enough, I'll be bound. But I ought not to talk about her at all; it might be as much as my place is worth to mention her—only you saw her first yourself, so there can be no great harm in speaking of her now."

"How long has this lady been here?" continued I.

"She came early on the morning after your ladyship's arrival," answered she; "but do not ask me anymore, for the master would think nothing of turning me out of doors for daring to speak of her at all, much less to you, my lady."

I did not like to press the poor woman further, for her reluctance to speak on this topic was evident and strong.

You will readily believe that upon the very slight grounds which my information afforded, contradicted as it was by the solemn oath of my husband, and derived from what was, at best, a very questionable source, I could not take any very decisive measure whatever; and as to the menace of the strange woman who had thus unaccountably twice intruded herself into my chamber, although, at the moment, it occasioned me some uneasiness, it was not, even in my eyes, sufficiently formidable to induce my departure from Cahergillagh.

A few nights after the scene which I have just mentioned, Lord Glenfallen having, as usual, early retired to his study, I was left alone in the parlour to amuse myself as best I might.

It was not strange that my thoughts should often recur to the agitating scenes in which I had recently taken a part.

The subject of my reflections, the solitude, the silence, and the lateness of the hour, as also the depression of spirits to which I had of late been a constant prey, tended to produce that nervous excitement which places us wholly at the mercy of the imagination.

In order to calm my spirits I was endeavouring to direct my thoughts into some more pleasing channel, when I heard, or thought I heard, uttered, within a few yards of me, in an odd, half-sneering tone, the words,

"There is blood upon your ladyship's throat."

So vivid was the impression that I started to my feet, and involuntarily placed my hand upon my neck.

I looked around the room for the speaker, but in vain.

I went then to the room-door, which I opened, and peered into the passage, nearly faint with horror lest some leering, shapeless thing should greet me upon the threshold.

When I had gazed long enough to assure myself that no strange object was within sight, "I have been too much of a rake lately; I am racking out my nerves," said I, speaking aloud, with a view to reassure myself.

I rang the bell, and, attended by old Martha, I retired to settle for the night.

While the servant was—as was her custom—arranging the lamp which I have already stated always burned during the night in my chamber, I was employed in undressing, and, in doing so, I had recourse to a large looking-glass which occupied a considerable portion of the wall in which it was fixed, rising from the ground to a height of about six feet—this mirror filled the space of a large panel in the wainscoting opposite the foot of the bed.

I had hardly been before it for the lapse of a minute when something like a black pall was slowly waved between me and it.

"Oh, God! there it is," I exclaimed, wildly. "I have seen it again, Martha—the black cloth."

"God be merciful to us, then!" answered she, tremulously crossing herself. "Some misfortune is over us."

"No, no, Martha," said I, almost instantly recovering my collectedness; for, although of a nervous temperament, I had never been superstitious. "I do not believe in omens. You know I saw, or fancied I saw, this thing before, and nothing followed."

"The Dutch lady came the next morning," replied she.

"But surely her coming scarcely deserved such a dreadful warning," I replied.

"She is a strange woman, my lady," said Martha; "and she is not Gone yet—mark my words."

"Well, well, Martha," said I, "I have not wit enough to change your opinions, nor inclination to alter mine; so I will talk no more of the matter. Goodnight," and so I was left to my reflections.

After lying for about an hour awake, I at length fell into a kind of doze; but my imagination was still busy, for I was startled from this unrefreshing sleep by fancying that I heard a voice close to my face exclaim as before:

"There is blood upon your ladyship's throat."

The words were instantly followed by a loud burst of laughter.

Quaking with horror, I awakened, and heard my husband enter the room. Even this was it relief.

Scared as I was, however, by the tricks which my imagination had played me, I preferred remaining silent, and pretending to sleep, to attempting to engage my husband in conversation, for I well knew that his mood was such, that his words would not, in all probability, convey anything that had not better be unsaid and unheard.

Lord Glenfallen went into his dressing-room, which lay upon the right-hand side of the bed. The door lying open, I could see him by himself, at full length upon a sofa, and, in about half an hour, I became aware, by his deep and regularly drawn respiration, that he was fast asleep.

When slumber refuses to visit one, there is something peculiarly irritating, not to the temper, but to the nerves, in the consciousness that someone is in your immediate presence, actually enjoying the boon which you are seeking in vain; at least, I have always found it so, and never more than upon the present occasion.

A thousand annoying imaginations harassed and excited me; every object which I looked upon, though ever so familiar, seemed to have acquired a strange phantom-like character, the varying shadows thrown by the flickering of the lamplight, seemed shaping themselves into grotesque and unearthly forms, and whenever my eyes wandered to the

JOSEPH SHERIDAN LE FANU

sleeping figure of my husband, his features appeared to undergo the strangest and most demoniacal contortions.

Hour after hour was told by the old clock, and each succeeding one found me, if possible, less inclined to sleep than its predecessor.

It was now considerably past three; my eyes, in their involuntary wanderings, happened to alight upon the large mirror which was, as I have said, fixed in the wall opposite the foot of the bed. A view of it was commanded from where I lay, through the curtains. As I gazed fixedly upon it, I thought I perceived the broad sheet of glass shifting its position in relation to the bed; I riveted my eyes upon it with intense scrutiny; it was no deception, the mirror, as if acting of its own impulse, moved slowly aside, and disclosed a dark aperture in the wall, nearly as large as an ordinary door; a figure evidently stood in this, but the light was too dim to define it accurately.

It stepped cautiously into the chamber, and with so little noise, that had I not actually seen it, I do not think I should have been aware of its presence. It was arrayed in a kind of woollen night-dress, and a white handkerchief or cloth was bound tightly about the head; I had no difficulty, spite of the strangeness of the attire, in recognising the blind woman whom I so much dreaded.

She stooped down, bringing her head nearly to the ground, and in that attitude she remained motionless for some moments, no doubt in order to ascertain if any suspicious sound were stirring.

She was apparently satisfied by her observations, for she immediately recommenced her silent progress towards a ponderous mahogany dressing-table of my husband's. When she had reached it, she paused again, and appeared to listen attentively for some minutes; she then noiselessly opened one of the drawers, from which, having groped for sometime, she took something, which I soon perceived to be a case of razors. She opened it, and tried the edge of each of the two instruments upon the skin of her hand; she quickly selected one, which she fixed firmly in her grasp. She now stooped down as before, and having listened for a time, she, with the hand that was disengaged, groped her way into the dressing-room where Lord Glenfallen lay fast asleep.

I was fixed as if in the tremendous spell of a nightmare. I could not stir even a finger; I could not lift my voice; I could not even breathe; and though I expected every moment to see the sleeping man murdered, I could not even close my eyes to shut out the horrible spectacle, which I had not the power to avert.

I saw the woman approach the sleeping figure, she laid the unoccupied hand lightly along his clothes, and having thus ascertained his identity, she, after a brief interval, turned back and again entered my chamber; here she bent down again to listen.

I had now not a doubt but that the razor was intended for my throat; yet the terrific fascination which had locked all my powers so long, still continued to bind me fast.

I felt that my life depended upon the slightest ordinary exertion, and yet I could not stir one joint from the position in which I lay, nor even make noise enough to waken Lord Glenfallen.

The murderous woman now, with long, silent steps, approached the bed; my very heart seemed turning to ice; her left hand, that which was disengaged, was upon the pillow; she gradually slid it forward towards my head, and in an instant, with the speed of lightning, it was clutched in my hair, while, with the other hand, she dashed the razor at my throat.

A slight inaccuracy saved me from instant death; the blow fell short, the point of the razor grazing my throat. In a moment, I know not how, I found myself at the other side of the bed, uttering shriek after shriek; the wretch was, however, determined if possible to murder me.

Scrambling along by the curtains, she rushed round the bed towards me; I seized the handle of the door to make my escape. It was, however, fastened. At all events, I could not open it. From the mere instinct of recoiling terror, I shrunk back into a corner. She was now within a yard of me. Her hand was upon my face.

I closed my eyes fast, expecting never to open them again, when a blow, inflicted from behind by a strong arm, stretched the monster senseless at my feet. At the same moment the door opened, and several domestics, alarmed by my cries, entered the apartment.

I do not recollect what followed, for I fainted. One swoon succeeded another, so long and death-like, that my life was considered very doubtful.

At about ten o'clock, however, I sunk into a deep and refreshing sleep, from which I was awakened at about two, that I might swear my deposition before a magistrate, who attended for that purpose.

I accordingly did so, as did also Lord Glenfallen, and the woman was fully committed to stand her trial at the ensuing assizes.

I shall never forget the scene which the examination of the blind woman and of the other parties afforded.

She was brought into the room in the custody of two servants. She wore a kind of flannel wrapper which had not been changed since the night before. It was torn and soiled, and here and there smeared with blood, which had flowed in large quantities from a wound in her head. The white handkerchief had fallen off in the scuffle, and her grizzled hair fell in masses about her wild and deadly pale countenance.

She appeared perfectly composed, however, and the only regret she expressed throughout, was at not having succeeded in her attempt, the object of which she did not pretend to conceal.

On being asked her name, she called herself the Countess Glenfallen, and refused to give any other title.

"The woman's name is Flora Van-Kemp," said Lord Glenfallen.

"It WAS, it WAS, you perjured traitor and cheat!" screamed the woman; and then there followed a volley of words in some foreign language. "Is there a magistrate here?" she resumed; "I am Lord Glenfallen's wife—I'll prove it—write down my words. I am willing to be hanged or burned, so HE meets his deserts. I did try to kill that doll of his; but it was he who put it into my head to do it—two wives were too many; I was to murder her, or she was to hang me; listen to all I have to say."

Here Lord Glenfallen interrupted.

"I think, sir," said he, addressing the magistrate, "that we had better proceed to business; this unhappy woman's furious recriminations but waste our time. If she refuses to answer your questions, you had better, I presume, take my depositions."

"And are you going to swear away my life, you black-perjured murderer?" shrieked the woman. "Sir, sir, sir, you must hear me," she continued, addressing the magistrate; "I can convict him—he bid me murder that girl, and then, when I failed, he came behind me, and struck me down, and now he wants to swear away my life. Take down all I say."

"If it is your intention," said the magistrate, "to confess the crime with which you stand charged, you may, upon producing sufficient evidence, criminate whom you please."

"Evidence!—I have no evidence but myself," said the woman. "I will swear it all—write down my testimony—write it down, I say—we shall hang side by side, my brave lord—all your own handy-work, my gentle husband."

This was followed by a low, insolent, and sneering laugh, which, from one in her situation, was sufficiently horrible.

"I will not at present hear anything," replied he, "but distinct answers to the questions which I shall put to you upon this matter."

"Then you shall hear nothing," replied she sullenly, and no inducement or intimidation could bring her to speak again.

Lord Glenfallen's deposition and mine were then given, as also those of the servants who had entered the room at the moment of my rescue.

The magistrate then intimated that she was committed, and must proceed directly to gaol, whither she was brought in a carriage; of Lord Glenfallen's, for his lordship was naturally by no means indifferent to the effect which her vehement accusations against himself might produce, if uttered before every chance hearer whom she might meet with between Cahergillagh and the place of confinement whither she was despatched.

During the time which intervened between the committal and the trial of the prisoner, Lord Glenfallen seemed to suffer agonies of mind which baffle all description; he hardly ever slept, and when he did, his slumbers seemed but the instruments of new tortures, and his waking hours were, if possible, exceeded in intensity of terrors by the dreams which disturbed his sleep.

Lord Glenfallen rested, if to lie in the mere attitude of repose were to do so, in his dressing-room, and thus I had an opportunity of witnessing, far oftener than I wished it, the fearful workings of his mind. His agony often broke out into such fearful paroxysms that delirium and total loss of reason appeared to be impending. He frequently spoke of flying from the country, and bringing with him all the witnesses of the appalling scene upon which the prosecution was founded; then, again, he would fiercely lament that the blow which he had inflicted had not ended all.

The assizes arrived, however, and upon the day appointed Lord Glenfallen and I attended in order to give our evidence.

The cause was called on, and the prisoner appeared at the bar.

Great curiosity and interest were felt respecting the trial, so that the court was crowded to excess.

The prisoner, however, without appearing to take the trouble of listening to the indictment, pleaded guilty, and no representations on the part of the court availed to induce her to retract her plea.

After much time had been wasted in a fruitless attempt to prevail upon her to reconsider her words, the court proceeded, according to the usual form, to pass sentence.

This having been done, the prisoner was about to be removed, when she said, in a low, distinct voice:

JOSEPH SHERIDAN LE FANU

"A word—a word, my lord!—Is Lord Glenfallen here in the court?"

On being told that he was, she raised her voice to a tone of loud menace, and continued:

"Hardress, Earl of Glenfallen, I accuse you here in this court of justice of two crimes,—first, that you married a second wife, while the first was living; and again, that you prompted me to the murder, for attempting which I am to die. Secure him—chain him—bring him here."

There was a laugh through the court at these words, which were naturally treated by the judge as a violent extemporary recrimination, and the woman was desired to be silent.

"You won't take him, then?" she said; "you won't try him? You'll let him go free?"

It was intimated by the court that he would certainly be allowed "to go free," and she was ordered again to be removed.

Before, however, the mandate was executed, she threw her arms wildly into the air, and uttered one piercing shriek so full of preternatural rage and despair, that it might fitly have ushered a soul into those realms where hope can come no more.

The sound still rang in my ears, months after the voice that had uttered it was forever silent.

The wretched woman was executed in accordance with the sentence which had been pronounced.

For sometime after this event, Lord Glenfallen appeared, if possible, to suffer more than he had done before, and altogether his language, which often amounted to half confessions of the guilt imputed to him, and all the circumstances connected with the late occurrences, formed a mass of evidence so convincing that I wrote to my father, detailing the grounds of my fears, and imploring him to come to Cahergillagh without delay, in order to remove me from my husband's control, previously to taking legal steps for a final separation.

Circumstanced as I was, my existence was little short of intolerable, for, besides the fearful suspicions which attached to my husband, I plainly perceived that if Lord Glenfallen were not relieved, and that speedily, insanity must supervene. I therefore expected my father's arrival, or at least a letter to announce it, with indescribable impatience.

About a week after the execution had taken place, Lord Glenfallen one morning met me with an unusually sprightly air.

"Fanny," said he, "I have it now for the first time in my power to explain to your satisfaction everything which has hitherto appeared suspicious or mysterious in my conduct. After breakfast come with me to my study, and I shall, I hope, make all things clear."

This invitation afforded me more real pleasure than I had experienced for months. Something had certainly occurred to tranquillize my husband's mind in no ordinary degree, and I thought it by no means impossible that he would, in the proposed interview, prove himself the most injured and innocent of men.

Full of this hope, I repaired to his study at the appointed hour. He was writing busily when I entered the room, and just raising his eyes, he requested me to be seated.

I took a chair as he desired, and remained silently awaiting his leisure, while he finished, folded, directed, and sealed his letter. Laying it then upon the table with the address downward, he said,

"My dearest Fanny, I know I must have appeared very strange to you and very unkind—often even cruel. Before the end of this week I will show you the necessity of my conduct—how impossible it was that I should have seemed otherwise. I am conscious that many acts of mine must have inevitably given rise to painful suspicions—suspicions which, indeed, upon one occasion, you very properly communicated to me. I have got two letters from a quarter which commands respect, containing information as to the course by which I may be enabled to prove the negative of all the crimes which even the most credulous suspicion could lay to my charge. I expected a third by this morning's post, containing documents which will set the matter forever at rest, but owing, no doubt, to some neglect, or, perhaps, to some difficulty in collecting the papers, some inevitable delay, it has not come to hand this morning, according to my expectation. I was finishing one to the very same quarter when you came in, and if a sound rousing be worth anything, I think I shall have a special messenger before two days have passed. I have been anxiously considering with myself, as to whether I had better imperfectly clear up your doubts by submitting to your inspection the two letters which I have already received, or wait till I can triumphantly vindicate myself by the production of the documents which I have already mentioned, and I have, I think, not unnaturally decided upon the latter course. However, there is a person in the next room whose testimony is not without its value excuse me for one moment."

So saying, he arose and went to the door of a closet which opened from the study; this he unlocked, and half opening the door, he said,

"It is only I," and then slipped into the room and carefully closed and locked the door behind him.

I immediately heard his voice in animated conversation. My curiosity upon the subject of the letter was naturally great, so, smothering any little scruples which I might have felt, I resolved to look at the address of the letter which lay, as my husband had left it, with its face upon the table. I accordingly drew it over to me and turned up the direction.

For two or three moments I could scarce believe my eyes, but there could be no mistake—in large characters were traced the words, "To the Archangel Gabriel in Heaven."

I had scarcely returned the letter to its original position, and in some degree recovered the shock which this unequivocal proof of insanity produced, when the closet door was unlocked, and Lord Glenfallen re-entered the study, carefully closing and locking the door again upon the outside.

"Whom have you there?" inquired I, making a strong effort to appear calm.

"Perhaps," said he, musingly, "you might have some objection to seeing her, at least for a time."

"Who is it?" repeated I.

"Why," said he, "I see no use in hiding it—the blind Dutchwoman. I have been with her the whole morning. She is very anxious to get out of that closet; but you know she is odd, she is scarcely to be trusted."

A heavy gust of wind shook the door at this moment with a sound as if something more substantial were pushing against it.

"Ha, ha, ha!—do you hear her?" said he, with an obstreperous burst of laughter.

The wind died away in a long howl, and Lord Glenfallen, suddenly checking his merriment, shrugged his shoulders, and muttered:

"Poor devil, she has been hardly used."

"We had better not tease her at present with questions," said I, in as unconcerned a tone as I could assume, although I felt every moment as if I should faint.

"Humph! may be so," said he. "Well, come back in an hour or two, or when you please, and you will find us here."

He again unlocked the door, and entered with the same precautions which he had adopted before, locking the door upon the inside; and as I hurried from the room, I heard his voice again exerted as if in eager parley.

I can hardly describe my emotions; my hopes had been raised to the highest, and now, in an instant, all was gone—the dreadful consummation was accomplished—the fearful retribution had fallen upon the guilty man—the mind was destroyed—the power to repent was gone.

The agony of the hours which followed what I would still call my AWFUL interview with Lord Glenfallen, I cannot describe; my solitude was, however, broken in upon by Martha, who came to inform me of the arrival of a gentleman, who expected me in the parlour.

I accordingly descended, and, to my great joy, found my father seated by the fire.

This expedition upon his part was easily accounted for: my communications had touched the honour of the family. I speedily informed him of the dreadful malady which had fallen upon the wretched man.

My father suggested the necessity of placing some person to watch him, to prevent his injuring himself or others.

I rang the bell, and desired that one Edward Cooke, an attached servant of the family, should be sent to me.

I told him distinctly and briefly the nature of the service required of him, and, attended by him, my father and I proceeded at once to the study. The door of the inner room was still closed, and everything in the outer chamber remained in the same order in which I had left it.

We then advanced to the closet-door, at which we knocked, but without receiving any answer.

We next tried to open the door, but in vain—it was locked upon the inside. We knocked more loudly, but in vain.

Seriously alarmed, I desired the servant to force the door, which was, after several violent efforts, accomplished, and we entered the closet.

Lord Glenfallen was lying on his face upon a sofa.

"Hush!" said I, "he is asleep." We paused for a moment.

"He is too still for that," said my father.

We all of us felt a strong reluctance to approach the figure.

"Edward," said I, "try whether your master sleeps."

The servant approached the sofa where Lord Glenfallen lay. He leant his ear towards the head of the recumbent figure, to ascertain whether the sound of breathing was audible. He turned towards us, and said:

"My lady, you had better not wait here; I am sure he is dead!"

"Let me see the face," said I, terribly agitated; "you MAY be mistaken."

The man then, in obedience to my command, turned the body round, and, gracious God! what a sight met my view. He was, indeed, perfectly dead.

The whole breast of the shirt, with its lace frill, was drenched with gore, as was the couch underneath the spot where he lay.

The head hung back, as it seemed, almost severed from the body by a frightful gash, which yawned across the throat. The instrument which had inflicted it was found under his body.

All, then, was over; I was never to learn the history in whose termination I had been so deeply and so tragically involved.

The severe discipline which my mind had undergone was not bestowed in vain. I directed my thoughts and my hopes to that place where there is no more sin, nor danger, nor sorrow.

Thus ends a brief tale whose prominent incidents many will recognise as having marked the history of a distinguished family; and though it refers to a somewhat distant date, we shall be found not to have taken, upon that account, any liberties with the facts, but in our statement of all the incidents to have rigorously and faithfully adhered to the truth.

An Authentic Narrative
of a Haunted House

W ithin the last eight years—the precise date I purposely omit—I was ordered by my physician, my health being in an unsatisfactory state, to change my residence to one upon the sea-coast; and accordingly, I took a house for a year in a fashionable watering-place, at a moderate distance from the city in which I had previously resided, and connected with it by a railway.

Winter was setting in when my removal thither was decided upon; but there was nothing whatever dismal or depressing in the change. The house I had taken was to all appearance, and in point of convenience, too, quite a modern one. It formed one in a cheerful row, with small gardens in front, facing the sea, and commanding sea air and sea views in perfection. In the rear it had coach-house and stable, and between them and the house a considerable grass-plot, with some flower-beds, interposed.

Our family consisted of my wife and myself, with three children, the eldest about nine years old, she and the next in age being girls; and the youngest, between six and seven, a boy. To these were added six servants, whom, although for certain reasons I decline giving their real names, I shall indicate, for the sake of clearness, by arbitrary ones. There was a nurse, Mrs. Southerland; a nursery-maid, Ellen Page; the cook, Mrs. Greenwood; and the housemaid, Ellen Faith; a butler, whom I shall call Smith, and his son, James, about two-and-twenty.

We came out to take possession at about seven o'clock in the evening; everything was comfortable and cheery; good fires lighted, the rooms neat and airy, and a general air of preparation and comfort, highly conducive to good spirits and pleasant anticipations.

The sitting-rooms were large and cheerful, and they and the bed-rooms more than ordinarily lofty, the kitchen and servants' rooms, on the same level, were well and comfortably furnished, and had, like the rest of the house, an air of recent painting and fitting up, and a completely modern character, which imparted a very cheerful air of cleanliness and convenience.

There had been just enough of the fuss of settling agreeably to occupy us, and to give a pleasant turn to our thoughts after we had retired to our rooms. Being an invalid, I had a small bed to myself—resigning the four-poster to my wife. The candle was extinguished, but a night-light was burning. I was coming up stairs, and she, already in bed, had just dismissed her maid, when we were both startled by a wild scream from her room; I found her in a state of the extremest agitation and terror. She insisted that she had seen an unnaturally tall figure come beside her bed and stand there. The light was too faint to enable her to define anything respecting this apparition, beyond the fact of her having most distinctly seen such a shape, colourless from the insufficiency of the light to disclose more than its dark outline.

We both endeavoured to re-assure her. The room once more looked so cheerful in the candlelight, that we were quite uninfluenced by the contagion of her terrors. The movements and voices of the servants down stairs still getting things into their places and completing our comfortable arrangements, had also their effect in steeling us against any such influence, and we set the whole thing down as a dream, or an imperfectly-seen outline of the bed-curtains. When, however, we were alone, my wife reiterated, still in great agitation, her clear assertion that she had most positively seen, being at the time as completely awake as ever she was, precisely what she had described to us. And in this conviction she continued perfectly firm.

A day or two after this, it came out that our servants were under an apprehension that, somehow or other, thieves had established a secret mode of access to the lower part of the house. The butler, Smith, had seen an ill-looking woman in his room on the first night of our arrival; and he and other servants constantly saw, for many days subsequently, glimpses of a retreating figure, which corresponded with that so seen by him, passing through a passage which led to a back area in which were some coal-vaults.

This figure was seen always in the act of retreating, its back turned, generally getting round the corner of the passage into the area, in a stealthy and hurried way, and, when closely followed, imperfectly seen again entering one of the coal-vaults, and when pursued into it, nowhere to be found.

The idea of anything supernatural in the matter had, strange to say, not yet entered the mind of anyone of the servants. They had heard some stories of smugglers having secret passages into houses, and using their means of access for purposes of pillage, or with a view to frighten superstitious people out of houses which they needed for their own objects, and a suspicion of similar practices here, caused them extreme uneasiness. The apparent anxiety also manifested by this retreating figure to escape observation, and her always appearing to make her egress at the same point, favoured this romantic hypothesis. The men, however, made a most careful examination of the back area, and of the coal-vaults, with a view to discover some mode of egress, but entirely without success. On the contrary, the result was, so far as it went, subversive of the theory; solid masonry met them on every hand.

I called the man, Smith, up, to hear from his own lips the particulars of what he had seen; and certainly his report was very curious. I give it as literally as my memory enables me:—

His son slept in the same room, and was sound asleep; but he lay awake, as men sometimes will on a change of bed, and having many things on his mind. He was lying with his face towards the wall, but observing a light and some little stir in the room, he turned round in his bed, and saw the figure of a woman, squalid, and ragged in dress; her figure rather low and broad; as well as I recollect, she had something—either a cloak or shawl—on, and wore a bonnet. Her back was turned, and she appeared to be searching or rummaging for something on the floor, and, without appearing to observe him, she turned in doing so towards him. The light, which was more like the intense glow of a coal, as he described it, being of a deep red colour, proceeded from the hollow of her hand, which she held beside her head, and he saw her perfectly distinctly. She appeared middle-aged, was deeply pitted with the smallpox, and blind of one eye. His phrase in describing her general appearance was, that she was "a miserable, poor-looking creature."

He was under the impression that she must be the woman who had been left by the proprietor in charge of the house, and who had that evening, after having given up the keys, remained for some little time with the female servants. He coughed, therefore, to apprize her of his presence, and turned again towards the wall. When he again looked round she and the light were gone; and odd as was her method of lighting herself in her search, the circumstances excited neither uneasiness nor curiosity in his mind, until he discovered next morning that the woman in question had left the house long before he had gone to his bed.

I examined the man very closely as to the appearance of the person who had visited him, and the result was what I have described. It struck me as an odd thing, that even then, considering how prone to superstition persons in his rank of life usually are, he did not seem to suspect anything supernatural in the occurrence; and, on the contrary, was thoroughly persuaded that his visitant was a living person, who had got into the house by some hidden entrance.

On Sunday, on his return from his place of worship, he told me that, when the service was ended, and the congregation making their way slowly out, he saw the very woman in the crowd, and kept his eye upon her for several minutes, but such was the crush, that all his efforts to reach her were unavailing, and when he got into the open street she was gone. He was quite positive as to his having distinctly seen her, however, for several minutes, and scouted the possibility of any mistake as to identity; and fully impressed with the substantial and living reality of his visitant, he was very much provoked at her having escaped him. He made inquiries also in the neighbourhood, but could procure no information, nor hear of any other persons having seen any woman corresponding with his visitant.

The cook and the housemaid occupied a bed-room on the kitchen floor. It had whitewashed walls, and they were actually terrified by the appearance of the shadow of a woman passing and repassing across the side wall opposite to their beds. They suspected that this had been going on much longer than they were aware, for its presence was discovered by a sort of accident, its movements happening to take a direction in distinct contrariety to theirs.

This shadow always moved upon one particular wall, returning after short intervals, and causing them extreme terror. They placed the candle, as the most obvious specific, so close to the infested wall, that the flame all but touched it; and believed for sometime that they had effectually got rid of this annoyance; but one night, notwithstanding this arrangement of the light, the shadow returned, passing and repassing, as heretofore, upon the same wall, although their only candle was burning within an inch of it, and it was obvious that no substance capable of casting such a shadow could have interposed; and, indeed, as they described it, the shadow seemed to have no sort of relation to the position of the light, and appeared, as I have said, in manifest defiance of the laws of optics.

I ought to mention that the housemaid was a particularly fearless sort of person, as well as a very honest one; and her companion, the cook, a scrupulously religious woman, and both agreed in every particular in their relation of what occurred.

Meanwhile, the nursery was not without its annoyances, though as yet of a comparatively trivial kind. Sometimes, at night, the handle of the door was turned hurriedly as if by a person trying to come in, and at others a knocking was made at it. These sounds occurred after the children had settled to sleep, and while the nurse still remained awake. Whenever she called to know "who is there," the sounds ceased; but several times, and particularly at first, she was under the impression that they were caused by her mistress, who had come to see the children, and thus impressed she had got up and opened the door, expecting to see her, but discovering only darkness, and receiving no answer to her inquiries.

With respect to this nurse, I must mention that I believe no more perfectly trustworthy servant was ever employed in her capacity; and, in addition to her integrity, she was remarkably gifted with sound common sense.

One morning, I think about three or four weeks after our arrival, I was sitting at the parlour window which looked to the front, when I saw the little iron door which admitted into the small garden that lay between the window where I was sitting and the public road, pushed open by a woman who so exactly answered the description given by Smith of the woman who had visited his room on the night of his arrival as instantaneously to impress me with the conviction that she must be the identical person. She was a square, short woman, dressed in soiled and tattered clothes, scarred and pitted with small-pox, and blind of an eye. She stepped hurriedly into the little enclosure, and peered from a distance of a few yards into the room where I was sitting. I felt that now was the moment to clear the matter up; but there was something stealthy in the manner and look of the woman which convinced me that I must not appear to notice her until her retreat was fairly cut off. Unfortunately, I was suffering from a lame foot, and could not reach the bell as quickly as I wished. I made all the haste I could, and rang violently to bring up the servant Smith. In the short interval that intervened, I observed the woman from the window, who having in a leisurely way, and with a kind of scrutiny, looked along the front windows of the house, passed quickly out again, closing the gate after her, and followed a lady who was walking along the footpath at a quick pace, as if with the intention of begging from her. The moment the man entered I told him—"the blind woman you described to me has this instant followed a lady in that direction, try to overtake her." He was, if possible, more eager than I in the chase, but returned in a short time after a vain pursuit, very hot, and utterly disappointed. And, thereafter, we saw her face no more.

JOSEPH SHERIDAN LE FANU

All this time, and up to the period of our leaving the house, which was not for two or three months later, there occurred at intervals the only phenomenon in the entire series having any resemblance to what we hear described of "Spiritualism." This was a knocking, like a soft hammering with a wooden mallet, as it seemed in the timbers between the bedroom ceilings and the roof. It had this special peculiarity, that it was always rythmical, and, I think, invariably, the emphasis upon the last stroke. It would sound rapidly "one, two, three, *four*—one, two, three, *four*"; or "one, two, *three*—one, two, *three*," and sometimes "one, *two*—one, *two*," &c., and this, with intervals and resumptions, monotonously for hours at a time.

At first this caused my wife, who was a good deal confined to her bed, much annoyance; and we sent to our neighbours to inquire if any hammering or carpentering was going on in their houses but were informed that nothing of the sort was taking place. I have myself heard it frequently, always in the same inaccessible part of the house, and with the same monotonous emphasis. One odd thing about it was, that on my wife's calling out, as she used to do when it became more than usually troublesome, "stop that noise," it was invariably arrested for a longer or shorter time.

Of course none of these occurrences were ever mentioned in hearing of the children. They would have been, no doubt, like most children, greatly terrified had they heard anything of the matter, and known that their elders were unable to account for what was passing; and their fears would have made them wretched and troublesome.

They used to play for some hours everyday in the back garden—the house forming one end of this oblong inclosure, the stable and coach-house the other, and two parallel walls of considerable height the sides. Here, as it afforded a perfectly safe playground, they were frequently left quite to themselves; and in talking over their days' adventures, as children will, they happened to mention a woman, or rather the woman, for they had long grown familiar with her appearance, whom they used to see in the garden while they were at play. They assumed that she came in and went out at the stable door, but they never actually saw her enter or depart. They merely saw a figure—that of a very poor woman, soiled and ragged—near the stable wall, stooping over the ground, and apparently grubbing in the loose clay in search of something. She did not disturb, or appear to observe them; and they left her in undisturbed possession of her nook of ground. When seen it was always in the same spot, and similarly occupied; and the description they gave of her general appearance—for they never saw her face—corresponded with that of the one-eyed woman whom Smith, and subsequently as it seemed, I had seen.

The other man, James, who looked after a mare which I had purchased for the purpose of riding exercise, had, like everyone else in the house, his little trouble to report, though it was not much. The stall in which, as the most comfortable, it was decided to place her, she peremptorily declined to enter. Though a very docile and gentle little animal, there was no getting her into it. She would snort and rear, and, in fact, do or suffer anything rather than set her hoof in it. He was fain, therefore, to place her in another. And on several occasions he found her there, exhibiting all the equine symptoms of extreme fear. Like the rest of us, however, this man was not troubled in the particular case with any superstitious qualms. The mare had evidently been frightened; and he was puzzled to find out how, or by whom, for the stable was well-secured, and had, I am nearly certain, a lock-up yard outside.

One morning I was greeted with the intelligence that robbers had certainly got into the house in the night; and that one of them had actually been seen in the nursery. The witness, I found, was my eldest child, then, as I have said, about nine years of age. Having awoke in the night, and lain awake for sometime in her bed, she heard the handle of the door turn, and a person whom she distinctly saw—for it was a light night, and the window-shutters unclosed—but whom she had never seen before, stepped in on tiptoe, and with an appearance of great caution. He was a rather small man, with a very red face; he wore an oddly cut frock coat, the collar of which stood up, and trousers, rough and wide, like those of a sailor, turned up at the ankles, and either short boots or clumsy shoes, covered with mud. This man listened beside the nurse's bed, which stood next the door, as if to satisfy himself that she was sleeping soundly; and having done so for some seconds, he began to move cautiously in a diagonal line, across the room to the chimney-piece, where he stood for a while, and so resumed his tiptoe walk, skirting the wall, until he reached a chest of drawers, some of which were open, and into which he looked, and began to rummage in a hurried way, as the child supposed, making search for something worth taking away. He then passed on to the window, where was a dressing-table, at which he also stopped, turning over the things upon it, and standing for sometime at the window as if looking out, and then resuming his walk by the side wall opposite to that by which he had moved up to the window, he returned in the same way toward the nurse's bed, so as to reach it at the foot. With its side to the end wall, in which was the door, was placed the little bed in which lay my eldest child, who watched his proceedings with the extremest terror. As he drew near she instinctively moved herself in the bed, with her head and shoulders to the wall, drawing up her feet; but he passed by without appearing to observe, or, at least, to care for her presence. Immediately after the nurse turned in her bed as if about to waken; and when the child, who had drawn the clothes about her head, again ventured to peep out, the man was gone.

The child had no idea of her having seen anything more formidable than a thief. With the prowling, cautious, and noiseless manner of proceeding common to such marauders, the air and movements of the man whom she had seen entirely corresponded. And on hearing her perfectly distinct and consistent account, I could myself arrive at no other conclusion than that a stranger had actually got into the house. I had, therefore, in the first instance, a most careful examination made to discover any traces of an entrance having been made by any window into the house. The doors had been found barred and locked as usual; but no sign of anything of the sort was discernible. I then had the various articles—plate, wearing apparel, books, &c., counted; and after having conned over and reckoned up everything, it became quite clear that nothing whatever had been removed from the house, nor was there the slightest indication of anything having been so much as disturbed there. I must here state that this child was remarkably clear, intelligent, and observant; and that her description of the man, and of all that had occurred, was most exact, and as detailed as the want of perfect light rendered possible.

I felt assured that an entrance had actually been effected into the house, though for what purpose was not easily to be conjectured. The man, Smith, was equally confident upon this point; and his theory was that the object was simply to frighten us out of the house by making us believe it haunted; and he was more than ever anxious and on the alert to discover the conspirators. It often since appeared to me odd. Every year, indeed, more odd, as this cumulative case of the marvellous becomes to my mind more and more inexplicable—that underlying my sense of mystery and puzzle, was all along the quiet assumption that all these occurrences were one way or another referable to natural causes. I could not account for them, indeed, myself; but during the whole period I inhabited that house, I never once felt, though much alone, and often up very late at night, any of those tremors and thrills which everyone has at times experienced when situation and the hour are favourable. Except the cook and housemaid, who were plagued with the shadow I mentioned crossing and recrossing upon the bedroom wall, we all, without exception, experienced the same strange sense of security, and regarded these phenomena rather with a perplexed sort of interest and curiosity, than with anymore unpleasant sensations.

The knockings which I have mentioned at the nursery door, preceded generally by the sound of a step on the lobby, meanwhile continued. At that time (for my wife, like myself, was an invalid) two eminent physicians, who came out occasionally by rail, were attending us. These gentlemen were at first only amused, but ultimately interested, and very much puzzled by the occurrences which we described. One of them, at last, recommended that a candle should be kept burning upon the lobby. It was in fact a recurrence to an old woman's recipe against ghosts—of course it might be serviceable, too, against impostors; at all events, seeming, as I have said, very much interested and puzzled, he advised it, and it was tried. We fancied that it was successful; for there was an interval of quiet for, I think, three or four nights. But after that, the noises—the footsteps on the lobby—the knocking at the door, and the turning of the handle recommenced in full force, notwithstanding the light upon the table outside; and these particular phenomena became only more perplexing than ever.

The alarm of robbers and smugglers gradually subsided after a week or two; but we were again to hear news from the nursery. Our second little girl, then between seven and eight years of age, saw in the night time— she alone being awake—a young woman, with black, or very dark hair, which hung loose, and with a black cloak on, standing near the middle of the floor, opposite the hearthstone, and fronting the foot of her bed. She appeared quite unobservant of the children and nurse sleeping in the room. She was very pale, and looked, the child said, both "sorry and frightened," and with something very peculiar and terrible about her eyes, which made the child conclude that she was dead. She was looking, not at, but in the direction of the child's bed, and there was a dark streak across her throat, like a scar with blood upon it. This figure was not motionless; but once or twice turned slowly, and without appearing to be conscious of the presence of the child, or the other occupants of the room, like a person in vacancy or abstraction. There was on this occasion a night-light burning in the chamber; and the child saw, or thought she saw, all these particulars with the most perfect distinctness. She got her head under the bed-clothes; and although a good many years have passed since then, she cannot recall the spectacle without feelings of peculiar horror.

One day, when the children were playing in the back garden, I asked them to point out to me the spot where they were accustomed to see the woman who occasionally showed herself as I have described, near the stable wall. There was no division of opinion as to this precise point, which they indicated in the most distinct and confident way. I suggested that, perhaps, something might be hidden there in the ground; and advised them digging a hole there with their little spades, to try for it. Accordingly, to work they went, and by my return in the evening they had grubbed up a piece of a jawbone, with several teeth in it. The bone was very much decayed, and ready to crumble to pieces, but the teeth were quite sound. I could not tell whether they were human grinders; but I showed the fossil to one of the physicians I have mentioned, who came out the next evening, and he pronounced them human teeth. The same conclusion was come to a day or two later by the other medical man. It appears to me now, on reviewing the whole matter, almost unaccountable that, with such evidence before me, I should not have got in a labourer, and had the spot effectually dug and searched. I can only say, that so it was. I was quite satisfied of the moral truth of every word that had been related to me, and which I have here set down with scrupulous accuracy. But I experienced an apathy, for which neither then nor afterwards did I quite know how to account. I had a vague, but immovable impression that the whole affair was referable to natural agencies. It was not until sometime after we had left the house, which, by-the-by, we afterwards found had had the reputation of being haunted before we had come to live in it, that on reconsideration I discovered the serious difficulty of accounting satisfactorily for all that had occurred upon ordinary principles. A great deal we might arbitrarily set down to imagination. But even in so doing there was, *in limine*, the oddity, not to say improbability, of so many different persons having nearly simultaneously suffered from different spectral and other illusions during the short period for which we had occupied that house, who never before, nor so far as we learned, afterwards were troubled by any fears or fancies of the sort. There were other things, too, not to be so accounted for. The odd knockings in the roof I frequently heard myself.

There were also, which I before forgot to mention, in the daytime, rappings at the doors of the sitting-rooms, which constantly deceived us; and it was not till our "come in" was unanswered, and the hall or passage outside the door was discovered to be empty, that we learned that whatever else caused them, human hands did not. All the persons who reported having seen the different persons or appearances here described by me, were just as confident of having literally and distinctly seen them, as I was of having seen the hard-featured woman with the blind eye, so remarkably corresponding with Smith's description.

About a week after the discovery of the teeth, which were found, I think, about two feet under the ground, a friend, much advanced in years, and who remembered the town in which we had now taken up our abode, for a very long time, happened to pay us a visit. He good-humouredly pooh-poohed the whole thing; but at the same time was evidently curious about it. "We might construct a sort of story," said I (I am giving, of course, the substance and purport, not the exact words, of our dialogue), "and assign to each of the three figures who appeared their respective parts in some dreadful tragedy enacted in this house. The male figure represents the murderer; the ill-looking, one-eyed woman his accomplice, who, we will suppose, buried the body where she is now so often seen grubbing in the earth, and where the human teeth and jawbone have so lately been disinterred; and the young woman with dishevelled tresses, and black cloak, and the bloody scar across her throat, their victim. A difficulty, however, which I cannot get over, exists in the cheerfulness, the great publicity, and the evident very recent date of the house." "Why, as to that," said he, "the house is *not* modern; it and those beside it formed an old government store, altered and fitted up recently as you see. I remember it well in my young days, fifty years ago, before the town had grown out in this direction, and a more entirely lonely spot, or one more fitted for the commission of a secret crime, could not have been imagined."

I have nothing to add, for very soon after this my physician pronounced a longer stay unnecessary for my health, and we took our departure for another place of abode. I may add, that although I have resided for considerable periods in many other houses, I never experienced any annoyances of a similar kind elsewhere; neither have I made (stupid dog! you will say), any inquiries respecting either the antecedents or subsequent history of the house in which we made so disturbed a sojourn. I was content with what I knew, and have here related as clearly as I could, and I think it a very pretty puzzle as it stands.

The Child That Went with the Fairies

E astward of the old city of Limerick, about ten Irish miles under the range of mountains known as the Slieveelim hills, famous as having afforded Sarsfield a shelter among their rocks and hollows, when he crossed them in his gallant descent upon the cannon and ammunition of King William, on its way to the beleaguering army, there runs a very old and narrow road. It connects the Limerick road to Tipperary with the old road from Limerick to Dublin, and runs by bog and pasture, hill and hollow, straw-thatched village, and roofless castle, not far from twenty miles.

Skirting the healthy mountains of which I have spoken, at one part it becomes singularly lonely. For more than three Irish miles it traverses a deserted country. A wide, black bog, level as a lake, skirted with copse, spreads at the left, as you journey northward, and the long and irregular line of mountain rises at the right, clothed in heath, broken with lines of grey rock that resemble the bold and irregular outlines of fortifications, and riven with many a gully, expanding here and there into rocky and wooded glens, which open as they approach the road.

A scanty pasturage, on which browsed a few scattered sheep or kine, skirts this solitary road for some miles, and under shelter of a hillock, and of two or three great ash-trees, stood, not many years ago, the little thatched cabin of a widow named Mary Ryan.

Poor was this widow in a land of poverty. The thatch had acquired the grey tint and sunken outlines, that show how the alternations of rain and sun have told upon that perishable shelter.

But whatever other dangers threatened, there was one well provided against by the care of other times. Round the cabin stood half a dozen mountain ashes, as the rowans, inimical to witches, are there called. On the worn planks of the door were nailed two horse-shoes, and over the lintel and spreading along the thatch, grew, luxuriant, patches of that ancient cure for many maladies, and prophylactic against the machinations of the evil one, the house-leek. Descending into the doorway, in the *chiaroscuro* of the interior, when your eye grew sufficiently accustomed to that dim light, you might discover, hanging at the head of the widow's wooden-roofed bed, her beads and a phial of holy water.

Here certainly were defences and bulwarks against the intrusion of that unearthly and evil power, of whose vicinity this solitary family were constantly reminded by the outline of Lisnavoura, that lonely hillhaunt of the "Good people," as the fairies are called euphemistically, whose strangely dome-like summit rose not half a mile away, looking like an outwork of the long line of mountain that sweeps by it.

It was at the fall of the leaf, and an autumnal sunset threw the lengthening shadow of haunted Lisnavoura, close in front of the solitary little cabin, over the undulating slopes and sides of Slieveelim. The birds were singing among the branches in the thinning leaves of the melancholy ash-trees that grew at the roadside in front of the door. The widow's three younger children were playing on the road, and their voices mingled with the evening song of the birds. Their elder sister, Nell, was "within in the house," as their phrase is, seeing after the boiling of the potatoes for supper.

Their mother had gone down to the bog, to carry up a hamper of turf on her back. It is, or was at least, a charitable custom—and if not disused, long may it continue—for the wealthier people when cutting their turf and stacking it in the bog, to make a smaller stack for the behoof of the poor, who were welcome to take from it so long as it lasted, and thus the potato pot was kept boiling, and hearth warm that would have been cold enough but for that good-natured bounty, through wintry months.

Moll Ryan trudged up the steep "bohereen" whose banks were overgrown with thorn and brambles, and stooping under her burden, re-entered her door, where her dark-haired daughter Nell met her with a welcome, and relieved her of her hamper.

Moll Ryan looked round with a sigh of relief, and drying her forehead, uttered the Munster exclamation:

"Eiah, wisha! It's tired I am with it, God bless it. And where's the craythurs, Nell?"

"Playin' out on the road, mother; didn't ye see them and you comin' up?"

"No; there was no one before me on the road," she said, uneasily; "not a soul, Nell; and why didn't ye keep an eye on them?"

"Well, they're in the haggard, playin' there, or round by the back o' the house. Will I call them in?"

"Do so, good girl, in the name o' God. The hens is comin' home, see, and the sun was just down over Knockdoulah, an' I comin' up."

So out ran tall, dark-haired Nell, and standing on the road, looked up and down it; but not a sign of her two little brothers, Con and Bill, or her little sister, Peg, could she see. She called them; but no answer came from the little haggard, fenced with straggling bushes. She listened, but the sound of their voices was missing. Over the stile, and behind the house she ran—but there all was silent and deserted.

She looked down toward the bog, as far as she could see; but they did not appear. Again she listened—but in vain. At first she had felt angry, but now a different feeling overcame her, and she grew pale. With an undefined boding she looked toward the heathy boss of Lisnavoura, now darkening into the deepest purple against the flaming sky of sunset.

Again she listened with a sinking heart, and heard nothing but the farewell twitter and whistle of the birds in the bushes around. How many stories had she listened to by the winter hearth, of children stolen by the fairies, at nightfall, in lonely places! With this fear she knew her mother was haunted.

No one in the country round gathered her little flock about her so early as this frightened widow, and no door "in the seven parishes" was barred so early.

Sufficiently fearful, as all young people in that part of the world are of such dreaded and subtle agents, Nell was even more than usually afraid of them, for her terrors were infected and redoubled by her mother's. She was looking towards Lisnavoura in a trance of fear, and crossed herself again and again, and whispered prayer after prayer. She was interrupted by her mother's voice on the road calling her loudly. She answered, and ran round to the front of the cabin, where she found her standing.

"And where in the world's the craythurs—did ye see sight o' them anywhere?" cried Mrs. Ryan, as the girl came over the stile.

"Arrah! mother, 'tis only what they're run down the road a bit. We'll see them this minute coming back. It's like goats they are, climbin' here and runnin' there; an' if I had them here, in my hand, maybe I wouldn't give them a hiding all round."

"May the Lord forgive you, Nell! the childhers gone. They're took, and not a soul near us, and Father Tom three miles away! And what'll I do, or who's to help us this night? Oh, wirristhru, wirristhru! The craythurs is gone!"

"Whisht, mother, be aisy: don't ye see them comin' up?"

And then she shouted in menacing accents, waving her arm, and beckoning the children, who were seen approaching on the road, which some little way off made a slight dip, which had concealed them. They were approaching from the westward, and from the direction of the dreaded hill of Lisnavoura.

But there were only two of the children, and one of them, the little girl, was crying. Their mother and sister hurried forward to meet them, more alarmed than ever.

"Where is Billy—where is he?" cried the mother, nearly breathless, so soon as she was within hearing.

"He's gone—they took him away; but they said he'll come back again," answered little Con, with the dark brown hair.

"He's gone away with the grand ladies," blubbered the little girl.

"What ladies—where? Oh, Leum, asthora! My darlin', are you gone away at last? Where is he? Who took him? What ladies are you talkin' about? What way did he go?" she cried in distraction.

"I couldn't see where he went, mother; 'twas like as if he was going to Lisnavoura."

With a wild exclamation the distracted woman ran on towards the hill alone, clapping her hands, and crying aloud the name of her lost child.

Scared and horrified, Nell, not daring to follow, gazed after her, and burst into tears; and the other children raised high their lamentations in shrill rivalry.

Twilight was deepening. It was long past the time when they were usually barred securely within their habitation. Nell led the younger children into the cabin, and made them sit down by the turf fire, while she stood in the open door, watching in great fear for the return of her mother.

After a long while they did see their mother return. She came in and sat down by the fire, and cried as if her heart would break.

"Will I bar the doore, mother?" asked Nell.

"Ay, do—didn't I lose enough, this night, without lavin' the doore open, for more o' yez to go; but first take an' sprinkle a dust o' the holy waters over ye, acuishla, and bring it here till I throw a taste iv it over myself and the craythurs; an' I wondher, Nell, you'd forget to do the like yourself, lettin' the craythurs out so near nightfall. Come here and sit on my knees, asthora, come to me, mavourneen, and hould me fast, in the name o' God, and I'll hould you fast that none can take yez from me, and tell me all about it, and what it was—the Lord between us and harm—an' how it happened, and who was in it."

And the door being barred, the two children, sometimes speaking together, often interrupting one another, often interrupted by their mother, managed to tell this strange story, which I had better relate connectedly and in my own language.

The Widow Ryan's three children were playing, as I have said, upon the narrow old road in front of her door. Little Bill or Leum, about five years old, with golden hair and large blue eyes, was a very pretty boy, with all the clear tints of healthy childhood, and that gaze of earnest simplicity which belongs not to town children of the same age. His little sister Peg, about a year older, and his brother Con, a little more than a year elder than she, made up the little group.

Under the great old ash-trees, whose last leaves were falling at their feet, in the light of an October sunset, they were playing with the hilarity and eagerness of rustic children, clamouring together, and their faces were turned toward the west and storied hill of Lisnavoura.

Suddenly a startling voice with a screech called to them from behind, ordering them to get out of the way, and turning, they saw a sight, such as they never beheld before. It was a carriage drawn by four horses that were pawing and snorting, in impatience, as it just pulled up. The children were almost under their feet, and scrambled to the side of the road next their own door.

This carriage and all its appointments were old-fashioned and gorgeous, and presented to the children, who had never seen anything finer than a turf car, and once, an old chaise that passed that way from Killaloe, a spectacle perfectly dazzling.

Here was antique splendour. The harness and trappings were scarlet, and blazing with gold. The horses were huge, and snow white, with great manes, that as they tossed and shook them in the air, seemed to stream and float sometimes longer and sometimes shorter, like so much smoke—their tails were long, and tied up in bows of broad scarlet and gold ribbon. The coach itself was glowing with colours, gilded and emblazoned. There were footmen in gay liveries, and three-cocked hats, like the coachman's; but he had a great wig, like a judge's, and their hair was frizzed out and powdered, and a long thick "pigtail," with a bow to it, hung down the back of each.

All these servants were diminutive, and ludicrously out of proportion with the enormous horses of the equipage, and had sharp, sallow features, and small, restless fiery eyes, and faces of cunning and malice that chilled the children. The little coachman was scowling and showing his white fangs under his cocked hat, and his little blazing beads of eyes were quivering with fury in their sockets as he whirled his whip round and round over their heads, till the lash of it looked like a streak of fire in the evening sun, and sounded like the cry of a legion of "fillapoueeks" in the air.

"Stop the princess on the highway!" cried the coachman, in a piercing treble.

"Stop the princess on the highway!" piped each footman in turn, scowling over his shoulder down on the children, and grinding his keen teeth.

The children were so frightened they could only gape and turn white in their panic. But a very sweet voice from the open window of the carriage reassured them, and arrested the attack of the lackeys.

A beautiful and "very grand-looking" lady was smiling from it on them, and they all felt pleased in the strange light of that smile.

"The boy with the golden hair, I think," said the lady, bending her large and wonderfully clear eyes on little Leum.

The upper sides of the carriage were chiefly of glass, so that the children could see another woman inside, whom they did not like so well.

This was a black woman, with a wonderfully long neck, hung round with many strings of large variously-coloured beads, and on her head was a sort of turban of silk striped with all the colours of the rainbow, and fixed in it was a golden star.

This black woman had a face as thin almost as a death's-head, with high cheekbones, and great goggle eyes, the whites of which, as well as her wide range of teeth, showed in brilliant contrast with her skin, as she looked over the beautiful lady's shoulder, and whispered something in her ear.

"Yes; the boy with the golden hair, I think," repeated the lady.

And her voice sounded sweet as a silver bell in the children's ears, and her smile beguiled them like the light of an enchanted lamp, as she leaned from the window with a look of ineffable fondness on the golden-haired boy, with the large blue eyes; insomuch that little Billy, looking up, smiled in return with a wondering fondness, and when she stooped down, and stretched her jewelled arms towards him, he stretched his little hands up, and how they touched the other children did not know; but, saying, "Come and give me a kiss, my darling," she raised him, and he seemed to ascend in her small fingers as lightly as a feather, and she held him in her lap and covered him with kisses.

Nothing daunted, the other children would have been only too happy to change places with their favoured little brother. There was only one thing that was unpleasant, and a little frightened them, and that was the black woman, who stood and stretched forward, in the carriage

JOSEPH SHERIDAN LE FANU

as before. She gathered a rich silk and gold handkerchief that was in her fingers up to her lips, and seemed to thrust ever so much of it, fold after fold, into her capacious mouth, as they thought to smother her laughter, with which she seemed convulsed, for she was shaking and quivering, as it seemed, with suppressed merriment; but her eyes, which remained uncovered, looked angrier than they had ever seen eyes look before.

But the lady was so beautiful they looked on her instead, and she continued to caress and kiss the little boy on her knee; and smiling at the other children she held up a large russet apple in her fingers, and the carriage began to move slowly on, and with a nod inviting them to take the fruit, she dropped it on the road from the window; it rolled some way beside the wheels, they following, and then she dropped another, and then another, and so on. And the same thing happened to all; for just as either of the children who ran beside had caught the rolling apple, somehow it slipt into a hole or ran into a ditch, and looking up they saw the lady drop another from the window, and so the chase was taken up and continued till they got, hardly knowing how far they had gone, to the old cross-road that leads to Owney. It seemed that there the horses' hoofs and carriage wheels rolled up a wonderful dust, which being caught in one of those eddies that whirl the dust up into a column, on the calmest day, enveloped the children for a moment, and passed whirling on towards Lisnavoura, the carriage, as they fancied, driving in the centre of it; but suddenly it subsided, the straws and leaves floated to the ground, the dust dissipated itself, but the white horses and the lackeys, the gilded carriage, the lady and their little golden-haired brother were gone.

At the same moment suddenly the upper rim of the clear setting sun disappeared behind the hill of Knockdoula, and it was twilight. Each child felt the transition like a shock—and the sight of the rounded summit of Lisnavoura, now closely overhanging them, struck them with a new fear.

They screamed their brother's name after him, but their cries were lost in the vacant air. At the same time they thought they heard a hollow voice say, close to them, "Go home."

Looking round and seeing no one, they were scared, and hand in hand—the little girl crying wildly, and the boy white as ashes, from fear, they trotted homeward, at their best speed, to tell, as we have seen, their strange story.

Molly Ryan never more saw her darling. But something of the lost little boy was seen by his former playmates.

Sometimes when their mother was away earning a trifle at haymaking, and Nelly washing the potatoes for their dinner, or "beatling" clothes in the little stream that flows in the hollow close by, they saw the pretty face of little Billy peeping in archly at the door, and smiling silently at them, and as they ran to embrace him, with cries of delight, he drew back, still smiling archly, and when they got out into the open day, he was gone, and they could see no trace of him anywhere.

This happened often, with slight variations in the circumstances of the visit. Sometimes he would peep for a longer time, sometimes for a shorter time, sometimes his little hand would come in, and, with bended finger, beckon them to follow; but always he was smiling with the same arch look and wary silence—and always he was gone when they reached the door. Gradually these visits grew less and less frequent, and in about eight months they ceased altogether, and little Billy, irretrievably lost, took rank in their memories with the dead.

One wintry morning, nearly a year and a half after his disappearance, their mother having set out for Limerick soon after cockcrow, to sell some fowls at the market, the little girl, lying by the side of her elder sister, who was fast asleep, just at the grey of the morning heard the latch lifted softly, and saw little Billy enter and close the door gently after him. There was light enough to see that he was barefoot and ragged, and looked pale and famished. He went straight to the fire, and cowered over the turf embers, and rubbed his hands slowly, and seemed to shiver as he gathered the smouldering turf together.

The little girl clutched her sister in terror and whispered, "Waken, Nelly, waken; here's Billy come back!"

Nelly slept soundly on, but the little boy, whose hands were extended close over the coals, turned and looked toward the bed, it seemed to her, in fear, and she saw the glare of the embers reflected on his thin cheek as he turned toward her. He rose and went, on tiptoe, quickly to the door, in silence, and let himself out as softly as he had come in.

After that, the little boy was never seen anymore by anyone of his kindred.

"Fairy doctors," as the dealers in the preternatural, who in such cases were called in, are termed, did all that in them lay—but in vain. Father Tom came down, and tried what holier rites could do, but equally without result. So little Billy was dead to mother, brother, and sisters; but no grave received him. Others whom affection cherished, lay in holy ground, in the old churchyard of Abington, with headstone to mark the spot over which the survivor might kneel and say a kind prayer for the peace of the departed soul. But there was no landmark to show where little Billy was hidden from their loving eyes, unless it was in the old hill of Lisnavoura, that cast its long shadow at sunset before the cabin-door; or that, white and filmy in the moonlight, in later years, would occupy his brother's gaze as he returned from fair or market, and draw from him a sigh and a prayer for the little brother he had lost so long ago, and was never to see again.

The Drunkard's Dream

"All this he *told with some confusion and*
Dismay, the usual consequence of dreams
Of the unpleasant kind, with none at hand
To expound their vain and visionary gleams.
I've known some odd ones which seemed really planned
Prophetically, as that which one deems
'A strange coincidence,' to use a phrase
By which such things are settled now-a-days."

—Byron

Dreams—What age, or what country of the world has not felt and acknowledged the mystery of their origin and end? I have thought not a little upon the subject, seeing it is one which has been often forced upon my attention, and sometimes strangely enough; and yet I have never arrived at anything which at all appeared a satisfactory conclusion. It does appear that a mental phenomenon so extraordinary cannot be wholly without its use. We know, indeed, that in the olden times it has been made the organ of communication between the Deity and his creatures; and when, as I have seen, a dream produces upon a mind, to all appearance hopelessly reprobate and depraved, an effect so powerful and so lasting as to break down the inveterate habits, and to reform the life of an abandoned sinner. We see in the result, in the reformation of morals, which appeared incorrigible in the reclamation of a human soul which seemed to be irretrievably lost, something more than could be produced by a mere chimaera of the slumbering fancy, something more than could arise from the capricious images of a terrified imagination; but once prevented, we behold in all these things, in the tremendous and mysterious results, the operation of the hand of God. And while Reason rejects as absurd the superstition which will read a prophecy in every dream, she may, without violence to herself, recognize, even in the wildest and most incongruous of the wanderings of a slumbering intellect, the evidences and the fragments of a language which may be spoken, which *has* been spoken to terrify, to warn, and to command. We have reason to believe too, by the promptness of action, which in the age of the prophets, followed all intimations of this kind, and by the strength of conviction and strange permanence of the effects resulting from certain dreams in latter times, which effects ourselves may have witnessed, that when this medium of communication has been employed by the Deity, the evidences of his presence have been unequivocal. My thoughts were directed to this subject, in a manner to leave a lasting impression upon my mind, by the events which I shall now relate, the statement of which, however extraordinary, is nevertheless *accurately correct*.

About the year 17— having been appointed to the living of C——h, I rented a small house in the town, which bears the same name: one morning, in the month of November, I was awakened before my usual time, by my servant, who bustled into my bedroom for the purpose of announcing a sick call. As the Catholic Church holds her last rites to be totally indispensable to the safety of the departing sinner, no conscientious clergyman can afford a moment's unnecessary delay, and in little more than five minutes I stood ready cloaked and booted for the road in the small front parlour, in which the messenger, who was to act as my guide, awaited my coming. I found a poor little girl crying piteously near the door, and after some slight difficulty I ascertained that her father was either dead, or just dying.

"And what may be your father's name, my poor child?" said I. She held down her head, as if ashamed. I repeated the question, and the wretched little creature burst into floods of tears, still more bitter than she had shed before. At length, almost provoked by conduct which appeared to me so unreasonable, I began to lose patience, spite of the pity which I could not help feeling towards her, and I said rather harshly, "If you will not tell me the name of the person to whom you would lead me, your silence can arise from no good motive, and I might be justified in refusing to go with you at all."

"Oh! don't say that, don't say that," cried she. "Oh! sir, it was that I was afeard of when I would not tell you—I was afeard when you heard his name you would not come with me; but it is no use hidin' it now— it's Pat Connell, the carpenter, your honour."

She looked in my face with the most earnest anxiety, as if her very existence depended upon what she should read there; but I relieved her at once. The name, indeed, was most unpleasantly familiar to me; but, however fruitless my visits and advice might have been at another time, the present was too fearful an occasion to suffer my doubts of their utility as my reluctance to re-attempting what appeared a hopeless task to weigh even against the lightest chance, that a consciousness of his imminent danger might produce in him a more docile and tractable disposition. Accordingly I told the child to lead the way, and followed her in silence. She hurried rapidly through the long narrow street which forms the great thoroughfare of the town. The darkness of the hour, rendered still deeper by the close approach of the old fashioned houses, which lowered in tall obscurity on either side of the way; the damp dreary chill which renders the advance of morning peculiarly cheerless, combined with the object of my walk, to visit the death-bed of a presumptuous sinner, to endeavour, almost against my own conviction, to infuse a hope into the heart of a dying reprobate—a drunkard, but too probably perishing under the consequences of some mad fit of intoxication; all these circumstances united served to enhance the gloom and solemnity of my feelings, as I silently followed my little guide, who with quick steps traversed the uneven pavement of the main street. After a walk of about five minutes she turned off into a narrow lane, of that obscure and comfortless class which are to be found in almost all small old fashioned towns, chill without ventilation, reeking with all manner of offensive effluviae, dingy, smoky, sickly and pent-up buildings, frequently not only in a wretched but in a dangerous condition.

"Your father has changed his abode since I last visited him, and, I am afraid, much for the worse," said I.

"Indeed he has, sir, but we must not complain," replied she; "we have to thank God that we have lodging and food, though it's poor enough, it is, your honour."

Poor child! thought I, how many an older head might learn wisdom from thee—how many a luxurious philosopher, who is skilled to preach but not to suffer, might not thy patient words put to the blush! The manner and language of this child were alike above her years and station; and, indeed, in all cases in which the cares and sorrows of life have anticipated their usual date, and have fallen, as they sometimes do, with melancholy prematurity to the lot of childhood, I have observed the result to have proved uniformly the same. A young mind, to which joy and indulgence have been strangers, and to which suffering and self-denial have been familiarised from the first, acquires a solidity and an elevation which no other discipline could have bestowed, and which, in the present case, communicated a striking but mournful peculiarity to the manners, even to the voice of the child. We paused before a narrow, crazy door, which she opened by means of a latch, and we forthwith

JOSEPH SHERIDAN LE FANU

began to ascend the steep and broken stairs, which led upwards to the sick man's room. As we mounted flight after flight towards the garret floor, I heard more and more distinctly the hurried talking of many voices. I could also distinguish the low sobbing of a female. On arriving upon the uppermost lobby, these sounds became fully audible.

"This way, your honor," said my little conductress, at the same time pushing open a door of patched and half rotten plank, she admitted me into the squalid chamber of death and misery. But one candle, held in the fingers of a scared and haggard-looking child, was burning in the room, and that so dim that all was twilight or darkness except within its immediate influence. The general obscurity, however, served to throw into prominent and startling relief the death-bed and its occupant. The light was nearly approximated to, and fell with horrible clearness upon, the blue and swollen features of the drunkard. I did not think it possible that a human countenance could look so terrific. The lips were black and drawn apart—the teeth were firmly set—the eyes a little unclosed, and nothing but the whites appearing—every feature was fixed and livid, and the whole face wore a ghastly and rigid expression of despairing terror such as I never saw equalled; his hands were crossed upon his breast, and firmly clenched, while, as if to add to the corpse-like effect of the whole, some white cloths, dipped in water, were wound about the forehead and temples. As soon as I could remove my eyes from this horrible spectacle, I observed my friend Dr. D——, one of the most humane of a humane profession, standing by the bedside. He had been attempting, but unsuccessfully, to bleed the patient, and had now applied his finger to the pulse.

"Is there any hope?" I inquired in a whisper.

A shake of the head was the reply. There was a pause while he continued to hold the wrist; but he waited in vain for the throb of life, it was not there, and when he let go the hand it fell stiffly back into its former position upon the other.

"The man is dead," said the physician, as he turned from the bed where the terrible figure lay.

Dead! thought I, scarcely venturing to look upon the tremendous and revolting spectacle—dead! without an hour for repentance, even a moment for reflection—dead! without the rites which even the best should have. Is there a hope for him? The glaring eyeball, the grinning mouth, the distorted brow—that unutterable look in which a painter would have sought to embody the fixed despair of the nethermost hell— these were my answer.

The poor wife sat at a little distance, crying as if her heart would break—the younger children clustered round the bed, looking, with wondering curiosity, upon the form of death, never seen before. When the first tumult of uncontrollable sorrow had passed away, availing myself of the solemnity and impressiveness of the scene, I desired the heart-stricken family to accompany me in prayer, and all knelt down, while I solemnly and fervently repeated some of those prayers which appeared most applicable to the occasion. I employed myself thus in a manner which, I trusted, was not unprofitable, at least to the living, for about ten minutes, and having accomplished my task, I was the first to arise. I looked upon the poor, sobbing, helpless creatures who knelt so humbly around me, and my heart bled for them. With a natural transition, I turned my eyes from them to the bed in which the body lay, and, great God! what was the revulsion, the horror which I experienced on seeing the corpse-like, terrific thing seated half upright before me—the white cloths, which had been wound about the head, had now partly slipped from their position, and were hanging in grotesque festoons about the face and shoulders, while the distorted eyes leered from amid them—

"A sight to dream of, not to tell."

I stood actually rivetted to the spot. The figure nodded its head and lifted its arm, I thought with a menacing gesture. A thousand confused and horrible thoughts at once rushed upon my mind. I had often read that the body of a presumptuous sinner, who, during life, had been the willing creature of every satanic impulse, after the human tenant had deserted it, had been known to become the horrible sport of demoniac possession. I was roused from the stupefaction of terror in which I stood, by the piercing scream of the mother, who now, for the first time, perceived the change which had taken place. She rushed towards the bed, but, stunned by the shock and overcome by the conflict of violent emotions, before she reached it, she fell prostrate upon the floor. I am perfectly convinced that had I not been startled from the torpidity of horror in which I was bound, by some powerful and arousing stimulant, I should have gazed upon this unearthly apparition until I had fairly lost my senses. As it was, however, the spell was broken, superstition gave way to reason: the man whom all believed to have been actually dead, was living! Dr. D—— was instantly standing by the bedside, and, upon examination, he found that a sudden and copious flow of blood had taken place from the wound which the lancet had left, and this, no doubt, had effected his sudden and almost preternatural restoration to an existence from which all thought he had been forever removed. The man was still speechless, but he seemed to understand the physician when he forbid his repeating the painful and fruitless attempts which he made to articulate, and he at once resigned himself quietly into his hands.

I left the patient with leeches upon his temples, and bleeding freely—apparently with little of the drowsiness which accompanies apoplexy; indeed, Dr. D—— told me that he had never before witnessed a seizure which seemed to combine the symptoms of so many kinds, and yet which belonged to none of the recognized classes; it certainly was not apoplexy, catalepsy, *nor delirium tremens*, and yet it seemed, in some degree, to partake of the properties of all—it was strange, but stranger things are coming.

During two or three days Dr. D—— would not allow his patient to converse in a manner which could excite or exhaust him, with anyone; he suffered him merely, as briefly as possible, to express his immediate wants, and it was not until the fourth day after my early visit, the particulars of which I have just detailed, that it was thought expedient that I should see him, and then only because it appeared that his extreme importunity and impatience were likely to retard his recovery more than the mere exhaustion attendant upon a short conversation could possibly do; perhaps, too, my friend entertained some hope that if by holy confession his patient's bosom were eased of the perilous stuff, which no doubt, oppressed it, his recovery would be more assured and rapid. It was, then, as I have said, upon the fourth day after my first professional call, that I found myself once more in the dreary chamber of want and sickness. The man was in bed, and appeared low and restless. On my entering the room he raised himself in the bed, and muttered twice or thrice—"Thank God! thank God." I signed to those of his family who stood by, to leave the room, and took a chair beside the bed. So soon as we were alone, he said, rather doggedly—"There's no use now in telling me of the sinfulness of bad ways—I know it all—I know where they lead to—I seen everything about it with my own eyesight, as plain as I see you." He rolled himself in the bed, as if to hide his face in the clothes, and then suddenly raising himself, he exclaimed with startling vehemence—"Look, sir, there is no use in mincing the matter; I'm blasted with the fires of hell; I have been in hell; what do you think of that?—in hell—I'm lost forever—I have not a chance—I am damned already—damned—damned—." The end of this sentence he actually shouted; his vehemence was perfectly terrific; he threw himself back, and laughed, and sobbed hysterically. I poured some water into a tea-cup, and gave it to him. After he had swallowed it, I told him if he had anything to communicate, to do so as briefly as he could, and in a manner as little agitating to himself as possible; threatening at the same time, though I had no intention of doing so, to leave him at once, in case he again gave way to such passionate excitement. "It's only foolishness," he continued, "for me to try to thank you for coming to such a villain as myself at all; it's no use for me to wish good to you, or to bless you; for such as me has no blessings to give." I told him that I had but done my duty, and urged him to proceed to the matter which weighed upon his mind; he then spoke nearly as follows:—"I came in drunk on Friday night last, and got to my bed here, I don't remember how; sometime in the night, it seemed to me, I wakened, and feeling unasy in myself, I got up out of the bed. I wanted the fresh air, but I would not make a noise to open the window, for fear I'd waken the crathurs. It was very dark, and throublesome to find the door; but at last I did get it, and I groped my way out, and went down as asy as I could. I felt quite sober, and I counted the steps one after another, as I was going down, that I might not stumble at the bottom. When I came to the first landing-place, God be about us always! the floor of it sunk under me, and I went down, down, down, till the senses almost left me. I do not know how long I was falling, but it seemed to me a great while. When I came rightly to myself at last, I was sitting at a great table, near the top of it; and I could not see the end of it, if it had any, it was so far off; and there was men beyond reckoning, sitting down, all along by it, at each side, as far as I could see at all. I did not know at first was it in the open air; but there was a close smothering feel in it, that was not natural, and there was a kind of light that my eyesight never saw before, red and unsteady, and I did not see for a long time where it was coming from, until I looked straight up, and then I seen that it came from great balls of blood-coloured fire, that were rolling high over head with a sort of rushing, trembling sound, and I perceived that they shone on the ribs of a great roof of rock that was arched overhead instead of the sky. When I seen this, scarce knowing what I did, I got up, and I said, 'I have no right to be here; I must go,' and the man that was sitting at my left hand, only smiled, and said, 'sit down again, you can *never* leave this place,' and his voice was weaker than any child's voice I ever heerd, and when he was done speaking he smiled again. Then I spoke out very loud and bold, and I said—'in the name of God, let me out of this bad place.' And there was a great man, that I did not see before, sitting at the end of

JOSEPH SHERIDAN LE FANU

the table that I was near, and he was taller than twelve men, and his face was very proud and terrible to look at, and he stood up and stretched out his hand before him, and when he stood up, all that was there, great and small, bowed down with a sighing sound, and a dread came on my heart, and he looked at me, and I could not speak. I felt I was his own, to do what he liked with, for I knew at once who he was, and he said, 'if you promise to return, you may depart for a season'; and the voice he spoke with was terrible and mournful, and the echoes of it went rolling and swelling down the endless cave, and mixing with the trembling of the fire overhead; so that, when he sate down, there was a sound after him, all through the place like the roaring of a furnace, and I said, with all the strength I had, 'I promise to come back; in God's name let me go,' and with that I lost the sight and the hearing of all that was there, and when my senses came to me again, I was sitting in the bed with the blood all over me, and you and the rest praying around the room." Here he paused and wiped away the chill drops of horror which hung upon his forehead.

I remained silent for some moments. The vision which he had just described struck my imagination not a little, for this was long before Vathek and the "Hall of Iblis" had delighted the world; and the description which he gave had, as I received it, all the attractions of novelty beside the impressiveness which always belongs to the narration of an *eye-witness*, whether in the body or in the spirit, of the scenes which he describes. There was something, too, in the stern horror with which the man related these things, and in the incongruity of his description, with the vulgarly received notions of the great place of punishment, and of its presiding spirit, which struck my mind with awe, almost with fear. At length he said, with an expression of horrible, imploring earnestness, which I shall never forget—"Well, sir, is there any hope; is there any chance at all? or, is my soul pledged and promised away forever? is it gone out of my power? must I go back to the place?"

In answering him I had no easy task to perform; for however clear might be my internal conviction of the groundlessness of his fears, and however strong my scepticism respecting the reality of what he had described, I nevertheless felt that his impression to the contrary, and his humility and terror resulting from it, might be made available as no mean engines in the work of his conversion from profligacy, and of his restoration to decent habits, and to religious feeling. I therefore told him that he was to regard his dream rather in the light of a warning than in that of a prophecy; that our salvation depended not upon the word or deed of a moment, but upon the habits of a life; that, in fine, if he at once discarded his idle companions and evil habits, and firmly adhered to a sober, industrious, and religious course of life, the powers of darkness might claim his soul in vain, for that there were higher and firmer pledges than human tongue could utter, which promised salvation to him who should repent and lead a new life.

I left him much comforted, and with a promise to return upon the next day. I did so, and found him much more cheerful, and without any remains of the dogged sullenness which I suppose had arisen from his despair. His promises of amendment were given in that tone of deliberate earnestness, which belongs to deep and solemn determination; and it was with no small delight that I observed, after repeated visits, that his good resolutions, so far from failing, did but gather strength by time; and when I saw that man shake off the idle and debauched companions, whose society had for years formed alike his amusement and his ruin, and revive his long discarded habits of industry and sobriety, I said within myself, there is something more in all this than the operation of an idle dream. One day, sometime after his perfect restoration to health, I was surprised on ascending the stairs, for the purpose of visiting this man, to find him busily employed in nailing down some planks upon the landing place, through which, at the commencement of his mysterious vision, it seemed to him that he had sunk. I perceived at once that he was strengthening the floor with a view to securing himself against such a catastrophe, and could scarcely forbear a smile as I bid "God bless his work."

He perceived my thoughts, I suppose, for he immediately said,

"I can never pass over that floor without trembling. I'd leave this house if I could, but I can't find another lodging in the town so cheap, and I'll not take a better till I've paid off all my debts, please God; but I could not be asy in my mind till I made it as safe as I could. You'll hardly believe me, your honor, that while I'm working, maybe a mile away, my heart is in a flutter the whole way back, with the bare thoughts of the two little steps I have to walk upon this bit of a floor. So it's no wonder, sir, I'd thry to make it sound and firm with any idle timber I have."

I applauded his resolution to pay off his debts, and the steadiness with which he pursued his plans of conscientious economy, and passed on.

Many months elapsed, and still there appeared no alteration in his resolutions of amendment. He was a good workman, and with his better habits he recovered his former extensive and profitable employment. Everything seemed to promise comfort and respectability. I have little more to add, and that shall be told quickly. I had one evening met Pat Connell, as he returned from his work, and as usual, after a mutual, and on his side respectful salutation, I spoke a few words of encouragement and approval. I left him industrious, active, healthy—when next I saw him, not three days after, he was a corpse. The circumstances which marked the event of his death were somewhat strange—I might say fearful. The unfortunate man had accidentally met an early friend, just returned, after a long absence, and in a moment of excitement, forgetting everything in the warmth of his joy, he yielded to his urgent invitation to accompany him into a public house, which lay close by the spot where the encounter had taken place. Connell, however, previously to entering the room, had announced his determination to take nothing more than the strictest temperance would warrant. But oh! who can describe the inveterate tenacity with which a drunkard's habits cling to him through life. He may repent—he may reform—he may look with actual abhorrence upon his past profligacy; but amid all this reformation and compunction, who can tell the moment in which the base and ruinous propensity may not recur, triumphing over resolution, remorse, shame, everything, and prostrating its victim once more in all that is destructive and revolting in that fatal vice.

The wretched man left the place in a state of utter intoxication. He was brought home nearly insensible, and placed in his bed, where he lay in the deep calm lethargy of drunkenness. The younger part of the family retired to rest much after their usual hour; but the poor wife remained up sitting by the fire, too much grieved and shocked at the recurrence of what she had so little expected, to settle to rest; fatigue, however, at length overcame her, and she sunk gradually into an uneasy slumber. She could not tell how long she had remained in this state, when she awakened, and immediately on opening her eyes, she perceived by the faint red light of the smouldering turf embers, two persons, one of whom she recognized as her husband noiselessly gliding out of the room.

"Pat, darling, where are you going?" said she. There was no answer—the door closed after them; but in a moment she was startled and terrified by a loud and heavy crash, as if some ponderous body had been hurled down the stair. Much alarmed, she started up, and going to the head of the staircase, she called repeatedly upon her husband, but in vain. She returned to the room, and with the assistance of her daughter, whom I had occasion to mention before, she succeeded in finding and lighting a candle, with which she hurried again to the head of the staircase. At the bottom lay what seemed to be a bundle of clothes, heaped together, motionless, lifeless—it was her husband. In going down the stairs, for what purpose can never now be known, he had fallen helplessly and violently to the bottom, and coming head foremost, the spine at the neck had been dislocated by the shock, and instant death must have ensued. The body lay upon that landing-place to which his dream had referred. It is scarcely worth endeavouring to clear up a single point in a narrative where all is mystery; yet I could not help suspecting that the second figure which had been seen in the room by Connell's wife on the night of his death, might have been no other than his own shadow. I suggested this solution of the difficulty; but she told me that the unknown person had been considerably in advance of the other, and on reaching the door, had turned back as if to communicate something to his companion—it was then a mystery. Was the dream verified?—whither had the disembodied spirit sped?— who can say? We know not. But I left the house of death that day in a state of horror which I could not describe. It seemed to me that I was scarce awake. I heard and saw everything as if under the spell of a nightmare. The coincidence was terrible.

The Fortunes of Sir Robert Ardagh

"The earth hath bubbles as the water hath—
And these are of them."

In the south of Ireland, and on the borders of the county of Limerick, there lies a district of two or three miles in length, which is rendered interesting by the fact that it is one of the very few spots throughout this country, in which some vestiges of aboriginal forest still remain. It has little or none of the lordly character of the American forest, for the axe has felled its oldest and its grandest trees; but in the close wood which survives, live all the wild and pleasing peculiarities of nature: its complete irregularity, its vistas, in whose perspective the quiet cattle are peacefully browsing; its refreshing glades, where the grey rocks arise from amid the nodding fern; the silvery shafts of the old birch trees; the knotted trunks of the hoary oak, the grotesque but graceful branches which never shed their honours under the tyrant pruning-hook; the soft green sward; the chequered light and shade; the wild luxuriant weeds; the lichen and the moss—all, all are beautiful alike in the green freshness of spring, or in the sadness and sere of autumn. Their beauty is of that kind which makes the heart full with joy—appealing to the affections with a power which belongs to nature only. This wood runs up, from below the base, to the ridge of a long line of irregular hills, having perhaps, in primitive times, formed but the skirting of some mighty forest which occupied the level below.

But now, alas! whither have we drifted? whither has the tide of civilisation borne us? It has passed over a land unprepared for it—it has left nakedness behind it; we have lost our forests, but our marauders remain; we have destroyed all that is picturesque, while we have retained everything that is revolting in barbarism. Through the midst of this woodland there runs a deep gully or glen, where the stillness of the scene is broken in upon by the brawling of a mountain-stream, which, however, in the winter season, swells into a rapid and formidable torrent.

There is one point at which the glen becomes extremely deep and narrow; the sides descend to the depth of some hundred feet, and are so steep as to be nearly perpendicular. The wild trees which have taken root in the crannies and chasms of the rock have so intersected and entangled, that one can with difficulty catch a glimpse of the stream, which wheels, flashes, and foams below, as if exulting in the surrounding silence and solitude.

This spot was not unwisely chosen, as a point of no ordinary strength, for the erection of a massive square tower or keep, one side of which rises as if in continuation of the precipitous cliff on which it is based. Originally, the only mode of ingress was by a narrow portal in the very wall which overtopped the precipice, opening upon a ledge of rock which afforded a precarious pathway, cautiously intersected, however, by a deep trench cut with great labour in the living rock; so that, in its original state, and before the introduction of artillery into the art of war, this tower might have been pronounced, and that not presumptuously, almost impregnable.

The progress of improvement and the increasing security of the times had, however, tempted its successive proprietors, if not to adorn, at least to enlarge their premises, and at about the middle of the last century, when the castle was last inhabited, the original square tower formed but a small part of the edifice.

The castle, and a wide tract of the surrounding country, had from time immemorial belonged to a family which, for distinctness, we shall call by the name of Ardagh; and owing to the associations which, in Ireland, almost always attach to scenes which have long witnessed alike the exercise of stern feudal authority, and of that savage hospitality which distinguished the good old times, this building has become the subject and the scene of many wild and extraordinary traditions. One of them I have been enabled, by a personal acquaintance with an eye-witness of the events, to trace to its origin; and yet it is hard to say whether the events which I am about to record appear more strange or improbable as seen through the distorting medium of tradition, or in the appalling dimness of uncertainty which surrounds the reality.

Tradition says that, sometime in the last century, Sir Robert Ardagh, a young man, and the last heir of that family, went abroad and served in foreign armies; and that, having acquired considerable honour and emolument, he settled at Castle Ardagh, the building we have just now attempted to describe. He was what the country people call a DARK man; that is, he was considered morose, reserved, and ill-tempered; and, as it was supposed from the utter solitude of his life, was upon no terms of cordiality with the other members of his family.

The only occasion upon which he broke through the solitary monotony of his life was during the continuance of the racing season, and immediately subsequent to it; at which time he was to be seen among the busiest upon the course, betting deeply and unhesitatingly, and invariably with success. Sir Robert was, however, too well known as a man of honour, and of too high a family, to be suspected of any unfair dealing. He was, moreover, a soldier, and a man of an intrepid as well as of a haughty character; and no one cared to hazard a surmise, the consequences of which would be felt most probably by its originator only.

Gossip, however, was not silent; it was remarked that Sir Robert never appeared at the race-ground, which was the only place of public resort which he frequented, except in company with a certain strange-looking person, who was never seen elsewhere, or under other circumstances. It was remarked, too, that this man, whose relation to Sir Robert was never distinctly ascertained, was the only person to whom he seemed to speak unnecessarily; it was observed that while with the country gentry he exchanged no further communication than what was unavoidable in arranging his sporting transactions, with this person he would converse earnestly and frequently. Tradition asserts that, to enhance the curiosity which this unaccountable and exclusive preference excited, the stranger possessed some striking and unpleasant peculiarities of person and of garb—she does not say, however, what these were—but they, in conjunction with Sir Robert's secluded habits and extraordinary run of luck—a success which was supposed to result from the suggestions and immediate advice of the unknown—were sufficient to warrant report in pronouncing that there was something QUEER in the wind, and in surmising that Sir Robert was playing a fearful and a hazardous game, and that, in short, his strange companion was little better than the devil himself.

Years, however, rolled quietly away, and nothing novel occurred in the arrangements of Castle Ardagh, excepting that Sir Robert parted with his odd companion, but as nobody could tell whence he came, so nobody could say whither he had gone. Sir Robert's habits, however, underwent no consequent change; he continued regularly to frequent the race meetings, without mixing at all in the convivialities of the gentry, and immediately afterwards to relapse into the secluded monotony of his ordinary life.

It was said that he had accumulated vast sums of money—and, as his bets were always successful, and always large, such must have been the case. He did not suffer the acquisition of wealth, however, to influence his hospitality or his housekeeping—he neither purchased land, nor extended his establishment; and his mode of enjoying his money must have been altogether that of the miser—consisting merely in the pleasure of touching and telling his gold, and in the consciousness of wealth.

Sir Robert's temper, so far from improving, became more than ever gloomy and morose. He sometimes carried the indulgence of his evil dispositions to such a height that it bordered upon insanity. During these paroxysms he would neither eat, drink, nor sleep. On such occasions he insisted on perfect privacy, even from the intrusion of his most trusted servants; his voice was frequently heard, sometimes in earnest supplication, sometime as if in loud and angry altercation with some unknown visitant; sometimes he would, for hours together, walk to and fro throughout the long oak wainscoted apartment, which he generally occupied, with wild gesticulations and agitated pace, in the manner of one who has been roused to a state of unnatural excitement by some sudden and appalling intimation.

These paroxysms of apparent lunacy were so frightful, that during their continuance even his oldest and most-faithful domestics dared not approach him; consequently, his hours of agony were never intruded upon, and the mysterious causes of his sufferings appeared likely to remain hidden forever.

On one occasion a fit of this kind continued for an unusual time, the ordinary term of their duration—about two days—had been long past, and the old servant who generally waited upon Sir Robert after these visitations, having in vain listened for the well-known tinkle of his master's hand-bell, began to feel extremely anxious; he feared that his master might have died from sheer exhaustion, or perhaps put an end to his own existence during his miserable depression. These fears at length became so strong, that having in vain urged some of his brother servants to accompany him, he determined to go up alone, and himself see whether any accident had befallen Sir Robert.

He traversed the several passages which conducted from the new to the more ancient parts of the mansion, and having arrived in the old hall of the castle, the utter silence of the hour, for it was very late in the night, the idea of the nature of the enterprise in which he was engaging himself, a sensation of remoteness from anything like human companionship, but, more than all, the vivid but undefined anticipation of something horrible, came upon him with such oppressive weight that he hesitated as to whether he should proceed. Real uneasiness, however, respecting the fate of his master, for whom he felt that kind of attachment which the force of habitual intercourse not unfrequently engenders respecting objects not in themselves amiable, and also a latent unwillingness to expose his weakness to the ridicule of his fellow-servants, combined to overcome his reluctance; and he had just placed his foot upon the first step of the staircase which conducted to his master's chamber, when his attention was arrested by a low but distinct knocking at the hall-door. Not, perhaps, very sorry at finding thus an excuse even for deferring his intended expedition, he placed the candle upon a stone block which lay in the hall, and approached the door, uncertain whether his ears had not deceived him. This doubt was justified by the circumstance that the hall entrance had been for nearly fifty years disused as a mode of ingress to the castle. The situation of this gate also, which we have endeavoured to describe, opening upon a narrow ledge of rock which overhangs a perilous cliff, rendered it at all times, but particularly at night, a dangerous entrance. This shelving platform of rock, which formed the only avenue to the door, was divided, as I have already stated, by a broad chasm, the planks across which had long disappeared by decay or otherwise, so that it seemed at least highly improbable that any man could have found his way across the passage in safety to the door, more particularly on a night like that, of singular darkness. The old man, therefore, listened attentively, to ascertain whether the first application should be followed by another. He had not long to wait; the same low but singularly distinct knocking was repeated; so low that it seemed as if the applicant had employed no harder or heavier instrument than his hand, and yet, despite the immense thickness of the door, with such strength that the sound was distinctly audible.

The knock was repeated a third time, without any increase of loudness; and the old man, obeying an impulse for which to his dying hour he could never account, proceeded to remove, one by one, the three great oaken bars which secured the door. Time and damp had effectually corroded the iron chambers of the lock, so that it afforded little resistance. With some effort, as he believed, assisted from without, the old servant succeeded in opening the door; and a low, square-built figure, apparently that of a man wrapped in a large black cloak, entered the hall. The servant could not see much of this visitant with any distinctness; his dress appeared foreign, the skirt of his ample cloak was thrown over one shoulder; he wore a large felt hat, with a very heavy leaf, from under which escaped what appeared to be a mass of long sooty-black hair; his feet were cased in heavy riding-boots. Such were the few particulars which the servant had time and light to observe. The stranger desired him to let his master know instantly that a friend had come, by appointment, to settle some business with him. The servant hesitated, but a slight motion on the part of his visitor, as if to possess himself of the candle, determined him; so, taking it in his hand, he ascended the castle stairs, leaving his guest in the hall.

On reaching the apartment which opened upon the oak-chamber he was surprised to observe the door of that room partly open, and the room itself lit up. He paused, but there was no sound; he looked in, and saw Sir Robert, his head and the upper part of his body reclining on a table, upon which burned a lamp; his arms were stretched forward on either side, and perfectly motionless; it appeared that, having been sitting at the table, he had thus sunk forward, either dead or in a swoon. There was no sound of breathing; all was silent, except the sharp ticking of a watch, which lay beside the lamp. The servant coughed twice or thrice, but with no effect; his fears now almost amounted to certainty, and he was approaching the table on which his master partly lay, to satisfy himself of his death, when Sir Robert slowly raised his head, and throwing himself back in his chair, fixed his eyes in a ghastly and uncertain gaze upon his attendant. At length he said, slowly and painfully, as if he dreaded the answer:

"In God's name, what are you?"

"Sir," said the servant, "a strange gentleman wants to see you below."

At this intimation Sir Robert, starting on his feet and tossing his arms wildly upwards, uttered a shriek of such appalling and despairing terror that it was almost too fearful for human endurance; and long after the sound had ceased it seemed to the terrified imagination of the old servant to roll through the deserted passages in bursts of unnatural laughter. After a few moments Sir Robert said:

"Can't you send him away? Why does he come so soon? O God! O God! let him leave me for an hour; a little time. I can't see him now; try to get him away. You see I can't go down now; I have not strength. O God! O God! let him come back in an hour; it is not long to wait. He cannot lose anything by it; nothing, nothing, nothing. Tell him that; say anything to him."

The servant went down. In his own words, he did not feel the stairs under him till he got to the hall. The figure stood exactly as he had left it. He delivered his master's message as coherently as he could. The stranger replied in a careless tone:

"If Sir Robert will not come down to me, I must go up to him."

The man returned, and to his surprise he found his master much more composed in manner. He listened to the message, and though the cold perspiration rose in drops upon his forehead faster than he could wipe it away, his manner had lost the dreadful agitation which had marked it before. He rose feebly, and casting a last look of agony behind him, passed from the room to the lobby, where he signed to his attendant not to follow him. The man moved as far as the head of the staircase, from whence he had a tolerably distinct view of the hall, which was imperfectly lighted by the candle he had left there.

He saw his master reel, rather than walk down the stairs, clinging all the way to the banisters. He walked on, as if about to sink every moment from weakness. The figure advanced as if to meet him, and in passing struck down the light. The servant could see no more; but there was a sound of struggling, renewed at intervals with silent but fearful energy. It was evident, however, that the parties were approaching the door, for he heard the solid oak sound twice or thrice, as the feet of the combatants, in shuffling hither and thither over the floor, struck upon it. After a slight pause he heard the door thrown open with such violence that the leaf seemed to strike the side-wall of the hall, for it was so dark without that this could only be surmised by the sound. The struggle was renewed with an agony and intenseness of energy that betrayed itself in deep-drawn gasps. One desperate effort, which terminated in the breaking of some part of the door, producing a sound as if the door-post was wrenched from its position, was followed by another wrestle, evidently upon the narrow ledge which ran outside the door, overtopping the precipice. This proved to be the final struggle, for it was followed by a crashing sound as if some heavy body had fallen over, and was rushing down the precipice, through the light boughs that crossed near the top. All then became still as the grave, except when the moan of the night wind sighed up the wooded glen.

The old servant had not nerve to return through the hall, and to him the darkness seemed all but endless; but morning at length came, and with it the disclosure of the events of the night. Near the door, upon the ground, lay Sir Robert's sword-belt, which had given way in the scuffle. A huge splinter from the massive door-post had been wrenched off by an almost superhuman effort—one which nothing but the gripe of a despairing man could have severed—and on the rock outside were left the marks of the slipping and sliding of feet.

At the foot of the precipice, not immediately under the castle, but dragged some way up the glen, were found the remains of Sir Robert, with hardly a vestige of a limb or feature left distinguishable. The right hand, however, was uninjured, and in its fingers were clutched, with the fixedness of death, a long lock of coarse sooty hair—the only direct circumstantial evidence of the presence of a second person. So says tradition.

This story, as I have mentioned, was current among the dealers in such lore; but the original facts are so dissimilar in all but the name of the principal person mentioned and his mode of life, and the fact that his death was accompanied with circumstances of extraordinary mystery, that the two narratives are totally irreconcilable (even allowing the utmost for the exaggerating influence of tradition), except by supposing report to have combined and blended together the fabulous histories of several distinct bearers of the family name. However this may be, I shall lay before the reader a distinct recital of the events from which the foregoing tradition arose. With respect to these there can be no mistake; they are authenticated as fully as anything can be by human testimony; and I state them principally upon the evidence of a lady who herself bore a prominent part in the strange events which she related, and which I now record as being among the few well-attested tales of the marvellous which it has been my fate to hear. I shall, as far as I am able, arrange in one combined narrative the evidence of several distinct persons who were eye-witnesses of what they related, and with the truth of whose testimony I am solemnly and deeply impressed.

Sir Robert Ardagh, as we choose to call him, was the heir and representative of the family whose name he bore; but owing to the prodigality of his father, the estates descended to him in a very impaired condition. Urged by the restless spirit of youth, or more probably by a feeling of pride which could not submit to witness, in the paternal mansion, what he considered a humiliating alteration in the style and hospitality which up to that time had distinguished his family, Sir Robert left Ireland and went abroad. How he occupied himself, or what countries he visited during his absence, was never known, nor did he afterwards make any allusion or encourage any inquiries touching his foreign sojourn. He left Ireland in the year 1742, being then just of age, and was not heard of until the year 1760—about eighteen years afterwards—at which time he returned. His personal appearance was, as might have been expected, very greatly altered, more altered, indeed, than the time of his absence might have warranted one in supposing likely. But to counterbalance the unfavourable change which time had wrought in his form and features, he had acquired all the advantages of polish of manner and refinement of taste which foreign travel is supposed to bestow. But what was truly surprising was that it soon became evident that Sir Robert was very wealthy—wealthy to an extraordinary and unaccountable degree; and this fact was made manifest, not only by his expensive style of living, but by his proceeding to disembarrass his property, and to purchase extensive estates in addition. Moreover, there could be nothing deceptive in these appearances, for he paid ready money for everything, from the most important purchase to the most trifling.

Sir Robert was a remarkably agreeable man, and possessing the combined advantages of birth and property, he was, as a matter of course, gladly received into the highest society which the metropolis then commanded. It was thus that he became acquainted with the two beautiful Miss F——ds, then among the brightest ornaments of the highest circle of Dublin fashion. Their family was in more than one direction allied to nobility; and Lady D——, their elder sister by many years, and sometime married to a once well-known nobleman, was now their protectress. These considerations, beside the fact that the young ladies were what is usually termed heiresses, though not to a very great amount, secured to them a high position in the best society which Ireland then produced. The two young ladies differed strongly, alike in appearance and in character. The elder of the two, Emily, was generally considered the handsomer—for her beauty was of that impressive kind which never failed to strike even at the first glance, possessing as it did all the advantages of a fine person and a commanding carriage. The beauty of her features strikingly assorted in character with that of her figure and deportment. Her hair was raven-black and richly luxuriant, beautifully contrasting with the perfect whiteness of her forehead—her finely pencilled brows were black as the ringlets that clustered near them—and her blue eyes, full, lustrous, and animated, possessed all the power and brilliancy of brown ones, with more than their softness and variety of expression. She was not, however, merely the tragedy queen. When she smiled, and that was not seldom, the dimpling of cheek and chin, the laughing display of the small and beautiful teeth—but, more than all, the roguish archness of her deep, bright eye, showed that nature had not neglected in her the lighter and the softer characteristics of woman.

Her younger sister Mary was, as I believe not unfrequently occurs in the case of sisters, quite in the opposite style of beauty. She was light-haired, had more colour, had nearly equal grace, with much more liveliness of manner. Her eyes were of that dark grey which poets so much admire—full of expression and vivacity. She was altogether a very beautiful and animated girl—though as unlike her sister as the presence of those two qualities would permit her to be. Their dissimilarity did not stop here—it was deeper than mere appearance—the character of their minds differed almost as strikingly as did their complexion. The fair-haired beauty had a large proportion of that softness and pliability of temper which physiognomists assign as the characteristics of such complexions. She was much more the creature of impulse than of feeling, and consequently more the victim of extrinsic circumstances than was her sister. Emily, on the contrary, possessed considerable firmness and decision. She was less excitable, but when excited her feelings were more intense and enduring. She wanted much of the gaiety, but with it the volatility of her younger sister. Her opinions were adopted, and her friendships formed more reflectively, and her affections seemed to move, as it were, more slowly, but more determinedly. This firmness of character did not amount to anything masculine, and did not at all impair the feminine grace of her manners.

Sir Robert Ardagh was for a long time apparently equally attentive to the two sisters, and many were the conjectures and the surmises as to which would be the lady of his choice. At length, however, these doubts were determined; he proposed for and was accepted by the dark beauty, Emily F——d.

The bridals were celebrated in a manner becoming the wealth and connections of the parties; and Sir Robert and Lady Ardagh left Dublin to pass the honeymoon at the family mansion, Castle Ardagh, which had lately been fitted up in a style bordering upon magnificent. Whether in compliance with the wishes of his lady, or owing to some whim of his own, his habits were henceforward strikingly altered; and from having moved among the gayest if not the most profligate of the votaries of fashion, he suddenly settled down into a quiet, domestic, country gentleman, and seldom, if ever, visited the capital, and then his sojourns were as brief as the nature of his business would permit.

Lady Ardagh, however, did not suffer from this change further than in being secluded from general society; for Sir Robert's wealth, and the hospitality which he had established in the family mansion, commanded that of such of his lady's friends and relatives as had leisure or inclination to visit the castle; and as their style of living was very handsome, and its internal resources of amusement considerable, few invitations from Sir Robert or his lady were neglected.

Many years passed quietly away, during which Sir Robert's and Lady Ardagh's hopes of issue were several times disappointed. In the lapse of all this time there occurred but one event worth recording. Sir Robert had brought with him from abroad a valet, who sometimes professed himself to be French, at others Italian, and at others again German. He spoke all these languages with equal fluency, and seemed to take a kind of pleasure in puzzling the sagacity and balking the curiosity of such of the visitors at the castle as at anytime happened to enter into conversation with him, or who, struck by his singularities, became inquisitive respecting his country and origin. Sir Robert called him by the French name, JACQUE, and among the lower orders he was familiarly known by the title of "Jack, the devil," an appellation which originated in a supposed malignity of disposition and a real reluctance to mix in the society of those who were believed to be his equals. This morose reserve, coupled with the mystery which enveloped all about him, rendered him an object of suspicion and inquiry to his fellow-servants, amongst whom it was whispered that this man in secret governed the actions of Sir Robert with a despotic dictation, and that, as if to indemnify himself for his public and apparent servitude and self-denial, he in private exacted a degree of respectful homage from his so-called master, totally inconsistent with the relation generally supposed to exist between them.

This man's personal appearance was, to say the least of it, extremely odd; he was low in stature; and this defect was enhanced by a distortion of the spine, so considerable as almost to amount to a hunch; his features, too, had all that sharpness and sickliness of hue which generally accompany deformity; he wore his hair, which was black as soot, in heavy neglected ringlets about his shoulders, and always without powder—a peculiarity in those days. There was something unpleasant, too, in the circumstance that he never raised his eyes to meet those of another; this fact was often cited as a proof of his being something not quite right, and said to result not from the timidity which is supposed in most cases to induce this habit, but from a consciousness that his eye possessed a power which, if exhibited, would betray a supernatural origin. Once, and once only, had he violated this sinister observance: it was on the occasion of Sir Robert's hopes having been most bitterly disappointed; his lady, after a severe and dangerous confinement, gave birth to a dead child. Immediately after the intelligence had been made known, a servant, having upon some business passed outside the gate of the castle-yard, was met by Jacque, who, contrary to his wont, accosted him, observing, "So, after all the pother, the son and heir is still-born." This remark was accompanied by a chuckling laugh, the only approach to merriment which he was ever known to exhibit. The servant, who was really disappointed, having hoped for holiday times, feasting and debauchery with impunity during the rejoicings which would have accompanied a christening, turned tartly upon the little valet, telling him that he should let Sir Robert know how he had received the tidings which should have filled any faithful servant with sorrow; and having once broken the ice, he was proceeding with increasing fluency, when his harangue was cut short and his temerity punished, by the little man raising his head and treating him to a scowl so fearful, half-demoniac, half-insane, that it haunted his imagination in nightmares and nervous tremors for months after.

To this man Lady Ardagh had, at first sight, conceived an antipathy amounting to horror, a mixture of loathing and dread so very powerful that she had made it a particular and urgent request to Sir Robert, that he would dismiss him, offering herself, from that property which Sir Robert had by the marriage settlements left at her own disposal, to provide handsomely for him, provided only she might be relieved from the continual anxiety and discomfort which the fear of encountering him induced.

Sir Robert, however, would not hear of it; the request seemed at first to agitate and distress him; but when still urged in defiance of his peremptory refusal, he burst into a violent fit of fury; he spoke darkly of great sacrifices which he had made, and threatened that if the request were at anytime renewed he would leave both her and the country forever. This was, however, a solitary instance of violence; his general conduct towards Lady Ardagh, though at no time uxorious, was certainly kind and respectful, and he was more than repaid in the fervent attachment which she bore him in return.

Some short time after this strange interview between Sir Robert and Lady Ardagh; one night after the family had retired to bed, and when everything had been quiet for sometime, the bell of Sir Robert's dressing-room rang suddenly and violently; the ringing was repeated again and again at still shorter intervals, and with increasing violence, as if the person who pulled the bell was agitated by the presence of some terrifying and imminent danger. A servant named Donovan was the first to answer it; he threw on his clothes, and hurried to the room.

Sir Robert had selected for his private room an apartment remote from the bed-chambers of the castle, most of which lay in the more modern parts of the mansion, and secured at its entrance by a double door. As the servant opened the first of these, Sir Robert's bell again sounded with a longer and louder peal; the inner door resisted his efforts to open it; but after a few violent struggles, not having been perfectly secured, or owing to the inadequacy of the bolt itself, it gave way, and the servant rushed into the apartment, advancing several paces before he could recover himself. As he entered, he heard Sir Robert's voice exclaiming loudly—"Wait without, do not come in yet"; but the prohibition came too late. Near a low truckle-bed, upon which Sir Robert sometimes slept, for he was a whimsical man, in a large armchair, sat, or rather lounged, the form of the valet Jacque, his arms folded, and his heels stretched forward on the floor, so as fully to exhibit his misshapen legs, his head thrown back, and his eyes fixed upon his master with a look of indescribable defiance and derision, while, as if to add to the strange insolence of his attitude and expression, he had placed upon his head the black cloth cap which it was his habit to wear.

Sir Robert was standing before him, at the distance of several yards, in a posture expressive of despair, terror, and what might be called an agony of humility. He waved his hand twice or thrice, as if to dismiss the servant, who, however, remained fixed on the spot where he had first stood; and then, as if forgetting everything but the agony within him, he pressed his clenched hands on his cold damp brow, and dashed away the heavy drops that gathered chill and thickly there.

Jacque broke the silence.

"Donovan," said he, "shake up that drone and drunkard, Carlton; tell him that his master directs that the travelling carriage shall be at the door within half-an-hour."

The servant paused, as if in doubt as to what he should do; but his scruples were resolved by Sir Robert's saying hurriedly, "Go—go, do whatever he directs; his commands are mine; tell Carlton the same."

The servant hurried to obey, and in about half-an-hour the carriage was at the door, and Jacque, having directed the coachman to drive to B——n, a small town at about the distance of twelve miles—the nearest point, however, at which post-horses could be obtained—stepped into the vehicle, which accordingly quitted the castle immediately.

Although it was a fine moonlight night, the carriage made its way but very slowly, and after the lapse of two hours the travellers had arrived at a point about eight miles from the castle, at which the road strikes through a desolate and heathy flat, sloping up distantly at either side into bleak undulatory hills, in whose monotonous sweep the imagination beholds the heaving of some dark sluggish sea, arrested in its first commotion by some preternatural power. It is a gloomy and divested spot; there is neither tree nor habitation near it; its monotony is unbroken, except by here and there the grey front of a rock peering above the heath, and the effect is rendered yet more dreary and spectral by the exaggerated and misty shadows which the moon casts along the sloping sides of the hills.

When they had gained about the centre of this tract, Carlton, the coachman, was surprised to see a figure standing at some distance in advance, immediately beside the road, and still more so when, on coming up, he observed that it was no other than Jacque whom he believed to be at that moment quietly seated in the carriage; the coachman drew up, and nodding to him, the little valet exclaimed:

"Carlton, I have got the start of you; the roads are heavy, so I shall even take care of myself the rest of the way. Do you make your way back as best you can, and I shall follow my own nose."

So saying, he chucked a purse into the lap of the coachman, and turning off at a right angle with the road, he began to move rapidly away in the direction of the dark ridge that lowered in the distance.

The servant watched him until he was lost in the shadowy haze of night; and neither he nor any of the inmates of the castle saw Jacque again. His disappearance, as might have been expected, did not cause any regret among the servants and dependants at the castle; and Lady Ardagh did not attempt to conceal her delight; but with Sir Robert matters were different, for two or three days subsequent to this event he confined himself to his room, and when he did return to his ordinary occupations, it was with a gloomy indifference, which showed that he did so more from habit than from any interest he felt in them. He appeared from that moment unaccountably and strikingly changed, and thenceforward walked through life as a thing from which he could derive neither profit nor pleasure. His temper, however, so far from growing wayward or morose, became, though gloomy, very—almost unnaturally—placid and cold; but his spirits totally failed, and he grew silent and abstracted.

These sombre habits of mind, as might have been anticipated, very materially affected the gay house-keeping of the castle; and the dark and melancholy spirit of its master seemed to have communicated itself to the very domestics, almost to the very walls of the mansion.

Several years rolled on in this way, and the sounds of mirth and wassail had long been strangers to the castle, when Sir Robert requested his lady, to her great astonishment, to invite some twenty or thirty of their friends to spend the Christmas, which was fast approaching, at the castle. Lady Ardagh gladly complied, and her sister Mary, who still continued unmarried, and Lady D—— were of course included in the invitations. Lady Ardagh had requested her sisters to set forward as early as possible, in order that she might enjoy a little of their society before the arrival of the other guests; and in compliance with this request they left Dublin almost immediately upon receiving the invitation, a little more than a week before the arrival of the festival which was to be the period at which the whole party were to muster.

For expedition's sake it was arranged that they should post, while Lady D——'s groom was to follow with her horses, she taking with herself her own maid and one male servant. They left the city when the day was considerably spent, and consequently made but three stages in the first day; upon the second, at about eight in the evening, they had reached the town of K——k, distant about fifteen miles from Castle Ardagh. Here, owing to Miss F——d's great fatigue, she having been for a considerable time in a very delicate state of health, it was determined to put up for the night. They, accordingly, took possession of the best sitting-room which the inn commanded, and Lady D—— remained in it to direct and urge the preparations for some refreshment, which the fatigues of the day had rendered necessary, while her younger sister retired to her bed-chamber to rest there for a little time, as the parlour commanded no such luxury as a sofa.

Miss F——d was, as I have already stated, at this time in very delicate health; and upon this occasion the exhaustion of fatigue, and the dreary badness of the weather, combined to depress her spirits. Lady D—— had not been left long to herself, when the door communicating with the passage was abruptly opened, and her sister Mary entered in a state of great agitation; she sat down pale and trembling upon one of the chairs, and it was not until a copious flood of tears had relieved her, that she became sufficiently calm to relate the cause of her excitement and distress. It was simply this. Almost immediately upon lying down upon the bed she sank into a feverish and unrefreshing slumber; images of all grotesque shapes and startling colours flitted before her sleeping fancy with all the rapidity and variety of the changes in a kaleidoscope. At length, as she described it, a mist seemed to interpose itself between her sight and the ever-shifting scenery which sported before her imagination, and out of this cloudy shadow gradually emerged a figure whose back seemed turned towards the sleeper; it was that of a lady, who, in perfect silence, was expressing as far as pantomimic gesture could, by wringing her hands, and throwing her head from side to side, in the manner of one who is exhausted by the over indulgence, by the very sickness and impatience of grief, the extremity of misery. For a long time she sought in vain to catch a glimpse of the face of the apparition, who thus seemed to stir and live before her. But at length the figure seemed to move with an air of authority, as if about to give directions to some inferior, and in doing so, it turned its head so as to display, with a ghastly distinctness, the features of Lady Ardagh, pale as death, with her dark hair all dishevelled, and her eyes dim and sunken with weeping. The revulsion of feeling which Miss F——d experienced at this disclosure—for up to that point she had contemplated the appearance rather with a sense of curiosity and of interest, than of anything deeper—was so horrible, that the shock awoke her perfectly. She sat up in the bed, and looked fearfully around the room, which was imperfectly lighted by a single candle burning dimly, as if she almost expected to see the reality of her dreadful vision lurking in some corner of the chamber. Her fears were, however, verified, though not in the way she expected; yet in a manner sufficiently horrible—for she had hardly time to breathe and to collect her thoughts, when she heard, or thought she heard, the voice of her sister, Lady Ardagh, sometimes sobbing violently, and sometimes almost shrieking as if in terror, and calling upon her and Lady D——, with the most imploring earnestness of despair, for God's sake to lose no time in coming to her. All this was so horribly distinct, that it seemed as if the mourner was standing within a few yards of the spot where Miss F——d lay. She sprang from the bed, and leaving the candle in the room behind her, she made her way in the dark through the passage, the voice still following her, until as she arrived at the door of the sitting-room it seemed to die away in low sobbing.

As soon as Miss F——d was tolerably recovered, she declared her determination to proceed directly, and without further loss of time, to

JOSEPH SHERIDAN LE FANU

Castle Ardagh. It was not without much difficulty that Lady D——
at length prevailed upon her to consent to remain where they then
were, until morning should arrive, when it was to be expected that the
young lady would be much refreshed by at least remaining quiet for the
night, even though sleep were out of the question. Lady D—— was
convinced, from the nervous and feverish symptoms which her sister
exhibited, that she had already done too much, and was more than ever
satisfied of the necessity of prosecuting the journey no further upon
that day. After sometime she persuaded her sister to return to her room,
where she remained with her until she had gone to bed, and appeared
comparatively composed. Lady D—— then returned to the parlour,
and not finding herself sleepy, she remained sitting by the fire. Her
solitude was a second time broken in upon, by the entrance of her sister,
who now appeared, if possible, more agitated than before. She said that
Lady D—— had not long left the room, when she was roused by a
repetition of the same wailing and lamentations, accompanied by the
wildest and most agonized supplications that no time should be lost in
coming to Castle Ardagh, and all in her sister's voice, and uttered at the
same proximity as before. This time the voice had followed her to the
very door of the sitting-room, and until she closed it, seemed to pour
forth its cries and sobs at the very threshold.

Miss F——d now most positively declared that nothing should
prevent her proceeding instantly to the castle, adding that if Lady D——
would not accompany her, she would go on by herself. Superstitious
feelings are at all times more or less contagious, and the last century
afforded a soil much more congenial to their growth than the present.
Lady D—— was so far affected by her sister's terrors, that she became,
at least, uneasy; and seeing that her sister was immovably determined
upon setting forward immediately, she consented to accompany her
forthwith. After a slight delay, fresh horses were procured, and the
two ladies and their attendants renewed their journey, with strong
injunctions to the driver to quicken their rate of travelling as much as
possible, and promises of reward in case of his doing so.

Roads were then in much worse condition throughout the south,
even than they now are; and the fifteen miles which modern posting
would have passed in little more than an hour and a half, were not
completed even with every possible exertion in twice the time. Miss
F——d had been nervously restless during the journey. Her head had
been constantly out of the carriage window; and as they approached the

entrance to the castle demesne, which lay about a mile from the building, her anxiety began to communicate itself to her sister. The postillion had just dismounted, and was endeavouring to open the gate—at that time a necessary trouble; for in the middle of the last century porter's lodges were not common in the south of Ireland, and locks and keys almost unknown. He had just succeeded in rolling back the heavy oaken gate so as to admit the vehicle, when a mounted servant rode rapidly down the avenue, and drawing up at the carriage, asked of the postillion who the party were; and on hearing, he rode round to the carriage window and handed in a note, which Lady D—— received. By the assistance of one of the coach-lamps they succeeded in deciphering it. It was scrawled in great agitation, and ran thus:

My Dear Sister—My Dear Sisters Both,
    In God's name lose no time, I am frightened and miserable; I cannot explain all till you come. I am too much terrified to write coherently; but understand me—hasten— do not waste a minute. I am afraid you will come too late.

E. A.

The servant could tell nothing more than that the castle was in great confusion, and that Lady Ardagh had been crying bitterly all the night. Sir Robert was perfectly well. Altogether at a loss as to the cause of Lady Ardagh's great distress, they urged their way up the steep and broken avenue which wound through the crowding trees, whose wild and grotesque branches, now left stripped and naked by the blasts of winter, stretched drearily across the road. As the carriage drew up in the area before the door, the anxiety of the ladies almost amounted to agony; and scarcely waiting for the assistance of their attendant, they sprang to the ground, and in an instant stood at the castle door. From within were distinctly audible the sounds of lamentation and weeping, and the suppressed hum of voices as if of those endeavouring to soothe the mourner. The door was speedily opened, and when the ladies entered, the first object which met their view was their sister, Lady Ardagh, sitting on a form in the hall, weeping and wringing her hands in deep agony. Beside her stood two old, withered crones, who were each endeavouring in their own way to administer consolation, without even knowing or caring what the subject of her grief might be.

Immediately on Lady Ardagh's seeing her sisters, she started up, fell on their necks, and kissed them again and again without speaking, and then taking them each by a hand, still weeping bitterly, she led them into a small room adjoining the hall, in which burned a light, and, having closed the door, she sat down between them. After thanking them for the haste they had made, she proceeded to tell them, in words incoherent from agitation, that Sir Robert had in private, and in the most solemn manner, told her that he should die upon that night, and that he had occupied himself during the evening in giving minute directions respecting the arrangements of his funeral. Lady D—— here suggested the possibility of his labouring under the hallucinations of a fever; but to this Lady Ardagh quickly replied:

"Oh! no, no! Would to God I could think it. Oh! no, no! Wait till you have seen him. There is a frightful calmness about all he says and does; and his directions are all so clear, and his mind so perfectly collected, it is impossible, quite impossible." And she wept yet more bitterly.

At that moment Sir Robert's voice was heard in issuing some directions, as he came downstairs; and Lady Ardagh exclaimed, hurriedly:

"Go now and see him yourself. He is in the hall."

Lady D—— accordingly went out into the hall, where Sir Robert met her; and, saluting her with kind politeness, he said, after a pause:

"You are come upon a melancholy mission—the house is in great confusion, and some of its inmates in considerable grief." He took her hand, and looking fixedly in her face, continued: "I shall not live to see tomorrow's sun shine."

"You are ill, sir, I have no doubt," replied she; "but I am very certain we shall see you much better tomorrow, and still better the day following."

"I am NOT ill, sister," replied he. "Feel my temples, they are cool; lay your finger to my pulse, its throb is slow and temperate. I never was more perfectly in health, and yet do I know that ere three hours be past, I shall be no more."

"Sir, sir," said she, a good deal startled, but wishing to conceal the impression which the calm solemnity of his manner had, in her own despite, made upon her, "Sir, you should not jest; you should not even speak lightly upon such subjects. You trifle with what is sacred—you are sporting with the best affections of your wife—"

"Stay, my good lady," said he; "if when this clock shall strike the hour of three, I shall be anything but a helpless clod, then upbraid me. Pray return now to your sister. Lady Ardagh is, indeed, much to be pitied;

but what is past cannot now be helped. I have now a few papers to arrange, and some to destroy. I shall see you and Lady Ardagh before my death; try to compose her—her sufferings distress me much; but what is past cannot now be mended."

Thus saying, he went upstairs, and Lady D—— returned to the room where her sisters were sitting.

"Well," exclaimed Lady Ardagh, as she re-entered, "is it not so?—do you still doubt?—do you think there is any hope?"

Lady D—— was silent.

"Oh! none, none, none," continued she; "I see, I see you are convinced." And she wrung her hands in bitter agony.

"My dear sister," said Lady D——, "there is, no doubt, something strange in all that has appeared in this matter; but still I cannot but hope that there may be something deceptive in all the apparent calmness of Sir Robert. I still must believe that some latent fever has affected his mind, or that, owing to the state of nervous depression into which he has been sinking, some trivial occurrence has been converted, in his disordered imagination, into an augury foreboding his immediate dissolution."

In such suggestions, unsatisfactory even to those who originated them, and doubly so to her whom they were intended to comfort, more than two hours passed; and Lady D—— was beginning to hope that the fated term might elapse without the occurrence of any tragical event, when Sir Robert entered the room. On coming in, he placed his finger with a warning gesture upon his lips, as if to enjoin silence; and then having successively pressed the hands of his two sisters-in-law, he stooped sadly over the fainting form of his lady, and twice pressed her cold, pale forehead, with his lips, and then passed silently out of the room.

Lady D——, starting up, followed to the door, and saw him take a candle in the hall, and walk deliberately up the stairs. Stimulated by a feeling of horrible curiosity, she continued to follow him at a distance. She saw him enter his own private room, and heard him close and lock the door after him. Continuing to follow him as far as she could, she placed herself at the door of the chamber, as noiselessly as possible, where after a little time she was joined by her two sisters, Lady Ardagh and Miss F——d. In breathless silence they listened to what should pass within. They distinctly heard Sir Robert pacing up and down the room for sometime; and then, after a pause, a sound as if someone had thrown himself heavily upon the bed. At this moment Lady D——, forgetting that the door had been secured within, turned the handle for the purpose of entering; when someone from the inside, close to the door, said, "Hush! hush!" The same lady, now much alarmed, knocked violently at the door; there was no answer. She knocked again more violently, with no further success. Lady Ardagh, now uttering a piercing shriek, sank in a swoon upon the floor. Three or four servants, alarmed by the noise, now hurried upstairs, and Lady Ardagh was carried apparently lifeless to her own chamber. They then, after having knocked long and loudly in vain, applied themselves to forcing an entrance into Sir Robert's room. After resisting some violent efforts, the door at length gave way, and all entered the room nearly together. There was a single candle burning upon a table at the far end of the apartment; and stretched upon the bed lay Sir Robert Ardagh. He was a corpse—the eyes were open—no convulsion had passed over the features, or distorted the limbs—it seemed as if the soul had sped from the body without a struggle to remain there. On touching the body it was found to be cold as clay—all lingering of the vital heat had left it. They closed the ghastly eyes of the corpse, and leaving it to the care of those who seem to consider it a privilege of their age and sex to gloat over the revolting spectacle of death in all its stages, they returned to Lady Ardagh, now a widow. The party assembled at the castle, but the atmosphere was tainted with death. Grief there was not much, but awe and panic were expressed in every face. The guests talked in whispers, and the servants walked on tiptoe, as if afraid of the very noise of their own footsteps.

The funeral was conducted almost with splendour. The body, having been conveyed, in compliance with Sir Robert's last directions, to Dublin, was there laid within the ancient walls of St. Audoen's Church—where I have read the epitaph, telling the age and titles of the departed dust. Neither painted escutcheon, nor marble slab, have served to rescue from oblivion the story of the dead, whose very name will ere long moulder from their tracery,

"Et sunt sua fata sepulchris."[1]

---

1. This prophecy has since been realised; for the aisle in which Sir Robert's remains were laid has been suffered to fall completely to decay; and the tomb which marked his grave, and other monuments more curious, form now one indistinguishable mass of rubbish.

The events which I have recorded are not imaginary. They are FACTS; and there lives one whose authority none would venture to question, who could vindicate the accuracy of every statement which I have set down, and that, too, with all the circumstantiality of an eye-witness.[2]

---

2. This paper, from a memorandum, I find to have been written in 1803. The lady to whom allusion is made, I believe to be Miss Mary F——d. She never married, and survived both her sisters, living to a very advanced age.

The Murdered Cousin

*"And they lay wait for their own blood: they lurk privily for their own
lives."*

*"So are the ways of everyone that is greedy of gain; which taketh
away the life of the owner thereof."*

This story of the Irish peerage is written, as nearly as possible, in
the very words in which it was related by its "heroine," the late
Countess D——, and is therefore told in the first person.

My mother died when I was an infant, and of her I have no
recollection, even the faintest. By her death my education was left
solely to the direction of my surviving parent. He entered upon his
task with a stern appreciation of the responsibility thus cast upon him.
My religious instruction was prosecuted with an almost exaggerated
anxiety; and I had, of course, the best masters to perfect me in all those
accomplishments which my station and wealth might seem to require.
My father was what is called an oddity, and his treatment of me, though
uniformly kind, was governed less by affection and tenderness, than
by a high and unbending sense of duty. Indeed I seldom saw or spoke
to him except at meal-times, and then, though gentle, he was usually
reserved and gloomy. His leisure hours, which were many, were passed
either in his study or in solitary walks; in short, he seemed to take no
further interest in my happiness or improvement, than a conscientious
regard to the discharge of his own duty would seem to impose.

Shortly before my birth an event occurred which had contributed
much to induce and to confirm my father's unsocial habits; it was the
fact that a suspicion of *murder* had fallen upon his younger brother,
though not sufficiently definite to lead to any public proceedings, yet
strong enough to ruin him in public opinion. This disgraceful and
dreadful doubt cast upon the family name, my father felt deeply and
bitterly, and not the less so that he himself was thoroughly convinced of
his brother's innocence. The sincerity and strength of this conviction he
shortly afterwards proved in a manner which produced the catastrophe
of my story.

Before, however, I enter upon my immediate adventures, I ought to
relate the circumstances which had awakened that suspicion to which
I have referred, inasmuch as they are in themselves somewhat curious,

and in their effects most intimately connected with my own after-history.

My uncle, Sir Arthur Tyrrell, was a gay and extravagant man, and, among other vices, was ruinously addicted to gaming. This unfortunate propensity, even after his fortune had suffered so severely as to render retrenchment imperative, nevertheless continued to engross him, nearly to the exclusion of every other pursuit. He was, however, a proud, or rather a vain man, and could not bear to make the diminution of his income a matter of triumph to those with whom he had hitherto competed; and the consequence was, that he frequented no longer the expensive haunts of his dissipation, and retired from the gay world, leaving his coterie to discover his reasons as best they might. He did not, however, forego his favourite vice, for though he could not worship his great divinity in those costly temples where he was formerly wont to take his place, yet he found it very possible to bring about him a sufficient number of the votaries of chance to answer all his ends. The consequence was, that Carrickleigh, which was the name of my uncle's residence, was never without one or more of such visiters as I have described. It happened that upon one occasion he was visited by one Hugh Tisdall, a gentleman of loose, and, indeed, low habits, but of considerable wealth, and who had, in early youth, travelled with my uncle upon the Continent. The period of this visit was winter, and, consequently, the house was nearly deserted excepting by its ordinary inmates; it was, therefore, highly acceptable, particularly as my uncle was aware that his visiter's tastes accorded exactly with his own.

Both parties seemed determined to avail themselves of their mutual suitability during the brief stay which Mr. Tisdall had promised; the consequence was, that they shut themselves up in Sir Arthur's private room for nearly all the day and the greater part of the night, during the space of almost a week, at the end of which the servant having one morning, as usual, knocked at Mr. Tisdall's bed-room door repeatedly, received no answer, and, upon attempting to enter, found that it was locked. This appeared suspicious, and the inmates of the house having been alarmed, the door was forced open, and, on proceeding to the bed, they found the body of its occupant perfectly lifeless, and hanging halfway out, the head downwards, and near the floor. One deep wound had been inflicted upon the temple, apparently with some blunt instrument, which had penetrated the brain, and another blow, less effective—probably the first aimed—had grazed his head, removing some of the scalp. The door had been double locked upon the *inside*, in evidence of which the key still lay where it had been placed in the lock. The window, though not secured on the interior, was closed; a circumstance not a little puzzling, as it afforded the only other mode of escape from the room. It looked out, too, upon a kind of court-yard, round which the old buildings stood, formerly accessible by a narrow doorway and passage lying in the oldest side of the quadrangle, but which had since been built up, so as to preclude all ingress or egress; the room was also upon the second story, and the height of the window considerable; in addition to all which the stone window-sill was much too narrow to allow of anyone's standing upon it when the window was closed. Near the bed were found a pair of razors belonging to the murdered man, one of them upon the ground, and both of them open. The weapon which inflicted the mortal wound was not to be found in the room, nor were any footsteps or other traces of the murderer discoverable. At the suggestion of Sir Arthur himself, the coroner was instantly summoned to attend, and an inquest was held. Nothing, however, in any degree conclusive was elicited. The walls, ceiling, and floor of the room were carefully examined, in order to ascertain whether they contained a trap-door or other concealed mode of entrance, but no such thing appeared. Such was the minuteness of investigation employed, that, although the grate had contained a large fire during the night, they proceeded to examine even the very chimney, in order to discover whether escape by it were possible. But this attempt, too, was fruitless, for the chimney, built in the old fashion, rose in a perfectly perpendicular line from the hearth, to a height of nearly fourteen feet above the roof, affording in its interior scarcely the possibility of ascent, the flue being smoothly plastered, and sloping towards the top like an inverted funnel; promising, too, even if the summit were attained, owing to its great height, but a precarious descent upon the sharp and steep-ridged roof; the ashes, too, which lay in the grate, and the soot, as far as it could be seen, were undisturbed, a circumstance almost conclusive upon the point.

Sir Arthur was of course examined. His evidence was given with clearness and unreserve, which seemed calculated to silence all suspicion. He stated that, up to the day and night immediately preceding the catastrophe, he had lost to a heavy amount, but that, at their last sitting, he had not only won back his original loss, but upwards of £4,000 in addition; in evidence of which he produced an acknowledgment of debt to that amount in the handwriting of the deceased, bearing date the night of the catastrophe. He had mentioned the circumstance to Lady Tyrrell, and in presence of some of his domestics; which statement was supported by *their* respective evidence. One of the jury shrewdly observed, that the circumstance of Mr. Tisdall's having sustained so heavy a loss might have suggested to some ill-minded persons, accidentally hearing it, the plan of robbing him, after having murdered him in such a manner as might make it appear that he had committed suicide; a supposition which was strongly supported by the razors having been found thus displaced and removed from their case. Two persons had probably been engaged in the attempt, one watching by the sleeping man, and ready to strike him in case of his awakening suddenly, while the other was procuring the razors and employed in inflicting the fatal gash, so as to make it appear to have been the act of the murdered man himself. It was said that while the juror was making this suggestion Sir Arthur changed colour. There was nothing, however, like legal evidence to implicate him, and the consequence was that the verdict was found against a person or persons unknown, and for sometime the matter was suffered to rest, until, after about five months, my father received a letter from a person signing himself Andrew Collis, and representing himself to be the cousin of the deceased. This letter stated that his brother, Sir Arthur, was likely to incur not merely suspicion but personal risk, unless he could account for certain circumstances connected with the recent murder, and contained a copy of a letter written by the deceased, and dated the very day upon the night of which the murder had been perpetrated. Tisdall's letter contained, among a great deal of other matter, the passages which follow:—

"I have had sharp work with Sir Arthur: he tried some of his stale tricks, but soon found that *I* was Yorkshire, too; it would not do—you understand me. We went to the work like good ones, head, heart, and soul; and in fact, since I came here, I have lost no time. I am rather fagged, but I am sure to be well paid for my hardship; I never want sleep so long as I can have the music of a dice-box, and wherewithal to pay the piper. As I told you, he tried some of his queer turns, but I foiled him like a man, and, in return, gave him more than he could relish of the genuine *dead knowledge*. In short, I have plucked the old baronet as never baronet was plucked before; I have scarce left him the stump of a quill. I have got promissory notes in his hand to the amount of—; if you like round numbers, say five-and-twenty thousand pounds, safely deposited in my portable strong box, alias, double-clasped pocket-book. I leave this ruinous old rat-hole early on tomorrow, for two reasons: first, I do not want to play with Sir Arthur deeper than I think his security would warrant; and, secondly, because I am safer a hundred miles away from Sir Arthur than in the house with him. Look you, my worthy, I tell you this between ourselves—I may be wrong—but, by—, I am sure as that I am now living, that Sir A—— attempted to poison me last night. So much for old friendship on both sides. When I won the last stake, a heavy one enough, my friend leant his forehead upon his hands, and you'll laugh when I tell you that his head literally smoked like a hot dumpling. I do not know whether his agitation was produced by the plan which he had against me, or by his having lost so heavily; though it must be allowed that he had reason to be a little funked, whichever way his thoughts went; but he pulled the bell, and ordered two bottles of Champagne. While the fellow was bringing them, he wrote a promissory note to the full amount, which he signed, and, as the man came in with the bottles and glasses, he desired him to be off. He filled a glass for me, and, while he thought my eyes were off, for I was putting up his note at the time, he dropped something slyly into it, no doubt to sweeten it; but I saw it all, and, when he handed it to me, I said, with an emphasis which he might easily understand, 'There is some sediment in it, I'll not drink it.' 'Is there?' said he, and at the same time snatched it from my hand and threw it into the fire. What do you think of that? Have I not a tender bird in hand? Win or lose, I will not play beyond five thousand tonight, and tomorrow sees me safe out of the reach of Sir Arthur's Champagne."

Of the authenticity of this document, I never heard my father express a doubt; and I am satisfied that, owing to his strong conviction in favour of his brother, he would not have admitted it without sufficient inquiry, inasmuch as it tended to confirm the suspicions which already existed to his prejudice. Now, the only point in this letter which made strongly against my uncle, was the mention of the "double-clasped pocket-book," as the receptacle of the papers likely to involve him, for this pocket-book was not forthcoming, nor anywhere to be found, nor had any papers referring to his gaming transactions been discovered upon the dead man.

But whatever might have been the original intention of this man, Collis, neither my uncle nor my father ever heard more of him; he published the letter, however, in Faulkner's newspaper, which was shortly afterwards made the vehicle of a much more mysterious attack. The passage in that journal to which I allude, appeared about four years afterwards, and while the fatal occurrence was still fresh in public recollection. It commenced by a rambling preface, stating that "a *certain person* whom *certain* persons thought to be dead, was not so, but living, and in full possession of his memory, and moreover, ready and able to make *great* delinquents tremble": it then went on to describe the murder, without, however, mentioning names; and in doing so, it entered into minute and circumstantial particulars of which none but an *eye-witness* could have been possessed, and by implications almost too unequivocal to be regarded in the light of insinuation, to involve the "*titled gambler*" in the guilt of the transaction.

My father at once urged Sir Arthur to proceed against the paper in an action of libel, but he would not hear of it, nor consent to my father's taking any legal steps whatever in the matter. My father, however, wrote in a threatening tone to Faulkner, demanding a surrender of the author of the obnoxious article; the answer to this application is still in my possession, and is penned in an apologetic tone: it states that the manuscript had been handed in, paid for, and inserted as an advertisement, without sufficient inquiry, or any knowledge as to whom it referred. No step, however, was taken to clear my uncle's character in the judgment of the public; and, as he immediately sold a small property, the application of the proceeds of which were known to none, he was said to have disposed of it to enable himself to buy off the threatened information; however the truth might have been, it is certain that no charges respecting the mysterious murder were afterwards publicly made against my uncle, and, as far as external disturbances were concerned, he enjoyed henceforward perfect security and quiet.

A deep and lasting impression, however, had been made upon the public mind, and Sir Arthur Tyrrell was no longer visited or noticed by the gentry of the county, whose attentions he had hitherto received. He accordingly affected to despise those courtesies which he no longer enjoyed, and shunned even that society which he might have commanded. This is all that I need recapitulate of my uncle's history, and I now recur to my own.

Although my father had never, within my recollection, visited, or been visited by my uncle, each being of unsocial, procrastinating, and indolent habits, and their respective residences being very far apart— the one lying in the county of Galway, the other in that of Cork—he was strongly attached to his brother, and evinced his affection by an active correspondence, and by deeply and proudly resenting that neglect which had branded Sir Arthur as unfit to mix in society.

When I was about eighteen years of age, my father, whose health had been gradually declining, died, leaving me in heart wretched and desolate, and, owing to his habitual seclusion, with few acquaintances, and almost no friends. The provisions of his will were curious, and when I was sufficiently come to myself to listen to, or comprehend them, surprised me not a little: all his vast property was left to me, and to the heirs of my body, forever; and, in default of such heirs, it was to go after my death to my uncle, Sir Arthur, without any entail. At the same time, the will appointed him my guardian, desiring that I might be received within his house, and reside with his family, and under his care, during the term of my minority; and in consideration of the increased expense consequent upon such an arrangement, a handsome allowance was allotted to him during the term of my proposed residence. The object of this last provision I at once understood; my father desired, by making it the direct apparent interest of Sir Arthur that I should die without issue, while at the same time he placed my person wholly in his power, to prove to the world how great and unshaken was his confidence in his brother's innocence and honour. It was a strange, perhaps an idle scheme, but as I had been always brought up in the habit of considering my uncle as a deeply injured man, and had been taught, almost as a part of my religion, to regard him as the very soul of honour, I felt no further uneasiness respecting the arrangement than that likely to affect a shy and timid girl at the immediate prospect of taking up her abode for the first time in her life among strangers. Previous to leaving my home, which I felt I should do with a heavy heart, I received a most tender and affectionate letter from my uncle, calculated, if anything could do so, to remove the bitterness of parting from scenes familiar and dear from my earliest childhood, and in some degree to reconcile me to the measure. It was upon a fine autumn day that I approached the old domain of Carrickleigh. I shall not soon forget the impression of sadness and of gloom which all that I saw produced upon my mind; the sunbeams were falling with a rich and melancholy lustre upon the fine old trees, which stood in lordly groups, casting their long sweeping shadows over rock and sward; there was an air of neglect and decay about the spot, which amounted almost to desolation, and mournfully increased as we approached the building itself, near which the ground had been originally more artificially and carefully cultivated than elsewhere, and where consequently neglect more immediately and strikingly betrayed itself.

As we proceeded, the road wound near the beds of what had been formerly two fish-ponds, which were now nothing more than stagnant swamps, overgrown with rank weeds, and here and there encroached upon by the straggling underwood; the avenue itself was much broken; and in many places the stones were almost concealed by grass and nettles; the loose stone walls which had here and there intersected the broad park, were, in many places, broken down, so as no longer to answer their original purpose as fences; piers were now and then to be seen, but the gates were gone; and to add to the general air of dilapidation, some huge trunks were lying scattered through the venerable old trees, either the work of the winter storms, or perhaps the victims of some extensive but desultory scheme of denudation, which the projector had not capital or perseverance to carry into full effect.

After the carriage had travelled a full mile of this avenue, we reached the summit of a rather abrupt eminence, one of the many which added to the picturesqueness, if not to the convenience of this rude approach; from the top of this ridge the grey walls of Carrickleigh were visible, rising at a small distance in front, and darkened by the hoary wood which crowded around them; it was a quadrangular building of considerable extent, and the front, where the great entrance was placed, lay towards us, and bore unequivocal marks of antiquity; the time-worn, solemn aspect of the old building, the ruinous and deserted appearance of the whole place, and the associations which connected it with a dark page in the history of my family, combined to depress spirits already predisposed for the reception of sombre and dejecting impressions. When the carriage drew up in the grass-grown court-yard before the hall-door, two lazy-looking men, whose appearance well accorded with that of the place which they tenanted, alarmed by the obstreperous barking of a great chained dog, ran out from some half-ruinous outhouses, and took charge of the horses; the hall-door stood open, and I entered a gloomy and imperfectly-lighted apartment, and found no one within it. However, I had not long to wait in this awkward predicament, for before my luggage had been deposited in the house, indeed before I had well removed my cloak and other muffles, so as to enable me to look around, a young girl ran lightly into the hall, and kissing me heartily and somewhat boisterously exclaimed,

"My dear cousin, my dear Margaret—I am so delighted—so out of breath, we did not expect you till ten o'clock; my father is somewhere about the place, he must be close at hand. James—Corney—run out and tell your master; my brother is seldom at home, at least at any reasonable hour; you must be so tired—so fatigued—let me show you to your room; see that Lady Margaret's luggage is all brought up; you must lie down and rest yourself. Deborah, bring some coffee—up these stairs; we are so delighted to see you—you cannot think how lonely I have been; how steep these stairs are, are not they? I am so glad you are come—I could hardly bring myself to believe that you were really coming; how good of you, dear Lady Margaret." There was real good nature and delight in my cousin's greeting, and a kind of constitutional confidence of manner which placed me at once at ease, and made me feel immediately upon terms of intimacy with her. The room into which she ushered me, although partaking in the general air of decay which pervaded the mansion and all about it, had, nevertheless, been fitted up with evident attention to comfort, and even with some dingy attempt at luxury; but what pleased me most was that it opened, by a second door, upon a lobby which communicated with my fair cousin's apartment; a circumstance which divested the room, in my eyes, of the air of solitude and sadness which would otherwise have characterised it, to a degree almost painful to one so depressed and agitated as I was.

After such arrangements as I found necessary were completed, we both went down to the parlour, a large wainscotted room, hung round with grim old portraits, and, as I was not sorry to see, containing, in its ample grate, a large and cheerful fire. Here my cousin had leisure to talk more at her ease; and from her I learned something of the manners and the habits of the two remaining members of her family, whom I had not yet seen. On my arrival I had known nothing of the family among whom I was come to reside, except that it consisted of three individuals, my uncle, and his son and daughter, Lady Tyrrell having been long dead; in addition to this very scanty stock of information, I shortly learned from my communicative companion, that my uncle was, as I had suspected, completely retired in his habits, and besides that, having been, so far back as she could well recollect, always rather strict, as reformed rakes frequently become, he had latterly been growing more gloomily and sternly religious than heretofore. Her account of her brother was far less favourable, though she did not say anything directly to his disadvantage. From all that I could gather from her, I was led to suppose that he was a specimen of the idle, coarse-mannered, profligate "*squirearchy*"—a result which might naturally have followed from the circumstance of his being, as it were, outlawed from society, and driven for companionship to grades below his own—enjoying, too, the dangerous prerogative of spending a good deal of money. However, you may easily suppose that I found nothing in my cousin's communication fully to bear me out in so very decided a conclusion.

I awaited the arrival of my uncle, which was every moment to be expected, with feelings half of alarm, half of curiosity—a sensation which I have often since experienced, though to a less degree, when upon the point of standing for the first time in the presence of one of whom I have long been in the habit of hearing or thinking with interest. It was, therefore, with some little perturbation that I heard, first a slight bustle at the outer door, then a slow step traverse the hall, and finally witnessed the door open, and my uncle enter the room. He was a striking looking man; from peculiarities both of person and of dress, the whole effect of his appearance amounted to extreme singularity. He was tall, and when young his figure must have been strikingly elegant; as it was, however, its effect was marred by a very decided stoop; his dress was of a sober colour, and in fashion anterior to anything which I could remember. It was, however, handsome, and by no means carelessly put on; but what completed the singularity of his appearance was his uncut, white hair, which hung in long, but not at all neglected curls, even so far as his shoulders, and which combined with his regularly classic features, and fine dark eyes, to bestow upon him an air of venerable dignity and pride, which I have seldom seen equalled elsewhere. I rose as he entered, and met him about the middle of the room; he kissed my cheek and both my hands, saying—

"You are most welcome, dear child, as welcome as the command of this poor place and all that it contains can make you. I am rejoiced to see you—truly rejoiced. I trust that you are not much fatigued; pray be seated again." He led me to my chair, and continued, "I am glad to perceive you have made acquaintance with Emily already; I see, in your being thus brought together, the foundation of a lasting friendship. You are both innocent, and both young. God bless you—God bless you, and make you all that I could wish."

He raised his eyes, and remained for a few moments silent, as if in secret prayer. I felt that it was impossible that this man, with feelings manifestly so tender, could be the wretch that public opinion had represented him to be. I was more than ever convinced of his innocence.

His manners were, or appeared to me, most fascinating. I know not how the lights of experience might have altered this estimate. But I was then very young, and I beheld in him a perfect mingling of the courtesy of polished life with the gentlest and most genial virtues of the heart. A feeling of affection and respect towards him began to spring up within me, the more earnest that I remembered how sorely he had suffered in fortune and how cruelly in fame. My uncle having given me fully to understand that I was most welcome, and might command whatever was his own, pressed me to take some supper; and on my refusing, he observed that, before bidding me goodnight, he had one duty further to perform, one in which he was convinced I would cheerfully acquiesce. He then proceeded to read a chapter from the Bible; after which he took his leave with the same affectionate kindness with which he had greeted me, having repeated his desire that I should consider everything in his house as altogether at my disposal. It is needless to say how much I was pleased with my uncle—it was impossible to avoid being so; and I could not help saying to myself, if such a man as this is not safe from the assaults of slander, who is? I felt much happier than I had done since my father's death, and enjoyed that night the first refreshing sleep which had visited me since that calamity. My curiosity respecting my male cousin did not long remain unsatisfied; he appeared upon the next day at dinner. His manners, though not so coarse as I had expected, were exceedingly disagreeable; there was an assurance and a forwardness for which I was not prepared; there was less of the vulgarity of manner, and almost more of that of the mind, than I had anticipated. I felt quite uncomfortable in his presence; there was just that confidence in his look and tone, which would read encouragement even in mere toleration; and I felt more disgusted and annoyed at the coarse and extravagant compliments which he was pleased from time to time to pay me, than perhaps the extent of the atrocity might fully have warranted. It was, however, one consolation that he did not often appear, being much engrossed by pursuits about which I neither knew nor cared anything; but when he did, his attentions, either with a view to his amusement, or to some more serious object, were so obviously and perseveringly directed to me, that young and inexperienced as I was, even *I* could not be ignorant of their significance. I felt more provoked by this odious persecution than I can express, and discouraged him with so much vigour, that I did not stop even at rudeness to convince him that his assiduities were unwelcome; but all in vain.

This had gone on for nearly a twelvemonth, to my infinite annoyance, when one day, as I was sitting at some needlework with my companion, Emily, as was my habit, in the parlour, the door opened, and my cousin Edward entered the room. There was something, I thought, odd in his manner, a kind of struggle between shame and impudence, a kind of flurry and ambiguity, which made him appear, if possible, more than ordinarily disagreeable.

"Your servant, ladies," he said, seating himself at the same time; "sorry to spoil your *tête-à-tête*; but never mind, I'll only take Emily's place for a minute or two, and then we part for a while, fair cousin. Emily, my father wants you in the corner turret; no shilly, shally, he's in a hurry." She hesitated. "Be off—tramp, march, I say," he exclaimed, in a tone which the poor girl dared not disobey.

She left the room, and Edward followed her to the door. He stood there for a minute or two, as if reflecting what he should say, perhaps satisfying himself that no one was within hearing in the hall. At length he turned about, having closed the door, as if carelessly, with his foot, and advancing slowly, in deep thought, he took his seat at the side of the table opposite to mine. There was a brief interval of silence, after which he said:—

"I imagine that you have a shrewd suspicion of the object of my early visit; but I suppose I must go into particulars. Must I?"

"I have no conception," I replied, "what your object may be."

"Well, well," said he becoming more at his ease as he proceeded, "it may be told in a few words. You know that it is totally impossible, quite out of the question, that an off-hand young fellow like me, and a good-looking girl like yourself, could meet continually as you and I have done, without an attachment—a liking growing up on one side or other; in short, I think I have let you know as plainly as if I spoke it, that I have been in love with you, almost from the first time I saw you." He paused, but I was too much horrified to speak. He interpreted my silence favourably. "I can tell you," he continued, "I'm reckoned rather hard to please, and very hard to *hit*. I can't say when I was taken with a girl before, so you see fortune reserved me—."

Here the odious wretch actually put his arm round my waist: the action at once restored me to utterance, and with the most indignant vehemence I released myself from his hold, and at the same time said:—

"I *have*, sir, of course, perceived your most disagreeable attentions; they have long been a source of great annoyance to me; and you must be aware that I have marked my disapprobation, my disgust, as unequivocally as I possibly could, without actual indelicacy."

I paused, almost out of breath from the rapidity with which I had spoken; and without giving him time to renew the conversation, I hastily quitted the room, leaving him in a paroxysm of rage and mortification. As I ascended the stairs, I heard him open the parlour-door with violence, and take two or three rapid strides in the direction in which I was moving. I was now much frightened, and ran the whole way until I reached my room, and having locked the door, I listened breathlessly, but heard no sound. This relieved me for the present; but so much had I been overcome by the agitation and annoyance attendant upon the scene which I had just passed through, that when my cousin Emily knocked at the door, I was weeping in great agitation. You will readily conceive my distress, when you reflect upon my strong dislike to my cousin Edward, combined with my youth and extreme inexperience. Any proposal of such a nature must have agitated me; but that it should come from the man whom, of all others, I instinctively most loathed and abhorred, and to whom I had, as clearly as manner could do it, expressed the state of my feelings, was almost too annoying to be borne; it was a calamity, too, in which I could not claim the sympathy of my cousin Emily, which had always been extended to me in my minor grievances. Still I hoped that it might not be unattended with good; for I thought that one inevitable and most welcome consequence would result from this painful *éclaircissement*, in the discontinuance of my cousin's odious persecution.

When I arose next morning, it was with the fervent hope that I might never again behold his face, or even hear his name; but such a consummation, though devoutedly to be wished, was hardly likely to occur. The painful impressions of yesterday were too vivid to be at once erased; and I could not help feeling some dim foreboding of coming annoyance and evil. To expect on my cousin's part anything like delicacy or consideration for me, was out of the question. I saw that he had set his heart upon my property, and that he was not likely easily to forego such a prize, possessing what might have been considered opportunities and facilities almost to compel my compliance. I now keenly felt the unreasonableness of my father's conduct in placing me to reside with a family, with all the members of which, with one exception, he was wholly unacquainted, and I bitterly felt the helplessness of my situation. I determined, however, in the event of my cousin's persevering in his addresses, to lay all the particulars before my uncle, although he had never, in kindness or intimacy, gone a step beyond our first interview, and to throw myself upon his hospitality and his sense of honour for protection against a repetition of such annoyances.

My cousin's conduct may appear to have been an inadequate cause for such serious uneasiness; but my alarm was awakened neither by his acts nor by words, but entirely by his manner, which was strange and even intimidating. At the beginning of our yesterday's interview, there was a sort of bullying swagger in his air, which, towards the end, gave place to something bordering upon the brutal vehemence of an undisguised ruffian, a transition which had tempted me into a belief that he might seek, even forcibly, to extort from me a consent to his wishes, or by means still more horrible, of which I scarcely dared to trust myself to think, to possess himself of my property.

I was early next day summoned to attend my uncle in his private room, which lay in a corner turret of the old building; and thither I accordingly went, wondering all the way what this unusual measure might prelude. When I entered the room, he did not rise in his usual courteous way to greet me, but simply pointed to a chair opposite to his own; this boded nothing agreeable. I sat down, however, silently waiting until he should open the conversation.

"Lady Margaret," at length he said, in a tone of greater sternness than I thought him capable of using, "I have hitherto spoken to you as a friend, but I have not forgotten that I am also your guardian, and that my authority as such gives me a right to controul your conduct. I shall put a question to you, and I expect and will demand a plain, direct answer. Have I rightly been informed that you have contemptuously rejected the suit and hand of my son Edward?"

I stammered forth with a good deal of trepidation:—

"I believe, that is, I have, sir, rejected my cousin's proposals; and my coldness and discouragement might have convinced him that I had determined to do so."

"Madame," replied he, with suppressed, but, as it appeared to me, intense anger, "I have lived long enough to know that *coldness and discouragement*, and such terms, form the common cant of a worthless coquette. You know to the full, as well as I, that *coldness and discouragement* may be so exhibited as to convince their object that he is neither distasteful nor indifferent to the person who wears that manner. You know, too, none better, that an affected neglect, when skillfully managed, is amongst the most formidable of the allurements which artful beauty can employ. I tell you, madame, that having, without one word spoken in discouragement, permitted my son's most marked attentions for a twelvemonth or more, you have no *right* to dismiss him with no further explanation than demurely telling him that you had always looked coldly upon him, and neither your wealth nor *your ladyship* (there was an emphasis of scorn on the word which would have become Sir Giles Overreach himself) can warrant you in treating with contempt the affectionate regard of an honest heart."

I was too much shocked at this undisguised attempt to bully me into an acquiescence in the interested and unprincipled plan for their own aggrandisement, which I now perceived my uncle and his son had deliberately formed, at once to find strength or collectedness to frame an answer to what he had said. At length I replied, with a firmness that surprised myself:—

"In all that you have just now said, sir, you have grossly misstated my conduct and motives. Your information must have been most incorrect, as far as it regards my conduct towards my cousin; my manner towards him could have conveyed nothing but dislike; and if anything could have added to the strong aversion which I have long felt towards him, it would be his attempting thus to frighten me into a marriage which he knows to be revolting to me, and which is sought by him only as a means for securing to himself whatever property is mine."

As I said this, I fixed my eyes upon those of my uncle, but he was too old in the world's ways to falter beneath the gaze of more searching eyes than mine; he simply said—

"Are you acquainted with the provisions of your father's will?"

I answered in the affirmative; and he continued:—"Then you must be aware that if my son Edward were, which God forbid, the unprincipled, reckless man, the ruffian you pretend to think him"—(here he spoke very slowly, as if he intended that every word which escaped him should be registered in my memory, while at the same time the expression of his countenance underwent a gradual but horrible change, and the eyes which he fixed upon me became so darkly vivid, that I almost lost sight of everything else)—"if he were what you have described him, do you think, child, he would have found no shorter way than marriage to gain his ends? A single blow, an outrage not a degree worse than you insinuate, would transfer your property to us!!"

I stood staring at him for many minutes after he had ceased to speak, fascinated by the terrible, serpent-like gaze, until he continued with a welcome change of countenance:—

"I will not speak again to you, upon this topic, until one month has passed. You shall have time to consider the relative advantages of the two courses which are open to you. I should be sorry to hurry you to a decision. I am satisfied with having stated my feelings upon the subject, and pointed out to you the path of duty. Remember this day month; not one word sooner."

He then rose, and I left the room, much agitated and exhausted.

This interview, all the circumstances attending it, but most particularly the formidable expression of my uncle's countenance while he talked, though hypothetically, of *murder*, combined to arouse all my worst suspicions of him. I dreaded to look upon the face that had so recently worn the appalling livery of guilt and malignity. I regarded it with the mingled fear and loathing with which one looks upon an object which has tortured them in a night-mare.

In a few days after the interview, the particulars of which I have just detailed, I found a note upon my toilet-table, and on opening it I read as follows:—

My Dear Lady Margaret,

You will be, perhaps, surprised to see a strange face in your room today. I have dismissed your Irish maid, and secured a French one to wait upon you; a step rendered necessary by my proposing shortly to visit the Continent with all my family.

Your faithful guardian,
ARTHUR TYRELL

On inquiry, I found that my faithful attendant was actually gone, and far on her way to the town of Galway; and in her stead there appeared a tall, raw-boned, ill-looking, elderly Frenchwoman, whose sullen and presuming manners seemed to imply that her vocation had never before been that of a lady's-maid. I could not help regarding her as a creature of my uncle's, and therefore to be dreaded, even had she been in no other way suspicious.

Days and weeks passed away without any, even a momentary doubt upon my part, as to the course to be pursued by me. The allotted period had at length elapsed; the day arrived upon which I was to communicate my decision to my uncle. Although my resolution had never for a moment wavered, I could not shake off the dread of the approaching colloquy; and my heart sank within me as I heard the expected summons. I had not seen my cousin Edward since the occurrence of the grand *éclaircissement*; he must have studiously avoided me; I suppose from policy, it could not have been from delicacy. I was prepared for a terrific burst of fury from my uncle, as soon as I should make known my determination; and I not unreasonably feared that some act of violence or of intimidation would next be resorted to. Filled with these dreary forebodings, I fearfully opened the study door, and the next minute I stood in my uncle's presence. He received me with a courtesy which I dreaded, as arguing a favourable anticipation respecting the answer which I was to give; and after some slight delay he began by saying—

"It will be a relief to both of us, I believe, to bring this conversation as soon as possible to an issue. You will excuse me, then, my dear niece, for speaking with a bluntness which, under other circumstances, would be unpardonable. You have, I am certain, given the subject of our last interview fair and serious consideration; and I trust that you are now prepared with candour to lay your answer before me. A few words will suffice; we perfectly understand one another."

He paused; and I, though feeling that I stood upon a mine which might in an instant explode, nevertheless answered with perfect composure: "I must now, sir, make the same reply which I did upon the last occasion, and I reiterate the declaration which I then made, that I never can nor will, while life and reason remain, consent to a union with my cousin Edward."

This announcement wrought no apparent change in Sir Arthur, except that he became deadly, almost lividly pale. He seemed lost in dark thought for a minute, and then, with a slight effort, said, "You have answered me honestly and directly; and you say your resolution is unchangeable; well, would it had been otherwise—would it had been otherwise—but be it as it is; I am satisfied."

He gave me his hand—it was cold and damp as death; under an assumed calmness, it was evident that he was fearfully agitated. He continued to hold my hand with an almost painful pressure, while, as if unconsciously, seeming to forget my presence, he muttered, "Strange, strange, strange, indeed! fatuity, helpless fatuity!" there was here a long pause. "Madness *indeed* to strain a cable that is rotten to the very heart; it must break—and then—all goes." There was again a pause of some minutes, after which, suddenly changing his voice and manner to one of wakeful alacrity, he exclaimed,

"Margaret, my son Edward shall plague you no more. He leaves this country tomorrow for France; he shall speak no more upon this subject— never, never more; whatever events depended upon your answer must now take their own course; but as for this fruitless proposal, it has been tried enough; it can be repeated no more."

At these words he coldly suffered my hand to drop, as if to express his total abandonment of all his projected schemes of alliance; and certainly the action, with the accompanying words, produced upon my mind a more solemn and depressing effect than I believed possible to have been caused by the course which I had determined to pursue; it struck upon my heart with an awe and heaviness which *will* accompany the accomplishment of an important and irrevocable act, even though no doubt or scruple remains to make it possible that the agent should wish it undone.

"Well," said my uncle, after a little time, "we now cease to speak upon this topic, never to resume it again. Remember you shall have no farther uneasiness from Edward; he leaves Ireland for France tomorrow; this will be a relief to you; may I depend upon your *honour* that no word touching the subject of this interview shall ever escape you?" I gave him the desired assurance; he said, "It is well; I am satisfied; we have nothing more, I believe, to say upon either side, and my presence must be a restraint upon you, I shall therefore bid you farewell." I then left the apartment, scarcely knowing what to think of the strange interview which had just taken place.

On the next day my uncle took occasion to tell me that Edward had actually sailed, if his intention had not been prevented by adverse winds or weather; and two days after he actually produced a letter from his son, written, as it said, *on board*, and despatched while the ship was getting under weigh. This was a great satisfaction to me, and as being likely to prove so, it was no doubt communicated to me by Sir Arthur.

During all this trying period I had found infinite consolation in the society and sympathy of my dear cousin Emily. I never, in after-life, formed a friendship so close, so fervent, and upon which, in all its progress, I could look back with feelings of such unalloyed pleasure, upon whose termination I must ever dwell with so deep, so yet unembittered a sorrow. In cheerful converse with her I soon recovered my spirits considerably, and passed my time agreeably enough, although still in the utmost seclusion. Matters went on smoothly enough, although I could not help sometimes feeling a momentary, but horrible uncertainty respecting my uncle's character; which was not altogether unwarranted by the circumstances of the two trying interviews, the particulars of which I have just detailed. The unpleasant impression which these conferences were calculated to leave upon my mind was fast wearing away, when there occurred a circumstance, slight indeed in itself, but calculated irrepressibly to awaken all my worst suspicions, and to overwhelm me again with anxiety and terror.

I had one day left the house with my cousin Emily, in order to take a ramble of considerable length, for the purpose of sketching some favourite views, and we had walked about half a mile when I perceived that we had forgotten our drawing materials, the absence of which would have defeated the object of our walk. Laughing at our own thoughtlessness, we returned to the house, and leaving Emily outside, I ran upstairs to procure the drawing-books and pencils which lay in my bed-room. As I ran up the stairs, I was met by the tall, ill-looking Frenchwoman, evidently a good deal flurried; "Que veut Madame?" said she, with a more decided effort to be polite, than I had ever known her make before. "No, no—no matter," said I, hastily running by her in the direction of my room. "Madame," cried she, in a high key, "restez ici s'il vous plaît, votre chambre n'est pas faite." I continued to move on without heeding her. She was some way behind me, and feeling that she could not otherwise prevent my entrance, for I was now upon the very lobby, she made a desperate attempt to seize hold of my person; she succeeded in grasping the end of my shawl, which she drew from my shoulders, but slipping at the same time upon the polished oak floor, she fell at full length upon the boards. A little frightened as well as angry at the rudeness of this strange woman, I hastily pushed open the door of my room, at which I now stood, in order to escape from her; but great was my amazement on entering to find the apartment preoccupied. The window was open, and beside it stood two male figures; they appeared to be examining the fastenings of the casement, and their backs were turned towards the door. One of them was my uncle; they both had turned on my entrance, as if startled; the stranger was booted and cloaked, and wore a heavy, broad-leafed hat over his brows; he turned but for a moment, and averted his face; but I had seen enough to convince me that he was no other than my cousin Edward. My uncle had some iron instrument in his hand, which he hastily concealed behind his back; and coming towards me, said something as if in an explanatory tone; but I was too much shocked and confounded to understand what it might be. He said something about "*repairs*—window-frames—cold, and safety." I did not wait, however, to ask or to receive explanations, but hastily left the room. As I went down stairs I thought I heard the voice of the Frenchwoman in all the shrill volubility of excuse, and others uttering suppressed but vehement imprecations, or what seemed to me to be such.

I joined my cousin Emily quite out of breath. I need not say that my head was too full of other things to think much of drawing for that day. I imparted to her frankly the cause of my alarms, but, at the same time, as gently as I could; and with tears she promised vigilance, devotion, and love. I never had reason for a moment to repent the unreserved confidence which I then reposed in her. She was no less surprised than I at the unexpected appearance of Edward, whose departure for France neither of us had for a moment doubted, but which was now proved by his actual presence to be nothing more than an imposture practised, I feared, for no good end. The situation in which I had found my uncle had very nearly removed all my doubts as to his designs; I magnified suspicions into certainties, and dreaded night after night that I should be murdered in my bed. The nervousness produced by sleepless nights and days of anxious fears increased the horrors of my situation to such a degree, that I at length wrote a letter to a Mr. Jefferies, an old and faithful friend of my father's, and perfectly acquainted with all his affairs, praying him, for God's sake, to relieve me from my present terrible situation, and communicating without reserve the nature and grounds of my suspicions. This letter I kept sealed and directed for two or three days always about my person, for discovery would have been ruinous, in expectation of an opportunity, which might be safely trusted, of having it placed in the post-office; as neither Emily nor I were permitted to pass beyond the precincts of the demesne itself, which was surrounded by high walls formed of dry stone, the difficulty of procuring such an opportunity was greatly enhanced.

At this time Emily had a short conversation with her father, which she reported to me instantly. After some indifferent matter, he had asked her whether she and I were upon good terms, and whether I was unreserved in my disposition. She answered in the affirmative; and he then inquired whether I had been much surprised to find him in my chamber on the other day. She answered that I had been both surprised and amused. "And what did she think of George Wilson's appearance?" "Who?" inquired she. "Oh! the architect," he answered, "who is to

contract for the repairs of the house; he is accounted a handsome fellow."
"She could not see his face," said Emily, "and she was in such a hurry to
escape that she scarcely observed him." Sir Arthur appeared satisfied,
and the conversation ended.

This slight conversation, repeated accurately to me by Emily, had the
effect of confirming, if indeed anything was required to do so, all that
I had before believed as to Edward's actual presence; and I naturally
became, if possible, more anxious than ever to despatch the letter to
Mr. Jefferies. An opportunity at length occurred. As Emily and I were
walking one day near the gate of the demesne, a lad from the village
happened to be passing down the avenue from the house; the spot was
secluded, and as this person was not connected by service with those
whose observation I dreaded, I committed the letter to his keeping, with
strict injunctions that he should put it, without delay, into the receiver
of the town post-office; at the same time I added a suitable gratuity, and
the man having made many protestations of punctuality, was soon out
of sight. He was hardly gone when I began to doubt my discretion in
having trusted him; but I had no better or safer means of despatching
the letter, and I was not warranted in suspecting him of such wanton
dishonesty as a disposition to tamper with it; but I could not be quite
satisfied of its safety until I had received an answer, which could not
arrive for a few days. Before I did, however, an event occurred which
a little surprised me. I was sitting in my bed-room early in the day,
reading by myself, when I heard a knock at the door. "Come in," said I,
and my uncle entered the room. "Will you excuse me," said he, "I sought
you in the parlour, and thence I have come here. I desired to say a word
to you. I trust that you have hitherto found my conduct to you such as
that of a guardian towards his ward should be." I dared not withhold my
assent. "And," he continued, "I trust that you have not found me harsh
or unjust, and that you have perceived, my dear niece, that I have sought
to make this poor place as agreeable to you as may be?" I assented again;
and he put his hand in his pocket, whence he drew a folded paper, and
dashing it upon the table with startling emphasis he said, "Did you
write that letter?" The sudden and fearful alteration of his voice, manner,
and face, but more than all, the unexpected production of my letter to
Mr. Jefferies, which I at once recognised, so confounded and terrified
me, that I felt almost choking. I could not utter a word. "Did you write
that letter?" he repeated, with slow and intense emphasis. "You did, liar
and hypocrite. You dared to write that foul and infamous libel; but it

shall be your last. Men will universally believe you mad, if I choose to call for an inquiry. I can make you appear so. The suspicions expressed in this letter are the hallucinations and alarms of a moping lunatic. I have defeated your first attempt, madam; and by the holy God, if ever you make another, chains, darkness, and the keeper's whip shall be your portion." With these astounding words he left the room, leaving me almost fainting.

I was now almost reduced to despair; my last cast had failed; I had no course left but that of escaping secretly from the castle, and placing myself under the protection of the nearest magistrate. I felt if this were not done, and speedily, that I should be *murdered*. No one, from mere description, can have an idea of the unmitigated horror of my situation; a helpless, weak, inexperienced girl, placed under the power, and wholly at the mercy of evil men, and feeling that I had it not in my power to escape for one moment from the malignant influences under which I was probably doomed to fall; with a consciousness, too, that if violence, if murder were designed, no human being would be near to aid me; my dying shriek would be lost in void space.

I had seen Edward but once during his visit, and as I did not meet him again, I began to think that he must have taken his departure; a conviction which was to a certain degree satisfactory, as I regarded his absence as indicating the removal of immediate danger. Emily also arrived circuitously at the same conclusion, and not without good grounds, for she managed indirectly to learn that Edward's black horse had actually been for a day and part of a night in the castle stables, just at the time of her brother's supposed visit. The horse had gone, and as she argued, the rider must have departed with it.

This point being so far settled, I felt a little less uncomfortable; when being one day alone in my bed-room, I happened to look out from the window, and to my unutterable horror, I beheld peering through an opposite casement, my cousin Edward's face. Had I seen the evil one himself in bodily shape, I could not have experienced a more sickening revulsion. I was too much appalled to move at once from the window, but I did so soon enough to avoid his eye. He was looking fixedly down into the narrow quadrangle upon which the window opened. I shrunk back unperceived, to pass the rest of the day in terror and despair. I went to my room early that night, but I was too miserable to sleep.

At about twelve o'clock, feeling very nervous, I determined to call my cousin Emily, who slept, you will remember, in the next room, which communicated with mine by a second door. By this private entrance I found my way into her chamber, and without difficulty persuaded her to return to my room and sleep with me. We accordingly lay down together, she undressed, and I with my clothes on, for I was every moment walking up and down the room, and felt too nervous and miserable to think of rest or comfort. Emily was soon fast asleep, and I lay awake, fervently longing for the first pale gleam of morning, and reckoning every stroke of the old clock with an impatience which made every hour appear like six.

It must have been about one o'clock when I thought I heard a slight noise at the partition door between Emily's room and mine, as if caused by somebody's turning the key in the lock. I held my breath, and the same sound was repeated at the second door of my room, that which opened upon the lobby; the sound was here distinctly caused by the revolution of the bolt in the lock, and it was followed by a slight pressure upon the door itself, as if to ascertain the security of the lock. The person, whoever it might be, was probably satisfied, for I heard the old boards of the lobby creak and strain, as if under the weight of somebody moving cautiously over them. My sense of hearing became unnaturally, almost painfully acute. I suppose the imagination added distinctness to sounds vague in themselves. I thought that I could actually hear the breathing of the person who was slowly returning along the lobby.

At the head of the stair-case there appeared to occur a pause; and I could distinctly hear two or three sentences hastily whispered; the steps then descended the stairs with apparently less caution. I ventured to walk quickly and lightly to the lobby door, and attempted to open it; it was indeed fast locked upon the outside, as was also the other. I now felt that the dreadful hour was come; but one desperate expedient remained—it was to awaken Emily, and by our united strength, to attempt to force the partition door, which was slighter than the other, and through this to pass to the lower part of the house, whence it might be possible to escape to the grounds, and so to the village. I returned to the bedside, and shook Emily, but in vain; nothing that I could do availed to produce from her more than a few incoherent words; it was a death-like sleep. She had certainly drunk of some narcotic, as, probably, had I also, in spite of all the caution with which I had examined everything presented to us to eat or drink. I now attempted, with as little noise as possible, to force first one door, then the other; but all in vain. I believe no strength could have affected my object, for both doors opened inwards. I therefore collected whatever moveables I could carry thither, and piled them against the doors, so as to assist me in whatever attempts I should make to resist the entrance of those without. I then returned to the bed and endeavoured again, but fruitlessly, to awaken my cousin. It was not sleep, it was torpor, lethargy, death. I knelt down and prayed with an agony of earnestness; and then seating myself upon the bed, I awaited my fate with a kind of terrible tranquillity.

I heard a faint clanking sound from the narrow court which I have already mentioned, as if caused by the scraping of some iron instrument against stones or rubbish. I at first determined not to disturb the calmness which I now experienced, by uselessly watching the proceedings of those who sought my life; but as the sounds continued, the horrible curiosity which I felt overcame every other emotion, and I determined, at all hazards, to gratify it. I, therefore, crawled upon my knees to the window, so as to let the smallest possible portion of my head appear above the sill.

The moon was shining with an uncertain radiance upon the antique grey buildings, and obliquely upon the narrow court beneath; one side of it was therefore clearly illuminated, while the other was lost in obscurity, the sharp outlines of the old gables, with their nodding clusters of ivy, being at first alone visible. Whoever or whatever occasioned the noise which had excited my curiosity, was concealed under the shadow of the dark side of the quadrangle. I placed my hand over my eyes to shade them from the moonlight, which was so bright as to be almost dazzling, and, peering into the darkness, I first dimly, but afterwards gradually, almost with full distinctness, beheld the form of a man engaged in digging what appeared to be a rude hole close under the wall. Some implements, probably a shovel and pickaxe, lay beside him, and to these he every now and then applied himself as the nature of the ground required. He pursued his task rapidly, and with as little noise as possible. "So," thought I, as shovelful after shovelful, the dislodged rubbish mounted into a heap, "they are digging the grave in which, before two hours pass, I must lie, a cold, mangled corpse. I am *theirs*—I cannot escape." I felt as if my reason was leaving me. I started to my feet, and in mere despair I applied myself again to each of the two doors alternately. I strained every nerve and sinew, but I might as well have attempted, with my single strength, to force the building itself from its foundations. I threw myself madly upon the ground, and clasped my hands over my eyes as if to shut out the horrible images which crowded upon me.

The paroxysm passed away. I prayed once more with the bitter, agonised fervour of one who feels that the hour of death is present and inevitable. When I arose, I went once more to the window and looked out, just in time to see a shadowy figure glide stealthily along the wall. The task was finished. The catastrophe of the tragedy must soon be accomplished. I determined now to defend my life to the last; and that I might be able to do so with some effect, I searched the room for something which might serve as a weapon; but either through accident, or else in anticipation of such a possibility, everything which might have been made available for such a purpose had been removed.

I must then die tamely and without an effort to defend myself. A thought suddenly struck me; might it not be possible to escape through the door, which the assassin must open in order to enter the room? I resolved to make the attempt. I felt assured that the door through which ingress to the room would be effected was that which opened upon the lobby. It was the more direct way, besides being, for obvious reasons, less liable to interruption than the other. I resolved, then, to place myself behind a projection of the wall, the shadow would serve fully to conceal me, and when the door should be opened, and before they should have discovered the identity of the occupant of the bed, to creep noiselessly from the room, and then to trust to Providence for escape. In order to facilitate this scheme, I removed all the lumber which I had heaped against the door; and I had nearly completed my arrangements, when I perceived the room suddenly darkened, by the close approach of some shadowy object to the window. On turning my eyes in that direction, I observed at the top of the casement, as if suspended from above, first the feet, then the legs, then the body, and at length the whole figure of a man present itself. It was Edward Tyrrell. He appeared to be guiding his descent so as to bring his feet upon the centre of the stone block which occupied the lower part of window; and having secured his footing upon this, he kneeled down and began to gaze into the room. As the moon was gleaming into the chamber, and the bed-curtains were drawn, he was able to distinguish the bed itself and its contents. He appeared satisfied with his scrutiny, for he looked up and made a sign with his hand. He then applied his hands to the window-frame, which must have been ingeniously contrived for the purpose, for with apparently no resistance the whole frame, containing casement and all, slipped from its position in the wall, and was by him lowered into the room. The cold night wind waved the bed-curtains, and he paused for a moment; all was still again, and he stepped in upon the floor of the room. He held in his hand what appeared to be a steel instrument, shaped something like a long hammer.

This he held rather behind him, while, with three long, *tip-toe* strides, he brought himself to the bedside. I felt that the discovery must now be made, and held my breath in momentary expectation of the execration in which he would vent his surprise and disappointment. I closed my eyes; there was a pause, but it was a short one. I heard two dull blows, given in rapid succession; a quivering sigh, and the long-drawn, heavy breathing of the sleeper was forever suspended. I unclosed my eyes, and saw the murderer fling the quilt across the head of his victim; he then, with the instrument of death still in his hand, proceeded to the lobby-door, upon which he tapped sharply twice or thrice. A quick step was then heard approaching, and a voice whispered something from without. Edward answered, with a kind of shuddering chuckle, "Her ladyship is past complaining; unlock the door, in the devil's name, unless you're afraid to come in, and help me to lift her out of the window." The key was turned in the lock, the door opened, and my uncle entered the room. I have told you already that I had placed myself under the shade of a projection of the wall, close to the door. I had instinctively shrunk down cowering towards the ground on the entrance of Edward through the window. When my uncle entered the room, he and his son both stood so very close to me that his hand was every moment upon the point of touching my face. I held my breath, and remained motionless as death.

"You had no interruption from the next room?" said my uncle.

"No," was the brief reply.

"Secure the jewels, Ned; the French harpy must not lay her claws upon them. You're a steady hand, by G—d; not much blood—eh?"

"Not twenty drops," replied his son, "and those on the quilt."

"I'm glad it's over," whispered my uncle again; "we must lift the—the *thing* through the window, and lay the rubbish over it."

They then turned to the bedside, and, winding the bed-clothes round the body, carried it between them slowly to the window, and exchanging a few brief words with someone below, they shoved it over the window-sill, and I heard it fall heavily on the ground underneath.

"I'll take the jewels," said my uncle; "there are two caskets in the lower drawer."

He proceeded, with an accuracy which, had I been more at ease, would have furnished me with matter of astonishment, to lay his hand upon the very spot where my jewels lay; and having possessed himself of them, he called to his son:—

"Is the rope made fast above?"

"I'm no fool; to be sure it is," replied he.

They then lowered themselves from the window; and I rose lightly and cautiously, scarcely daring to breathe, from my place of concealment, and was creeping towards the door, when I heard my uncle's voice, in a sharp whisper, exclaim, "Get up again; G—d d—n you, you've forgot to lock the room door"; and I perceived, by the straining of the rope which hung from above, that the mandate was instantly obeyed. Not a second was to be lost. I passed through the door, which was only closed, and moved as rapidly as I could, consistently with stillness, along the lobby. Before I had gone many yards, I heard the door through which I had just passed roughly locked on the inside. I glided down the stairs in terror, lest, at every corner, I should meet the murderer or one of his accomplices. I reached the hall, and listened, for a moment, to ascertain whether all was silent around. No sound was audible; the parlour windows opened on the park, and through one of them I might, I thought, easily effect my escape. Accordingly, I hastily entered; but, to my consternation, a candle was burning in the room, and by its light I saw a figure seated at the dinner-table, upon which lay glasses, bottles, and the other accompaniments of a drinking party. Two or three chairs were placed about the table, irregularly, as if hastily abandoned by their occupants. A single glance satisfied me that the figure was that of my French attendant. She was fast asleep, having, probably, drank deeply. There was something malignant and ghastly in the calmness of this bad woman's features, dimly illuminated as they were by the flickering blaze of the candle. A knife lay upon the table, and the terrible thought struck me—"Should I kill this sleeping accomplice in the guilt of the murderer, and thus secure my retreat?" Nothing could be easier; it was but to draw the blade across her throat, the work of a second.

An instant's pause, however, corrected me. "No," thought I, "the God who has conducted me thus far through the valley of the shadow of death, will not abandon me now. I will fall into their hands, or I will escape hence, but it shall be free from the stain of blood; His will be done." I felt a confidence arising from this reflection, an assurance of protection which I cannot describe. There were no other means of escape, so I advanced, with a firm step and collected mind, to the window. I noiselessly withdrew the bars, and unclosed the shutters; I pushed open the casement, and without waiting to look behind me, I ran with my utmost speed, scarcely feeling the ground beneath me, down the avenue, taking care to keep upon the grass which bordered it. I did not for a moment slacken my speed, and I had now gained the central point between the park-gate and the mansion-house. Here the avenue made a wider circuit, and in order to avoid delay, I directed my way across the smooth sward round which the carriageway wound, intending, at the opposite side of the level, at a point which I distinguished by a group of old birch trees, to enter again upon the beaten track, which was from thence tolerably direct to the gate. I had, with my utmost speed, got about half way across this broad flat, when the rapid tramp of a horse's hoofs struck upon my ear. My heart swelled in my bosom, as though I would smother. The clattering of galloping hoofs approached; I was pursued; they were now upon the sward on which I was running; there was not a bush or a bramble to shelter me; and, as if to render escape altogether desperate, the moon, which had hitherto been obscured, at this moment shone forth with a broad, clear light, which made every object distinctly visible. The sounds were now close behind me. I felt my knees bending under me, with the sensation which unnerves one in a dream. I reeled, I stumbled, I fell; and at the same instant the cause of my alarm wheeled past me at full gallop. It was one of the young fillies which pastured loose about the park, whose frolics had thus all but maddened me with terror. I scrambled to my feet, and rushed on with weak but rapid steps, my sportive companion still galloping round and round me with many a frisk and fling, until, at length, more dead than alive, I reached the avenue-gate, and crossed the stile, I scarce knew how. I ran through the village, in which all was silent as the grave, until my progress was arrested by the hoarse voice of a sentinel, who cried "Who goes there?" I felt that I was now safe. I turned in the direction of the voice, and fell fainting at the soldier's feet. When I came to myself, I was sitting in a miserable hovel, surrounded by strange faces, all bespeaking curiosity and compassion. Many soldiers were in it also; indeed, as I afterwards found, it was employed as a guard-room by a detachment of troops quartered for that night in the town. In a few words I informed their officer of the circumstances which had occurred, describing also the appearance of the persons engaged in the murder; and he, without further loss of time than was necessary to procure the attendance of a magistrate, proceeded to the mansion-house of Carrickleigh, taking with him a party of his men. But the villains had discovered their mistake, and had effected their escape before the arrival of the military.

The Frenchwoman was, however, arrested in the neighbourhood upon the next day. She was tried and condemned at the ensuing assizes;

and previous to her execution confessed that "*she had a hand in making Hugh Tisdall's bed.*" She had been a housekeeper in the castle at the time, and a *chère amie* of my uncle's. She was, in reality, able to speak English like a native, but had exclusively used the French language, I suppose to facilitate her designs. She died the same hardened wretch she had lived, confessing her crimes only, as she alleged, that her doing so might involve Sir Arthur Tyrrell, the great author of her guilt and misery, and whom she now regarded with unmitigated detestation.

With the particulars of Sir Arthur's and his son's escape, as far as they are known, you are acquainted. You are also in possession of their after fate; the terrible, the tremendous retribution which, after long delays of many years, finally overtook and crushed them. Wonderful and inscrutable are the dealings of God with his creatures!

Deep and fervent as must always be my gratitude to heaven for my deliverance, effected by a chain of providential occurrences, the failing of a single link of which must have ensured my destruction, it was long before I could look back upon it with other feelings than those of bitterness, almost of agony. The only being that had ever really loved me, my nearest and dearest friend, ever ready to sympathise, to counsel, and to assist; the gayest, the gentlest, the warmest heart; the only creature on earth that cared for me; *her* life had been the price of my deliverance; and I then uttered the wish, which no event of my long and sorrowful life has taught me to recall, that she had been spared, and that, in her stead, *I* were mouldering in the grave, forgotten, and at rest.

THE MYSTERIOUS LODGER

Part I

ABOUT THE YEAR 1822 I resided in a comfortable and roomy old house, the exact locality of which I need not particularise, further than to say that it was not very far from Old Brompton, in the immediate neighbourhood, or rather continuity (as even my Connemara readers perfectly well know), of the renowned city of London.

Though this house was roomy and comfortable, as I have said, it was not, by any means, a handsome one. It was composed of dark red brick, with small windows, and thick white sashes; a porch, too—none of your flimsy trellis-work, but a solid projection of the same vermillion masonry—surmounted by a leaded balcony, with heavy, half-rotten balustrades, darkened the hall-door with a perennial gloom. The mansion itself stood in a walled enclosure, which had, perhaps, from the date of the erection itself, been devoted to shrubs and flowers. Some of the former had grown there almost to the dignity of trees; and two dark little yews stood at each side of the porch, like swart and inauspicious dwarfs, guarding the entrance of an enchanted castle. Not that my domicile in any respect deserved the comparison: it had no reputation as a haunted house; if it ever had any ghosts, nobody remembered them. Its history was not known to me: it may have witnessed plots, cabals, and forgeries, bloody suicides and cruel murders. It was certainly old enough to have become acquainted with iniquity; a small stone slab, under the balustrade, and over the arch of the porch I mentioned, had the date 1672, and a half-effaced coat of arms, which I might have deciphered any day, had I taken the trouble to get a ladder, but always put it off. All I can say for the house is, that it was well stricken in years, with a certain air of sombre comfort about it; contained a vast number of rooms and closets; and, what was of far greater importance, was got by me a dead bargain.

Its individuality attracted me. I grew fond of it for itself, and for its associations, until other associations of a hateful kind first disturbed, and then destroyed, their charm. I forgave its dull red brick, and pinched white windows, for the sake of the beloved and cheerful faces within: its ugliness was softened by its age; and its sombre evergreens, and moss-grown stone flower-pots, were relieved by the brilliant hues of a thousand gay and graceful flowers that peeped among them, or nodded over the grass.

Within that old house lay my life's treasure! I had a darling little girl of nine, and another little darling—a boy—just four years of age; and dearer, unspeakably, than either—a wife—the prettiest, gayest, best little wife in all London. When I tell you that our income was scarcely £380 a-year, you will perceive that our establishment cannot have been a magnificent one; yet, I do assure you, we were more comfortable than a great many lords, and happier, I dare say, than the whole peerage put together.

This happiness was not, however, what it ought to have been. The reader will understand at once, and save me a world of moralising circumlocution, when he learns, bluntly and nakedly, that, among all my comforts and blessings, I was an infidel.

I had not been without religious training; on the contrary, more than average pains had been bestowed upon my religious instruction from my earliest childhood. My father, a good, plain, country clergyman, had worked hard to make me as good as himself; and had succeeded, at least, in training me in godly habits. He died, however, when I was but twelve years of age; and fate had long before deprived me of the gentle care of a mother. A boarding-school, followed by a college life, where nobody having any very direct interest in realising in my behalf the ancient blessing, that in fulness of time I should "die a good old man," I was left very much to my own devices, which, in truth, were none of the best.

Among these were the study of Voltaire, Tom Paine, Hume, Shelley, and the whole school of infidels, poetical as well as prose. This pursuit, and the all but blasphemous vehemence with which I gave myself up to it, was, perhaps, partly reactionary. A somewhat injudicious austerity and precision had indissolubly associated in my childish days the ideas of restraint and gloom with religion. I bore it a grudge; and so, when I became thus early my own master, I set about paying off, after my own fashion, the old score I owed it. I was besides, like every other young infidel whom it has been my fate to meet, a conceited coxcomb. A smattering of literature, without any real knowledge, and a great assortment of all the cut-and-dry flippancies of the school I had embraced, constituted my intellectual stock in trade. I was, like most of my school of philosophy, very proud of being an unbeliever; and fancied myself, in the complacency of my wretched ignorance, at an immeasurable elevation above the church-going, Bible-reading herd, whom I treated with a good-humoured superciliousness which I thought vastly indulgent.

My wife was an excellent little creature and truly pious. She had married me in the full confidence that my levity was merely put on, and would at once give way before the influence she hoped to exert upon my mind. Poor little thing! she deceived herself. I allowed her, indeed, to do entirely as she pleased; but for myself, I carried my infidelity to the length of an absolute superstition. I made an ostentation of it. I would rather have been in a "hell" than in a church on Sunday; and though I did not prevent my wife's instilling her own principles into the minds of our children, I, in turn, took especial care to deliver mine upon all occasions in their hearing, by which means I trusted to sow the seeds of that unprejudiced scepticism in which I prided myself, at least as early as my good little partner dropped those of her own gentle "superstition" into their infant minds. Had I had my own absurd and impious will in this matter, my children should have had absolutely no religious education whatsoever, and been left wholly unshackled to choose for themselves among all existing systems, infidelity included, precisely as chance, fancy, or interest might hereafter determine.

It is not to be supposed that such a state of things did not afford her great uneasiness. Nevertheless, we were so very fond of one another, and in our humble way enjoyed so many blessings, that we were as entirely happy as any pair can be without the holy influence of religious sympathy.

But the even flow of prosperity which had for so long gladdened my little household was not destined to last forever. It was ordained that I should experience the bitter truth of more than one of the wise man's proverbs, and first, especially, of that which declares that "he that hateth suretyship is sure." I found myself involved (as how many have been before) by a "d—d good-natured friend," for more than two hundred pounds. This agreeable intelligence was conveyed to me in an attorney's letter, which, to obviate unpleasant measures, considerately advised my paying the entire amount within just one week of the date of his pleasant epistle. Had I been called upon within that time to produce the Pitt diamond, or to make title to the Buckingham estates, the demand would have been just as easily complied with.

I have no wish to bore my reader further with this little worry—a very serious one to me, however—and it will be enough to mention, that the kindness of a friend extricated me from the clutches of the law by a timely advance, which, however, I was bound to replace within two years. To enable me to fulfill this engagement, my wife and I, after repeated consultations, resolved upon the course which resulted in the odd and unpleasant consequences which form the subject of this narrative.

We resolved to advertise for a lodger, with or without board, &c.; and by resolutely submitting, for a single year, to the economy we had prescribed for ourselves, as well as to the annoyance of a stranger's intrusion, we calculated that at the end of that term we should have liquidated our debt.

Accordingly, without losing time, we composed an advertisement in the most tempting phraseology we could devise, consistently with that economic laconism which the cost per line in the columns of the *Times* newspaper imposes upon the rhetoric of the advertising public.

Somehow we were unlucky; for although we repeated our public notification three times in the course of a fortnight, we had but two applications. The one was from a clergyman in ill health—a man of great ability and zealous piety, whom we both knew by reputation, and who has since been called to his rest. My good little wife was very anxious that we should close with his offer, which was very considerably under what we had fixed upon; and I have no doubt that she was influenced by the hope that his talents and zeal might exert a happy influence upon my stubborn and unbelieving heart. For my part, his religious character displeased me. I did not wish my children's heads to be filled with mythic dogmas—for so I judged the doctrines of our holy faith— and instinctively wished him away. I therefore declined his offer; and I have often since thought not quite so graciously as I ought to have done. The other offer—if so it can be called—was so very inadequate that we could not entertain it.

I was now beginning to grow seriously uneasy—our little project, so far from bringing in the gains on which we had calculated, had put me considerably out of pocket; for, independently of the cost of the advertisement I have mentioned, there were sundry little expenses involved in preparing for the meet reception of our expected inmate, which, under ordinary circumstances, we should not have dreamed of. Matters were in this posture, when an occurrence took place which immediately revived my flagging hopes.

As we had no superfluity of servants, our children were early obliged to acquire habits of independence; and my little girl, then just nine years of age, was frequently consigned with no other care than that of her own good sense, to the companionship of a little band of playmates, pretty similarly circumstanced, with whom it was her wont to play. Having one fine summer afternoon gone out as usual with these little companions, she did not return quite so soon as we had expected her; when she did so, she was out of breath, and excited.

"Oh, papa," she said, "I have seen such a nice old, kind gentleman, and he told me to tell you that he has a particular friend who wants a lodging in a quiet place, and that he thinks your house would suit him exactly, and ever so much more; and, look here, he gave me this."

She opened her hand, and shewed me a sovereign.

"Well, this does look promisingly," I said, my wife and I having first exchanged a smiling glance.

"And what kind of gentleman was he, dear?" inquired she. "Was he well dressed—whom was he like?"

"He was not like anyone that I know," she answered; "but he had very nice new clothes on, and he was one of the fattest men I ever saw; and I am sure he is sick, for he looks very pale, and he had a crutch beside him."

"Dear me, how strange!" exclaimed my wife; though, in truth there was nothing very wonderful in the matter. "Go on, child," I said; "let us hear it all out."

"Well, papa, he had such an immense yellow waistcoat!—I never did see such a waistcoat," she resumed; "and he was sitting or leaning, I can't say which, against the bank of the green lane; I suppose to rest himself, for he seems very weak, poor gentleman!"

"And how did you happen to speak to him?" asked my wife.

"When we were passing by, none of us saw him at all but I suppose he heard them talking to me, and saying my name; for he said, 'Fanny—little Fanny—so, that's your name—come here child, I have a question to ask you.'"

"And so you went to him?" I said.

"Yes," she continued, "he beckoned to me, and I did go over to him, but not very near, for I was greatly afraid of him at first."

"Afraid! dear, and why afraid?" asked I.

"I was afraid, because he looked very old, very frightful, and as if he would hurt me."

"What was there so old and frightful about him?" I asked.

She paused and reflected a little, and then said—

"His face was very large and pale, and it was looking upwards: it seemed very angry, I thought, but maybe it was angry from pain; and sometimes one side of it used to twitch and tremble for a minute, and then to grow quite still again; and all the time he was speaking to me, he never looked at me once, but always kept his face and eyes turned upwards; but his voice was very soft, and he called me little Fanny, and gave me this pound to buy toys with; so I was not so frightened in a little time, and then he sent a long message to you, papa, and told me if I forgot it he would beat me; but I knew he was only joking, so that did not frighten me either."

"And what was the message, my girl?" I asked, patting her pretty head with my hand.

"Now, let me remember it all," she said, reflectively; "for he told it to me twice. He asked me if there was a good bedroom at the top of the house, standing by itself—and you know there is, so I told him so; it was exactly the kind of room that he described. And then he said that his friend would pay two hundred pounds a-year for that bedroom, his board and attendance; and he told me to ask you, and have your answer when he should next meet me."

"Two hundred pounds!" exclaimed my poor little wife; "why that is nearly twice as much as we expected."

"But did he say that his friend was sick, or very old; or that he had any servant to be supported also?" I asked.

"Oh! no; he told me that he was quite able to take care of himself, and that he had, I think he called it, an asthma, but nothing else the matter; and that he would give no trouble at all, and that any friend who came to see him, he would see, not in the house, but only in the garden."

"In the garden!" I echoed, laughing in spite of myself.

"Yes, indeed he said so; and he told me to say that he would pay one hundred pounds when he came here, and the next hundred in six months, and so on," continued she.

"Oh, ho! half-yearly in advance—better and better," said I.

"And he bid me say, too, if you should ask about his character, that he is just as good as the master of the house himself," she added; "and when he said that, he laughed a little."

"Why, if he gives us a hundred pounds in advance," I answered, turning to my wife, "we are safe enough; for he will not find half that value in plate and jewels in the entire household, if he is disposed to rob us. So I see no reason against closing with the offer, should it be seriously meant—do you, dear?"

"Quite the contrary, love," said she. "I think it most desirable—indeed, most *providential*."

"Providential! my dear little bigot!" I repeated, with a smile. "Well, be it so. I call it *lucky* merely; but, perhaps, you are happier in your faith, than I in my philosophy. Yes, you are *grateful* for the chance that I only rejoice at. You receive it as a proof of a divine and tender love—I as an accident. Delusions are often more elevating than truth."

And so saying, I kissed away the saddened cloud that for a moment overcast her face.

"Papa, he bid me be sure to have an answer for him when we meet again," resumed the child. "What shall I say to him when he asks me?"

"Say that we agree to his proposal, my dear—or stay," I said, addressing my wife, "may it not be prudent to reduce what the child says to writing, and accept the offer so? This will prevent misunderstanding, as she may possibly have made some mistake."

My wife agreed, and I wrote a brief note, stating that I was willing to receive an inmate upon the terms recounted by little Fanny, and which I distinctly specified, so that no mistake could possibly arise owing to the vagueness of what lawyers term a parole agreement. This important memorandum I placed in the hands of my little girl, who was to deliver it whenever the old gentleman in the yellow waistcoat should chance to meet her. And all these arrangements completed, I awaited the issue of the affair with as much patience as I could affect. Meanwhile, my wife and I talked it over incessantly; and she, good little soul, almost wore herself to death in settling and unsettling the furniture and decorations of our expected inmate's apartments. Days passed away—days of hopes deferred, tedious and anxious. We were beginning to despond again, when one morning our little girl ran into the breakfast-parlour, more excited even than she had been before, and fresh from a new interview with the gentleman in the yellow waistcoat. She had encountered him suddenly, pretty nearly where she had met him before, and the result was, that he had read the little note I have mentioned, and desired the child to inform me that his friend, *Mr. Smith*, would take possession of the apartments I proposed setting, on the terms agreed between us, that very evening.

"This evening!" exclaimed my wife and I simultaneously—*I* full of the idea of making a first instalment on the day following; *she*, of the hundred-and-one preparations which still remained to be completed.

"And so Smith is his name! Well, that does not tell us much," said I; "but where did you meet your friend on this occasion, and how long is it since?"

"Near the corner of the wall-flower lane (so we indicated one which abounded in these fragrant plants); he was leaning with his back against the old tree you cut my name on, and his crutch was under his arm."

"But how long ago?" I urged.

"Only this moment; I ran home as fast as I could," she replied.

"Why, you little blockhead, you should have told me that at first," I cried, snatching up my hat, and darting away in pursuit of the yellow waistcoat, whose acquaintance I not unnaturally coveted, inasmuch as a man who, for the first time, admits a stranger into his house, on the footing of permanent residence, desires generally to know a little more about him than that his name is Smith.

The place indicated was only, as we say, a step away; and as yellow waistcoat was fat, and used a crutch, I calculated on easily overtaking him. I was, however, disappointed; crutch, waistcoat, and all had disappeared. I climbed to the top of the wall, and from this commanding point of view made a sweeping observation—but in vain. I returned home, cursing my ill-luck, the child's dulness, and the fat old fellow's activity.

I need hardly say that Mr. Smith, in all his aspects, moral, social, physical, and monetary, formed a fruitful and interesting topic of speculation during dinner. How many phantom Smiths, short and long, stout and lean, ill-tempered and well-tempered—rich, respectable, or highly dangerous merchants, spies, forgers, nabobs, swindlers, danced before us, in the endless mazes of fanciful conjecture, during that anxious *tête-à-tête*, which was probably to be interrupted by the arrival of the gentleman himself.

My wife and I puzzled over the problem as people would over the possible *dénouement* of a French novel; and at last, by mutual consent, we came to the conclusion that Smith could, and would turn out to be no other than the good-natured valetudinarian in the yellow waistcoat himself, a humorist, as was evident enough, and a millionaire, as we unhesitatingly pronounced, who had no immediate relatives, and as I hoped, and my wife "was certain," taken a decided fancy to our little Fanny; I patted the child's head with something akin to pride, as I thought of the magnificent, though remote possibilities, in store for her.

Meanwhile, hour after hour stole away. It was a beautiful autumn evening, and the amber lustre of the declining sun fell softly upon the yews and flowers, and gave an air, half melancholy, half cheerful, to the dark-red brick piers surmounted with their cracked and grass-grown stone urns, and furnished with the light foliage of untended creeping plants. Down the short broad walk leading to this sombre entrance, my eye constantly wandered; but no impatient rattle on the latch, no battering at the gate, indicated the presence of a visited, and the lazy bell hung dumbly among the honey-suckles.

"When will he come? Yellow waistcoat promised *this evening*! It has been evening a good hour and a half, and yet he is not here. When will he come? It will soon be dark—the evening will have passed—will he come at all?"

Such were the uneasy speculations which began to trouble us. Redder and duskier grew the light of the setting sun, till it saddened into the mists of night. Twilight came, and then darkness, and still no arrival, no summons at the gate. I would not admit even to my wife the excess of my own impatience. I could, however, stand it no longer; so I took my hat and walked to the gate, where I stood by the side of the public road, watching every vehicle and person that approached, in a fever of expectation. Even these, however, began to fail me, and the road grew comparatively quiet and deserted. Having kept guard like a sentinel for more than half an hour, I returned in no very good humour, with the punctuality of an expected inmate—ordered the servant to draw the curtains and secure the hall-door; and so my wife and I sate down to our disconsolate cup of tea. It must have been about ten o'clock, and we were both sitting silently—she working, I looking moodily into a paper—and neither of us any longer entertaining a hope that anything but disappointment would come of the matter, when a sudden tapping, very loud and sustained, upon the window pane, startled us both in an instant from our reveries.

I am not sure whether I mentioned before that the sitting-room we occupied was upon the ground-floor, and the sward came close under the window. I drew the curtains, and opened the shutters with a revived hope; and looking out, saw a very tall thin figure, a good deal wrapped up, standing about a yard before me, and motioning with head and hand impatiently towards the hall-door. Though the night was clear, there was no moon, and therefore I could see no more than the black outline, like that of an *ombre chinoise* figure, signing to me with mop and moe. In a moment I was at the hall-door, candle in hand; the stranger stept in—his long fingers clutched in the handle of a valise, and a bag which trailed upon the ground behind him.

The light fell full upon him. He wore a long, ill-made, black surtout, buttoned across, and which wrinkled and bagged about his lank figure; his hat was none of the best, and rather broad in the brim; a sort of white woollen muffler enveloped the lower part of his face; a pair of prominent green goggles, fenced round with leather, completely concealed his eyes; and nothing of the genuine man, but a little bit of yellow forehead, and a small transverse segment of equally yellow cheek and nose, encountered the curious gaze of your humble servant.

"You are—I suppose"—I began; for I really was a little doubtful about my man.

"Mr. Smith—the same; be good enough to show me to my bedchamber," interrupted the stranger, brusquely, and in a tone which, spite of the muffler that enveloped his mouth, was sharp and grating enough.

"Ha!—Mr. Smith—so I supposed. I hope you may find everything as comfortable as we desire to make it—"

I was about making a speech, but was cut short by a slight bow, and a decisive gesture of the hand in the direction of the staircase. It was plain that the stranger hated ceremony.

Together, accordingly, we mounted the staircase; he still pulling his luggage after him, and striding lightly up without articulating a word; and on reaching his bedroom, he immediately removed his hat, showing a sinister, black scratch-wig underneath, and then began unrolling the mighty woolen wrapping of his mouth and chin.

"Come," thought I, "we *shall* see something of your face after all."

This something, however, proved to be very little; for under his muffler was a loose cravat, which stood up in front of his chin and upon his mouth, he wore a respirator—an instrument which I had never seen before, and of the use of which I was wholly ignorant.

There was something so excessively odd in the effect of this piece of unknown mechanism upon his mouth, surmounted by the huge goggles which encased his eyes, that I believe I should have laughed outright, were it not for a certain unpleasant and peculiar impressiveness in the *tout ensemble* of the narrow-chested, long-limbed, and cadaverous figure in black. As it was, we stood looking at one another in silence for several seconds.

"Thank you, sir," at last he said, abruptly. "I shan't want anything whatever tonight; if you can only spare me this candle."

I assented; and, becoming more communicative, he added—

"I am, though an invalid, an independent sort of fellow enough. I am a bit of a philosopher; I am my own servant, and, I hope, my own master, too. I rely upon myself in matters of the body and of the mind. I place valets and priests in the same category—fellows who live by our laziness, intellectual or corporeal. I am a Voltaire, without his luxuries—a Robinson Crusoe, without his Bible—an anchorite, without a superstition—in short, my indulgence is asceticism, and my faith infidelity. Therefore, I shan't disturb your servants much with my bell, nor yourselves with my psalmody. You have got a rational lodger, who knows how to attend upon himself."

During this singular address he was drawing off his ill-fitting black gloves, and when he had done so, a bank-note, which had been slipped underneath for safety, remained in his hand.

"Punctuality, sir, is one of my poor pleasures," he said; "will you allow me to enjoy it now? Tomorrow you may acknowledge this; I should not rest were you to decline it."

He extended his bony and discoloured fingers, and placed the note in my hand. Oh, Fortune and Plutus! It was a £100 bank-note.

"Pray, not one word, my dear sir," he continued, unbending still further; "it is simply done pursuant to agreement. We shall know one another better, I hope, in a little time; you will find me always equally punctual. At present pray give yourself no further trouble; I require nothing more. Goodnight."

I returned the valediction, closed his door, and groped my way down the stairs. It was not until I had nearly reached the hall, that I recollected that I had omitted to ask our new inmate at what hour he would desire to be called in the morning, and so I groped my way back again. As I reached the lobby on which his chamber opened, I perceived a long line of light issuing from the partially-opened door, within which stood Mr. Smith, the same odd figure I had just left; while along the boards was creeping towards him across the lobby, a great, big-headed, buff-coloured cat. I had never seen this ugly animal before; and it had reached the threshold of his door, arching its back, and rubbing itself on the post, before either appeared conscious of my approach, when, with an angry growl, it sprang into the stranger's room.

"What do you want?" he demanded, sharply, standing in the doorway.

I explained my errand.

"I shall call myself," was his sole reply; and he shut the door with a crash that indicated no very pleasurable emotions.

I cared very little about my lodger's temper. The stealthy rustle of his bank-note in my waistcoat pocket was music enough to sweeten the harshest tones of his voice, and to keep alive a cheerful good humour in my heart; and although there was, indisputably, something queer about him, I was, on the whole, very well pleased with my bargain.

The next day our new inmate did not ring his bell until noon. As soon as he had had some breakfast, of which he very sparingly partook, he told the servant that, for the future, he desired that a certain quantity of milk and bread might be left outside his door; and this being done, he would dispense with regular meals. He desired, too, that, on my return, I should be acquainted that he wished to see me in his own room at about nine o'clock; and, meanwhile, he directed that he should be left undisturbed. I found my little wife full of astonishment at Mr. Smith's strange frugality and seclusion, and very curious to learn the object of the interview he had desired with me. At nine o'clock I repaired to his room.

I found him in precisely the costume in which I had left him—the same green goggles—the same muffling of the mouth, except that being now no more than a broadly-folded black silk handkerchief, very loose, and covering even the lower part of the nose, it was obviously intended for the sole purpose of concealment. It was plain I was not to see more of his features than he had chosen to disclose at our first interview. The effect was as if the lower part of his face had some hideous wound or sore. He closed the door with his own hand on my entrance, nodded slightly, and took his seat. I expected him to begin, but he was so long silent that I was at last constrained to address him.

I said, for want of something more to the purpose, that I hoped he had not been tormented by the strange cat the night before.

"What cat?" he asked, abruptly; "what the plague do you mean?"

"Why, I certainly did see a cat go into your room last night," I resumed.

"Hey, and what if you did—though I fancy you dreamed it—I'm not afraid of a cat; are you?" he interrupted, tartly.

At this moment there came a low growling mew from the closet which opened from the room in which we sat.

"Talk of the devil," said I, pointing towards the closet. My companion, without any exact change of expression, looked, I thought, somehow still more sinister and lowering; and I felt for a moment a sort of superstitious misgiving, which made the rest of the sentence die away on my lips.

Perhaps Mr. Smith perceived this, for he said, in a tone calculated to reassure me—

"Well, sir, I think I am bound to tell you that I like my apartments very well; they suit me, and I shall probably be your tenant for much longer than at first you anticipated."

I expressed my gratification.

He then began to talk, something in the strain in which he had spoken of his own peculiarities of habit and thinking upon the previous evening. He disposed of all classes and denominations of superstition with an easy sarcastic slang, which for me was so captivating, that I soon lost all reserve, and found myself listening and suggesting by turns—acquiescent and pleased—sometimes hazarding dissent; but whenever I did, foiled and floored by a few pointed satirical sentences, whose sophistry, for such I must now believe it, confounded me with a rapidity which, were it not for the admiration with which he had insensibly inspired me, would have piqued and irritated my vanity not a little.

While this was going on, from time to time the mewing and growling of a cat within the closet became more and more audible. At last these sounds became so loud, accompanied by scratching at the door, that I paused in the midst of a sentence, and observed—

"There certainly is a cat shut up in the closet?"

"Is there?" he exclaimed, in a surprised tone; "nay, I do not hear it."

He rose abruptly and approached the door; his back was towards me, but I observed he raised the goggles which usually covered his eyes, and looked steadfastly at the closet door. The angry sounds all died away into a low, protracted growl, which again subsided into silence. He continued in the same attitude for some moments, and then returned.

"I do not hear it," he said, as he resumed his place, and taking a book from his capacious pocket, asked me if I had seen it before? I never had, and this surprised me, for I had flattered myself that I knew, at least by name, every work published in England during the last fifty years in favour of that philosophy in which we both delighted. The book, moreover, was an odd one, as both its title and table of contents demonstrated.

While we were discoursing upon these subjects, I became more and more distinctly conscious of a new class of sounds proceeding from the same closet. I plainly heard a measured and heavy tread, accompanied by the tapping of some hard and heavy substance like the end of a staff, pass up and down the floor—first, as it seemed, stealthily, and then more and more unconcealedly. I began to feel very uncomfortable and suspicious. As the noise proceeded, and became more and more unequivocal, Mr. Smith abruptly rose, opened the closet door, just enough to admit his own lath-like person, and steal within the threshold for some seconds. What he did I could not see—I felt conscious he had an associate concealed there; and though my eyes remained fixed on the book, I could not avoid listening for some audible words, or signal of caution. I heard, however, nothing of the kind. Mr. Smith turned back—walked a step or two towards me, and said—

"I fancied I heard a sound from that closet, but there is nothing—nothing—nothing whatever; bring the candle, let us both look."

I obeyed with some little trepidation, for I fully anticipated that I should detect the intruder, of whose presence my own ears had given me, for nearly half an hour, the most unequivocal proofs. We entered the closet together; it contained but a few chairs and a small spider table. At the far end of the room there was a sort of grey woollen cloth upon the floor, and a bundle of something underneath it. I looked jealously at it, and half thought I could trace the outline of a human figure; but, if so, it was perfectly motionless.

"Some of my poor wardrobe," he muttered, as he pointed his lean finger in the direction. "It did not sound like a cat, did it—hey—did it?" he muttered; and without attending to my answer, he went about the apartment, clapping his hands, and crying, "Hish—hish—hish!"

The game, however, whatever it was, did not start. As I entered I had seen, however, a large crutch reposing against the wall in the corner opposite to the door. This was the only article in the room, except that I have mentioned, with which I was not familiar. With the exception of our two selves, there was not a living creature to be seen there; no shadow but ours upon the bare walls; no feet but our own upon the comfortless floor.

I had never before felt so strange and unpleasant a sensation.

"There is nothing unusual in the room but that crutch," I said.

"What crutch, you dolt? I see no crutch," he exclaimed, in a tone of sudden but suppressed fury.

"Why, *that* crutch," I answered (for somehow I neither felt nor resented his rudeness), turning and pointing to the spot where I had seen it. It was gone!—it was neither there nor anywhere else. It must have been an illusion—rather an odd one, to be sure. And yet I could at this moment, with a safe conscience, *swear* that I never saw an object more distinctly than I had seen it but a second before.

My companion was muttering fast to himself as we withdrew; his presence rather scared than reassured me; and I felt something almost amounting to horror, as, holding the candle above his cadaverous and sable figure, he stood at his threshold, while I descended the stairs, and said, in a sort of whisper—

"Why, but that I am, like yourself, a philosopher, I should say that your house is—is—a—ha! ha! ha!—HAUNTED!"

"You look very pale, my love," said my wife, as I entered the drawing-room, where she had been long awaiting my return. "Nothing unpleasant has happened?"

"Nothing, nothing, I assure you. Pale!—*do* I look pale?" I answered. "We are excellent friends, I assure you. So far from having had the smallest disagreement, there is every prospect of our agreeing but too well, as you will say; for I find that he holds all my opinions upon speculative subjects. We have had a great deal of conversation this evening, I assure you; and I never met, I think, so scholarlike and able a man."

"I am sorry for it, dearest," she said, sadly. "The greater his talents, if such be his opinions, the more dangerous a companion is he."

We turned, however, to more cheerful topics, and it was late before we retired to rest. I believe it was pride—perhaps only vanity—but, at all events, some obstructive and stubborn instinct of my nature, which I could not overcome—that prevented my telling my wife the odd occurrences which had disturbed my visit to our guest. I was unable or ashamed to confess that so slight a matter had disturbed me; and, above all, that any accident could possibly have clouded, even for a moment, the frosty clearness of my pure and lofty scepticism with the shadows of superstition.

Almost everyday seemed to develop some new eccentricity of our strange guest. His dietary consisted, without any variety or relief, of the monotonous bread and milk with which he started; his bed had not been made for nearly a week; nobody had been admitted into his room since my visit, just described; and he never ventured down stairs, or out of doors, until after nightfall, when he used sometimes to glide swiftly round our little enclosed shrubbery, and at others stand quite motionless, composed, as if in an attitude of deep attention. After employing about an hour in this way, he would return, and steal up stairs to his room, when he would shut himself up, and not be seen again until the next night—or, it might be, the night after that—when, perhaps, he would repeat his odd excursion.

Strange as his habits were, their eccentricity was all upon the side least troublesome to us. He required literally no attendance; and as to his occasional night ramble, even *it* caused not the slightest disturbance of our routine hour for securing the house and locking up the hall-door for the night, inasmuch as he had invariably retired before that hour arrived.

All this stimulated curiosity, and, in no small degree, that of my wife, who, notwithstanding her vigilance and her anxiety to see our strange inmate, had been hitherto foiled by a series of cross accidents. We were sitting together somewhere about ten o'clock at night, when there came a tap at the room-door. We had just been discussing the unaccountable Smith; and I felt a sheepish consciousness that he might be himself at the door, and have possibly even overheard our speculation— some of them anything but complimentary, respecting himself.

"Come in," cried, I, with an effort; and the tall form of our lodger glided into the room. My wife was positively frightened, and stood looking at him, as he advanced, with a stare of manifest apprehension, and even recoiled mechanically, and caught my hand.

Sensitiveness, however, was not his fault: he made a kind of stiff nod as I mumbled an introduction; and seating himself unasked, began at once to chat in that odd, off-hand, and sneering style, in which he excelled, and which had, as he wielded it, a sort of fascination of which I can pretend to convey no idea.

My wife's alarm subsided, and although she still manifestly felt some sort of misgiving about our visitor, she yet listened to his conversation, and, spite of herself, soon began to enjoy it. He stayed for nearly half an hour. But although he glanced at a great variety of topics, he did not approach the subject of religion. As soon as he was gone, my wife delivered judgment upon him in form. She admitted he was agreeable; but then he was such an unnatural, awful-looking object: there was, besides, something indescribably frightful, she thought, in his manner—the very tone of his voice was strange and hateful; and, on the whole, she felt unutterably relieved at his departure.

A few days after, on my return, I found my poor little wife agitated and dispirited. Mr. Smith had paid her a visit, and brought with him a book, which he stated he had been reading, and which contained some references to the Bible which he begged of her to explain in that profounder and less obvious sense in which they had been cited. This she had endeavoured to do; and affecting to be much gratified by her satisfactory exposition, he had requested her to reconcile some discrepancies which he said had often troubled him when reading the Scriptures. Some of them were quite new to my good little wife; they startled and even horrified her. He pursued this theme, still pretending only to seek for information to quiet his own doubts, while in reality he was sowing in her mind the seeds of the first perturbations that had ever troubled the sources of her peace. He had been with her, she thought, no more than a quarter of an hour; but he had contrived to leave her abundant topics on which to ruminate for days. I found her shocked and horrified at the doubts which this potent Magus had summoned from the pit—doubts which she knew not how to combat, and from the torment of which she could not escape.

"He has made me very miserable with his deceitful questions. I never thought of them before; and, merciful Heaven! I cannot answer them! What am I to do? My serenity is gone; I shall never be happy again."

In truth, she was so very miserable, and, as it seemed to me, so disproportionately excited, that, inconsistent in me as the task would have been, I would gladly have explained away her difficulties, and restored to her mind its wonted confidence and serenity, had I possessed sufficient knowledge for the purpose. I really pitied her, and heartily wished Mr. Smith, for the nonce, at the devil.

I observed after this that my wife's spirits appeared permanently affected. There was a constantly-recurring anxiety, and I thought something was lying still more heavily at her heart than the uncertainties inspired by our lodger.

One evening, as we two were sitting together, after a long silence, she suddenly laid her hand upon my arm, and said—

"Oh, Richard, my darling! would to God you could pray for me!"

There was something so agitated, and even terrified, in her manner, that I was absolutely startled. I urged her to disclose whatever preyed upon her mind.

"You can't sympathise with me—you can't help me—you can scarcely compassionate me in my misery! Oh, dearest Richard! Some evil influence has been gaining upon my heart, dulling and destroying my convictions, killing all my holy affections, and—and absolutely transforming me. I look inward upon myself with amazement, with terror—with—oh, God!—with actual despair!"

Saying this, she threw herself on her knees, and wept an agonised flood of tears, with her head reposing in my lap.

Poor little thing, my heart bled for her! But what could I do or say?

All I could suggest was what I really thought, that she was unwell—hysterical—and needed to take better care of her precious self; that her change of feeling was fancied, not real; and that a few days would restore her to her old health and former spirits and serenity.

"And sometimes," she resumed, after I had ended a consolatory discussion, which it was but too manifest had fallen unprofitably upon her ear, "such dreadful, impious thoughts come into my mind, whether I choose it or not; they come, and stay, and return, strive as I may; and I can't pray against them. They are forced upon me with the strength of an independent will; and oh!—horrible—frightful—they blaspheme the character of God himself. They upbraid the Almighty upon his throne, and I can't pray against them; there is something in me now that resists prayer."

There was such a real and fearful anguish in the agitation of my gentle companion, that it shook my very soul within me, even while I was affecting to make light of her confessions. I had never before witnessed a struggle at all like this, and I was awe-struck at the spectacle.

At length she became comparatively calm. I did gradually succeed, though very imperfectly, in reassuring her. She strove hard against her depression, and recovered a little of her wonted cheerfulness.

After a while, however, the cloud returned. She grew sad and earnest, though no longer excited; and entreated, or rather implored, of me to grant her one special favour, and this was, to avoid the society of our lodger.

"I never," she said, "could understand till now the instinctive dread with which poor Margaret, in *Faust*, shrinks from the hateful presence of Mephistopheles. I now feel it in myself. The dislike and suspicion I first felt for that man—Smith, or whatever else he may call himself—has grown into literal detestation and terror. I hate him—I am afraid of him—I never knew what anguish of mind was until he entered our doors; and would to God—would to God he were gone."

I reasoned with her—kissed her—laughed at her; but could not dissipate, in the least degree, the intense and preternatural horror with which she had grown to regard the poor philosophic invalid, who was probably, at that moment, poring over some metaphysical book in his solitary bedchamber.

The circumstance I am about to mention will give you some notion of the extreme to which these excited feelings had worked upon her nerves. I was that night suddenly awakened by a piercing scream—I started upright in the bed, and saw my wife standing at the bedside, white as ashes with terror. It was some seconds, so startled was I, before I could find words to ask her the cause of her affright. She caught my wrist in her icy grasp, and climbed, trembling violently, into bed. Notwithstanding my repeated entreaties, she continued for a long time stupified and dumb. At length, however, she told me, that having lain awake for a long time, she felt, on a sudden, that she could pray, and lighting the candle, she had stolen from beside me, and kneeled down for the purpose. She had, however, scarcely assumed the attitude of prayer, when somebody, she said, clutched her arm violently near the wrist, and she heard, at the same instant, some blasphemous menace, the import of which escaped her the moment it was spoken, muttered close in her ear. This terrifying interruption was the cause of the scream which had awakened me; and the condition in which she continued during the remainder of the night confirmed me more than ever in the conviction, that she was suffering under some morbid action of the nervous system.

After this event, which *I* had no hesitation in attributing to fancy, she became literally afraid to pray, and her misery and despondency increased proportionately.

It was shortly after this that an unusual pressure of business called me into town one evening after office hours. I had left my dear little wife tolerably well, and little Fanny was to be her companion until I returned. She and her little companion occupied the same room in which we sat on the memorable evening which witnessed the arrival of our eccentric guest. Though usually a lively child, it most provokingly happened upon this night that Fanny was heavy and drowsy to excess. Her mamma would have sent her to bed, but that she now literally feared to be left alone; although, however, she could not so far overcome her horror of solitude as to do this, she yet would not persist in combating the poor child's sleepiness.

Accordingly, little Fanny was soon locked in a sound sleep, while her mamma quietly pursued her work beside her. They had been perhaps some ten minutes thus circumstanced, when my wife heard the window softly raised from without—a bony hand parted the curtains, and Mr. Smith leaned into the room.

She was so utterly overpowered at sight of this apparition, that even had it, as she expected, climbed into the room, she told me she could not have uttered a sound, or stirred from the spot where she sate transfixed and petrified.

"Ha, ha!" he said gently, "I hope you'll excuse this, I must admit, very odd intrusion; but I knew I should find you here, and could not resist the opportunity of raising the window just for a moment, to look in upon a little family picture, and say a word to yourself. I understand that you are troubled, because for some cause you cannot say your prayers—because what you call your 'faith' is, so to speak, dead and gone, and also because what *you* consider bad thoughts are constantly recurring to your mind. Now, all that is very silly. If it is really impossible for you to believe and to pray, what are you to infer from that? It is perfectly plain your Christian system can't be a true one—faith and *prayer* it everywhere represents as the conditions of grace, acceptance, and salvation; and yet your Creator will not *permit* you either to believe or pray. The Christian system is, forsooth, a *free* gift, and yet he who formed *you* and *it*, makes it absolutely impossible for you to accept it. *Is* it, I ask you, from your own experience—is it a free gift? And if your own experience, in which you can't be mistaken, gives its pretensions the lie, why, in the name of common sense, will you persist in believing it? I say it is downright blasphemy to think it has emanated from the Good Spirit—assuming that there is one. It tells you that you must be tormented hereafter in a way only to be made intelligible by the image of eternal fires—pretty strong, we must all allow—unless you comply with certain conditions, which it pretends are so easy that it is a positive pleasure to embrace and perform them; and yet, for the life of you, you can't—physically *can't*— do either. Is this truth and mercy?—or is it swindling and cruelty? Is it the part of the Redeemer, or that of the tyrant, deceiver, and tormentor?"

Up to that moment, my wife had sate breathless and motionless, listening, in the catalepsy of nightmare, to a sort of echo of the vile and impious reasoning which had haunted her for so long. At the last words of the sentence his voice became harsh and thrilling; and his whole manner bespoke a sort of crouching and terrific hatred, the like of which she could not have conceived.

Whatever may have been the cause, she was on a sudden disenchanted. She started to her feet; and, freezing with horror though she was, in a shrill cry of agony commanded him, in the name of God, to depart from her. His whole frame seemed to darken; he drew back silently; the curtains dropped into their places, the window was let down again as stealthily as it had just been raised; and my wife found herself alone in the chamber with our little child, who had been startled from her sleep by her mother's cry of anguish, and with the fearful words, "tempter," "destroyer," "devil," still ringing in her ears, was weeping bitterly, and holding her terrified mother's hand.

There is nothing, I believe, more infectious than that species of nervousness which shows itself in superstitious fears. I began—although I could not bring myself to admit anything the least like it—to partake insensibly, but strongly of the peculiar feelings with which my wife, and indeed my whole household, already regarded the lodger up stairs. The fact was, beside, that the state of my poor wife's mind began to make me seriously uneasy; and, although I was fully sensible of the pecuniary and other advantages attendant upon his stay, they were yet far from outweighing the constant gloom and frequent misery in which the protracted sojourn was involving my once cheerful house. I resolved, therefore, at whatever monetary sacrifice, to put an end to these commotions; and, after several debates with my wife, in which the subject was, as usual, turned in all its possible and impossible bearings, we agreed that, deducting a fair proportion for his five weeks' sojourn, I should return the remainder of his £100, and request immediate possession of his apartments. Like a man suddenly relieved of an insufferable load, and breathing freely once more, I instantly prepared to carry into effect the result of our deliberations.

In pursuance of this resolution, I waited upon Mr. Smith. This time my call was made in the morning, somewhere about nine o'clock. He received me at his door, standing as usual in the stealthy opening which barely admitted his lank person. There he stood, fully equipped with goggles and respirator, and swathed, rather than dressed, in his puckered black garments.

As he did not seem disposed to invite me into his apartment, although I had announced my visit as one of business, I was obliged to open my errand where I stood; and after a great deal of fumbling and muttering, I contrived to place before him distinctly the resolution to which I had come.

"But I can't think of taking back any portion of the sum I have paid you," said he, with a cool, dry emphasis.

"Your reluctance to do so, Mr. Smith, is most handsome, and I assure you, appreciated," I replied. "It is very generous; but, at the same time, it is quite impossible for me to accept what I have no right to take, and I must beg of you not to mention that part of the subject again."

"And why should *I* take it?" demanded Mr. Smith.

"Because you have paid this hundred pounds for six months, and you are leaving me with nearly five months of the term still unexpired," I replied. "I expect to receive fair play myself, and always give it."

"But who on earth said that I was going away so soon?" pursued Mr. Smith, in the same dry, sarcastic key. "*I* have not said so—because I really don't intend it; I mean to stay here to the last day of the six months for which I have paid you. I have no notion of vacating my hired lodgings, simply because you say, *go*. I shan't quarrel with you—I never quarrel with anybody. I'm as much your friend as ever; but, without the least wish to disoblige, I can't do this, positively I cannot. Is there anything else?"

I had not anticipated in the least the difficulty which thus encountered and upset our plans. I had so set my heart upon effecting the immediate retirement of our inauspicious inmate, that the disappointment literally stunned me for a moment. I, however, returned to the charge: I urged, and prayed, and almost besought him to give up his apartments, and to leave us. I offered to repay every farthing of the sum he had paid me—reserving nothing on account of the time he had already been with us. I suggested all the disadvantages of the house. I shifted my ground, and told him that my wife wanted the rooms; I pressed his gallantry—his good nature—his economy; in short, I assailed him upon every point—but in vain, he did not even take the trouble of repeating what he had said before—he neither relented, nor showed the least irritation, but simply said—

"I can't do this; here I am, and here I stay until the half-year has expired. You wanted a lodger, and you have got one—the quietest, least troublesome, least expensive person you could have; and though your house, servants, and furniture are none of the best, I don't care for that. I pursue my own poor business and enjoyments here entirely to my satisfaction."

Having thus spoken, he gave me a sort of nod, and closed the door.

So, instead of getting rid of him the next day, as we had hoped, we had nearly five months more of his company in expectancy; I hated, and my wife dreaded the prospect. She was literally miserable and panic-struck at her disappointment—and grew so nervous and wretched that I made up my mind to look out for lodgings for her and the children (subversive of all our schemes of retrenchment as such a step would be), and surrendering the house absolutely to Mr. Smith and the servants during the remainder of his term.

Circumstances, however, occurred to prevent our putting this plan in execution. My wife, meanwhile, was, if possible, more depressed and nervous everyday. The servants seemed to sympathise in the dread and gloom which involved ourselves; the very children grew timid and spiritless, without knowing why—and the entire house was pervaded with an atmosphere of uncertainty and fear. A poorhouse or a dungeon would have been cheerful, compared with a dwelling haunted unceasingly with unearthly suspicions and alarms. I would have made any sacrifice short of ruin, to emancipate our household from the odious mental and moral thraldom which was invisibly established over us—overcasting us with strange anxieties and an undefined terror.

About this time my wife had a dream which troubled her much, although she could not explain its supposed significance satisfactorily by any of the ordinary rules of interpretation in such matters. The vision was as follows.

She dreamed that we were busily employed in carrying out our scheme of removal, and that I came into the parlour where she was making some arrangements, and, with rather an agitated manner, told her that the carriage had come for the children. She thought she went out to the hall, in consequence, holding little Fanny by one hand, and the boy—or, as we still called him, "baby,"—by the other, and feeling, as she did so, an unaccountable gloom, almost amounting to terror, steal over her. The children, too, seemed, she thought, frightened, and disposed to cry.

So close to the hall-door as to exclude the light, stood some kind of vehicle, of which she could see nothing but that its door was wide open, and the interior involved in total darkness. The children, she thought, shrunk back in great trepidation, and she addressed herself to induce them, by persuasion, to enter, telling them that they were only "going to their new home." So, in a while, little Fanny approached it; but, at the same instant, some person came swiftly up from behind, and, raising the little boy in his hands, said fiercely, "No, the baby first"; and placed him in the carriage. This person was our lodger, Mr. Smith, and was gone as soon as seen. My wife, even in her dream, could not act or speak; but as the child was lifted into the carriage-door, a man, whose face was full of beautiful tenderness and compassion, leaned forward from the carriage and received the little child, which, stretching his arms to the stranger, looked back with a strange smile upon his mother.

"He is safe with me, and I will deliver him to you when you come."

These words the man spoke, looking upon her, as he received him, and immediately the carriage-door shut, and the noise of its closing wakened my wife from her nightmare.

This dream troubled her very much, and even haunted my mind unpleasantly too. We agreed, however, not to speak of it to anybody, not to divulge any of our misgivings respecting the stranger. We were anxious that neither the children nor the servants should catch the contagion of those fears which had seized upon my poor little wife, and, if truth were spoken, upon myself in some degree also. But this precaution was, I believe, needless, for, as I said before, everybody under the same roof with Mr. Smith was, to a certain extent, affected with the same nervous gloom and apprehension.

And now commences a melancholy chapter in my life. My poor little Fanny was attacked with a cough which soon grew very violent, and after a time degenerated into a sharp attack of inflammation. We were seriously alarmed for her life, and nothing that care and medicine could effect was spared to save it. Her mother was indefatigable, and scarcely left her night or day; and, indeed, for sometime, we all but despaired of her recovery.

One night, when she was at the worst, her poor mother, who had sat for many a melancholy hour listening, by her bedside, to those plaintive incoherences of delirium and moanings of fever, which have harrowed so many a fond heart, gained gradually from her very despair the courage which she had so long wanted, and knelt down at the side of her sick darling's bed to pray for her deliverance.

With clasped hands, in an agony of supplication, she prayed that God would, in his mercy, spare her little child—that, justly as she herself deserved the sorest chastisement his hand could inflict, he would yet deal patiently and tenderly with her in this one thing. She poured out her sorrows before the mercy-seat—she opened her heart, and declared her only hope to be in his pity; without which, she felt that her darling would only leave the bed where she was lying for her grave.

Exactly as she came to this part of her supplication, the child, who had grown, as it seemed, more and more restless, and moaned and muttered with increasing pain and irritation, on a sudden started upright in her bed, and, in a thrilling voice, cried—

"No! no!—the baby first."

The mysterious sentence which had secretly tormented her for so long, thus piercingly uttered by this delirious, and, perhaps, dying child, with what seemed a preternatural earnestness and strength, arrested her devotions, and froze her with a feeling akin to terror.

"Hush, hush, my darling!" said the poor mother, almost wildly, as she clasped the attenuated frame of the sick child in her arms; "hush, my darling; don't cry out so loudly—there—there—my own love."

The child did not appear to see or hear her, but sate up still with feverish cheeks, and bright unsteady eyes, while her dry lips were muttering inaudible words.

"Lie down, my sweet child—lie down, for your own mother," she said; "if you tire yourself, you can't grow well, and your poor mother will lose you."

At these words, the child suddenly cried out again, in precisely the same loud, strong voice—"No! no! the baby first, the baby first"—and immediately afterwards lay down, and fell, for the first time since her illness into a tranquil sleep.

My good little wife sate, crying bitterly by her bedside. The child was better—*that* was, indeed, delightful. But then there was an omen in the words, thus echoed from her dream, which she dared not trust herself to interpret, and which yet had seized, with a grasp of iron, upon every fibre of her brain.

"Oh, Richard," she cried, as she threw her arms about my neck, "I am terrified at this horrible menace from the unseen world. Oh! poor, darling little baby, I shall lose you—I am sure I shall lose you. Comfort me, darling, and say he is not to die."

And so I did; and tasked all my powers of argument and persuasion to convince her how unsubstantial was the ground of her anxiety. The little boy was perfectly well, and, even were he to die before his sister that event might not occur for seventy years to come. I could not, however, conceal from myself that there was something odd and unpleasant in the coincidence; and my poor wife had grown so nervous and excitable, that a much less ominous conjecture would have sufficed to alarm her.

Meanwhile, the unaccountable terror which our lodger's presence inspired continued to increase. One of our maids gave us warning, solely from her dread of our queer inmate, and the strange accessories which haunted him. She said—and this was corroborated by her fellow-servant—that Mr. Smith seemed to have constantly a companion in his room; that although they never heard them speak, they continually and distinctly heard the tread of two persons walking up and down the room together, and described accurately the peculiar sound of a stick or crutch tapping upon the floor, which my own ears had heard. They also had seen the large, ill-conditioned cat I have mentioned, frequently steal in and out of the stranger's room; and observed that when our little girl was in greatest danger, the hateful animal was constantly writhing, fawning, and crawling about the door of the sick room after nightfall. They were thoroughly persuaded that this ill-omened beast was the foul fiend himself, and I confess I could not—sceptic as I was—bring myself absolutely to the belief that he was nothing more than a "harmless, necessary cat." These and similar reports—implicitly believed as they palpably were by those who made them—were certainly little calculated to allay the perturbation and alarm with which our household was filled.

The evenings had by this time shortened very much, and darkness often overtook us before we sate down to our early tea. It happened just at this period of which I have been speaking, after my little girl had begun decidedly to mend, that I was sitting in our dining-parlour, with my little boy fast asleep upon my knees, and thinking of I know not what, my wife having gone up stairs, as usual, to sit in the room with little Fanny. As I thus sate in what was to me, in effect, total solitude, darkness unperceived stole on us.

On a sudden, as I sate, with my elbow leaning upon the table, and my other arm round the sleeping child, I felt, as I thought, a cold current of air faintly blowing upon my forehead. I raised my head, and saw, as nearly as I could calculate, at the far end of the table on which my arm rested, two large green eyes confronting me. I could see no more, but instantly concluded they were those of the abominable cat. Yielding to an impulse of horror and abhorrence, I caught a water-croft that was close to my hand, and threw it full at it with all my force. I must have missed my object, for the shining eyes continued fixed for a second, and then glided still nearer to me, and then a little nearer still. The noise of the glass smashed with so much force upon the table called in the servant, who happened to be passing. She had a candle in her hand, and, perhaps, the light alarmed the odious beast, for as she came in it was gone.

I had had an undefined idea that its approach was somehow connected with a designed injury of some sort to the sleeping child. I could not be mistaken as to the fact that I had plainly seen the two broad, glaring, green eyes. Where the cursed animal had gone I had not observed: it might, indeed, easily have run out at the door as the servant opened it, but neither of us had seen it do so; and we were everyone of us in such a state of nervous excitement, that even this incident was something in the catalogue of our ambiguous experiences.

It was a great happiness to see our darling little Fanny everyday mending, and now quite out of danger: this was cheering and delightful. It was also something to know that more than two months of our lodger's term of occupation had already expired; and to realise, as we now could do, by anticipation, the unspeakable relief of his departure.

My wife strove hard to turn our dear child's recovery to good account for me; but the impressions of fear soon depart, and those of religious gratitude must be preceded by religious faith. All as yet was but as seed strewn upon the rock.

Little Fanny, though recovering rapidly, was still very weak, and her mother usually passed a considerable part of every evening in her bedroom—for the child was sometimes uneasy and restless at night. It happened at this period that, sitting as usual at Fanny's bedside, she witnessed an occurrence which agitated her not a little.

The child had been, as it seems, growing sleepy, and was lying listlessly, with eyes half open, apparently taking no note of what was passing. Suddenly, however, with an expression of the wildest terror, she drew up her limbs, and cowered in the bed's head, gazing at some object; which, judging from the motion of her eyes, must have been slowly advancing from the end of the room next the door.

The child made a low shuddering cry, as she grasped her mother's hand, and, with features white and tense with terror, slowly following with her eyes the noiseless course of some unseen spectre, shrinking more and more fearfully backward every moment.

"What is it? Where? What is it that frightens you, my darling?" asked the poor mother, who, thrilled with horror, looked in vain for the apparition which seemed to have all but bereft the child of reason.

"Stay with me—save me—keep it away—look, look at it—making signs to me—don't let it hurt me—it is angry—Oh! mamma, save me, save me!"

The child said this, all the time clinging to her with both her hands, in an ecstasy of panic.

"There—there, my darling," said my poor wife, "don't be afraid; there's nothing but me—your own mamma—and little baby in the room; nothing, my darling; nothing indeed."

JOSEPH SHERIDAN LE FANU

"Mamma, mamma, don't move; don't go near him"; the child continued wildly. "It's only his back now; don't make him turn again; he's untying his handkerchief. Oh! baby, baby; he'll *kill* baby! and he's lifting up those green things from his eyes; don't you see him doing it? Mamma, mamma, why does he come here? Oh, mamma, poor baby—poor little baby!"

She was looking with a terrified gaze at the little boy's bed, which lay directly opposite to her own, and in which he was sleeping calmly.

"Hush, hush, my darling child," said my wife, with difficulty restraining an hysterical burst of tears; "for God's sake don't speak so wildly, my own precious love—there, there—don't be frightened—there, darling, there."

"Oh! poor baby—poor little darling baby," the child continued as before; "will no one save him—tell that wicked man to go away—oh—there—why, mamma—don't—oh, sure you won't let him—don't—don't—he'll take the child's life—will you let him lie down that way on the bed—save poor little baby—oh, baby, baby, waken—his head is on your face."

As she said this she raised her voice to a cry of despairing terror which made the whole room ring again.

This cry, or rather yell, reached my ears as I sate reading in the parlour by myself, and fearing I knew not what, I rushed to the apartment; before I reached it, the sound had subsided into low but violent sobbing; and, just as I arrived at the threshold I heard, close at my feet, a fierce protracted growl, and something rubbing along the surbase. I was in the dark, but, with a feeling of mingled terror and fury, I stamped and struck at the abhorred brute with my feet, but in vain. The next moment I was in the room, and heard little Fanny, through her sobs, cry—

"Oh, poor baby is killed—that wicked man has killed him—he uncovered his face, and put it on him, and lay upon the bed and killed poor baby. I knew he came to kill him. Ah, papa, papa, why did you not come up before he went?—he is gone, he went away as soon as he killed our poor little darling baby."

I could not conceal my agitation, quite, and I said to my wife—

"Has he, Smith, been here?"

"No."

"What is it, then?"

"The child has seen *some*one."

"Seen whom? Who? Who has been here?"

"I did not see it; but—but I am sure the child saw—that is, *thought* she saw *him*;—the person you have named. Oh, God, in mercy deliver us! What shall I do—what shall I do!"

Thus saying, the dear little woman burst into tears, and crying, as if her heart would break, sobbed out an entreaty that I would look at baby; adding, that she herself had not courage to see whether her darling was sleeping or dead.

"Dead!" I exclaimed. "Tut, tut, my darling; you must not give way to such morbid fancies—he is very well, I see him breathing"; and so saying, I went over to the bed where our little boy was lying. He was slumbering; though it seemed to me very heavily, and his cheeks were flushed.

"Sleeping tranquilly, my darling—tranquilly, and deeply; and with a warm colour in his cheeks," I said, rearranging the coverlet, and retiring to my wife, who sate almost breathless whilst I was looking at our little boy.

"Thank God—thank God," she said quietly; and she wept again; and rising, came to his bedside.

"Yes, yes—alive; thank God; but it seems to me he is breathing very short, and with difficulty, and he looks—*does* he not look hot and feverish? Yes, he *is* very hot; feel his little hand—feel his neck; merciful heaven! he is burning."

It was, indeed, very true, that his skin was unnaturally dry and hot; his little pulse, too, was going at a fearful rate.

"I do think," said I—resolved to conceal the extent of my own apprehensions—"I do think that he is just a *little* feverish; but he has often been much more so; and will, I dare say, in the morning, be perfectly well again. I dare say, but for little Fanny's *dream*, we should not have observed it at all."

"Oh, my darling, my darling, my darling!" sobbed the poor little woman, leaning over the bed, with her hands locked together, and looking the very picture of despair. "Oh, my darling, what has happened to you? I put you into your bed, looking so well and beautiful, this evening, and here you are, stricken with sickness, my own little love. Oh, you will not—you cannot, leave your poor mother!"

It was quite plain that she despaired of the child from the moment we had ascertained that it was unwell. As it happened, her presentiment was but too truly prophetic. The apothecary said the child's ailment was "suppressed small-pox"; the physician pronounced it "typhus." The only certainty about it was the issue—the child died.

JOSEPH SHERIDAN LE FANU

To me few things appear so beautiful as a very young child in its shroud. The little innocent face looks so sublimely simple and confiding amongst the cold terrors of death—crimeless, and fearless, that little mortal has passed alone under the shadow, and explored the mystery of dissolution. There is death in its sublimest and purest image—no hatred, no hypocrisy, no suspicion, no care for the morrow ever darkened that little face; death has come lovingly upon it; there is nothing cruel, or harsh, in his victory. The yearnings of love, indeed, cannot be stifled; for the prattle, and smiles, and all the little world of thoughts that were so delightful, are gone forever. Awe, too, will overcast us in its presence—for we are looking on death; but we do not fear for the little, lonely voyager—for the child has gone, simple and trusting, into the presence of its all-wise Father; and of such, we know, is the kingdom of heaven.

And so we parted from poor little baby. I and his poor old nurse drove in a mourning carriage, in which lay the little coffin, early in the morning, to the churchyard of—. Sore, indeed, was my heart, as I followed that little coffin to the grave! Another burial had just concluded as we entered the churchyard, and the mourners stood in clusters round the grave, into which the sexton was now shovelling the mould.

As I stood, with head uncovered, listening to the sublime and touching service which our ritual prescribes, I found that a gentleman had drawn near also, and was standing at my elbow. I did not turn to look at him until the earth had closed over my darling boy; I then walked a little way apart, that I might be alone, and drying my eyes, sat down upon a tombstone, to let the confusion of my mind subside.

While I was thus lost in a sorrowful reverie, the gentleman who had stood near me at the grave was once more at my side. The face of the stranger, though I could not call it handsome, was very remarkable; its expression was the purest and noblest I could conceive, and it was made very beautiful by a look of such compassion as I never saw before.

"Why do you sorrow as one without hope?" he said, gently.

"I *have* no hope," I answered.

"Nay, I think you have," he answered again; "and I am sure you will soon have more. That little child for which you grieve, has escaped the dangers and miseries of life; its body has perished; but he will receive in the end the crown of life. God has given him an early victory."

I know not what it was in him that rebuked my sullen pride, and humbled and saddened me, as I listened to this man. He was dressed in deep mourning, and looked more serene, noble, and sweet than any I had ever seen. He was young, too, as I have said, and his voice very clear and harmonious. He talked to me for a long time, and I listened to him with involuntary reverence. At last, however, he left me, saying he had often seen me walking into town, about the same hour that he used to go that way, and that if he saw me again he would walk with me, and so we might reason of these things together.

It was late when I returned to my home, now a house of mourning.

Part II

OUR HOME WAS ONE OF sorrow and of fear. The child's death had stricken us with terror no less than grief. Referring it, as we both tacitly did, to the mysterious and fiendish agency of the abhorred being whom, in an evil hour, we had admitted into our house, we both viewed him with a degree and species of fear for which I can find no name.

I felt that some further calamity was impending. I could not hope that we were to be delivered from the presence of the malignant agent who haunted, rather than inhabited our home, without some additional proofs alike of his malice and his power.

My poor wife's presentiments were still more terrible and overpowering, though not more defined, than my own. She was never tranquil while our little girl was out of her sight; always dreading and expecting some new revelation of the evil influence which, as we were indeed both persuaded, had bereft our darling little boy of life. Against an hostility so unearthly and intangible there was no guarding, and the sense of helplessness intensified the misery of our situation. Tormented with doubts of the very basis of her religion, and recoiling from the ordeal of prayer with the strange horror with which the victim of hydrophobia repels the pure water, she no longer found the consolation which, had sorrow reached her in any other shape, she would have drawn from the healing influence of religion. We were both of us unhappy, dismayed, DEMON-STRICKEN.

Meanwhile, our lodger's habits continued precisely the same. If, indeed, the sounds which came from his apartments were to be trusted, he and his agents were more on the alert than ever. I can convey to you, good reader, no notion, even the faintest, of the dreadful sensation always more or less present to my mind, and sometimes with a reality which thrilled me almost to frenzy—the apprehension that I had admitted into my house the incarnate spirit of the dead or damned, to torment me and my family.

It was some nights after the burial of our dear little baby; we had not gone to bed until late, and I had slept, I suppose, some hours, when I was awakened by my wife, who clung to me with the energy of terror. She said nothing, but grasped and shook me with more than her natural strength. She had crept close to me, and was cowering with her head under the bedclothes.

The room was perfectly dark, as usual, for we burned no night-light; but from the side of the bed next her proceeded a voice as of one sitting there with his head within a foot of the curtains—and, merciful heavens! it was the voice of our lodger.

He was discoursing of the death of our baby, and inveighing, in the old mocking tone of hate and suppressed fury, against the justice, mercy, and goodness of God. He did this with a terrible plausibility of sophistry, and with a resolute emphasis and precision, which seemed to imply, "I have got something to tell you, and, whether you like it or like it not, I *will* say out my say."

To pretend that I felt anger at his intrusion, or emotion of any sort, save the one sense of palsied terror, would be to depart from the truth. I lay, cold and breathless, as if frozen to death—unable to move, unable to utter a cry—with the voice of that demon pouring, in the dark, his undisguised blasphemies and temptations close into my ears. At last the dreadful voice ceased—whether the speaker went or stayed I could not tell—the silence, which he might be improving for the purpose of some hellish strategem, was to me more tremendous even than his speech.

We both lay awake, not daring to move or speak, scarcely even breathing, but clasping one another fast, until at length the welcome light of day streamed into the room through the opening door, as the servant came in to call us. I need not say that our nocturnal visitant had left us.

The magnanimous reader will, perhaps, pronounce that I ought to have pulled on my boots and inexpressibles with all available despatch, run to my lodger's bedroom, and kicked him forthwith downstairs, and the entire way moreover out to the public road, as some compensation for the scandalous affront put upon me and my wife by his impertinent visit. Now, at that time, I had no scruples against what are termed the laws of honour, was by no means deficient in "pluck," and gifted, moreover, with a somewhat excitable temper. Yet, I will honestly avow that, so far from courting a collision with the dreaded stranger, I would have recoiled at his very sight, and given my eyes to avoid him, such was the ascendancy which he had acquired over me, as well as everybody else in my household, in his own quiet, irresistible, hellish way.

The shuddering antipathy which our guest inspired did not rob his infernal homily of its effect. It was not a new or strange thing which he presented to our minds. There was an awful subtlety in the train of his suggestions. All that he had said had floated through my own mind before, without order, indeed, or shew of logic. From my own rebellious heart the same evil thoughts had risen, like pale apparitions hovering and lost in the fumes of a necromancer's cauldron. His was like the summing up of all this—a reflection of my own feelings and fancies—but reduced to an awful order and definiteness, and clothed with a sophistical form of argument. The effect of it was powerful. It revived and exaggerated these bad emotions—it methodised and justified them—and gave to impulses and impressions, vague and desultory before, something of the compactness of a system.

My misfortune, therefore, did not soften, it exasperated me. I regarded the Great Disposer of events as a persecutor of the human race, who took delight in their miseries. I asked why my innocent child had been smitten down into the grave?—and why my darling wife, whose first object, I knew, had ever been to serve and glorify her Maker, should have been thus tortured and desolated by the cruelest calamity which the malignity of a demon could have devised? I railed and blasphemed, and even in my agony defied God with the impotent rage and desperation of a devil, in his everlasting torment.

In my bitterness, I could not forbear speaking these impenitent repetitions of the language of our nightly visitant, even in the presence of my wife. She heard me with agony, almost with terror. I pitied and loved her too much not to respect even her weaknesses—for so I characterised her humble submission to the chastisements of heaven. But even while I spared her reverential sensitiveness, the spectacle of her patience but enhanced my own gloomy and impenitent rage.

I was walking into town in this evil mood, when I was overtaken by the gentleman whom I had spoken with in the churchyard on the morning when my little boy was buried. I call him *gentleman*, but I could not say *what* was his rank—I never thought about it; there was a grace, a purity, a compassion, and a grandeur of intellect in his countenance, in his language, in his mien, that was beautiful and kinglike. I felt, in his company, a delightful awe, and an humbleness more gratifying than any elation of earthly pride.

He divined my state of feeling, but he said nothing harsh. He did not rebuke, but he reasoned with me—and oh! how mighty was that reasoning—without formality—without effort—as the flower grows and blossoms. Its process was in harmony with the successions of nature—gentle, spontaneous, irresistible.

At last he left me. I was grieved at his departure—I was wonder-stricken. His discourse had made me cry tears at once sweet and bitter; it had sounded depths I knew not of, and my heart was disquieted within me. Yet my trouble was happier than the resentful and defiant calm that had reigned within me before.

When I came home, I told my wife of my having met the same good, wise man I had first seen by the grave of my child. I recounted to her his discourse, and, as I brought it again to mind, my tears flowed afresh, and I was happy while I wept.

I now see that the calamity which bore at first such evil fruit, was good for me. It fixed my mind, however rebelliously, upon God, and it stirred up all the passions of my heart. Levity, inattention, and self-complacency are obstacles harder to be overcome than the violence of evil passions—the transition from hate is easier than from indifference, to love. A mighty change was making on my mind.

I need not particularise the occasions upon which I again met my friend, for so I knew him to be, nor detail the train of reasoning and feeling which in such interviews he followed out; it is enough to say, that he assiduously cultivated the good seed he had sown, and that his benignant teachings took deep root, and flourished in my soul, heretofore so barren.

One evening, having enjoyed on the morning of the same day another of those delightful and convincing conversations, I was returning on foot homeward; and as darkness had nearly closed, and the night threatened cold and fog, the footpaths were nearly deserted.

As I walked on, deeply absorbed in the discourse I had heard on the same morning, a person overtook me, and continued to walk, without much increasing the interval between us, a little in advance of me. There came upon me, at the same moment, an indefinable sinking of the heart, a strange and unaccountable fear. The pleasing topics of my meditations melted away, and gave place to a sense of danger, all the more unpleasant that it was vague and objectless. I looked up. What was that which moved before me? I stared—I faltered; my heart fluttered as if it would choke me, and then stood still. It was the peculiar and unmistakeable form of our lodger.

Exactly as I looked at him, he turned his head, and looked at me over his shoulder. His face was muffled as usual. I cannot have seen its features with any completeness, yet I felt that his look was one of fury. The next instant he was at my side; and my heart quailed within me—my limbs all but refused their office; yet the very emotions of terror, which might have overcome me, acted as a stimulus, and I quickened my pace.

"Hey! what a pious person! So I suppose you have learned at last that 'evil communications corrupt good manners'; and you are absolutely afraid of the old infidel, the old blasphemer, hey?"

I made him no answer; I was indeed too much agitated to speak.

"You'll make a good Christian, no doubt," he continued; "the independent man, who thinks for himself, reasons his way to his principles, and sticks fast to them, is sure to be true to whatever system he embraces. You have been so consistent a philosopher, that I am sure you will make a steady Christian. You're not the man to be led by the nose by a sophistical mumbler. *You* could never be made the prey of a grasping proselytism; *you* are not the sport of every whiff of doctrine, nor the facile slave of whatever superstition is last buzzed in your ear. No, no: you've got a masculine intellect, and think for yourself, hey?"

I was incapable of answering him. I quickened my pace to escape from his detested persecution; but he was close beside me still.

We walked on together thus for a time, during which I heard him muttering fast to himself, like a man under fierce and malignant excitement. We reached, at length, the gateway of my dwelling; and I turned the latch-key in the wicket, and entered the enclosure. As we stood together within, he turned full upon me, and confronting me with an aspect whose character I felt rather than saw, he said—

"And so you mean to be a Christian, after all! Now just reflect how very absurdly you are choosing. Leave the Bible to that class of fanatics who may hope to be saved under its system, and, in the name of common sense, study the Koran, or some less ascetic tome. Don't be gulled by a plausible slave, who wants nothing more than to multiply *professors* of his theory. Why don't you *read* the Bible, you miserable, puling poltroon, before you hug it as a treasure? Why don't you read it, and learn out of the mouth of the founder of Christianity, that there is one sin for which there is *no* forgiveness—blasphemy against the Holy Ghost, hey?—and that sin I myself have heard you commit by the hour—in my presence—in my room. I have heard you commit it in our free discussions a dozen times. The Bible seals against you the lips of mercy. If *it* be true, you are this moment as irrevocably damned as if you had died with those blasphemies on your lips."

Having thus spoken, he glided into the house. I followed slowly.

His words rang in my ears—I was stunned. What he had said I feared might be true. Giant despair felled me to the earth. He had recalled, and lighted up with a glare from the pit, remembrances with which I knew not how to cope. It was true I had spoken with daring impiety of subjects whose sacredness I now began to appreciate. With trembling hands I opened the Bible. I read and re-read the mysterious doom recorded by the Redeemer himself against blasphemers of the Holy Ghost—monsters set apart from the human race, and damned and dead, even while they live and walk upon the earth. I groaned—I wept. Henceforward the Bible, I thought, must be to me a dreadful record of despair. I dared not read it.

I will not weary you with all my mental agonies. My dear little wife did something toward relieving my mind, but it was reserved for the friend, to whose heavenly society I owed so much, to tranquillise it once more. He talked this time to me longer, and even more earnestly than before. I soon encountered him again. He expounded to me the ways of Providence, and showed me how needful sorrow was for every servant of God. How mercy was disguised in tribulation, and our best happiness came to us, like our children, in tears and wailing. He showed me that trials were sent to call us up, with a voice of preternatural power, from the mortal apathy of sin and the world. And then, again, in our new and better state, to prove our patience and our faith—

"The more trouble befalls you, the nearer is God to you. He visits you in sorrow—and sorrow, as well as joy, is a sign of his presence. If, then, other griefs overtake you, remember this—be patient, be faithful; and bless the name of God."

I returned home comforted and happy, although I felt assured that some further and sadder trial was before me.

Still our household was overcast by the same insurmountable dread of our tenant. The same strange habits characterised him, and the same unaccountable sounds disquieted us—an atmosphere of death and malice hovered about his door, and we all hated and feared to pass it.

Let me now tell, as well and briefly as I may, the dreadful circumstances of my last great trial. One morning, my wife being about her household affairs, and I on the point of starting for town, I went into the parlour for some letters which I was to take with me. I cannot easily describe my consternation when, on entering the room, I saw our lodger seated near the window, with our darling little girl upon his knee.

His back was toward the door, but I could plainly perceive that the respirator had been removed from his mouth, and that the odious green goggles were raised. He was sitting, as it seemed, absolutely without motion, and his face was advanced close to that of the child.

I stood looking at this group in a state of stupor for some seconds. He was, I suppose, conscious of my presence, for although he did not turn his head, or otherwise take any note of my arrival, he readjusted the muffler which usually covered his mouth, and lowered the clumsy spectacles to their proper place.

The child was sitting upon his knee as motionless as he himself, with a countenance white and rigid as that of a corpse, and from which every trace of meaning, except some vague character of terror, had fled, and staring with a fixed and dilated gaze into his face.

As it seemed, she did not perceive my presence. Her eyes were transfixed and fascinated. She did not even seem to me to breathe. Horror and anguish at last overcame my stupefaction.

"What—what is it?" I cried; "what ails my child, my darling child?"

"I'd be glad to know, myself," he replied, coolly; "it is certainly something very queer."

"What is it, darling?" I repeated, frantically, addressing the child.

"What is it?" he reiterated. "Why it's pretty plain, I should suppose, that the child is ill."

"Oh merciful God!" I cried, half furious, half terrified—"You have injured her—you have terrified her. Give me my child—give her to me."

These words I absolutely shouted, and stamped upon the floor in my horrid excitement.

"Pooh, pooh!" he said, with a sort of ugly sneer; "the child is nervous—you'll make her more so—be quiet and she'll probably find her tongue presently. I have had her on my knee some minutes, but the sweet bird could not tell what ails her."

"Let the child go," I shouted in a voice of thunder; "let her go, I say—let her go."

He took the passive, death-like child, and placed her standing by the window, and rising, he simply said—

"As soon as you grow cool, you are welcome to ask me what questions you like. The child is plainly ill. I should not wonder if she had seen something that frightened her."

JOSEPH SHERIDAN LE FANU

Having thus spoken, he passed from the room. I felt as if I spoke, saw, and walked in a horrid dream. I seized the darling child in my arms, and bore her away to her mother.

"What is it—for mercy's sake what is the matter?" she cried, growing in an instant as pale as the poor child herself.

"I found that—that *demon*—in the parlour with the child on his lap, staring in her face. She is manifestly terrified."

"Oh! gracious God! she is lost—she is killed," cried the poor mother, frantically looking into the white, apathetic, meaningless face of the child.

"Fanny, darling Fanny, tell us if you are ill," I cried, pressing the little girl in terror to my heart.

"Tell your own mother, my darling," echoed my poor little wife. "Oh! darling, darling child, speak to your poor mother."

It was all in vain. Still the same dilated, imploring gaze—the same pale face—wild and dumb. We brought her to the open window—we gave her cold water to drink—we sprinkled it in her face. We sent for the apothecary, who lived hard by, and he arrived in a few moments, with a parcel of tranquillising medicines. These, however, were equally unavailing.

Hour after hour passed away. The darling child looked upon us as if she would have given the world to speak to us, or to weep, but she uttered no sound. Now and then she drew a long breath as though preparing to say something, but still she was mute. She often put her hand to her throat, as if there was some pain or obstruction there.

I never can, while I live, lose one line of that mournful and terrible portrait—the face of my stricken child. As hour after hour passed away, without bringing the smallest change or amendment, we grew both alarmed, and at length absolutely terrified for her safety.

We called in a physician toward night, and told him that we had reason to suspect that the child had somehow been frightened, and that in no other way could we at all account for the extraordinary condition in which he found her.

This was a man, I may as well observe, though I do not name him, of the highest eminence in his profession, and one in whose skill, from past personal experience, I had the best possible reasons for implicitly confiding.

He asked a multiplicity of questions, the answers to which seemed to baffle his attempts to arrive at a satisfactory diagnosis. There was something undoubtedly anomalous in the case, and I saw plainly that there were features in it which puzzled and perplexed him not a little.

At length, however, he wrote his prescription, and promised to return at nine o'clock. I remember there was something to be rubbed along her spine, and some medicines beside.

But these remedies were as entirely unavailing as the others. In a state of dismay and distraction we watched by the bed in which, in accordance with the physician's direction, we had placed her. The absolute changelessness of her condition filled us with despair. The day which had elapsed had not witnessed even a transitory variation in the dreadful character of her seizure. Any change, even a change for the worse, would have been better than this sluggish, hopeless monotony of suffering.

At the appointed hour the physician returned. He appeared disappointed, almost shocked, at the failure of his prescriptions. On feeling her pulse he declared that she must have a little wine. There had been a wonderful prostration of all the vital powers since he had seen her before. He evidently thought the case a strange and precarious one.

She was made to swallow the wine, and her pulse rallied for a time, but soon subsided again. I and the physician were standing by the fire, talking in whispers of the darling child's symptoms, and likelihood of recovery, when we were arrested in our conversation by a cry of anguish from the poor mother, who had never left the bedside of her little child, and this cry broke into bitter and convulsive weeping.

The poor little child had, on a sudden, stretched down her little hands and feet, and died. There is no mistaking the features of death: the filmy eye and dropt jaw once seen, are recognised whenever we meet them again. Yet, spite of our belief, we cling to hope; and the distracted mother called on the physician, in accents which might have moved a statue, to say that her darling was not dead, not quite dead—that something might still be done—that it could not be all over. Silently he satisfied himself that no throb of life still fluttered in that little frame.

"It is, indeed, all over," he said, in tones scarce above a whisper; and pressing my hand kindly, he said, "comfort your poor wife"; and so, after a momentary pause, he left the room.

This blow had smitten me with stunning suddenness. I looked at the dead child, and from her to her poor mother. Grief and pity were both swallowed up in transports of fury and detestation with which the presence in my house of the wretch who had wrought all this destruction and misery filled my soul. My heart swelled with ungovernable rage; for a moment my habitual fear of him was neutralised by the vehemence of these passions. I seized a candle in silence, and mounted the stairs. The sight of the accursed cat, flitting across the lobby, and the loneliness of the hour, made me hesitate for an instant. I had, however, gone so far, that shame sustained me. Overcoming a momentary thrill of dismay, and determined to repel and defy the influence that had so long awed me, I knocked sharply at the door, and, almost at the same instant, pushed it open, and entered our lodger's chamber.

He had had no candle in the room, and it was lighted only by the "darkness visible" that entered through the window. The candle which I held very imperfectly illuminated the large apartment; but I saw his spectral form floating, rather than walking, back and forward in front of the windows.

At sight of him, though I hated him more than ever, my instinctive fear returned. He confronted me, and drew nearer and nearer, without speaking. There was something indefinably fearful in the silent attraction which seemed to be drawing him to me. I could not help recoiling, little by little, as he came toward me, and with an effort I said—

"You know why I have come: the child—she's dead!"

"Dead—ha!—*dead*—is she?" he said, in his odious, mocking tone.

"Yes—dead!" I cried, with an excitement which chilled my very marrow with horror; "and *you* have killed her, as you killed my other."

"How?—I killed her!—eh?—ha, ha!" he said, still edging nearer and nearer.

"Yes; I say you!" I shouted, trembling in every joint, but possessed by that unaccountable infatuation which has made men invoke, spite of themselves, their own destruction, and which I was powerless to resist— "deny it as you may, it is you who killed her—wretch!—Fiend!—no wonder she could not stand the breath and glare of Hell!"

"And you are one of those who believe that not a sparrow falls to the ground without your Creator's consent," he said, with icy sarcasm; "and this is a specimen of Christian resignation—hey? You charge his act upon a poor fellow like me, simply that you may cheat the devil, and rave and rebel against the decrees of heaven, under pretence of abusing me. The breath and flare of hell!—eh? You mean that I removed this and these (touching the covering of his mouth and eyes successively) as I *shall* do now again, and show you there's no great harm in that."

There was a tone of menace in his concluding words not to be mistaken.

"Murderer and liar from the beginning, as you are, I defy you!" I shouted, in a frenzy of hate and horror, stamping furiously on the floor.

As I said this, it seemed to me that he darkened and dilated before my eyes. My senses, thoughts, consciousness, grew horribly confused, as if some powerful, extraneous will, were seizing upon the functions of my brain. Whether I were to be mastered by death, or madness, or possession, I knew not; but hideous destruction of some sort was impending: all hung upon the moment, and I cried aloud, in my agony, an adjuration in the name of the three persons of the Trinity, that he should not torment me.

Stunned, bewildered, like a man recovered from a drunken fall, I stood, freezing and breathless, in the same spot, looking into the room, which wore, in my eyes, a strange, unearthly character. Mr. Smith was cowering darkly in the window, and, after a silence, spoke to me in a croaking, sulky tone, which was, however, unusually submissive.

"Don't it strike you as an odd procedure to break into a gentleman's apartment at such an hour, for the purpose of railing at him in the coarsest language? If you have any charge to make against me, do so; I invite inquiry and defy your worst. If you think you can bring home to me the smallest share of blame in this unlucky matter, call the coroner, and let his inquest examine and cross-examine me, and sift the matter— if, indeed, there is anything to *be* sifted—to the bottom. Meanwhile, go you about your business, and leave me to mine. But I see how the wind sits; you want to get rid of me, and so you make the place odious to me. But it won't do; and if you take to making criminal charges against me, you had better look to yourself; for two can play at that game."

There was a suppressed whine in all this, which strangely contrasted with the cool and threatening tone of his previous conversation.

Without answering a word I hurried from the room, and scarcely felt secure, even when once more in the melancholy chamber, where my poor wife was weeping.

Miserable, horrible was the night that followed. The loss of our child was a calamity which we had not dared to think of. It had come, and with a suddenness enough to bereave me of reason. It seemed all unreal, all fantastic. It needed an effort to convince me, minute after minute, that the dreadful truth was so; and the old accustomed feeling that she was still alive, still running from room to room, and the expectation that I should hear her step and her voice, and see her entering at the door, would return. But still the sense of dismay, of having received some stunning, irreparable blow, remained behind; and then came the horrible effort, like that with which one rouses himself from a haunted sleep, the question, "What disaster is this that has befallen?"—answered, alas! but too easily, too terribly! Amidst all this was perpetually rising before my fancy the obscure, dilated figure of our lodger, as he had confronted me in his malign power that night. I dismissed the image with a shudder as often as it recurred; and even now, at this distance of time, I have felt more than I could well describe in the mere effort to fix my recollection upon its hated traits, while writing the passages I have just concluded.

This hateful scene I did not recount to my poor wife. Its horrors were too fresh upon me. I had not courage to trust myself with the agitating narrative; and so I sate beside her, with her hand locked in mine: I had no comfort to offer but the dear love I bore her.

At last, like a child, she cried herself to sleep—the dull, heavy slumber of worn-out grief. As for me, the agitation of my soul was too fearful and profound for repose. My eye accidentally rested on the holy volume, which lay upon the table open, as I had left it in the morning; and the first words which met my eye were these—"For our light affliction, which is but for a moment, worketh for us a far more exceeding and eternal weight of glory." This blessed sentence riveted my attention, and shed a stream of solemn joy upon my heart; and so the greater part of that mournful night, I continued to draw comfort and heavenly wisdom from the same inspired source.

Next day brought the odious incident, the visit of the undertaker—the carpentery, upholstery, and millinery of death. Why has not civilisation abolished these repulsive and shocking formalities? What has the poor corpse to do with frills, and pillows, and napkins, and all the equipage in which it rides on its last journey? There is no intrusion so jarring to the decent grief of surviving affection, no conceivable mummery more derisive of mortality.

In the room which we had been so long used to call "the nursery," now desolate and mute, the unclosed coffin lay, with our darling shrouded in it. Before we went to our rest at night we visited it. In the morning the lid was to close over that sweet face, and I was to see the child laid by her little brother. We looked upon the well-known and loved features, purified in the sublime serenity of death, for a long time, whispering to one another, among our sobs, how sweet and beautiful we thought she looked; and at length, weeping bitterly, we tore ourselves away.

We talked and wept for many hours, and at last, in sheer exhaustion, dropt asleep. My little wife awaked me, and said—

"I think they have come—the—the undertakers."

It was still dark, so I could not consult my watch; but they were to have arrived early, and as it was winter, and the nights long, the hour of their visit might well have arrived.

"What, darling, is your reason for thinking so?" I asked.

"I am sure I have heard them for sometime in the nursery," she answered. "Oh! dear, dear little Fanny! Don't allow them to close the coffin until I have seen my darling once more."

I got up, and threw some clothes hastily about me. I opened the door and listened. A sound like a muffled knocking reached me from the nursery.

"Yes, my darling!" I said, "I think they have come. I will go and desire them to wait until you have seen her again."

And, so saying, I hastened from the room.

Our bedchamber lay at the end of a short corridor, opening from the lobby, at the head of the stairs, and the nursery was situated nearly at the end of a corresponding passage, which opened from the same lobby at the opposite side As I hurried along I distinctly heard the same sounds. The light of dawn had not yet appeared, but there was a strong moonlight shining through the windows. I thought the morning could hardly be so far advanced as we had at first supposed; but still, strangely as it now seems to me, suspecting nothing amiss, I walked on in noiseless, slippered feet, to the nursery-door. It stood half open; someone had unquestionably visited it since we had been there. I stepped forward, and entered. At the threshold horror arrested my advance.

The coffin was placed upon tressles at the further extremity of the chamber, with the foot of it nearly towards the door, and a large window at the side of it admitted the cold lustre of the moon full upon the apparatus of mortality, and the objects immediately about it.

At the foot of the coffin stood the ungainly form of our lodger. He seemed to be intently watching the face of the corpse, and was stooped a little, while with his hands he tapped sharply, from time to time at the sides of the coffin, like one who designs to awaken a slumberer. Perched upon the body of the child, and nuzzling among the grave-clothes, with a strange kind of ecstasy, was the detested brute, the cat I have so often mentioned.

The group thus revealed, I looked upon but for one instant; in the next I shouted, in absolute terror—

"In God's name! what are you doing?"

Our lodger shuffled away abruptly, as if disconcerted; but the ill-favoured cat, whisking round, stood like a demon sentinel upon the corpse, growling and hissing, with arched back and glaring eyes.

The lodger, turning abruptly toward me, motioned me to one side. Mechanically I obeyed his gesture, and he hurried hastily from the room.

Sick and dizzy, I returned to my own chamber. I confess I had not nerve to combat the infernal brute, which still held possession of the room, and so I left it undisturbed.

This incident I did not tell to my wife until sometime afterwards; and I mention it here because it was, and is, in my mind associated with a painful circumstance which very soon afterwards came to light.

That morning I witnessed the burial of my darling child. Sore and desolate was my heart; but with infinite gratitude to the great controller of all events, I recognised in it a change which nothing but the spirit of all good can effect. The love and fear of God had grown strong within me—in humbleness I bowed to his awful will—with a sincere trust I relied upon the goodness, the wisdom, and the mercy of him who had sent this great affliction. But a further incident connected with this very calamity was to test this trust and patience to the uttermost.

It was still early when I returned, having completed the last sad office. My wife, as I afterwards learned, still lay weeping upon her bed. But somebody awaited my return in the hall, and opened the door, anticipating my knock. This person was our lodger.

I was too much appalled by the sudden presentation of this abhorred spectre even to retreat, as my instinct would have directed, through the open door.

"I have been expecting your return," he said, "with the design of saying something which it might have profited you to learn, but now I apprehend it is too late. What a pity you are so violent and impatient; you would not have heard me, in all probability, this morning. You cannot think how cross-grained and intemperate you have grown since you became a saint—but that is your affair, not mine. You have buried your little daughter this morning. It requires a good deal of that new attribute of yours, *faith*, which judges all things by a rule of contraries, and can never see anything but kindness in the worst afflictions which malignity could devise, to discover benignity and mercy in the torturing calamity which has just punished you and your wife for *nothing*! But I fancy that it will be harder still when I tell you what I more than suspect—ha, ha. It would be really ridiculous, if it were not heart-rending; that your little girl has been actually buried *alive*; do you comprehend me?—alive. For, upon my life, I fancy she was not dead as she lay in her coffin."

I knew the wretch was exulting in the fresh anguish he had just inflicted. I know not how it was, but any announcement of *disaster* from his lips, seemed to me to be necessarily true. Half-stifled with the dreadful emotions he had raised, palpitating between hope and terror, I rushed frantically back again, the way I had just come, running as fast as my speed could carry me, toward the, alas! distant burial-ground where my darling lay.

I stopped a cab slowly returning to town, at the corner of the lane, sprang into it, directed the man to drive to the church of—, and promised him anything and everything for despatch. The man seemed amazed; doubtful, perhaps, whether he carried a maniac or a malefactor. Still he took his chance for the promised reward, and galloped his horse, while I, tortured with suspense, yelled my frantic incentives to further speed.

At last, in a space immeasurably short, but which to me was protracted almost beyond endurance, we reached the spot. I hallooed to the sexton, who was now employed upon another grave, to follow me. I myself seized a mattock, and in obedience to my incoherent and agonised commands, he worked as he had never worked before. The crumbling mould flew swiftly to the upper soil—deeper and deeper, every moment, grew the narrow grave—at last I sobbed, "Thank God—thank God," as I saw the face of the coffin emerge; a few seconds more and it lay upon the sward beside me, and we both, with the edges of our spades, ripped up the lid.

There was the corpse—but not the tranquil statue I had seen it last. Its knees were both raised, and one of its little hands drawn up and clenched near its throat, as if in a feeble but agonised struggle to force up the superincumbent mass. The eyes, that I had last seen closed, were now open, and the face no longer serenely pale, but livid and distorted.

I had time to see all in an instant; the whole scene reeled and darkened before me, and I swooned away.

When I came to myself, I found that I had been removed to the vestry-room. The open coffin was in the aisle of the church, surrounded by a curious crowd. A medical gentleman had examined the body carefully, and had pronounced life totally extinct. The trepidation and horror I experienced were indescribable. I felt like the murderer of my own child. Desperate as I was of any chance of its life, I dispatched messengers for no less than three of the most eminent physicians then practising in London. All concurred—the child was now as dead as any other, the oldest tenant of the churchyard.

Notwithstanding which, I would not permit the body to be reinterred for several days, until the symptoms of decay became unequivocal, and the most fantastic imagination could no longer cherish a doubt. This, however, I mention only parenthetically, as I hasten to the conclusion of my narrative. The circumstance which I have last described found its way to the public, and caused no small sensation at the time.

I drove part of the way home, and then discharged the cab, and walked the remainder. On my way, with an emotion of ecstasy I cannot describe, I met the good being to whom I owed so much. I ran to meet him, and felt as if I could throw myself at his feet, and kiss the very ground before him. I knew by his heavenly countenance he was come to speak comfort and healing to my heart.

With humbleness and gratitude, I drank in his sage and holy discourse. I need not follow the gracious and delightful exposition of God's revealed will and character with which he cheered and confirmed my faltering spirit. A solemn joy, a peace and trust, streamed on my heart. The wreck and desolation there, lost their bleak and ghastly character, like ruins illuminated by the mellow beams of a solemn summer sunset.

In this conversation, I told him what I had never revealed to anyone before—the absolute terror, in all its stupendous and maddening amplitude, with which I regarded our ill-omened lodger, and my agonised anxiety to rid my house of him. My companion answered me—

"I know the person of whom you speak—he designs no good for you or any other. He, too, knows me, and I have intimated to him that he must now leave you, and visit you no more. Be firm and bold, trusting in God, through his Son, like a good soldier, and you will win the victory from a greater and even worse than he—the *unseen* enemy of mankind. You need not see or speak with your evil tenant anymore. Call to him from your hall, in the name of the Most Holy, to leave you bodily, with all that appertains to him, this evening. He knows that he must go, and will obey you. But leave the house as soon as may be yourself; you will scarce have peace in it. Your own remembrances will trouble you and *other minds have established associations within its walls and chambers too.*"

These words sounded mysteriously in my ears.

Let me say here, before I bring my reminiscences to a close, a word or two about the house in which these detested scenes occurred, and which I did not long continue to inhabit. What I afterwards learned of it, seemed to supply in part a dim explanation of these words.

In a country village there is no difficulty in accounting for the tenacity with which the sinister character of a haunted tenement cleaves to it. Thin neighbourhoods are favourable to scandal; and in such localities the reputation of a house, like that of a woman, once blown upon, never quite recovers. In huge London, however, it is quite another matter; and, therefore, it was with some surprise that, five years after I had vacated the house in which the occurrences I have described took place, I learned that a respectable family who had taken it were obliged to give it up, on account of annoyances, for which they could not account, and all proceeding from the apartments formerly occupied by our "lodger." Among the sounds described were footsteps restlessly traversing the floor of that room, accompanied by the peculiar tapping of the crutch.

I was so anxious about this occurrence, that I contrived to have strict inquiries made into the matter. The result, however, added little to what I had at first learned—except, indeed, that our old friend, the cat, bore a part in the transaction as I suspected; for the servant, who had been placed to sleep in the room, complained that something bounded on and off, and ran to-and-fro along the foot of the bed, in the dark. The same servant, while in the room, in the broad daylight, had heard the sound of walking, and even the rustling of clothes near him, as of people passing and repassing; and, although he had never seen anything, he yet became so terrified that he would not remain in the house, and ultimately, in a short time, left his situation.

These sounds, attention having been called to them, were now incessantly observed—the measured walking up and down the room, the opening and closing of the door, and the teazing tap of the crutch—all these sounds were continually repeated, until at last, worn out, frightened, and worried, its occupants resolved on abandoning the house.

About four years since, having had occasion to visit the capital, I resolved on a ramble by Old Brompton, just to see if the house were still inhabited. I searched for it, however, in vain, and at length, with difficulty, ascertained its site, upon which now stood two small, staring, bran-new brick houses, with each a gay enclosure of flowers. Every trace of our old mansion, and, let us hope, of our "mysterious lodger," had entirely vanished.

Let me, however, return to my narrative where I left it.

Discoursing upon heavenly matters, my good and gracious friend accompanied me even within the outer gate of my own house. I asked him to come in and rest himself, but he would not; and before he turned to depart, he lifted up his hand, and blessed me and my household.

Having done this, he went away. My eyes followed him till he disappeared, and I turned to the house. My darling wife was standing at the window of the parlour. There was a seraphic smile on her face— pale, pure, and beautiful as death. She was gazing with an humble, heavenly earnestness on us. The parting blessing of the stranger shed a sweet and hallowed influence on my heart. I went into the parlour, to my darling: childless she was now; I had now need to be a tender companion to her.

She raised her arms in a sort of transport, with the same smile of gratitude and purity, and, throwing them round my neck, she said—

"I have seen him—it is he—the man that came with you to the door, and blessed us as he went away—is the same I saw in my dream—the same who took little baby in his arms, and said he would take care of him, and give him safely to me again."

More than a quarter of a century has glided away since then; other children have been given us by the good God—children who have been, from infancy to maturity, a pride and blessing to us. Sorrows and reverses, too, have occasionally visited us; yet, on the whole, we have been greatly blessed; prosperity has long since ended all the cares of the *res angusta domi*, and expanded our power of doing good to our fellow-creatures. God has given it; and God, we trust, directs its dispensation. In our children, and—would you think it?—our *grand*-children, too, the same beneficent God has given us objects that elicit and return all the delightful affections, and exchange the sweet converse that makes home and family dearer than aught else, save that blessed home where the Christian family shall meet at last.

The dear companion of my early love and sorrows still lives, blessed be Heaven! The evening tints of life have fallen upon her; but the dear remembrance of a first love, that never grew cold, makes her beauty changeless for me. As for your humble servant, he is considerably her senior, and looks it: time has stolen away his raven locks, and given him a *chevelure* of snow instead. But, as I said before, I and my wife love, and, I believe, *admire* one another more than ever; and I have often seen our elder children smile archly at one another, when they thought we did not observe them, thinking, no doubt, how like a pair of lovers we two were.

The Phantom Fourth

They were three.

It was in the cheap night-service train from Paris to Calais that I first met them.

Railways, as a rule, are among the many things which they do *not* order better in France, and the French Northern line is one of the worst managed in the world, barring none, not even the Italian *vie ferrate*. I make it a rule, therefore, to punish the directors of, and the shareholders in, that undertaking to the utmost within my limited ability, by spending as little money on their line as I can help.

It was, then, in a third-class compartment of the train that I met the three.

Three as hearty, jolly-looking Saxon faces, with stalwart frames to match, as one would be likely to meet in an hour's walk from the Regent's Park to the Mansion House.

One of the three was dark, the other two were fair. The dark one was the senior of the party. He wore an incipient full beard, evidently in process of training, with a considerable amount of grizzle in it.

The face of one of his companions was graced with a magnificent flowing beard. The third of the party, a fair-haired youth of some twenty-three or four summers, showed a scrupulously smooth-shaven face.

They looked all three much flushed and slightly excited, and, I must say, they turned out the most boisterous set of fellows I ever met.

They were clearly gentlemen, however, and men of education, with considerable linguistic acquirements; for they chatted and sang, and declaimed and "did orations" all the way from Paris to Calais, in a slightly bewildering variety of tongues.

Their jollity had, perhaps, just a little over-tinge of the slap-bang jolly-dog style in it; but there was so much heartiness and good-nature in all they said and in all they did, that it was quite impossible for any of the other occupants of the carriage to vote them a nuisance; and even the sourest of the officials, whom they chaffed most unmercifully and unremittingly at every station on the line, took their punishment with a shrug and a grin. The only person, indeed, who rose against them in indignant protestation was the head-waiter at the Calais station refreshment-room, to whom they would persist in propounding puzzling problems, such as, for instance, "If you charge two shillings for one-and-a-half-ounce slice of breast of veal, how many fools will it take to buy the joint off you?"—and what *he* got by the attempt to stop their chaff was a caution to any other sinner who might have felt similarly inclined.

As for me, I could only give half my sense of hearing to their utterings, the other half being put under strict sequester at the time by my friend O'Kweene, the great Irish philosopher, who was delivering to me, for my own special behoof and benefit, a brilliant, albeit somewhat abstruse, dissertation on the "visible and palpable outward manifestations of the inner consciousness of the soul in a trance"; which occupied all the time from Paris to Calais, full eight hours, and which, to judge from my feelings at the time, would certainly afford matter for three heavy volumes of reading in bed, in cases of inveterate sleeplessness—a hint to enterprising publishers.

My friend O'Kweene, who intended to stay a few days at Calais, took leave of me on the pier, and I went on board the steamer that was to carry us and the mail over to Dover.

Here I found our trio of the railway-car, snugly ensconced under an extemporized awning, artfully constructed with railway-rugs and greatcoats, supported partly against the luggage, and partly upon several oars, purloined from the boats, and turned into tent-poles for the nonce—which made the skipper swear wofully when he found it out sometime after.

The three were even more cheery and boisterous on board than they had been on shore. From what I could make out in the dark, they were discussing the contents of divers bottles of liquor; I counted four dead men dropped quietly overboard by them in the course of the hour and a half we had to wait for the arrival of the mail-train, which was late, as usual on this line.

At last we were off, about half-past two o'clock in the morning. It was a beautiful, clear, moonlit night, so clear, indeed, that we could see the Dover lights almost from Calais harbor. But we had considerably more than a capful of wind, and there was a turgent ground-swell on, which made our boat—double-engined, and as trim and tidy a craft as ever sped across the span from shore to shore—behave rather lively, with sportive indulgence in a brisk game of pitch-and-toss that proved anything but comfortable to most of the passengers.

When we were steaming out of Calais harbor, our three friends, emerging from beneath their tent, struck up in chorus Campbell's noble song, "Ye Mariners of England," finishing up with a stave from "Rule, Britannia!"

But, alas for them! however loudly their throats were shouting forth the sway proverbially held by Albion and her sons over the waves, on this occasion at least the said waves seemed determined upon ruling these particular three Britons with a rod of antimony; for barely a few seconds after the last vibrating echoes of the "Britons never, never, never shall be slaves!" had died away upon the wind, I beheld the three leaning lovingly together, in fast friendship linked, over the rail, conversing in deep ventriguttural accents with the denizens of Neptune's watery realm.

We had one of the quickest passages on record—ninety-three minutes' steaming carried us across from shore to shore. When we were just on the point of landing, I heard the dark senior of the party mutter to his companions, in a hollow whisper and mysterious manner, "He is gone again"; to which the others, the bearded and the smooth-shaven, responded in the same way, with deep sighs of evident relief, "Ay, marry! so he is at last."

This mysterious communication roused my curiosity. Who was the party that was said to be gone at last? Where had he come from? where had he been hiding, that *I* had not seen him? and where was he gone to now? I determined to know; if but the opportunity would offer, to screw, by cunning questioning, the secret out of either of the three.

Fate favored my design.

For some inscrutable reason, known only to the company's officials, we cheap-trainers were not permitted to proceed on our journey to London along with the mail, but were left to kick our heels for some two hours at the Dover station.

I went into the refreshment-room to look for my party; I had a notion I should find them where the Briton's unswerving and unerring instinct would be most likely to lead them. It turned out that I was right in my conjecture. There they were, seated round a table with huge bowls of steaming tea and monster piles of buttered toast and muffins spread on the festive board before them. Ay, indeed, there they were; but *quantum mutati ab illis*! how strangely changed from the noisy, rollicking set I had known them in the railway-car and on board the steamer, ere yet the demon of sea-sickness had claimed them for his own! How ghastly sober they looked now, to be sure! And how sternly and silently bent upon devoting themselves to the swilling of the Chinese shrub infusion and to the gorging of indigestible muffins. It was quite clear to me that it would have been worse than folly to venture upon addressing them while thus absorbed in absorbing. So I resolved to await a more favorable opening, and went out meanwhile to walk on the platform.

A short time I was left in solitary possession of the promenade; then I became suddenly aware that another traveller was treading the same ground with me—it was the dark elderly leader of the three. I glanced at him as he passed me under one of the lamps. He looked pale and sad. The furrowed lines on his brow bespoke deliberation deep and pondering profound. All the infinite mirth of the preceding few hours had departed from him, leaving him but a wretched wreck of his former reckless self.

"A fine night, sir," I said to break the ice—"for the season of the year," I added by way of a saving clause, to tone down the absoluteness of the assertion.

He looked at me abstractedly, merely reëchoing my own words, "A fine night, sir, for the season of the year."

"Why look ye so sad now, who were erst so jolly?" I bluntly asked, determined to force him into conversation.

"Ay, indeed, why so sad now?" he replied, looking me full in the face; then, suddenly clasping my arm with a spasmodic grip, he continued hurriedly, "I think I had best confide our secret to you. You seem a man of thought. I witnessed and admired the patient attention with which you listened to your friend's abstruse talk in the railway-car. Maybe you can find the solution of a mystery which defies the ponderings of our poor brains—mine and my two friends."

Then he proceeded to pour into my attentive ear this gruesome tale of mystery:

"We three—that is, myself, yon tall bearded Briton," pointing to the glass door of the refreshment-room, "whose name is Jack Hobson, and young Emmanuel Topp, junior partner in a great beer firm, whom you may behold now at his fifth bowl of tea and his seventh muffin—are teetotallers—"

"Teetotallers!" I could not help exclaiming. "Lord bless me! that is certainly about the last thing I should have taken you for, either of you."

"Well," he replied with some slight confusion, "at least, we *were total* teetotallers, though I admit we can now only claim the character of partial abstainers. The fact is, when, about a fortnight ago, we were discussing the plan of our projected visit to the great Paris Exhibition, Topp suggested that while in France we should do as the French do, to which Jack Hobson assented, remarking that the French knew nothing about tea, and that a Frenchman's tea would be sure to prove an Englishman's poison. So we resolved to suspend the pledge during our visit to France.

"It was on the second day after our arrival in Paris. We were dining in a private cabinet at Désiré Beaurain's, one of the leading restaurants on the fashionable side of the Montmartre—Italiens Boulevard. Our dinner was what an Irishman might call a most 'illigant' affair. We had sipped several bottles of Sauterne, and tasted a few of Tavel, and we were just topping the entertainment with a solitary bottle of champagne, when I became suddenly aware of the presence of another party in the room—a *fourth man*—who sat him down at our table, and helped himself liberally to our liquor. From what I ascertained afterward from Jack Hobson and Emmanuel Topp, the intruder's presence became revealed to them also, either about the same time or a little later. What was he like? I cannot tell. His figure and face remained indistinct throughout—phantom-like. His features seemed endowed with a stronge weird mobility that would defyingly elude the fixing grasp of our eager eyes. Now, and to my two companions, he would look marvellously like me; then, to me, he would stalk and rave about in the likeness of Jack Hobson; again, he would seem the counterfeit of Emmanuel Topp; then he would look like all the three of us put together; then like neither of us, nor like anybody else. Oh, sir, it was a woful thing to be haunted by this phantom apparition. Yet the strangest part of the affair was that neither of us seemed to feel a whit surprised at the dread presence; that we quietly and uncomplainingly let him drink our wine, and actually give orders for more; that we never objected, in fact, to any of his sayings and doings. What seemed also strange was that the waiter, while yet receiving and executing his orders, was evidently pretending to ignore his presence. But then, as I dare say you know as well as I do, French waiters are *such* actors!

"Well, to resume, there he was, this fourth man, seated at our table and feasting at our expense. And the pranks that he would play us—they were truly stupendous. He began his little game by ordering in half-a-dozen of champagne. And when the waiter seemed slightly doubtful and hesitating about executing the order, Topp, forsooth, must put in his oar, and indorse the command, actually pretending that *I*, who am now speaking to you, and who am the very last man in the world likely to dream of such a preposterous thing, had given the order, and that I was a jolly old brick, and the best of boon companions. Surprise at this barefaced assertion kept me mute, and so, of course, the champagne was brought in, and I thought the best thing to do under the circumstances was to have my share of it at least; and so I had—my fair share; but, bless you, it was nothing to what that fourth man drank of it. In fact, the amount of liquor *he* would swill on this and on the many subsequent occasions he intruded his presence upon us, was a caution.

"We paid our little bill without grumbling, though the presence of the fourth man at our table had added rather heavily to the *addition*, as they call bills at French restaurants.

"We sallied forth into the street to get a whiff of fresh air. *He*, the demon, pertinaciously stuck to us; he familiarly linked his arm through mine, and, suggesting coffee as rather a good thing to take after dinner, took us over to the Café du Cardinal, where he, however, took none of the Arabian beverage himself (there being only three cups placed for us, as I distinctly saw), but drank an interminable succession of *chasse-café*, utterly regardless of the divisional lines of the cognac *carafon*. Part of these he would take neat, another portion he would burn over sugar, gloating glaringly over the bluish flame, while gleams of demoniac delight would flit across his ever-changing features. Jack Hobson and Topp, I am sorry to say, joined him with a will in this double-distilled debauch; and when I attempted to remonstrate with them, they brazenly asserted that *I*, who am now speaking to you, who have always, publicly and privately, declared brandy to be the worst of evil spirits, had taken more of it, to my own cheek, as they slangily expressed it, than the two of them together; and the waiter, who had evidently been bribed by them, boldly maintained that *le vieux monsieur*, as he had the impudence to call me, had swallowed *plus de trois carafons de fine*; whereupon the fourth man, stepping up to him, punched his head, which served him right. Now you will hardly believe me when I tell you that at that very instant Topp forced me back into my chair, while Jack Hobson pinioned my arms from behind, and the waiter had the unblushing effrontery to stamp and rave at me like a maniac, demanding satisfaction or compensation at my hands for the unprovoked assault committed upon him by *me, coram populo*!—by *me*, who, I beg to assure you, am the most peaceable man living, and am actually famed for the mildness of my disposition and the sweetness and suavity of my temper. And, would you believe it? everybody present, waiters and guests, and my own two bosom-friends, joined in the conspiracy against me, and I actually had to give the wretch of a waiter ten francs as a plaster for his broken pate, and a salve for his wounded honor! Where was the

JOSEPH SHERIDAN LE FANU

real culprit all this time, you ask me—the fourth man? Why, he quietly stood by grinning, and they all and everyone of them pretended not to see him, though Topp and Jack Hobson next morning confessed to me that they certainly had an indistinct consciousness of the presence throughout of this miserable intruder.

"How we finished that night I remember not; nor could Jack Hobson or Emmanuel Topp. All we could conscientiously stand by, if we were questioned, is that we awoke next morning—the three of us—with some slight swimming in our heads, and a hazy recollection of a gorgeous dream of brilliant lights and sounds of music and revelry, and bright visions of groves and grottoes, and dancing houris (or hussies, as moral Jack Hobson calls the poor things), and a hot supper at a certain place in the Passage des Princes, of which I think the name is Peter's.

"I will not tire your courteous patience by a detailed narrative of our experiences day after day, during our fortnight's stay in Paris. Suffice it to tell you that from that time forward to yesterday, when we left, the *fourth man*, as we, by mutual consent, agreed to call the phantom apparition, came in regularly to our dinner; with the dessert or a little after; that he would constantly suggest a fresh supply of Côte St. Jacques, Moulin-à-Vent, Beaune, Chambertin, Roederer Carte Blanche, and a variety of other, generally rather more than less expensive, wines—and that he somehow would manage to make us have them, too.

"Then he would sally forth with us to the café, where he would indulge in irritating chaff of the waiters, and in slighting comments upon the great French nation in general, and the Parisians in particular, and upon their institutions and manners and customs.

"He would insist upon singing the Marseillaise; he would speak disparagingly of the Emperor, whom he would irreverently call Lambert; he would pass cutting and unsavory remarks upon the glorious system of the night-carts; he would call down the judgment of Heaven upon the devoted head of poor Mr. Haussmann; he would go up to some unhappy sergent-de-ville, who might, however unwittingly, excite his ire, and tell him a bit of his mind in English, with sarcastic allusions to his cocket-hat and his toasting-fork, and polite inquiries after the health of *ce cher* Monsieur Lambert, or the whereabouts of *cet excellent* Monsieur Godinot. The worst of the matter was that I suppose for the reason that man is an imitative animal, a sort of πιθηκος μυωρος, or Monboddian monkey minus the tail—my two companions were, somehow, always sure to join the wretch in his evil behavior, and to go on just as bad as he did. No wonder, then, that we got into no end of rows, and it is a marvel to me now, how ever we have managed to get off with a whole skin to our bodies.

"He would insist upon taking us to Mabille, the Closerie des Lilas, and the Châteaurouge, where he would indulge in the maddest pranks and antics, and somehow lead us to join in the wildest dances, and make us lift our legs as high as the highest lifter among the *habitués*, male or female.

"One night, at about half-past two in the morning (*Hibernicè*), he had the cool assurance to drag us along with him to the then closed entrance to the Passage des Princes, where he frantically shook the gate, and insisted to the frightened concierge, who came running up in his night-shirt, that Peter's must and ought to be open still, as *we* had not had our supper yet; and Topp and Jack Hobson, forsooth, must join in the row. I have no distinct recollection of whether it was our phantom guest or either of my companions that madly strove to detain the hastily retreating form of the concierge by a desperate clutch at the tail of his shirt; I only remember that the garment gave way in the struggle, and that the unhappy functionary was reduced nearly altogether to the primitive buff costume of the father of man in Paradise ere he had put his teeth into that unlucky apple of which, the pips keep so inconveniently sticking in poor humanity's gizzard to the present day. And what I remember also to my cost is, that the sergent-de-ville, whom the bereaved man's shouts of distress brought to the scene, fastened upon *me*, the most inoffensive of mortals, for a compensation fine of twenty francs, as if *I* had been the culprit. And deuced glad we were, I assure you, to get off without more serious damage to our pocket and reputation than this, and a copious volley of *sacrés ivrognes Anglais*, fired at us by the wretched concierge and his friend of the police, who, I am quite sure, went halves with him in the compensation. Ah! they are a lawless set, these French.

"On another occasion we three went to the Exhibition, where we visited one of our colonial departments, in company with several English friends, and some French gentlemen appointed on the wine jury. We went to taste a few samples of colonial wines. *He* was not with us *then*. Barely, however, had we uncorked a poor dozen bottles, which turned out rather good for colonial, though a little raw and slightly uneducated, when *who* should stalk in but our fourth man, as jaunty and unconcerned as ever. Well, *he* fell to tasting, and he soon grew eloquent in praise of the colonial juice, which he declared would, in another twenty years' time, be

JOSEPH SHERIDAN LE FANU

fit to compete successfully with the best French vintages. Of course, the French gentlemen with us could not stand *this*; they spoke slightingly of the British colonial, and one of them even went so far as to call it rotgut. I cannot say whether it was the spirit of the uncompromising opinion thus pronounced, or the coarsely indelicate way in which the judgment of our French friend was expressed, that riled our phantom guest—enough, it brought him down in full force upon the offender and his countrymen, with most fluent French vituperation and an unconscionable amount of bad jokes and worse puns, finishing up with a general address to them as members of the *disgusting* jury, instead of jury of *dégustation*. Now, this I should not have minded so much; for, I must confess, I felt rather nettled at the national conceit and prejudice of these French. But the wretch, in the impetuous utterance of his invective, must somehow—though I was not aware of it at the time—have mimicked my gestures and imitated the very tones and accent of my voice so closely as to deceive even some of my English companions: or how else to account for the fact of their calling me a noisy brawler and a pestilent nuisance? *me*, the gentlest and mildest-spoken of mortals!

"Before our departure from London we had calculated our probable expenses on a most liberal scale, and we had made comfortable provision accordingly for a few weeks' stay in Paris. But with the additional heavy burden of the franking of so copious an imbiber as our fourth man thus unexpectedly thrown on our shoulders, it was no great wonder that we should find our resources go much faster than we had anticipated; so we had already been forcedly led to bethink ourselves of shortening our intended stay in the French capital when a fresh exploit of the phantom fourth, climaxing all his past misdeeds, brought matters to a crisis.

"It was the day before yesterday, the 4th of September. We had been dining at Marigny, and dancing at Mabille. Our eccentric guest had come in, as usual, with the champagne, and had of course, after dinner, taken us over to the enchanted gardens. We were all very jolly. *He* suggested supper at the Cascades, in the Bois de Boulogne. We chartered a *fiacre* to take us there and back. We supped rather copiously. *He* somehow made our coachman drunk, and took upon himself to drive us home. Need I tell you that he upset us in the Avenue de l'Impératrice, and that we had to walk it, and pretty fast too? It was a mercy there were no bones broken.

"Well, as we were walking along, just barely recovering from the shock of the accident, he suddenly took some new whim into his confounded noddle. Nothing would do for him but he must drag us along with him to the great entrance of the Elysée Napoléon (which erst was, and maybe is soon likely to be once more, the Elysée Bourbon), where he had the brazen impudence to claim admittance, as the Emperor, he pretended, had been graciously pleased to offer us the splendid hospitality of that renowned mansion. What further happened here, neither I nor either of my friends can tell. Our recollections from this period till next morning are doubtful and indistinct. All we can state for certain is, that yesterday morning we awoke, the three of us, in a most wretched state, in a strange, nasty place. We learn soon after from a gentleman in a cocked hat, who came to visit us on business, that the imperial hospitality which we had claimed last night had indeed been extended to us—only in the *violon*, instead of the Elysée. Our phantom guest was gone: he would alway, somehow sneak away in the morning, when there was nothing left for him to drink—the guzzling villain!

"The gentleman in the cocked-hat pressingly invited us to pay a visit to the Commissaire du Quartier. That formidable functionary received us with the customary French-polished veneer of urbanity which, as a rule, constitutes the *suaviter in modo* of the higher class of Gallic officials. He read us a severe lecture, however, upon the alleged impropriety of our conduct; and when I ventured to protest that it was not to us the blame ought to be imputed, but to the *quatrième*, he mistook my meaning, and, ere I could explain myself, he cut me short with a polite remark that the French used the cardinal instead of the ordinal numbers in stating the days of the month, with the exception of the first, and that he had had too much trouble with our countrymen (he took us for Yankees!) on the 4th of July, to be disposed to look with an over-lenient eye upon the vagaries we had chosen to commit on the 4th of September, which he supposed was another great national day with us. He would, however, let us off this time with a simple reprimand, upon payment of one hundred francs, compensation for damage done to the coach—drunken cabby having turned up, of course, to testify against us. Well, we paid the money, and handed the worthy magistrate twenty francs besides, for the benefit of the poor, by way of acknowledgment for the imperial hospitality we had enjoyed. We were then allowed to depart in peace.

"Now, you'll hardly believe it, I dare say, but it is the truth notwithstanding, that we three, who have been fast friends for years, actually began to quarrel among ourselves now, mutually imputing to one another the blame of all our misadventures and misfortunes since our arrival in Paris, while yet we clearly knew and felt, each and every of us, that it was all the doings of that phantom fourth.

"One thing, however, we all agreed to do—to leave Paris by the first train.

"To fortify ourselves for the coming journey, we went to indulge in the luxury of a farewell breakfast at Désiré Beaurain's. Of course we emptied a few bottles to our reconciliation. I do not exactly remember how many, but this I *do* remember, that our irrepressible incubus walked in again, and took his place in the midst of us rather sooner even than he had been wont to do; and he never left us from that time to the moment of our landing at Dover harbor, when he took his, I hope and trust final, departure with a ghastly grin.

"I dare say you must have thought us a most noisy and obstreperous lot: well, with my hand on my heart, I can assure you, on my conscience, that a quieter and milder set of fellows than us three you are not likely to find on this or the other side the Channel. But for that mysterious phantom fourth—"

Here the whistle sounded, and the guard came up to us with a hurried, "Now then, gents, take your seats, please; train is off in half a minnit!"

"What can have become of Topp and Jack Hobson?" muttered my new friend, looking around him with eager scrutiny. "I should not wonder if they were still refreshing." And he started off in the direction of the refreshment-room.

I took my seat. Immediately after the train whirled off. I cannot say whether the three were left behind; all I know is that I did not see them get out at London Bridge.

Remembering, however, that the appalling secret of the supernatural visitation which had thus harassed my three fellow-travellers had been confided to me under the impression that I might be likely to find a solution of the mystery, I have ever since deeply pondered thereon.

Shallow thinkers, and sneerers uncharitably given, may, from a consideration of the times, places, and circumstances at and under which the abnormal phenomena here recited were stated to have been observed, be led to attribute them simply to the promptings and imaginings of brains overheated by excessive indulgence in spirituous liquors. But I, striving to be mindful always of the great scriptural injunction to judge not, lest we be judged, and opportunely remembering my friend O'Kweene's learned dissertation above alluded to, feel disposed to pronounce the apparition of the phantom of the fourth man, and all the sayings, doings, and demeanings of the same, to have been simply so many visible and palpable outward manifestations of the inner consciousness of the souls of the three, and more notably of that of the elderly senior of the party, in a succession of vino-alcoholic trances.

My friend O'Kweene is, of course, welcome to such credit as may attach to this attempted solution of mine.

Sir Dominick's Bargain:
A Legend of Dunoran

In the early autumn of the year 1838, business called me to the south of Ireland. The weather was delightful, the scenery and people were new to me, and sending my luggage on by the mail-coach route in charge of a servant, I hired a serviceable nag at a posting-house, and, full of the curiosity of an explorer, I commenced a leisurely journey of five-and-twenty miles on horseback, by sequestered cross-roads, to my place of destination. By bog and hill, by plain and ruined castle, and many a winding stream, my picturesque road led me.

I had started late, and having made little more than half my journey, I was thinking of making a short halt at the next convenient place, and letting my horse have a rest and a feed, and making some provision also for the comforts of his rider.

It was about four o'clock when the road, ascending a gradual steep, found a passage through a rocky gorge between the abrupt termination of a range of mountain to my left and a rocky hill, that rose dark and sudden at my right. Below me lay a little thatched village, under a long line of gigantic beech-trees, through the boughs of which the lowly chimneys sent up their thin turf-smoke. To my left, stretched away for miles, ascending the mountain range I have mentioned, a wild park, through whose sward and ferns the rock broke, time-worn and lichen-stained. This park was studded with straggling wood, which thickened to something like a forest, behind and beyond the little village I was approaching, clothing the irregular ascent of the hillsides with beautiful, and in some places discoloured foliage.

As you descend, the road winds slightly, with the grey park-wall, built of loose stone, and mantled here and there with ivy, at its left, and crosses a shallow ford; and as I approached the village, through breaks in the woodlands, I caught glimpses of the long front of an old ruined house, placed among the trees, about half-way up the picturesque mountain-side.

The solitude and melancholy of this ruin piqued my curiosity, and when I had reached the rude thatched public-house, with the sign of St. Columbkill, with robes, mitre, and crozier displayed over its lintel, having seen to my horse and made a good meal myself on a rasher and eggs, I began to think again of the wooded park and the ruinous house, and resolved on a ramble of half an hour among its sylvan solitudes.

The name of the place, I found, was Dunoran; and beside the gate a stile admitted to the grounds, through which, with a pensive enjoyment, I began to saunter towards the dilapidated mansion.

A long grass-grown road, with many turns and windings, led up to the old house, under the shadow of the wood.

The road, as it approached the house skirted the edge of a precipitous glen, clothed with hazel, dwarf-oak, and thorn, and the silent house stood with its wide-open hall-door facing this dark ravine, the further edge of which was crowned with towering forest; and great trees stood about the house and its deserted courtyard and stables.

I walked in and looked about me, through passages overgrown with nettles and weeds; from room to room with ceilings rotted, and here and there a great beam dark and worn, with tendrils of ivy trailing over it. The tall walls with rotten plaster were stained and mouldy, and in some rooms the remains of decayed wainscoting crazily swung to and fro. The almost sashless windows were darkened also with ivy, and about the tall chimneys the jackdaws were wheeling, while from the huge trees that overhung the glen in sombre masses at the other side, the rooks kept up a ceaseless cawing.

As I walked through these melancholy passages—peeping only into some of the rooms, for the flooring was quite gone in the middle, and bowed down toward the centre, and the house was very nearly un-roofed, a state of things which made the exploration a little critical—I began to wonder why so grand a house, in the midst of scenery so picturesque, had been permitted to go to decay; I dreamed of the hospitalities of which it had long ago been the rallying place, and I thought what a scene of Redgauntlet revelries it might disclose at midnight.

The great staircase was of oak, which had stood the weather wonderfully, and I sat down upon its steps, musing vaguely on the transitoriness of all things under the sun.

Except for the hoarse and distant clamour of the rooks, hardly audible where I sat, no sound broke the profound stillness of the spot. Such a sense of solitude I have seldom experienced before. The air was stirless, there was not even the rustle of a withered leaf along the passage. It was oppressive. The tall trees that stood close about the building darkened it, and added something of awe to the melancholy of the scene.

In this mood I heard, with an unpleasant surprise, close to me, a voice that was drawling, and, I fancied, sneering, repeat the words: "Food for worms, dead and rotten; God over all."

There was a small window in the wall, here very thick, which had been built up, and in the dark recess of this, deep in the shadow, I now saw a sharp-featured man, sitting with his feet dangling. His keen eyes were fixed on me, and he was smiling cynically, and before I had well recovered my surprise, he repeated the distich:

"If death was a thing that money could buy,
The rich they would live, and the poor they would die.

"It was a grand house in its day, sir," he continued, "Dunoran House, and the Sarsfields. Sir Dominick Sarsfield was the last of the old stock. He lost his life not six foot away from where you are sitting."

As he thus spoke he let himself down, with a little jump, on to the ground.

He was a dark-faced, sharp-featured, little hunchback, and had a walking-stick in his hand, with the end of which he pointed to a rusty stain in the plaster of the wall.

"Do you mind that mark, sir?" he asked.

"Yes," I said, standing up, and looking at it, with a curious anticipation of something worth hearing.

"That's about seven or eight feet from the ground, sir, and you'll not guess what it is."

"I dare say not," said I, "unless it is a stain from the weather."

"'Tis nothing so lucky, sir," he answered, with the same cynical smile and a wag of his head, still pointing at the mark with his stick. "That's a splash of brains and blood. It's there this hundred years; and it will never leave it while the wall stands."

"He was murdered, then?"

"Worse than that, sir," he answered.

"He killed himself, perhaps?"

"Worse than that, itself, this cross between us and harm! I'm oulder than I look, sir; you wouldn't guess my years."

He became silent, and looked at me, evidently inviting a guess.

"Well, I should guess you to be about five-and-fifty."

He laughed, and took a pinch of snuff, and said:

"I'm that, your honour, and something to the back of it. I was seventy last Candlemas. You would not a' thought that, to look at me."

"Upon my word I should not; I can hardly believe it even now. Still, you don't remember Sir Dominick Sarsfield's death?" I said, glancing up at the ominous stain on the wall.

"No, sir, that was a long while before I was born. But my grandfather was butler here long ago, and many a time I heard tell how Sir Dominick came by his death. There was no masther in the great house ever sinst that happened. But there was two sarvants in care of it, and my aunt was one o' them; and she kep' me here wid her till I was nine year old, and she was lavin' the place to go to Dublin; and from that time it was let to go down. The wind sthript the roof, and the rain rotted the timber, and little by little, in sixty years' time, it kem to what you see. But I have a likin' for it still, for the sake of ould times; and I never come this way but I take a look in. I don't think it's many more times I'll be turnin' to see the ould place, for I'll be undher the sod myself before long."

"You'll outlive younger people," I said.

And, quitting that trite subject, I ran on:

"I don't wonder that you like this old place; it is a beautiful spot, such noble trees."

"I wish ye seen the glin when the nuts is ripe; they're the sweetest nuts in all Ireland, I think," he rejoined, with a practical sense of the picturesque. "You'd fill your pockets while you'd be lookin' about you."

"These are very fine old woods," I remarked. "I have not seen any in Ireland I thought so beautiful."

"Eiah! your honour, the woods about here is nothing to what they wor. Al the mountains along here was wood when my father was a gossoon, and Murroa Wood was the grandest of them all. All oak mostly, and all cut down as bare as the road. Not one left here that's fit to compare with them. Which way did your honour come hither—from Limerick?"

"No. Killaloe."

"Well, then, you passed the ground where Murroa Wood was in former times. You kem undher Lisnavourra, the steep knob of a hill about a mile above the village here. 'Twas near that Murroa Wood was, and 'twas there Sir Dominick Sarsfield first met the devil, the Lord between us and harm, and a bad meeting it was for him and his."

I had become interested in the adventure which had occurred in the very scenery which had so greatly attracted me, and my new acquaintance, the little hunchback, was easily entreated to tell me the story, and spoke thus, so soon as we had each resumed his seat:

"It was a fine estate when Sir Dominick came into it; and grand doings there was entirely, feasting and fiddling, free quarters for all the pipers in the counthry round, and a welcome for everyone that liked to come. There was wine, by the hogshead, for the quality; and potteen enough to set a town a-fire, and beer and cidher enough to float a navy, for the boys and girls, and the likes o' me. It was kep' up the best part of a month, till the weather broke, and the rain spoilt the sod for the moneen jigs, and the fair of Allybally Killudeen comin' on they wor obliged to give over their divarsion, and attind to the pigs.

But Sir Dominick was only beginnin' when they wor lavin' off. There was no way of gettin' rid of his money and estates he did not try—what with drinkin', dicin', racin', cards, and all soarts, it was not many years before the estates wor in debt, and Sir Dominick a distressed man. He showed a bold front to the world as long as he could; and then he sould off his dogs, and most of his horses, and gev out he was going to thravel in France, and the like; and so off with him for awhile; and no one in these parts heard tale or tidings of him for two or three years. Till at last quite unexpected, one night there comes a rapping at the big kitchen window. It was past ten o'clock, and old Connor Hanlon, the butler, my grandfather, was sittin' by the fire alone, warming his shins over it. There was keen east wind blowing along the mountains that night, and whistling cowld enough, through the tops of the trees, and soundin' lonesome through the long chimneys.

(And the story-teller glanced up at the nearest stack visible from his seat.)

So he wasn't quite sure of the knockin' at the window, and up he gets, and sees his master's face.

My grandfather was glad to see him safe, for it was a long time since there was any news of him; but he was sorry, too, for it was a changed place and only himself and old Juggy Broadrick in charge of the house, and a man in the stables, and it was a poor thing to see him comin' back to his own like that.

He shook Con by the hand, and says he:

"I came here to say a word to you. I left my horse with Dick in the stable; I may want him again before morning, or I may never want him."

And with that he turns into the big kitchen, and draws a stool, and sits down to take an air of the fire.

"Sit down, Connor, opposite me, and listen to what I tell you, and don't be afeard to say what you think."

He spoke all the time lookin' into the fire, with his hands stretched over it, and a tired man he looked.

"An' why should I be afeard, Masther Dominick?" says my grandfather. "Yourself was a good masther to me, and so was your father, rest his sould, before you, and I'll say the truth, and dar' the devil, and more than that, for any Sarsfield of Dunoran, much less yourself, and a good right I'd have."

"It's all over with me, Con," says Sir Dominick.

"Heaven forbid!" says my grandfather.

"'Tis past praying for," says Sir Dominick. "The last guinea's gone; the ould place will follow it. It must be sold, and I'm come here, I don't know why, like a ghost to have a last look round me, and go off in the dark again."

And with that he tould him to be sure, in case he should hear of his death, to give the oak box, in the closet off his room, to his cousin, Pat Sarsfield, in Dublin, and the sword and pistols his grandfather carried in Aughrim, and two or three thrifling things of the kind.

And says he, "Con, they say if the divil gives you money overnight, you'll find nothing but a bagful of pebbles, and chips, and nutshells, in the morning. If I thought he played fair, I'm in the humour to make a bargain with him tonight."

"Lord forbid!" says my grandfather, standing up, with a start and crossing himself.

"They say the country's full of men, listin' sogers for the King o' France. If I light on one o' them, I'll not refuse his offer. How contrary things goes! How long is it since me an Captain Waller fought the jewel at New Castle?"

"Six years, Masther Dominick, and ye broke his thigh with the bullet the first shot."

"I did, Con," says he, "and I wish, instead, he had shot me through the heart. Have you any whisky?"

My grandfather took it out of the buffet, and the masther pours out some into a bowl, and drank it off.

"I'll go out and have a look at my horse," says he, standing up. There was sort of a stare in his eyes, as he pulled his riding-cloak about him, as if there was something bad in his thoughts.

"Sure, I won't be a minute running out myself to the stable, and looking after the horse for you myself," says my grandfather.

"I'm not goin' to the stable," says Sir Dominick; "I may as well tell you, for I see you found it out already—I'm goin' across the deer-park;

if I come back you'll see me in an hour's time. But, anyhow, you'd better not follow me, for if you do I'll shoot you, and that 'id be a bad ending to our friendship."

And with that he walks down this passage here, and turns the key in the side door at that end of it, and out wid him on the sod into the moonlight and the cowld wind; and my grandfather seen him walkin' hard towards the park-wall, and then he comes in and closes the door with a heavy heart.

Sir Dominick stopped to think when he got to the middle of the deer-park, for he had not made up his mind, when he left the house, and the whisky did not clear his head, only it gev him courage.

He did not feel the cowld wind now, nor fear death, nor think much of anything but the shame and fall of the old family.

And he made up his mind, if no better thought came to him between that and there, so soon as he came to Murroa Wood, he'd hang himself from one of the oak branches with his cravat.

It was a bright moonlight night, there was just a bit of a cloud driving across the moon now and then, but, only for that, as light a'most as day.

Down he goes, right for the wood of Murroa. It seemed to him every step he took was as long as three, and it was no time till he was among the big oak-trees with their roots spreading from one to another, and their branches stretching overhead like the timbers of a naked roof, and the moon shining down through them, and casting their shadows thick and twist abroad on the ground as black as my shoe.

He was sobering a bit by this time, and he slacked his pace, and he thought 'twould be better to list in the French king's army, and thry what that might do for him, for he knew a man might take his own life anytime, but it would puzzle him to take it back again when he liked.

Just as he made up his mind not to make away with himself, what should he hear but a step clinkin' along the dry ground under the trees, and soon he sees a grand gentleman right before him comin' up to meet him.

He was a handsome young man like himself, and he wore a cocked-hat with gold-lace round it, such as officers wears on their coats, and he had on a dress the same as French officers wore in them times.

He stopped opposite Sir Dominick, and he cum to a standstill also.

The two gentlemen took off their hats to one another, and says the stranger:

"I am recruiting, sir," says he, "for my sovereign, and you'll find my money won't turn into pebbles, chips, and nutshells, by tomorrow."

At the same time he pulls out a big purse full of gold.

The minute he set eyes on that gentleman, Sir Dominick had his own opinion of him; and at those words he felt the very hair standing up on his head.

"Don't be afraid," says he, "the money won't burn you. If it proves honest gold, and if it prospers with you, I'm willing to make a bargain. This is the last day of February," says he; "I'll serve you seven years, and at the end of that time you shall serve me, and I'll come for you when the seven years is over, when the clock turns the minute between February and March; and the first of March ye'll come away with me, or never. You'll not find me a bad master, anymore than a bad servant. I love my own; and I command all the pleasures and the glory of the world. The bargain dates from this day, and the lease is out at midnight on the last day I told you; and in the year"—he told him the year, it was easy reckoned, but I forget it—"and if you'd rather wait," he says, "for eight months and twenty eight days, before you sign the writin', you may, if you meet me here. But I can't do a great deal for you in the mean time; and if you don't sign then, all you get from me, up to that time, will vanish away, and you'll be just as you are tonight, and ready to hang yourself on the first tree you meet."

Well, the end of it was, Sir Dominick chose to wait, and he came back to the house with a big bag full of money, as round as your hat a'most.

My grandfather was glad enough, you may be sure, to see the master safe and sound again so soon. Into the kitchen he bangs again, and swings the bag o' money on the table; and he stands up straight, and heaves up his shoulders like a man that has just got shut of a load; and he looks at the bag, and my grandfather looks at him, and from him to it, and back again. Sir Dominick looked as white as a sheet, and says he:

"I don't know, Con, what's in it; it's the heaviest load I ever carried."

He seemed shy of openin' the bag; and he made my grandfather heap up a roaring fire of turf and wood, and then, at last, he opens it, and, sure enough, 'twas stuffed full o' golden guineas, bright and new, as if they were only that minute out o' the Mint.

Sir Dominick made my grandfather sit at his elbow while he counted every guinea in the bag.

When he was done countin', and it wasn't far from daylight when that time came, Sir Dominick made my grandfather swear not to tell a word about it. And a close secret it was for many a day after.

When the eight months and twenty-eight days were pretty near spent and ended, Sir Dominick returned to the house here with a troubled mind, in doubt what was best to be done, and no one alive but my grandfather knew anything about the matter, and he not half what had happened.

As the day drew near, towards the end of October, Sir Dominick grew only more and more troubled in mind.

One time he made up his mind to have no more to say to such things, nor to speak again with the like of them he met with in the wood of Murroa. Then, again, his heart failed him when he thought of his debts, and he not knowing where to turn. Then, only a week before the day, everything began to go wrong with him. One man wrote from London to say that Sir Dominick paid three thousand pounds to the wrong man, and must pay it over again; another demanded a debt he never heard of before; and another, in Dublin, denied the payment of a thundherin' big bill, and Sir Dominick could nowhere find the receipt, and so on, wid fifty other things as bad.

Well, by the time the night of the 28th of October came round, he was a'most ready to lose his senses with all the demands that was risin' up again him on all sides, and nothing to meet them but the help of the one dhreadful friend he had to depind on at night in the oak-wood down there below.

So there was nothing for it but to go through with the business that was begun already, and about the same hour as he went last, he takes off the little crucifix he wore round his neck, for he was a Catholic, and his gospel, and his bit o' the thrue cross that he had in a locket, for since he took the money from the Evil One he was growin' frightful in himself, and got all he could to guard him from the power of the devil. But tonight, for his life, he daren't take them with him. So he gives them into my grandfather's hands without a word, only he looked as white as a sheet o' paper; and he takes his hat and sword, and telling my grandfather to watch for him, away he goes, to try what would come of it.

It was a fine still night, and the moon—not so bright, though, now as the first time—was shinin' over heath and rock, and down on the lonesome oak-wood below him.

His heart beat thick as he drew near it. There was not a sound, not even the distant bark of a dog from the village behind him. There was not a lonesomer spot in the country round, and if it wasn't for his debts and losses that was drivin' him on half mad, in spite of his fears for his soul and his hopes of paradise, and all his good angel was whisperin' in his ear, he would a' turned back, and sent for his clargy, and made his confession and his penance, and changed his ways, and led a good life, for he was frightened enough to have done a great dale.

Softer and slower he stept as he got, once more, in undher the big branches of the oak-threes; and when he got in a bit, near where he met with the bad spirit before, he stopped and looked round him, and felt himself, every bit, turning as cowld as a dead man, and you may be sure he did not feel much betther when he seen the same man steppin' from behind the big tree that was touchin' his elbow a'most.

"You found the money good," says he, "but it was not enough. No matter, you shall have enough and to spare. I'll see after your luck, and I'll give you a hint whenever it can serve you; and anytime you want to see me you have only to come down here, and call my face to mind, and wish me present. You shan't owe a shilling by the end of the year, and you shall never miss the right card, the best throw, and the winning horse. Are you willing?"

The young gentleman's voice almost stuck in his throat, and his hair was rising on his head, but he did get out a word or two to signify that he consented; and with that the Evil One handed him a needle, and bid him give him three drops of blood from his arm; and he took them in the cup of an acorn, and gave him a pen, and bid him write some words that he repeated, and that Sir Dominick did not understand, on two thin slips of parchment. He took one himself and the other he sunk in Sir Dominick's arm at the place where he drew the blood, and he closed the flesh over it. And that's as true as you're sittin' there!

Well, Sir Dominick went home. He was a frightened man, and well he might be. But in a little time he began to grow aisier in his mind. Anyhow, he got out of debt very quick, and money came tumbling in to make him richer, and everything he took in hand prospered, and he never made a wager, or played a game, but he won; and for all that, there was not a poor man on the estate that was not happier than Sir Dominick.

So he took again to his old ways; for, when the money came back, all came back, and there were hounds and horses, and wine galore, and no end of company, and grand doin's, and divarsion, up here at the great house. And some said Sir Dominick was thinkin' of gettin' married; and more said he wasn't. But, anyhow, there was somethin' troublin' him more than common, and so one night, unknownst to all, away he goes to the lonesome oak-wood. It was something, maybe, my grandfather thought was troublin' him about a beautiful young lady he was jealous of, and mad in love with her. But that was only guess.

Well, when Sir Dominick got into the wood this time, he grew more in dread than ever; and he was on the point of turnin' and lavin' the place, when who should he see, close beside him, but my gentleman, seated on a big stone undher one of the trees. In place of looking the fine young gentleman in goold lace and grand clothes he appeared before, he was now in rags, he looked twice the size he had been, and his face smutted with soot, and he had a murtherin' big steel hammer, as heavy as a halfhundred, with a handle a yard long, across his knees. It was so dark under the tree, he did not see him quite clear for sometime.

He stood up, and he looked awful tall entirely. And what passed between them in that discourse my grandfather never heered. But Sir Dominick was as black as night afterwards, and hadn't a laugh for anything nor a word a'most for anyone, and he only grew worse and worse, and darker and darker. And now this thing, whatever it was, used to come to him of its own accord, whether he wanted it or no; sometimes in one shape, and sometimes in another, in lonesome places, and sometimes at his side by night when he'd be ridin' home alone, until at last he lost heart altogether and sent for the priest.

The priest was with him a long time, and when he heered the whole story, he rode off all the way for the bishop, and the bishop came here to the great house next day, and he gev Sir Dominick a good advice. He toult him he must give over dicin', and swearin', and drinkin', and all bad company, and live a vartuous steady life until the seven years bargain was out, and if the divil didn't come for him the minute afther the stroke of twelve the first morning of the month of March, he was safe out of the bargain. There was not more than eight or ten months to run now before the seven years wor out, and he lived all the time according to the bishop's advice, as strict as if he was "in retreat."

Well, you may guess he felt quare enough when the mornin' of the 28th of February came.

The priest came up by appointment, and Sir Dominick and his raverence wor together in the room you see there, and kep' up their prayers together till the clock struck twelve, and a good hour after, and not a sign of a disturbance, nor nothing came near them, and the priest slep' that night in the house in the room next Sir Dominick's, and all went over as comfortable as could be, and they shook hands and kissed like two comrades after winning a battle.

So, now, Sir Dominick thought he might as well have a pleasant evening, after all his fastin' and praying; and he sent round to half a dozen of the neighbouring gentlemen to come and dine with him, and his raverence stayed and dined also, and a roarin' bowl o' punch they had, and no end o' wine, and the swearin' and dice, and cards and guineas changing hands, and songs and stories, that wouldn't do anyone good to hear, and the priest slipped away, when he seen the turn things was takin', and it was not far from the stroke of twelve when Sir Dominick, sitting at the head of his table, swears, "this is the best first of March I ever sat down with my friends."

"It ain't the first o' March," says Mr. Hiffernan of Ballyvoreen. He was a scholard, and always kep' an almanack.

"What is it, then?" says Sir Dominick, startin' up, and dhroppin' the ladle into the bowl, and starin' at him as if he had two heads.

"'Tis the twenty-ninth of February, leap year," says he. And just as they were talkin', the clock strikes twelve; and my grandfather, who was half asleep in a chair by the fire in the hall, openin' his eyes, sees a short square fellow with a cloak on, and long black hair bushin' out from under his hat, standin' just there where you see the bit o' light shinin' again' the wall.

(My hunchbacked friend pointed with his stick to a little patch of red sunset light that relieved the deepening shadow of the passage.)

"Tell your master," says he, in an awful voice, like the growl of a baist, "that I'm here by appointment, and expect him downstairs this minute."

Up goes my grandfather, by these very steps you are sittin' on.

"Tell him I can't come down yet," says Sir Dominick, and he turns to the company in the room, and says he with a cold sweat shinin' on his face, "for God's sake, gentlemen, will any of you jump from the window and bring the priest here?" One looked at another and no one knew what to make of it, and in the mean time, up comes my grandfather again, and says he, tremblin', "He says, sir, unless you go down to him, he'll come up to you."

"I don't understand this, gentlemen, I'll see what it means," says Sir Dominick, trying to put a face on it, and walkin' out o' the room like a man through the press-room, with the hangman waitin' for him outside. Down the stairs he comes, and two or three of the gentlemen peeping over the banisters, to see. My grandfather was walking six or eight steps behind him, and he seen the stranger take a stride out to meet Sir Dominick, and catch him up in his arms, and whirl his head against the wall, and wi' that the hall-doore flies open, and out goes the candles, and the turf and wood-ashes flyin' with the wind out o' the hall-fire, ran in a drift o' sparks along the floore by his feet.

Down runs the gintlemen. Bang goes the hall-doore. Some comes runnin' up, and more runnin' down, with lights. It was all over with Sir Dominick. They lifted up the corpse, and put its shoulders again' the wall; but there was not a gasp left in him. He was cowld and stiffenin' already.

Pat Donovan was comin' up to the great house late that night and after he passed the little brook, that the carriage track up to the house crosses, and about fifty steps to this side of it, his dog, that was by his side, makes a sudden wheel, and springs over the wall, and sets up a yowlin' inside you'd hear a mile away; and that minute two men passed him by in silence, goin' down from the house, one of them short and square, and the other like Sir Dominick in shape, but there was little light under the trees where he was, and they looked only like shadows; and as they passed him by he could not hear the sound of their feet and he drew back to the wall frightened; and when he got up to the great house, he found all in confusion, and the master's body, with the head smashed to pieces, lying just on *that spot*.

The narrator stood up and indicated with the point of his stick the exact site of the body, and, as I looked, the shadow deepened, the red stain of sunlight vanished from the wall, and the sun had gone down behind the distant hill of New Castle, leaving the haunted scene in the deep grey of darkening twilight.

So I and the story-teller parted, not without good wishes on both sides, and a little "tip," which seemed not unwelcome, from me.

It was dusk and the moon up by the time I reached the village, remounted my nag, and looked my last on the scene of the terrible legend of Dunoran.

The Spectre Lovers

There lived some fifteen years since in a small and ruinous house, little better than a hovel, an old woman who was reported to have considerably exceeded her eightieth year, and who rejoiced in the name of Alice, or popularly, Ally Moran. Her society was not much courted, for she was neither rich, nor, as the reader may suppose, beautiful. In addition to a lean cur and a cat she had one human companion, her grandson, Peter Brien, whom, with laudable good nature, she had supported from the period of his orphanage down to that of my story, which finds him in his twentieth year. Peter was a good-natured slob of a fellow, much more addicted to wrestling, dancing, and love-making, than to hard work, and fonder of whiskey-punch than good advice. His grandmother had a high opinion of his accomplishments, which indeed was but natural, and also of his genius, for Peter had of late years begun to apply his mind to politics; and as it was plain that he had a mortal hatred of honest labour, his grandmother predicted, like a true fortuneteller, that he was born to marry an heiress, and Peter himself (who had no mind to forego his freedom even on such terms) that he was destined to find a pot of gold. Upon one point both agreed, that being unfitted by the peculiar bias of his genius for work, he was to acquire the immense fortune to which his merits entitled him by means of a pure run of good luck. This solution of Peter's future had the double effect of reconciling both himself and his grandmother to his idle courses, and also of maintaining that even flow of hilarious spirits which made him everywhere welcome, and which was in truth the natural result of his consciousness of approaching affluence.

It happened one night that Peter had enjoyed himself to a very late hour with two or three choice spirits near Palmerstown. They had talked politics and love, sung songs, and told stories, and, above all, had swallowed, in the chastened disguise of punch, at least a pint of good whiskey, every man.

It was considerably past one o'clock when Peter bid his companions goodbye, with a sigh and a hiccough, and lighting his pipe set forth on his solitary homeward way.

The bridge of Chapelizod was pretty nearly the midway point of his night march, and from one cause or another his progress was rather slow, and it was past two o'clock by the time he found himself leaning over its old battlements, and looking up the river, over whose winding current and wooded banks the soft moonlight was falling.

The cold breeze that blew lightly down the stream was grateful to him. It cooled his throbbing head, and he drank it in at his hot lips. The scene, too, had, without his being well sensible of it, a secret fascination. The village was sunk in the profoundest slumber, not a mortal stirring, not a sound afloat, a soft haze covered it all, and the fairy moonlight hovered over the entire landscape.

In a state between rumination and rapture, Peter continued to lean over the battlements of the old bridge, and as he did so he saw, or fancied he saw, emerging one after another along the river bank in the little gardens and enclosures in the rear of the street of Chapelizod, the queerest little white-washed huts and cabins he had ever seen there before. They had not been there that evening when he passed the bridge on the way to his merry tryst. But the most remarkable thing about it was the odd way in which these quaint little cabins showed themselves. First he saw one or two of them just with the corner of his eye, and when he looked full at them, strange to say, they faded away and disappeared. Then another and another came in view, but all in the same coy way, just appearing and gone again before he could well fix his gaze upon them; in a little while, however, they began to bear a fuller gaze, and he found, as it seemed to himself, that he was able by an effort of attention to fix the vision for a longer and a longer time, and when they waxed faint and nearly vanished, he had the power of recalling them into light and substance, until at last their vacillating indistinctness became less and less, and they assumed a permanent place in the moonlit landscape.

"Be the hokey," said Peter, lost in amazement, and dropping his pipe into the river unconsciously, "them is the quarist bits iv mud cabins I ever seen, growing up like musharoons in the dew of an evening, and poppin' up here and down again there, and up again in another place, like so many white rabbits in a warren; and there they stand at last as firm and fast as if they were there from the Deluge; bedad it's enough to make a man a'most believe in the fairies."

This latter was a large concession from Peter, who was a bit of a free-thinker, and spoke contemptuously in his ordinary conversation of that class of agencies.

Having treated himself to a long last stare at these mysterious fabrics, Peter prepared to pursue his homeward way; having crossed the bridge and passed the mill, he arrived at the corner of the main-street of the little town, and casting a careless look up the Dublin road, his eye was arrested by a most unexpected spectacle.

This was no other than a column of foot soldiers, marching with perfect regularity towards the village, and headed by an officer on horseback. They were at the far side of the turnpike, which was closed; but much to his perplexity he perceived that they marched on through it without appearing to sustain the least check from that barrier.

On they came at a slow march; and what was most singular in the matter was, that they were drawing several cannons along with them; some held ropes, others spoked the wheels, and others again marched in front of the guns and behind them, with muskets shouldered, giving a stately character of parade and regularity to this, as it seemed to Peter, most unmilitary procedure.

It was owing either to some temporary defect in Peter's vision, or to some illusion attendant upon mist and moonlight, or perhaps to someother cause, that the whole procession had a certain waving and vapoury character which perplexed and tasked his eyes not a little. It was like the pictured pageant of a phantasmagoria reflected upon smoke. It was as if every breath disturbed it; sometimes it was blurred, sometimes obliterated; now here, now there. Sometimes, while the upper part was quite distinct, the legs of the column would nearly fade away or vanish outright, and then again they would come out into clear relief, marching on with measured tread, while the cocked hats and shoulders grew, as it were, transparent, and all but disappeared.

Notwithstanding these strange optical fluctuations, however, the column continued steadily to advance. Peter crossed the street from the corner near the old bridge, running on tip-toe, and with his body stooped to avoid observation, and took up a position upon the raised footpath in the shadow of the houses, where, as the soldiers kept the middle of the road, he calculated that he might, himself undetected, see them distinctly enough as they passed.

"What the div—, what on airth," he muttered, checking the irreligious exclamation with which he was about to start, for certain queer misgivings were hovering about his heart, notwithstanding the factitious courage of the whiskey bottle. "What on airth is the manin' of all this? is it the French that's landed at last to give us a hand and help us in airnest to this blessed repale? If it is not them, I simply ask who the div—, I mane who on airth are they, for such sogers as them I never seen before in my born days?"

By this time the foremost of them were quite near, and truth to say they were the queerest soldiers he had ever seen in the course of his life. They wore long gaiters and leather breeches, three-cornered hats, bound with silver lace, long blue coats, with scarlet facings and linings, which latter were shewn by a fastening which held together the two opposite corners of the skirt behind; and in front the breasts were in like manner connected at a single point, where and below which they sloped back, disclosing a long-flapped waistcoat of snowy whiteness; they had very large, long cross-belts, and wore enormous pouches of white leather hung extraordinarily low, and on each of which a little silver star was glittering. But what struck him as most grotesque and outlandish in their costume was their extraordinary display of shirt-frill in front, and of ruffle about their wrists, and the strange manner in which their hair was frizzled out and powdered under their hats, and clubbed up into great rolls behind. But one of the party was mounted. He rode a tall white horse, with high action and arching neck; he had a snow-white feather in his three-cornered hat, and his coat was shimmering all over with a profusion of silver lace. From these circumstances Peter concluded that he must be the commander of the detachment, and examined him as he passed attentively. He was a slight, tall man, whose legs did not half fill his leather breeches, and he appeared to be at the wrong side of sixty. He had a shrunken, weather-beaten, mulberry-coloured face, carried a large black patch over one eye, and turned neither to the right nor to the left, but rode on at the head of his men, with a grim, military inflexibility.

The countenances of these soldiers, officers as well as men, seemed all full of trouble, and, so to speak, scared and wild. He watched in vain for a single contented or comely face. They had, one and all, a melancholy and hang-dog look; and as they passed by, Peter fancied that the air grew cold and thrilling.

He had seated himself upon a stone bench, from which, staring with all his might, he gazed upon the grotesque and noiseless procession as it filed by him. Noiseless it was; he could neither hear the jingle of accoutrements, the tread of feet, nor the rumble of the wheels; and when the old colonel turned his horse a little, and made as though he were giving the word of command, and a trumpeter, with a swollen blue nose and white feather fringe round his hat, who was walking beside him, turned about and put his bugle to his lips, still Peter heard nothing, although it was plain the sound had reached the soldiers, for they instantly changed their front to three abreast.

"Botheration!" muttered Peter, "is it deaf I'm growing?"

But that could not be, for he heard the sighing of the breeze and the rush of the neighbouring Liffey plain enough.

"Well," said he, in the same cautious key, "by the piper, this bangs Banagher fairly! It's either the Frinch army that's in it, come to take the town iv Chapelizod by surprise, an' makin' no noise for feard iv wakenin' the inhabitants; or else it's—it's—what it's—somethin' else. But, tundher-an-ouns, what's gone wid Fitzpatrick's shop across the way?"

The brown, dingy stone building at the opposite side of the street looked newer and cleaner than he had been used to see it; the front door of it stood open, and a sentry, in the same grotesque uniform, with shouldered musket, was pacing noiselessly to and fro before it. At the angle of this building, in like manner, a wide gate (of which Peter had no recollection whatever) stood open, before which, also, a similar sentry was gliding, and into this gateway the whole column gradually passed, and Peter finally lost sight of it.

"I'm not asleep; I'm not dhramin'," said he, rubbing his eyes, and stamping slightly on the pavement, to assure himself that he was wide awake. "It is a quare business, whatever it is; an' it's not alone that, but everything about town looks strange to me. There's Tresham's house new painted, bedad, an' them flowers in the windies! An' Delany's house, too, that had not a whole pane of glass in it this morning, and scarce a slate on the roof of it! It is not possible it's what it's dhrunk I am. Sure there's the big tree, and not a leaf of it changed since I passed, and the stars overhead, all right. I don't think it is in my eyes it is."

And so looking about him, and every moment finding or fancying new food for wonder, he walked along the pavement, intending, without further delay, to make his way home.

But his adventures for the night were not concluded. He had nearly reached the angle of the short land that leads up to the church, when for the first time he perceived that an officer, in the uniform he had just seen, was walking before, only a few yards in advance of him.

The officer was walking along at an easy, swinging gait, and carried his sword under his arm, and was looking down on the pavement with an air of reverie.

In the very fact that he seemed unconscious of Peter's presence, and disposed to keep his reflections to himself, there was something reassuring. Besides, the reader must please to remember that our hero had a quantum sufficit of good punch before his adventure commenced, and was thus fortified against those qualms and terrors under which, in a more reasonable state of mind, he might not impossibly have sunk.

The idea of the French invasion revived in full power in Peter's fuddled imagination, as he pursued the nonchalant swagger of the officer.

"Be the powers iv Moll Kelly, I'll ax him what it is," said Peter, with a sudden accession of rashness. "He may tell me or not, as he plases, but he can't be offinded, anyhow."

With this reflection having inspired himself, Peter cleared his voice and began—

"Captain!" said he, "I ax your pardon, captain, an' maybe you'd be so condescindin' to my ignorance as to tell me, if it's plasin' to yer honour, whether your honour is not a Frinchman, if it's plasin' to you."

This he asked, not thinking that, had it been as he suspected, not one word of his question in all probability would have been intelligible to the person he addressed. He was, however, understood, for the officer answered him in English, at the same time slackening his pace and moving a little to the side of the pathway, as if to invite his interrogator to take his place beside him.

"No; I am an Irishman," he answered.

"I humbly thank your honour," said Peter, drawing nearer—for the affability and the nativity of the officer encouraged him—"but maybe your honour is in the *sarvice* of the King of France?"

"I serve the same King as you do," he answered, with a sorrowful significance which Peter did not comprehend at the time; and, interrogating in turn, he asked, "But what calls you forth at this hour of the day?"

"The *day*, your honour!—the night, you mane."

"It was always our way to turn night into day, and we keep to it still," remarked the soldier. "But, no matter, come up here to my house; I have a job for you, if you wish to earn some money easily. I live here."

As he said this, he beckoned authoritatively to Peter, who followed almost mechanically at his heels, and they turned up a little lane near the old Roman Catholic chapel, at the end of which stood, in Peter's time, the ruins of a tall, stone-built house.

Like everything else in the town, it had suffered a metamorphosis. The stained and ragged walls were now erect, perfect, and covered with pebble-dash; window-panes glittered coldly in every window; the green hall-door had a bright brass knocker on it. Peter did not know whether to believe his previous or his present impressions; seeing is believing, and Peter could not dispute the reality of the scene. All the records of his memory seemed but the images of a tipsy dream. In a trance of astonishment and perplexity, therefore, he submitted himself to the chances of his adventure.

The door opened, the officer beckoned with a melancholy air of authority to Peter, and entered. Our hero followed him into a sort of hall, which was very dark, but he was guided by the steps of the soldier, and, in silence, they ascended the stairs. The moonlight, which shone in at the lobbies, showed an old, dark wainscoting, and a heavy, oak banister. They passed by closed doors at different landing-places, but all was dark and silent as, indeed, became that late hour of the night.

Now they ascended to the topmost floor. The captain paused for a minute at the nearest door, and, with a heavy groan, pushing it open, entered the room. Peter remained at the threshold. A slight female form in a sort of loose, white robe, and with a great deal of dark hair hanging loosely about her, was standing in the middle of the floor, with her back towards them.

The soldier stopped short before he reached her, and said, in a voice of great anguish, "Still the same, sweet bird—sweet bird! still the same." Whereupon, she turned suddenly, and threw her arms about the neck of the officer, with a gesture of fondness and despair, and her frame was agitated as if by a burst of sobs. He held her close to his breast in silence; and honest Peter felt a strange terror creep over him, as he witnessed these mysterious sorrows and endearments.

"Tonight, tonight—and then ten years more—ten long years—another ten years."

The officer and the lady seemed to speak these words together; her voice mingled with his in a musical and fearful wail, like a distant summer wind, in the dead hour of night, wandering through ruins. Then he heard the officer say, alone, in a voice of anguish—

"Upon me be it all, forever, sweet birdie, upon me."

And again they seemed to mourn together in the same soft and desolate wail, like sounds of grief heard from a great distance.

Peter was thrilled with horror, but he was also under a strange fascination; and an intense and dreadful curiosity held him fast.

The moon was shining obliquely into the room, and through the window Peter saw the familiar slopes of the Park, sleeping mistily under its shimmer. He could also see the furniture of the room with tolerable distinctness—the old balloon-backed chairs, a four-post bed in a sort of recess, and a rack against the wall, from which hung some military clothes and accoutrements; and the sight of all these homely objects reassured him somewhat, and he could not help feeling unspeakably curious to see the face of the girl whose long hair was streaming over the officer's epaulet.

Peter, accordingly, coughed, at first slightly, and afterward more loudly, to recall her from her reverie of grief; and, apparently, he succeeded; for she turned round, as did her companion, and both, standing hand in hand, gazed upon him fixedly. He thought he had never seen such large, strange eyes in all his life; and their gaze seemed to chill the very air around him, and arrest the pulses of his heart. An eternity of misery and remorse was in the shadowy faces that looked upon him.

If Peter had taken less whisky by a single thimbleful, it is probable that he would have lost heart altogether before these figures, which seemed every moment to assume a more marked and fearful, though hardly definable, contrast to ordinary human shapes.

"What is it you want with me?" he stammered.

"To bring my lost treasure to the churchyard," replied the lady, in a silvery voice of more than mortal desolation.

The word "treasure" revived the resolution of Peter, although a cold sweat was covering him, and his hair was bristling with horror; he believed, however, that he was on the brink of fortune, if he could but command nerve to brave the interview to its close.

"And where," he gasped, "is it hid—where will I find it?"

They both pointed to the sill of the window, through which the moon was shining at the far end of the room, and the soldier said—

"Under that stone."

Peter drew a long breath, and wiped the cold dew from his face, preparatory to passing to the window, where he expected to secure the reward of his protracted terrors. But looking steadfastly at the window, he saw the faint image of a new-born child sitting upon the sill in the moonlight, with its little arms stretched toward him, and a smile so heavenly as he never beheld before.

At sight of this, strange to say, his heart entirely failed him, he looked on the figures that stood near, and beheld them gazing on the infantine form with a smile so guilty and distorted, that he felt as if he were entering alive among the scenery of hell, and shuddering, he cried in an irrepressible agony of horror—

"I'll have nothing to say with you, and nothing to do with you; I don't know what yez are or what yez want iv me, but let me go this minute, everyone of yez, in the name of God."

With these words there came a strange rumbling and sighing about Peter's ears; he lost sight of everything, and felt that peculiar and not unpleasant sensation of falling softly, that sometimes supervenes in sleep, ending in a dull shock. After that he had neither dream nor consciousness till he wakened, chill and stiff, stretched between two piles of old rubbish, among the black and roofless walls of the ruined house.

We need hardly mention that the village had put on its wonted air of neglect and decay, or that Peter looked around him in vain for traces of those novelties which had so puzzled and distracted him upon the previous night.

"Ay, ay," said his grandmother, removing her pipe, as he ended his description of the view from the bridge, "sure enough I remember myself, when I was a slip of a girl, these little white cabins among the gardens by the river side. The artillery sogers that was married, or had not room in the barracks, used to be in them, but they're all gone long ago.

"The Lord be merciful to us!" she resumed, when he had described the military procession, "It's often I seen the regiment marchin' into the town, jist as you saw it last night, acushla. Oh, voch, but it makes my heart sore to think iv them days; they were pleasant times, sure enough; but is not it terrible, avick, to think it's what it was the ghost of the rigiment you seen? The Lord betune us an' harm, for it was nothing else, as sure as I'm sittin' here."

When he mentioned the peculiar physiognomy and figure of the old officer who rode at the head of the regiment—

"That," said the old crone, dogmatically, "was ould Colonel Grimshaw, the Lord presarve us! he's buried in the churchyard iv Chapelizod, and well I remember him, when I was a young thing, an' a cross ould floggin' fellow he was wid the men, an' a devil's boy among the girls—rest his soul!"

"Amen!" said Peter; "it's often I read his tombstone myself; but he's a long time dead."

"Sure, I tell you he died when I was no more nor a slip iv a girl—the Lord betune us and harm!"

"I'm afeard it is what I'm not long for this world myself, afther seeing such a sight as that," said Peter, fearfully.

"Nonsinse, avourneen," retorted his grandmother, indignantly, though she had herself misgivings on the subject; "sure there was Phil Doolan, the ferryman, that seen black Ann Scanlan in his own boat, and what harm ever kem of it?"

Peter proceeded with his narrative, but when he came to the description of the house, in which his adventure had had so sinister a conclusion, the old woman was at fault.

"I know the house and the ould walls well, an' I can remember the time there was a roof on it, and the doors an' windows in it, but it had a bad name about being haunted, but by who, or for what, I forget intirely."

"Did you ever hear was there goold or silver there?" he inquired.

"No, no, avick, don't be thinking about the likes; take a fool's advice, and never go next to near them ugly black walls again the longest day you have to live; an' I'd take my davy, it's what it's the same word the priest himself id be afther sayin' to you if you wor to ax his raverence consarnin' it, for it's plain to be seen it was nothing good you seen there, and there's neither luck nor grace about it."

Peter's adventure made no little noise in the neighbourhood, as the reader may well suppose; and a few evenings after it, being on an errand to old Major Vandeleur, who lived in a snug old-fashioned house, close by the river, under a perfect bower of ancient trees, he was called on to relate the story in the parlour.

The Major was, as I have said, an old man; he was small, lean, and upright, with a mahogany complexion, and a wooden inflexibility of face; he was a man, besides, of few words, and if *he* was old, it follows plainly that his mother was older still. Nobody could guess or tell *how* old, but it was admitted that her own generation had long passed away, and that she had not a competitor left. She had French blood in her veins, and although she did not retain her charms quite so well as Ninon de l'Enclos, she was in full possession of all her mental activity, and talked quite enough for herself and the Major.

"So, Peter," she said, "you have seen the dear, old Royal Irish again in the streets of Chapelizod. Make him a tumbler of punch, Frank; and Peter, sit down, and while you take it let us have the story."

Peter accordingly, seated, near the door, with a tumbler of the nectarian stimulant steaming beside him, proceeded with marvellous courage, considering they had no light but the uncertain glare of the fire, to relate with minute particularity his awful adventure. The old lady listened at first with a smile of good-natured incredulity; her cross-examination touching the drinking-bout at Palmerstown had been teazing, but as the narrative proceeded she became attentive, and at length absorbed, and once or twice she uttered exclamations of pity or awe. When it was over, the old lady looked with a somewhat sad and stern abstraction on the table, patting her cat assiduously meanwhile, and then suddenly looking upon her son, the Major, she said—

"Frank, as sure as I live he has seen the wicked Captain Devereux."

The Major uttered an inarticulate expression of wonder.

"The house was precisely that he has described. I have told you the story often, as I heard it from your dear grandmother, about the poor young lady he ruined, and the dreadful suspicion about the little baby. *She*, poor thing, died in that house heart-broken, and you know he was shot shortly after in a duel."

This was the only light that Peter ever received respecting his adventure. It was supposed, however, that he still clung to the hope that treasure of some sort was hidden about the old house, for he was often seen lurking about its walls, and at last his fate overtook him, poor fellow, in the pursuit; for climbing near the summit one day, his holding gave way, and he fell upon the hard uneven ground, fracturing a leg and a rib, and after a short interval died, and he, like the other heroes of these true tales, lies buried in the little churchyard of Chapelizod.

Squire Toby's Will: A Ghost Story

Anonymous in *Temple Bar* (1868, vol. xxii.). This story was written, it seems, contemporaneously with the novel *The Wyvern Mystery* (1868–9), and the old Squire in that book intimately resembles Squire Toby.

M any persons accustomed to travel the old York and London road, in the days of stage-coaches, will remember passing, in the afternoon, say, of an autumn day, in their journey to the capital, about three miles south of the town of Applebury, and a mile and a half before you reach the old Angel Inn, a large black-and-white house, as those old-fashioned cage-work habitations are termed, dilapidated and weather-stained, with broad lattice windows glimmering all over in the evening sun with little diamond panes, and thrown into relief by a dense background of ancient elms. A wide avenue, now overgrown like a churchyard with grass and weeds, and flanked by double rows of the same dark trees, old and gigantic, with here and there a gap in their solemn files, and sometimes a fallen tree lying across on the avenue, leads up to the hall-door.

Looking up its sombre and lifeless avenue from the top of the London coach, as I have often done, you are struck with so many signs of desertion and decay,—the tufted grass sprouting in the chinks of the steps and window-stones, the smokeless chimneys over which the jackdaws are wheeling, the absence of human life and all its evidence, that you conclude at once that the place is uninhabited and abandoned to decay. The name of this ancient house is Gylingden Hall. Tall hedges and old timber quickly shroud the old place from view, and about a quarter of a mile further on you pass, embowered in melancholy trees, a small and ruinous Saxon chapel, which, time out of mind, has been the burying-place of the family of Marston, and partakes of the neglect and desolation which brood over their ancient dwelling-place.

The grand melancholy of the secluded valley of Gylingden, lonely as an enchanted forest, in which the crows returning to their roosts among the trees, and the straggling deer who peep from beneath their branches, seem to hold a wild and undisturbed dominion, heightens the forlorn aspect of Gylingden Hall.

Of late years repairs have been neglected, and here and there the roof is stripped, and "the stitch in time" has been wanting. At the side of the house exposed to the gales that sweep through the valley like a torrent through its channel, there is not a perfect window left, and the shutters but imperfectly exclude the rain. The ceilings and walls are mildewed and green with damp stains. Here and there, where the drip falls from the ceiling, the floors are rotting. On stormy nights, as the guard described, you can hear the doors clapping in the old house, as far away as old Gryston bridge, and the howl and sobbing of the wind through its empty galleries.

About seventy years ago died the old Squire, Toby Marston, famous in that part of the world for his hounds, his hospitality, and his vices. He had done kind things, and he had fought duels: he had given away money and he had horse-whipped people. He carried with him some blessings and a good many curses, and left behind him an amount of debts and charges upon the estates which appalled his two sons, who had no taste for business or accounts, and had never suspected, till that wicked, open-handed, and swearing old gentleman died, how very nearly he had run the estates into insolvency.

They met at Gylingden Hall. They had the will before them, and lawyers to interpret, and information without stint, as to the encumbrances with which the deceased had saddled them. The will was so framed as to set the two brothers instantly at deadly feud.

These brothers differed in some points; but in one material characteristic they resembled one another, and also their departed father. They never went into a quarrel by halves, and once in, they did not stick at trifles.

The elder, Scroope Marston, the more dangerous man of the two, had never been a favourite of the old Squire. He had no taste for the sports of the field and the pleasures of a rustic life. He was no athlete, and he certainly was not handsome. All this the Squire resented. The young man, who had no respect for him, and outgrew his fear of his violence as he came to manhood, retorted. This aversion, therefore, in the ill-conditioned old man grew into positive hatred. He used to wish that d——d pippin-squeezing, hump-backed rascal Scroope, out of the way of better men— meaning his younger son Charles; and in his cups would talk in a way which even the old and young fellows who followed his hounds, and drank his port, and could stand a reasonable amount of brutality, did not like.

Scroope Marston was slightly deformed, and he had the lean sallow face, piercing black eyes, and black lank hair, which sometimes accompany deformity.

JOSEPH SHERIDAN LE FANU

"I'm no feyther o' that hog-backed creature. I'm no sire of hisn, d——n him! I'd as soon call that tongs son o' mine," the old man used to bawl, in allusion to his son's long, lank limbs: "Charlie's a man, but that's a jack-an-ape. He has no good-nature; there's nothing handy, nor manly, nor no one turn of a Marston in him."

And when he was pretty drunk, the old Squire used to swear he should never "sit at the head o' that board; nor frighten away folk from Gylingden Hall wi' his d——d hatchet-face—the black loon!"

"Handsome Charlie was the man for his money. He knew what a horse was, and could sit to his bottle; and the lasses were all clean *mad* about him. He was a Marston every inch of his six foot two."

Handsome Charlie and he, however, had also had a row or two. The old Squire was free with his horsewhip as with his tongue, and on occasion when neither weapon was quite practicable, had been known to give a fellow "a tap o' his knuckles." Handsome Charlie, however, thought there was a period at which personal chastisement should cease; and one night, when the port was flowing, there was some allusion to Marion Hayward, the miller's daughter, which for some reason the old gentleman did not like. Being "in liquor," and having clearer ideas about pugilism than self-government, he struck out, to the surprise of all present, at Handsome Charlie. The youth threw back his head scientifically, and nothing followed but the crash of a decanter on the floor. But the old Squire's blood was up, and he bounced from his chair. Up jumped Handsome Charlie, resolved to stand no nonsense. Drunken Squire Lilbourne, intending to mediate, fell flat on the floor, and cut his ear among the glasses. Handsome Charlie caught the thump which the old Squire discharged at him upon his open hand, and catching him by the cravat, swung him with his back to the wall. They said the old man never looked so purple, nor his eyes so goggle before; and then Handsome Charlie pinioned him tight to the wall by both arms.

"Well, I say—come, don't you talk no more nonsense o' that sort, and I won't lick you," croaked the old Squire. "You stopped that un clever, you did. Didn't he? Come, Charlie, man, gie us your hand, I say, and sit down again, lad." And so the battle ended; and I believe it was the last time the Squire raised his hand to Handsome Charlie.

But those days were over. Old Toby Marston lay cold and quiet enough now, under the drip of the mighty ash-tree within the Saxon ruin where so many of the old Marston race returned to dust, and were forgotten.

The weather-stained top-boots and leather-breeches, the three-cornered cocked hat to which old gentlemen of that day still clung, and the well-known red waistcoat that reached below his hips, and the fierce pug face of the old Squire, were now but a picture of memory. And the brothers between whom he had planted an irreconcilable quarrel, were now in their new mourning suits, with the gloss still on, debating furiously across the table in the great oak parlour, which had so often resounded to the banter and coarse songs, the oaths and laughter of the congenial neighbours whom the old Squire of Gylingden Hall loved to assemble there.

These young gentlemen, who had grown up in Gylingden Hall, were not accustomed to bridle their tongues, nor, if need be, to hesitate about a blow. Neither had been at the old man's funeral. His death had been sudden. Having been helped to his bed in that hilarious and quarrelsome state which was induced by port and punch, he was found dead in the morning,—his head hanging over the side of the bed, and his face very black and swollen.

Now the Squire's will despoiled his eldest son of Gylingden, which had descended to the heir time out of mind. Scroope Marston was furious. His deep stern voice was heard inveighing against his dead father and living brother, and the heavy thumps on the table with which he enforced his stormy recriminations resounded through the large chamber. Then broke in Charles's rougher voice, and then came a quick alternation of short sentences, and then both voices together in growing loudness and anger, and at last, swelling the tumult, the expostulations of pacific and frightened lawyers, and at last a sudden break up of the conference. Scroope broke out of the room, his pale furious face showing whiter against his long black hair, his dark fierce eyes blazing, his hands clenched, and looking more ungainly and deformed than ever in the convulsions of his fury.

Very violent words must have passed between them; for Charlie, though he was the winning man, was almost as angry as Scroope. The elder brother was for holding possession of the house, and putting his rival to legal process to oust him. But his legal advisers were clearly against it. So, with a heart boiling over with gall, up he went to London, and found the firm who had managed his father's business fair and communicative enough. They looked into the settlements, and found that Gylingden was excepted. It was very odd, but so it was, specially excepted; so that the right of the old Squire to deal with it by his will could not be questioned.

Notwithstanding all this, Scroope, breathing vengeance and aggression, and quite willing to wreck himself provided he could run his brother down, assailed Handsome Charlie, and battered old Squire Toby's will in the Prerogative Court and also at common law, and the feud between the brothers was knit, and every month their exasperation was heightened.

Scroope was beaten, and defeat did not soften him. Charles might have forgiven hard words; but he had been himself worsted during the long campaign in some of those skirmishes, special motions, and so forth, that constitute the episodes of a legal epic like that in which the Marston brothers figured as opposing combatants; and the blight of law costs had touched him, too, with the usual effect upon the temper of a man of embarrassed means.

Years flew, and brought no healing on their wings. On the contrary, the deep corrosion of this hatred bit deeper by time. Neither brother married. But an accident of a different kind befell the younger, Charles Marston, which abridged his enjoyments very materially.

This was a bad fall from his hunter. There were severe fractures, and there was concussion of the brain. For sometime it was thought that he could not recover. He disappointed these evil auguries, however. He did recover, but changed in two essential particulars. He had received an injury in his hip, which doomed him never more to sit in the saddle. And the rollicking animal spirits which hitherto had never failed him, had now taken flight forever.

He had been for five days in a state of coma—absolute insensibility—and when he recovered consciousness he was haunted by an indescribable anxiety.

Tom Cooper, who had been butler in the palmy days of Gylingden Hall, under old Squire Toby, still maintained his post with old-fashioned fidelity, in these days of faded splendour and frugal housekeeping. Twenty years had passed since the death of his old master. He had grown lean, and stooped, and his face, dark with the peculiar brown of age, furrowed and gnarled, and his temper, except with his master, had waxed surly.

His master had visited Bath and Buxton, and came back, as he went, lame, and halting gloomily about with the aid of a stick. When the hunter was sold, the last tradition of the old life at Gylingden disappeared. The young Squire, as he was still called, excluded by his mischance from the hunting-field, dropped into a solitary way of life, and halted slowly and solitarily about the old place, seldom raising his eyes, and with an appearance of indescribable gloom.

Old Cooper could talk freely on occasion with his master; and one day he said, as he handed him his hat and stick in the hall:

"You should rouse yourself up a bit, Master Charles!"

"It's past rousing with me, old Cooper."

"It's just this, I'm thinking: there's something on your mind, and you won't tell no one. There's no good keeping it on your stomach. You'll be a deal lighter if you tell it. Come, now, what is it, Master Charlie?"

The Squire looked with his round grey eyes straight into Cooper's eyes. He felt that there was a sort of spell broken. It was like the old rule of the ghost who can't speak till it is spoken to. He looked earnestly into old Cooper's face for some seconds, and sighed deeply.

"It ain't the first good guess you've made in your day, old Cooper, and I'm glad you've spoke. It's bin on my mind, sure enough, ever since I had that fall. Come in here after me, and shut the door."

The Squire pushed open the door of the oak parlour, and looked round on the pictures abstractedly. He had not been there for sometime, and, seating himself on the table, he looked again for a while in Cooper's face before he spoke.

"It's not a great deal, Cooper, but it troubles me, and I would not tell it to the parson nor the doctor; for, God knows what they'd say, though there's nothing to signify in it. But you were always true to the family, and I don't mind if I tell you."

"'Tis as safe with Cooper, Master Charles, as if 'twas locked in a chest, and sunk in a well."

"It's only this," said Charles Marston, looking down on the end of his stick, with which he was tracing lines and circles, "all the time I was lying like dead, as you thought, after that fall, I was with the old master." He raised his eyes to Cooper's again as he spoke, and with an awful oath he repeated—"I was with him, Cooper!"

"He was a good man, sir, in his way," repeated old Cooper, returning his gaze with awe." He was a good master to me, and a good father to you, and I hope he's happy. May God rest him!"

"Well," said Squire Charles, "it's only this: the whole of that time I was with him, or he was with me—I don't know which. The upshot is, we were together, and I thought I'd never get out of his hands again, and all the time he was bullying me about someone thing; and if it was to save my life, Tom Cooper, by —— from the time I waked I never could call to mind what it was; and I think I'd give that hand to know; and if you can think of anything it might be—for God's sake! don't be afraid, Tom Cooper, but speak it out, for he threatened me hard, and it was surely him."

Here ensued a silence.

"And what did you think it might be yourself, Master Charles?" said Cooper.

"I han't thought of aught that's likely. I'll never hit on't—*never*. I thought it might happen he knew something about that d—— hump-backed villain, Scroope, that swore before Lawyer Gingham I made away with a paper of settlements—me and father; and, as I hope to be saved, Tom Cooper, there never was a bigger lie! I'd a had the law of him for them identical words, and cast him for more than he's worth; only Lawyer Gingham never goes into nothing for me since money grew scarce in Gylingden; and I can't change my lawyer, I owe him such a hatful of money. But he did, he swore he'd hang me yet for it. He said it in them identical words—he'd never rest till he *hanged* me for it, and I think it was, like enough, something about *that*, the old master was troubled; but it's enough to drive a man mad. I *can't* bring it to mind—I can't remember a word he said, only he threatened awful, and looked— Lord a mercy on us!—frightful bad."

"There's no need he should. May the Lord a-mercy on him!" said the old butler.

"No, of course; and you're not to tell a soul, Cooper—not a living soul, mind, that I said he looked bad, nor nothing about it."

"God forbid!" said old Cooper, shaking his head. "But I was thinking, sir, it might ha' been about the slight that's bin so long put on him by having no stone over him, and never a scratch o' a chisel to say who he is."

"Ay! Well, I didn't think o' that. Put on your hat, old Cooper, and come down wi' me; for I'll look after that, at any rate."

There is a bye-path leading by a turnstile to the park, and thence to the picturesque old burying-place, which lies in a nook by the roadside, embowered in ancient trees. It was a fine autumnal sunset, and melancholy lights and long shadows spread their peculiar effects over the landscape as "Handsome Charlie" and the old butler made their way slowly toward the place where Handsome Charlie was himself to lie at last.

"Which of the dogs made that howling all last night?" asked the Squire, when they had got on a little way.

"'Twas a strange dog, Master Charlie, in front of the house; ours was all in the yard—a white dog wi' a black head, he looked to be, and he was smelling round them mounting-steps the old master, God be wi' him! set up, the time his knee was bad. When the tyke got up a' top of them, howlin' up at the windows, I'd a liked to shy something at him."

"Hullo! Is that like him?" said the Squire, stopping short, and pointing with his stick at a dirty-white dog, with a large black head, which was scampering round them in a wide circle, half crouching with that air of uncertainty and deprecation which dogs so well know how to assume.

He whistled the dog up. He was a large, half-starved bull-dog.

"That fellow has made a long journey—thin as a whipping-post, and stained all over, and his claws worn to the stumps," said the Squire, musingly. "He isn't a bad dog, Cooper. My poor father liked a good bull-dog, and knew a cur from a good 'un."

The dog was looking up into the Squire's face with the peculiar grim visage of his kind, and the Squire was thinking irreverently how strong a likeness it presented to the character of his father's fierce pug features when he was clutching his horsewhip and swearing at a keeper.

"If I did right I'd shoot him. He'll worry the cattle, and kill our dogs," said the Squire. "Hey, Cooper? I'll tell the keeper to look after him. That fellow could pull down a sheep, and he shan't live on my mutton."

But the dog was not to be shaken off. He looked wistfully after the Squire, and after they had got a little way on, he followed timidly.

It was vain trying to drive him off. The dog ran round them in wide circles, like the infernal dog in "Faust"; only he left no track of thin flame behind him. These man(oe)uvres were executed with a sort of beseeching air, which flattered and touched the object of this odd preference. So he called him up again, patted him, and then and there in a manner adopted him.

The dog now followed their steps dutifully, as if he had belonged to Handsome Charlie all his days. Cooper unlocked the little iron door, and the dog walked in close behind their heels, and followed them as they visited the roofless chapel.

The Marstons were lying under the floor of this little building in rows. There is not a vault. Each has his distinct grave enclosed in a lining of masonry. Each is surmounted by a stone kist, on the upper flag of which is enclosed his epitaph, except that of poor old Squire Toby. Over him was nothing but the grass and the line of masonry which indicate the site of the kist, whenever his family should afford him one like the rest.

"Well, it does look shabby. It's the elder brother's business; but if he won't, I'll see to it myself, and I'll take care, old boy, to cut sharp and deep in it, that the elder son having refused to lend a hand the stone was put there by the younger."

They strolled round this little burial-ground. The sun was now below the horizon, and the red metallic glow from the clouds, still illuminated by the departed sun, mingled luridly with the twilight. When Charlie peeped again into the little chapel, he saw the ugly dog stretched upon Squire Toby's grave, looking at least twice his natural length, and performing such antics as made the young Squire stare. If you have ever seen a cat stretched on the floor, with a bunch of Valerian, straining, writhing, rubbing its jaws in long-drawn caresses, and in the absorption of a sensual ecstasy, you have seen a phenomenon resembling that which Handsome Charlie witnessed on looking in.

The head of the brute looked so large, its body so long and thin, and its joints so ungainly and dislocated, that the Squire, with old Cooper beside him, looked on with a feeling of disgust and astonishment, which, in a moment or two more, brought the Squire's stick down upon him with a couple of heavy thumps. The beast awakened from his ecstasy, sprang to the head of the grave, and there on a sudden, thick and bandy as before, confronted the Squire, who stood at its foot, with a terrible grin, and eyes that glared with the peculiar green of canine fury.

The next moment the dog was crouching abjectly at the Squire's feet.

"Well, he's a rum 'un!" said old Cooper, looking hard at him.

"I like him," said the Squire.

"I don't," said Cooper.

"But he shan't come in here again," said the Squire.

"I shouldn't wonder if he was a witch," said old Cooper, who remembered more tales of witchcraft than are now current in that part of the world.

"He's a good dog," said the Squire, dreamily. "I remember the time I'd a given a handful for him—but I'll never be good for nothing again. Come along."

And he stooped down and patted him. So up jumped the dog and looked up in his face, as if watching for some sign, ever so slight, which he might obey.

Cooper did not like a bone in that dog's skin. He could not imagine what his master saw to admire in him. He kept him all night in the gun-room, and the dog accompanied him in his halting rambles about the place. The fonder his master grew of him, the less did Cooper and the other servants like him.

"He hasn't a point of a good dog about him," Cooper would growl. "I think Master Charlie be blind. And old Captain (an old red parrot, who sat chained to a perch in the oak parlour, and conversed with himself, and nibbled at his claws and bit his perch all day),—old Captain, the only living thing, except one or two of us, and the Squire himself, that remembers the old master, the minute he saw the dog, screeched as if he was struck, shakin' his feathers out quite wild, and drops down, poor old soul, a-hangin' by his foot, in a fit."

But there is no accounting for fancies, and the Squire was one of those dogged persons who persist more obstinately in their whims the more they are opposed. But Charles Marston's health suffered by his lameness. The transition from habitual and violent exercise to such a life as his privation now consigned him to, was never made without a risk to health; and a host of dyspeptic annoyances, the existence of which he had never dreamed of before, now beset him in sad earnest. Among these was the now not unfrequent troubling of his sleep with dreams and nightmares. In these his canine favourite invariably had a part and was generally a central, and sometimes a solitary figure. In these visions the dog seemed to stretch himself up the side of the Squire's bed, and in dilated proportions to sit at his feet, with a horrible likeness to the pug features of old Squire Toby, with his tricks of wagging his head and throwing up his chin; and then he would talk to him about Scroope, and tell him "all wasn't straight," and that he "must make it up wi' Scroope," that he, the old Squire, had "served him an ill turn," that "time was nigh up," and that "fair was fair," and he was "troubled where he was, about Scroope."

Then in his dream this semi-human brute would approach his face to his, crawling and crouching up his body, heavy as lead, till the face of the beast was laid on his, with the same odious caresses and stretchings and writhings which he had seen over the old Squire's grave. Then Charlie would wake up with a gasp and a howl, and start upright in the bed, bathed in a cold moisture, and fancy he saw something white sliding off the foot of the bed. Sometimes he thought it might be the curtain with white lining that slipped down, or the coverlet disturbed by his uneasy turnings; but he always fancied, at such moments, that he saw something white sliding hastily off the bed; and always when he had been visited by such dreams the dog next morning was more than usually caressing and servile, as if to obliterate, by a more than ordinary welcome, the sentiment of disgust which the horror of the night had left behind it.

The doctor half-satisfied the Squire that there was nothing in these dreams, which, in one shape or another, invariably attended forms of indigestion such as he was suffering from.

For a while, as if to corroborate this theory, the dog ceased altogether to figure in them. But at last there came a vision in which, more unpleasantly than before, he did resume his old place.

In his nightmare the room seemed all but dark; he heard what he knew to be the dog walking from the door round his bed slowly, to the side from which he always had come upon it. A portion of the room was uncarpeted, and he said he distinctly heard the peculiar tread of a dog, in which the faint clatter of the claws is audible. It was a light stealthy step, but at every tread the whole room shook heavily; he felt something place itself at the foot of his bed, and saw a pair of green eyes staring at him in the dark, from which he could not remove his own. Then he heard, as he thought, the old Squire Toby say—"The eleventh hour be passed, Charlie, and ye've done nothing—you and I 'a done Scroope a wrong!" and then came a good deal more, and then—"The time's nigh up, it's going to strike." And with a long low growl, the thing began to creep up upon his feet; the growl continued, and he saw the reflection of the up-turned green eyes upon the bed-clothes, as it began slowly to stretch itself up his body towards his face. With a loud scream, he waked. The light, which of late the Squire was accustomed to have in his bedroom, had accidentally gone out. He was afraid to get up, or even to look about the room for sometime; so sure did he feel of seeing the green eyes in the dark fixed on him from some corner. He had hardly recovered from the first agony which nightmare leaves behind it, and was beginning to collect his thoughts, when he heard the clock strike twelve. And he bethought him of the words "the eleventh hour be passed—time's nigh up—it's going to strike!" and he almost feared that he would hear the voice reopening the subject.

Next morning the Squire came down looking ill.

"Do you know a room, old Cooper," said he, "they used to call King Herod's Chamber?"

"Ay, sir; the story of King Herod was on the walls o't when I was a boy."

"There's a closet off it—is there?"

"I can't be sure o' that; but 'tisn't worth your looking at, now; the hangings was rotten, and took off the walls, before you was born; and there's nou't there but some old broken things and lumber. I seed them put there myself by poor Twinks; he was blind of an eye, and footman afterwards. You'll remember Twinks? He died here, about the time o' the great snow. There was a deal o' work to bury him, poor fellow!"

"Get the key, old Cooper; I'll look at the room," said the Squire.

"And what the devil can you want to look at it for?" said Cooper, with the old-world privilege of a rustic butler.

"And what the devil's that to you? But I don't mind if I tell you. I don't want that dog in the gun-room, and I'll put him somewhere else; and I don't care if I put him there."

"A bull-dog in a bedroom! Oons, sir! the folks 'ill say you're clean mad!"

"Well, let them; get you the key, and let us look at the room."

"You'd shoot him if you did right, Master Charlie. You never heard what a noise he kept up all last night in the gun-room, walking to and fro growling like a tiger in a show; and, say what you like, the dog's not worth his feed; he hasn't a point of a dog; he's a bad dog."

"I know a dog better than you—and he's a good dog!" said the Squire, testily.

"If you was a judge of a dog you'd hang that 'un," said Cooper.

"I'm not a-going to hang him, so there's an end. Go you, and get the key; and don't be talking, mind, when you go down. I may change my mind."

Now this freak of visiting King Herod's room had, in truth, a totally different object from that pretended by the Squire. The voice in his nightmare had uttered a particular direction, which haunted him, and would give him no peace until he had tested it. So far from liking that dog today, he was beginning to regard it with a horrible suspicion; and if old Cooper had not stirred his obstinate temper by seeming to dictate, I dare say he would have got rid of that inmate effectually before evening.

Up to the third storey, long disused, he and old Cooper mounted. At the end of a dusty gallery, the room lay. The old tapestry, from which the spacious chamber had taken its name, had long given place to modern paper, and this was mildewed, and in some places hanging from the walls. A thick mantle of dust lay over the floor. Some broken chairs and boards, thick with dust, lay, along with other lumber, piled together at one end of the room.

They entered the closet, which was quite empty. The Squire looked round, and you could hardly have said whether he was relieved or disappointed.

"No furniture here," said the Squire, and looked through the dusty window. "Did you say anything to me lately—I don't mean this morning—about this room, or the closet—or anything—I forget—"

"Lor' bless you! Not I. I han't been thinkin' o' this room this forty year."

"Is there any sort of old furniture called a *buffet*—do you remember?" asked the Squire.

"A buffet? why, yes—to be sure—there was a buffet, sure enough, in this closet, now you bring it to my mind," said Cooper. "But it's papered over."

"And what is it?"

"A little cupboard in the wall," answered the old man.

"Ho—I see—and there's such a thing here, is there, under the paper? Show me whereabouts it was."

"Well—I think it was somewhere about here," answered he, rapping his knuckles along the wall opposite the window. "Ay, there it is," he added, as the hollow sound of a wooden door was returned to his knock.

The Squire pulled the loose paper from the wall, and disclosed the doors of a small press, about two feet square, fixed in the wall.

"The very thing for my buckles and pistols, and the rest of my gimcracks," said the Squire. "Come away, we'll leave the dog where he is. Have you the key of that little press?"

No, he had not. The old master had emptied and locked it up, and desired that it should be papered over, and that was the history of it.

Down came the Squire, and took a strong turn-screw from his gun-case; and quietly he reascended to King Herod's room, and, with little trouble, forced the door of the small press in the closet wall. There were in it some letters and cancelled leases, and also a parchment deed which he took to the window and read with much agitation. It was a supplemental deed executed about a fortnight after the others, and previously to his father's marriage, placing Gylingden under strict settlement to the elder son, in what is called "tail male." Handsome Charlie, in his fraternal litigation, had acquired a smattering of technical knowledge, and he perfectly well knew that the effect of this would be not only to transfer the house and lands to his brother Scroope, but to leave him at the mercy of that exasperated brother, who might recover from him personally every guinea he had ever received by way of rent, from the date of his father's death.

It was a dismal, clouded day, with something threatening in its aspect, and the darkness, where he stood, was made deeper by the top of one of the huge old trees overhanging the window.

In a state of awful confusion he attempted to think over his position. He placed the deed in his pocket, and nearly made up his mind to destroy it. A short time ago he would not have hesitated for a moment under such circumstances; but now his health and his nerves were shattered, and he was under a supernatural alarm which the strange discovery of this deed had powerfully confirmed.

In this state of profound agitation he heard a sniffing at the closet-door, and then an impatient scratch and a long low growl. He screwed his courage up, and, not knowing what to expect, threw the door open and saw the dog, not in his dream-shape, but wriggling with joy, and crouching and fawning with eager submission; and then wandering about the closet, the brute growled awfully into the corners of it, and seemed in an unappeasable agitation.

Then the dog returned and fawned and crouched again at his feet.

After the first moment was over, the sensations of abhorrence and fear began to subside, and he almost reproached himself for requiting the affection of this poor friendless brute with the antipathy which he had really done nothing to earn.

The dog pattered after him down the stairs. Oddly enough, the sight of this animal, after the first revulsion, reassured him; it was, in his eyes, so attached, so good-natured, and palpably so mere a dog.

By the hour of evening the Squire had resolved on a middle course; he would not inform his brother of his discovery, nor yet would he destroy the deed. He would never marry. He was past that time. He would leave a letter, explaining the discovery of the deed, addressed to the only surviving trustee—who had probably forgotten everything about it—and having seen out his own tenure, he would provide that all should be set right after his death. Was not that fair? at all events it quite satisfied what he called his conscience, and he thought it a devilish good compromise for his brother; and he went out, towards sunset, to take his usual walk.

Returning in the darkening twilight, the dog, as usual attending him, began to grow frisky and wild, at first scampering round him in great circles, as before, nearly at the top of his speed, his great head between his paws as he raced. Gradually more excited grew the pace and narrower his circuit, louder and fiercer his continuous growl, and the Squire stopped and grasped his stick hard, for the lurid eyes and grin of the brute threatened an attack. Turning round and round as the excited brute encircled him, and striking vainly at him with his stick, he grew at last so tired that he almost despaired of keeping him longer at bay; when on a sudden the dog stopped short and crawled up to his feet wriggling and crouching submissively.

Nothing could be more apologetic and abject; and when the Squire dealt him two heavy thumps with his stick, the dog whimpered only, and writhed and licked his feet. The Squire sat down on a prostrate tree; and his dumb companion, recovering his wonted spirits immediately, began to sniff and nuzzle among the roots. The Squire felt in his breast-pocket for the deed—it was safe; and again he pondered, in this loneliest of spots, on the question whether he should preserve it for restoration after his death to his brother, or destroy it forthwith. He began rather to lean toward the latter solution, when the long low growl of the dog not far off startled him.

He was sitting in a melancholy grove of old trees, that slants gently westward. Exactly the same odd effect of light I have before described—a faint red glow reflected downward from the upper sky, after the sun had set, now gave to the growing darkness a lurid uncertainty. This grove, which lies in a gentle hollow, owing to its circumscribed horizon on all but one side, has a peculiar character of loneliness.

He got up and peeped over a sort of barrier, accidentally formed of the trunks of felled trees laid one over the other, and saw the dog straining up the other side of it, and hideously stretched out, his ugly head looking in consequence twice the natural size. His dream was coming over him again. And now between the trunks the brute's ungainly head was thrust, and the long neck came straining through, and the body, twining after it like a huge white lizard; and as it came striving and twisting through, it growled and glared as if it would devour him.

As swiftly as his lameness would allow, the Squire hurried from this solitary spot towards the house. What thoughts exactly passed through his mind as he did so, I am sure he could not have told. But when the dog came up with him it seemed appeased, and even in high good-humour, and no longer resembled the brute that haunted his dreams.

That night, near ten o'clock, the Squire, a good deal agitated, sent for the keeper, and told him that he believed the dog was mad, and that he must shoot him. He might shoot the dog in the gun-room, where he was—a grain of shot or two in the wainscot did not matter, and the dog must not have a chance of getting out.

The Squire gave the gamekeeper his double-barrelled gun, loaded with heavy shot. He did not go with him beyond the hall. He placed his hand on the keeper's arm; the keeper said his hand trembled, and that he looked "as white as curds."

"Listen a bit!" said the Squire under his breath.

They heard the dog in a state of high excitement in the room—growling ominously, jumping on the window-stool and down again, and running round the room.

"You'll need to be sharp, mind—don't give him a chance—slip in edgeways, d'ye see? and give him both barrels!"

"Not the first mad dog I've knocked over, sir," said the man, looking very serious as he cocked the gun.

As the keeper opened the door, the dog had sprung into the empty grate. He said he "never see sich a stark, staring devil." The beast made a twist round, as if, he thought, to jump up the chimney—"but that wasn't to be done at no price,"—and he made a yell—not like a dog—like a man caught in a mill-crank, and before he could spring at the keeper, he fired one barrel into him. The dog leaped towards him, and rolled over, receiving the second barrel in his head, as he lay snorting at the keeper's feet!

"I never seed the like; I never heard a screech like that!" said the keeper, recoiling. "It makes a fellow feel queer."

"Quite dead?" asked the Squire.

"Not a stir in him, sir," said the man, pulling him along the floor by the neck.

"Throw him outside the hall-door now," said the Squire"; and mind you pitch him outside the gate tonight—old Cooper says he's a witch," and the pale Squire smiled, "so he shan't lie in Gylingden."

Never was man more relieved than the Squire, and he slept better for a week after this than he had done for many weeks before.

It behoves us all to act promptly on our good resolutions. There is a determined gravitation towards evil, which, if left to itself, will bear down first intentions. If at one moment of superstitious fear, the Squire had made up his mind to a great sacrifice, and resolved in the matter of that deed so strangely recovered, to act honestly by his brother, that resolution very soon gave place to the compromise with fraud, which so conveniently postponed the restitution to the period when further enjoyment on his part was impossible. Then came more tidings of Scroope's violent and minatory language, with always the same burthen—that he would leave no stone unturned to show that there had existed a deed which Charles had either secreted or destroyed, and that he would never rest till he had hanged him.

This of course was wild talk. At first it had only enraged him; but, with his recent guilty knowledge and suppression, had come fear. His danger was the existence of the deed, and little by little he brought himself to a resolution to destroy it. There were many falterings and recoils before he could bring himself to commit this crime. At length, however, he did it, and got rid of the custody of that which at anytime might become the instrument of disgrace and ruin. There was relief in this, but also the new and terrible sense of actual guilt.

He had got pretty well rid of his supernatural qualms. It was a different kind of trouble that agitated him now.

But this night, he imagined, he was awakened by a violent shaking of his bed. He could see, in the very imperfect light, two figures at the foot of it, holding each a bed-post. One of these he half-fancied was his brother Scroope, but the other was the old Squire—of that he was sure—and he fancied that they had shaken him up from his sleep. Squire Toby was talking as Charlie wakened, and he heard him say:

"Put out of our own house by you! It won't hold for long. We'll come in together, friendly, and stay. Fore-warned, wi' yer eyes open, ye did it; and now Scroope'll hang you! We'll hang you together! Look at me, you devil's limb."

And the old Squire tremblingly stretched his face, torn with shot and bloody, and growing every moment more and more into the likeness of the dog, and began to stretch himself out and climb the bed over the foot-board; and he saw the figure at the other side, little more than a black shadow, begin also to scale the bed; and there was instantly a dreadful confusion and uproar in the room, and such a gabbling and laughing; he could not catch the words; but, with a scream, he woke, and found himself standing on the floor. The phantoms and the clamour were gone, but a crash and ringing of fragments was in his ears. The great china bowl, from which for generations the Marstons of Gylingden had been baptized, had fallen from the mantelpiece, and was smashed on the hearth-stone.

"I've bin dreamin' all night about Mr. Scroope, and I wouldn't wonder, old Cooper, if he was dead," said the Squire, when he came down in the morning.

"God forbid! I was adreamed about him, too, sir: I dreamed he was dammin' and sinkin' about a hole was burnt in his coat, and the old master, God be wi' him! said—quite plain—I'd 'a swore 'twas himself—'Cooper, get up, ye d——d land-loupin' thief, and lend a hand to hang him—for he's a daft cur, and no dog o' mine.' 'Twas the dog shot over night, I do suppose, as was runnin' in my old head. I thought old master gied me a punch wi' his knuckles, and says I, wakenin' up, 'At yer service, sir'; and for a while I couldn't get it out o' my head, master was in the room still."

Letters from town soon convinced the Squire that his brother Scroope, so far from being dead, was particularly active; and Charlie's attorney wrote to say, in serious alarm, that he had heard, accidentally, that he intended setting up a case, of a supplementary deed of settlement, of which he had secondary evidence, which would give him Gylingden. And at this menace Handsome Charlie snapped his fingers, and wrote courageously to his attorney; abiding what might follow with, however, a secret foreboding.

Scroope threatened loudly now, and swore after his bitter fashion, and reiterated his old promise of hanging that cheat at last. In the midst of these menaces and preparations, however, a sudden peace proclaimed itself: Scroope died, without time even to make provisions for a posthumous attack upon his brother. It was one of those cases of disease of the heart in which death is as sudden as by a bullet.

Charlie's exultation was undisguised. It was shocking. Not, of course, altogether malignant. For there was the expansion consequent on the removal of a secret fear. There was also the comic piece of luck, that only the day before Scroope had destroyed his old will, which left to a stranger every farthing he possessed, intending in a day or two to execute another to the same person, charged with the express condition of prosecuting the suit against Charlie.

The result was, that all his possessions went unconditionally to his brother Charles as his heir. Here were grounds for abundance of savage elation. But there was also the deep-seated hatred of half a life of mutual and persistent agression and revilings; and Handsome Charlie was capable of nursing a grudge, and enjoying a revenge with his whole heart.

He would gladly have prevented his brother's being buried in the old Gylingden chapel, where he wished to lie; but his lawyers doubted his power, and he was not quite proof against the scandal which would attend his turning back the funeral, which would, he knew, be attended by some of the country gentry and others, with an hereditary regard for the Marstons.

But he warned his servants that not one of them were to attend it; promising, with oaths and curses not to be disregarded, that anyone of them who did so, should find the door shut in his face on his return.

I don't think, with the exception of old Cooper, that the servants cared for this prohibition, except as it baulked a curiosity always strong in the solitude of the country. Cooper was very much vexed that the eldest son of the old Squire should be buried in the old family chapel, and no sign of decent respect from Gylingden Hall. He asked his master, whether he would not, at least, have some wine and refreshments in the oak parlour, in case any of the country gentlemen who paid this respect to the old family should come up to the house? But the Squire only swore at him, told him to mind his own business, and ordered him to say, if such a thing happened, that he was out, and no preparations made, and, in fact, to send them away as they came. Cooper expostulated stoutly, and the Squire grew angrier; and after a tempestuous scene, took his hat and stick and walked out, just as the funeral descending the valley from the direction of the "Old Angel Inn" came in sight.

Old Cooper prowled about disconsolately, and counted the carriages as well as he could from the gate. When the funeral was over, and they began to drive away, he returned to the hall, the door of which lay open, and as usual deserted. Before he reached it quite, a mourning coach drove up, and two gentlemen in black cloaks, and with crapes to their hats, got out, and without looking to the right or the left, went up the steps into the house. Cooper followed them slowly. The carriage had, he supposed, gone round to the yard, for, when he reached the door, it was no longer there.

So he followed the two mourners into the house. In the hall he found a fellow-servant, who said he had seen two gentlemen, in black cloaks, pass through the hall, and go up the stairs without removing their hats, or asking leave of anyone. This was very odd, old Cooper thought, and a great liberty; so upstairs he went to make them out.

But he could not find them then, nor ever. And from that hour the house was troubled.

In a little time there was not one of the servants who had not something to tell. Steps and voices followed them sometimes in the passages, and tittering whispers, always minatory, scared them at corners of the galleries, or from dark recesses; so that they would return panic-stricken to be rebuked by thin Mrs. Beckett, who looked on such stories as worse than idle. But Mrs. Beckett herself, a short time after, took a very different view of the matter.

She had herself begun to hear these voices, and with this formidable aggravation, that they came always when she was at her prayers, which she had been punctual in saying all her life, and utterly interrupted them. She was scared at such moments by dropping words and sentences, which grew, as she persisted, into threats and blasphemies.

These voices were not always in the room. They called, as she fancied, through the walls, very thick in that old house, from the neighbouring apartments, sometimes on one side, sometimes on the other; sometimes they seemed to holloa from distant lobbies, and came muffled, but threateningly, through the long panelled passages. As they approached they grew furious, as if several voices were speaking together. Whenever, as I said, this worthy woman applied herself to her devotions, these horrible sentences came hurrying towards the door, and, in panic, she would start from her knees, and all then would subside except the thumping of her heart against her stays, and the dreadful tremors of her nerves.

What these voices said, Mrs. Beckett never could quite remember one minute after they had ceased speaking; one sentence chased another away; gibe and menace and impious denunciation, each hideously articulate, were lost as soon as heard. And this added to the effect of these terrifying mockeries and invectives, that she could not, by any effort, retain their exact import, although their horrible character remained vividly present to her mind.

For a long time the Squire seemed to be the only person in the house absolutely unconscious of these annoyances. Mrs. Beckett had twice made up her mind within the week to leave. A prudent woman, however, who has been comfortable for more than twenty years in a place, thinks oftener than twice before she leaves it. She and old Cooper were the only servants in the house who remembered the good old housekeeping in Squire Toby's day. The others were few, and such as could hardly be accounted regular servants. Meg Dobbs, who acted as housemaid, would not sleep in the house, but walked home, in trepidation, to her father's, at the gate-house, under the escort of her little brother, every night. Old Mrs. Beckett, who was high and mighty with the make-shift servants of fallen Gylingden, let herself down all at once, and made Mrs. Kymes and the kitchenmaid move their beds into her large and faded room, and there, very frankly, shared her nightly terrors with them.

Old Cooper was testy and captious about these stories. He was already uncomfortable enough by reason of the entrance of the two muffled figures into the house, about which there could be no mistake. His own eyes had seen them. He refused to credit the stories of the women, and affected to think that the two mourners might have left the house and driven away, on finding no one to receive them.

Old Cooper was summoned at night to the oak parlour, where the Squire was smoking.

"I say, Cooper," said the Squire, looking pale and angry, "what for ha' you been frightenin' they crazy women wi' your plaguy stories? d—— me, if you see ghosts here it's no place for you, and it's time you should pack. I won't be left without servants. Here has been old Beckett, wi' the cook and the kitchenmaid, as white as pipe-clay, all in a row, to tell me I must have a parson to sleep among them, and preach down the devil! Upon my soul, you're a wise old body, filling their heads wi' maggots! and Meg goes down to the lodge every night, afeared to lie in the house—all your doing, wi' your old wives' stories,—ye withered old Tom o' Bedlam!"

"I'm not to blame, Master Charles. 'Tisn't along o' no stories o' mine, for I'm never done tellin' 'em it's all vanity and vapours. Mrs. Beckett 'ill tell you that, and there's been many a wry word betwixt us on the head o't. Whate'er I may *think*," said old Cooper, significantly, and looking askance, with the sternness of fear in the Squire's face.

The Squire averted his eyes, and muttered angrily to himself, and turned away to knock the ashes out of his pipe on the hob, and then turning suddenly round upon Cooper again, he spoke, with a pale face, but not quite so angrily as before.

"I know you're no fool, old Cooper, when you like. Suppose there was such a thing as a ghost here, don't you see, it ain't to them snipe-headed women it 'id go to tell its story. What ails you, man, that you should think aught about it, but just what *I* think? You had a good headpiece o' yer own once, Cooper, don't be you clappin' a goosecap over it, as my poor father used to say; d—— it, old boy, you mustn't let 'em be fools, settin' one another wild wi' their blether, and makin' the folk talk what they shouldn't, about Gylingden and the family. I don't think ye'd like that, old Cooper, I'm sure ye wouldn't. The women has gone out o' the kitchen, make up a bit o' fire, and get your pipe. I'll go to you, when I finish this one, and we'll smoke a bit together, and a glass o' brandy and water."

Down went the old butler, not altogether unused to such condescensions in that disorderly and lonely household; and let not those who can choose their company, be too hard on the Squire who couldn't.

When he had got things tidy, as he said, he sat down in that big old kitchen, with his feet on the fender, the kitchen candle burning in a great brass candlestick, which stood on the deal table at his elbow, with the brandy bottle and tumblers beside it, and Cooper's pipe also in readiness. And these preparations completed, the old butler, who had remembered other generations and better times, fell into rumination, and so, gradually, into a deep sleep.

Old Cooper was half awakened by someone laughing low, near his head. He was dreaming of old times in the Hall, and fancied one of "the young gentlemen" going to play him a trick, and he mumbled something in his sleep, from which he was awakened by a stern deep voice, saying, "You wern't at the funeral; I might take your life, I'll take your ear." At the same moment, the side of his head received a violent push, and he started to his feet. The fire had gone down, and he was chilled. The candle was expiring in the socket, and threw on the white wall long shadows, that danced up and down from the ceiling to the ground, and their black outlines he fancied resembled the two men in cloaks, whom he remembered with a profound horror.

He took the candle, with all the haste he could, getting along the passage, on whose walls the same dance of black shadows was continued, very anxious to reach his room before the light should go out. He was startled half out of his wits by the sudden clang of his master's bell, close over his head, ringing furiously.

"Ha, ha! There it goes—yes, sure enough," said Cooper, reassuring himself with the sound of his own voice, as he hastened on, hearing more and more distinct every moment the same furious ringing. "He's fell asleep, like me; that's it, and his lights is out, I lay you fifty—"

When he turned the handle of the door of the oak parlour, the Squire wildly called, "Who's *there*?" in the tone of a man who expects a robber.

"It's me, old Cooper, all right, Master Charlie, you didn't come to the kitchen after all, sir."

"I'm very bad, Cooper; I don't know how I've been. Did you meet anything?" asked the Squire.

"No," said Cooper.

They stared on one another.

"Come here—stay here! Don't you leave me! Look round the room, and say is all right; and gie us your hand, old Cooper, for I must hold it." The Squire's was damp and cold, and trembled very much. It was not very far from day-break now.

After a time he spoke again: "I'a done many a thing I shouldn't; I'm not fit to go, and wi' God's blessin' I'll look to it—why shouldn't I? I'm as lame as old Billy—I'll never be able to do any good no more, and I'll give over drinking, and marry, as I ought to 'a done long ago—none o' yer fine ladies, but a good homely wench; there's Farmer Crump's youngest daughter, a good lass, and discreet. What for shouldn't I take her? She'd take care o' me, and wouldn't bring a head full o' romances here, and mantua-makers' trumpery, and I'll talk with the parson, and I'll do what's fair wi' everyone; and mind, I said I'm sorry for many a thing I 'a done."

A wild cold dawn had by this time broken. The Squire, Cooper said, looked "awful bad," as he got his hat and stick, and sallied out for a walk, instead of going to his bed, as Cooper besought him, looking so wild and distracted, that it was plain his object was simply to escape from the house. It was twelve o'clock when the Squire walked into the kitchen, where he was sure of finding some of the servants, looking as if ten years had passed over him since yesterday. He pulled a stool by the fire, without speaking a word, and sat down. Cooper had sent to Applebury for the doctor, who had just arrived, but the Squire would not go to him. "If he wants to see me, he may come here," he muttered as often as Cooper urged him. So the doctor did come, charily enough, and found the Squire very much worse than he had expected.

The Squire resisted the order to get to his bed. But the doctor insisted under a threat of death, at which his patient quailed.

"Well, I'll do what you say—only this—you must let old Cooper and Dick Keeper stay wi' me. I mustn't be left alone, and they must keep awake o' nights; and stay a while, do *you*. When I get round a bit, I'll go and live in a town. It's dull livin' here, now that I can't do nou't, as I used, and I'll live a better life, mind ye; ye heard me say that, and I don't care who laughs, and I'll talk wi' the parson. I like 'em to laugh, hang 'em, it's a sign I'm doin' right, at last."

The doctor sent a couple of nurses from the County Hospital, not choosing to trust his patient to the management he had selected, and he went down himself to Gylingden to meet them in the evening. Old Cooper was ordered to occupy the dressing-room, and sit up at night, which satisfied the Squire, who was in a strangely excited state, very low, and threatened, the doctor said, with fever.

The clergyman came, an old, gentle, "book-learned" man, and talked and prayed with him late that evening. After he had gone the Squire called the nurses to his bedside, and said:

"There's a fellow sometimes comes; you'll never mind him. He looks in at the door and beckons,—a thin, hump-backed chap in mourning, wi' black gloves on; ye'll know him by his lean face, as brown as the wainscot: don't ye mind his smilin'. You don't go out to him, nor ask him in; he won't say nout; and if he grows anger'd and looks awry at ye, don't ye be afeared, for he can't hurt ye, and he'll grow tired waitin', and go away; and for God's sake mind ye don't ask him in, nor go out after him!"

The nurses put their heads together when this was over, and held afterwards a whispering conference with old Cooper. "Law bless ye!— no, there's no madman in the house," he protested; "not a soul but what ye saw,—it's just a trifle o' the fever in his head—no more."

The Squire grew worse as the night wore on. He was heavy and delirious, talking of all sorts of things—of wine, and dogs, and lawyers; and then he began to talk, as it were, to his brother Scroope. As he did so, Mrs. Oliver, the nurse, who was sitting up alone with him, heard, as she thought, a hand softly laid on the door-handle outside, and a stealthy attempt to turn it. "Lord bless us! who's there?" she cried, and her heart jumped into her mouth, as she thought of the hump-backed man in black, who was to put in his head smiling and beckoning— "Mr. Cooper! sir! are you there?" she cried. "Come here, Mr. Cooper, please—do, sir, quick!"

Old Cooper, called up from his doze by the fire, stumbled in from the dressing-room, and Mrs. Oliver seized him tightly as he emerged.

"The man with the hump has been atryin' the door, Mr. Cooper, as sure as I am here." The Squire was moaning and mumbling in his fever, understanding nothing, as she spoke. "No, no! Mrs. Oliver, ma'am, it's impossible, for there's no sich man in the house: what is Master Charlie sayin'?"

"He's saying *Scroope* every minute, whatever he means by that, and—and—hisht!—listen—there's the handle again," and, with a loud scream, she added—"Look at his head and neck in at the door!" and in her tremour she strained old Cooper in an agonizing embrace.

The candle was flaring, and there was a wavering shadow at the door that looked like the head of a man with a long neck, and a longish sharp nose, peeping in and drawing back.

"Don't be a d—— fool, ma'am!" cried Cooper, very white, and shaking her with all his might. "It's only the candle, I tell you—nothing in life but that. Don't you see?" and he raised the light; "and I'm sure there was no one at the door, and I'll try, if you let me go."

The other nurse was asleep on a sofa, and Mrs. Oliver called her up in a panic, for company, as old Cooper opened the door. There was no one near it, but at the angle of the gallery was a shadow resembling that which he had seen in the room. He raised the candle a little, and it seemed to beckon with a long hand as the head drew back. "Shadow from the candle!" exclaimed Cooper aloud, resolved not to yield to Mrs. Oliver's panic; and, candle in hand, he walked to the corner. There was nothing. He could not forbear peeping down the long gallery from this point, and as he moved the light, he saw precisely the same sort of shadow, a little further down, and as he advanced the same withdrawal, and beckon. "Gammon!" said he; "it is nout but the candle." And on he went, growing half angry and half frightened at the persistency with which this ugly shadow—a literal shadow he was sure it was—presented itself. As he drew near the point where it now appeared, it seemed to collect itself, and nearly dissolve in the central panel of an old carved cabinet which he was now approaching.

In the centre panel of this is a sort of boss carved into a wolf's head. The light fell oddly upon this, and the fugitive shadow seemed to be breaking up, and re-arranging itself as oddly. The eye-ball gleamed with a point of reflected light, which glittered also upon the grinning mouth, and he saw the long, sharp nose of Scroope Marston, and his fierce eye looking at him, he thought, with a steadfast meaning.

Old Cooper stood gazing upon this sight, unable to move, till he saw the face, and the figure that belonged to it, begin gradually to emerge from the wood. At the same time he heard voices approaching rapidly up a side gallery, and Cooper, with a loud "Lord a-mercy on us!" turned and ran back again, pursued by a sound that seemed to shake the old house like a mighty gust of wind.

Into his master's room burst old Cooper, half wild with fear, and clapped the door and turned the key in a twinkling, looking as if he had been pursued by murderers.

"Did you hear it?" whispered Cooper, now standing near the dressing-room door. They all listened, but not a sound from without disturbed the utter stillness of night. "God bless us! I doubt it's my old head that's gone crazy!" exclaimed Cooper.

He would tell them nothing but that he was himself "an old fool," to be frightened by their talk, and that "the rattle of a window, or the dropping o' a pin" was enough to scare him now; and so he helped himself through that night with brandy, and sat up talking by his master's fire.

The Squire recovered slowly from his brain fever, but not perfectly. A very little thing, the doctor said, would suffice to upset him. He was not yet sufficiently strong to remove for change of scene and air, which were necessary for his complete restoration.

Cooper slept in the dressing-room, and was now his only nightly attendant. The ways of the invalid were odd: he liked, half sitting up in his bed, to smoke his churchwarden o' nights, and made old Cooper smoke, for company, at the fireside. As the Squire and his humble friend indulged in it, smoking is a taciturn pleasure, and it was not until the Master of Gylingden had finished his third pipe that he essayed conversation, and when he did, the subject was not such as Cooper would have chosen.

"I say, old Cooper, look in my face, and don't be afeared to speak out," said the Squire, looking at him with a steady, cunning smile; "you know all this time, as well as I do, who's in the house. You needn't deny—hey?—Scroope and my father?"

"Don't you be talking like that, Charlie," said old Cooper, rather sternly and frightened, after a long silence; still looking in his face, which did not change.

"What's the good o' shammin', Cooper? Scroope's took the hearin' o' yer right ear—you know he did. He's looking angry. He's nigh took my life wi' this fever. But he's not done wi' me yet, and he looks awful wicked. Ye saw him—ye know ye did."

Cooper was awfully frightened, and the odd smile on the Squire's lips frightened him still more. He dropped his pipe, and stood gazing in silence at his master, and feeling as if he were in a dream.

"If ye think so, ye should not be smiling like that," said Cooper, grimly.

"I'm tired, Cooper, and it's as well to smile as t'other thing; so I'll even smile while I can. You know what they mean to do wi' me. That's all I wanted to say. Now, lad, go on wi' yer pipe—I'm goin' asleep."

So the Squire turned over in his bed, and lay down serenely, with his head on the pillow. Old Cooper looked at him, and glanced at the door, and then half-filled his tumbler with brandy, and drank it off, and felt better, and got to his bed in the dressing-room.

In the dead of night he was suddenly awakened by the Squire, who was standing, in his dressing-gown and slippers, by his bed.

"I've brought you a bit o' a present. I got the rents o' Hazelden yesterday, and ye'll keep that for yourself—it's a fifty—and give t' other to Nelly Carwell, tomorrow; I'll sleep the sounder; and I saw Scroope since; he's not such a bad 'un after all, old fellow! He's got a crape over his face—for I told him I couldn't bear it; and I'd do many a thing for him now. I never could stand shilly-shally. Goodnight, old Cooper!"

And the Squire laid his trembling hand kindly on the old man's shoulder, and returned to his own room. "I don't half like how he is. Doctor don't come half often enough. I don't like that queer smile o' his, and his hand was as cold as death. I hope in God his brain's not a-turnin'!"

With these reflections, he turned to the pleasanter subject of his present, and at last fell asleep.

In the morning, when he went into the Squire's room, the Squire had left his bed. "Never mind; he'll come back, like a bad shillin'," thought old Cooper, preparing the room as usual. But he did not return. Then began an uneasiness, succeeded by a panic, when it began to be plain that the Squire was not in the house. What had become of him? None of his clothes, but his dressing-gown and slippers, were missing. Had he left the house, in his present sickly state, in that garb? and, if so, could he be in his right senses; and was there a chance of his surviving a cold, damp night, so passed, in the open air?

Tom Edwards was up to the house, and told them, that, walking a mile or so that morning, at four o'clock—there being no moon—along with Farmer Nokes, who was driving his cart to market, in the dark, three men walked, in front of the horse, not twenty yards before them, all the way from near Gylingden Lodge to the burial-ground, the gate of which was opened for them from within, and the three men entered, and the gate was shut. Tom Edwards thought they were gone in to make preparation for a funeral of some member of the Marston family.

But the occurrence seemed to Cooper, who knew there was no such thing, horribly ominous.

He now commenced a careful search, and at last bethought him of the lonely upper storey, and King Herod's chamber. He saw nothing changed there, but the closet door was shut, and, dark as was the morning, something, like a large white knot sticking out over the door, caught his eye.

The door resisted his efforts to open it for a time; some great weight forced it down against the floor; at length, however, it did yield a little, and a heavy crash, shaking the whole floor, and sending an echo flying through all the silent corridors, with a sound like receding laughter, half stunned him.

When he pushed open the door, his master was lying dead upon the floor. His cravat was drawn halter-wise tight round his throat, and had done its work well. The body was cold, and had been long dead.

In due course the coroner held his inquest, and the jury pronounced, "that the deceased, Charles Marston, had died by his own hand, in a state of temporary insanity." But old Cooper had his own opinion about the Squire's death, though his lips were sealed, and he never spoke about it. He went and lived for the residue of his days in York, where there are still people who remember him, a taciturn and surly old man, who attended church regularly, and also drank a little, and was known to have saved some money.

Stories of Lough Guir

Anonymous in *All the Year Round* (1869–70). It differs from the other tales in this volume in being apparently a record of stories actually told to Le Fanu and not invented by him; and they purport to be, as the phrase goes, 'veridical.'

When the present writer was a boy of twelve or thirteen, he first made the acquaintance of Miss Anne Baily, of Lough Guir, in the county of Limerick. She and her sister were the last representatives at that place, of an extremely good old name in the county. They were both what is termed "old maids," and at that time past sixty. But never were old ladies more hospitable, lively, and kind, especially to young people. They were both remarkably agreeable and clever. Like all old county ladies of their time, they were great genealogists, and could recount the origin, generations, and intermarriages, of every county family of note.

These ladies were visited at their house at Lough Guir by Mr. Crofton Croker; and are, I think, mentioned, by name, in the second series of his fairy legends; the series in which (probably communicated by Miss Anne Baily), he recounts some of the picturesque traditions of those beautiful lakes—lakes, I should no longer say, for the smaller and prettier has since been drained, and gave up from its depths some long lost and very interesting relics.

In their drawing-room stood a curious relic of another sort: old enough, too, though belonging to a much more modern period. It was the ancient stirrup cup of the hospitable house of Lough Guir. Crofton Croker has preserved a sketch of this curious glass. I have often had it in my hand. It had a short stem; and the cup part, having the bottom rounded, rose cylindrically, and, being of a capacity to contain a whole bottle of claret, and almost as narrow as an old-fashioned ale glass, was tall to a degree that filled me with wonder. As it obliged the rider to extend his arm as he raised the glass, it must have tried a tipsy man, sitting in the saddle, pretty severely. The wonder was that the marvellous tall glass had come down to our times without a crack.

There was another glass worthy of remark in the same drawing-room. It was gigantic, and shaped conically, like one of those old-fashioned jelly glasses which used to be seen upon the shelves of confectioners. It was engraved round the rim with the words, "The glorious, pious, and immortal memory"; and on grand occasions, was filled to the brim, and after the manner of a loving cup, made the circuit of the Whig guests, who owed all to the hero whose memory its legend invoked.

It was now but the transparent phantom of those solemn convivialities of a generation, who lived, as it were, within hearing of the cannon and shoutings of those stirring times. When I saw it, this glass had long retired from politics and carousals, and stood peacefully on a little table in the drawing-room, where ladies' hands replenished it with fair water, and crowned it daily with flowers from the garden.

Miss Anne Baily's conversation ran oftener than her sister's upon the legendary and supernatural; she told her stories with the sympathy, the colour, and the mysterious air which contribute so powerfully to effect, and never wearied of answering questions about the old castle, and amusing her young audience with fascinating little glimpses of old adventure and bygone days. My memory retains the picture of my early friend very distinctly. A slim straight figure, above the middle height; a general likeness to the full-length portrait of that delightful Countess D'Aulnois, to whom we all owe our earliest and most brilliant glimpses of fairy-land; something of her gravely-pleasant countenance, plain, but refined and ladylike, with that kindly mystery in her sidelong glance and uplifted finger, which indicated the approaching climax of a tale of wonder.

Lough Guir is a kind of centre of the operations of the Munster fairies. When a child is stolen by the "good people," Lough Guir is conjectured to be the place of its unearthly transmutation from the human to the fairy state. And beneath its waters lie enchanted, the grand old castle of the Desmonds, the great earl himself, his beautiful young countess, and all the retinue that surrounded him in the years of his splendour, and at the moment of his catastrophe.

Here, too, are historic associations. The huge square tower that rises at one side of the stable-yard close to the old house, to a height that amazed my young eyes, though robbed of its battlements and one story, was a stronghold of the last rebellious Earl of Desmond, and is specially mentioned in that delightful old folio, the Hibernia Pacata, as having, with its Irish garrison on the battlements, defied the army of the lord deputy, then marching by upon the summits of the overhanging hills. The house, built under shelter of this stronghold of the once proud and turbulent Desmonds, is old, but snug, with a multitude of small low rooms, such as I have seen in houses of the same age in Shropshire and the neighbouring English counties.

The hills that overhang the lakes appeared to me, in my young days (and I have not seen them since), to be clothed with a short soft verdure, of a hue so dark and vivid as I had never seen before.

In one of the lakes is a small island, rocky and wooded, which is believed by the peasantry to represent the top of the highest tower of the castle which sank, under a spell, to the bottom. In certain states of the atmosphere, I have heard educated people say, when in a boat you have reached a certain distance, the island appears to rise some feet from the water, its rocks assume the appearance of masonry, and the whole circuit presents very much the effect of the battlements of a castle rising above the surface of the lake.

This was Miss Anne Baily's story of the submersion of this lost castle:

The Magician Earl

It is well known that the great Earl of Desmond, though history pretends to dispose of him differently, lives to this hour enchanted in his castle, with all his household, at the bottom of the lake.

There was not, in his day, in all the world, so accomplished a magician as he. His fairest castle stood upon an island in the lake, and to this he brought his young and beautiful bride, whom he loved but too well; for she prevailed upon his folly to risk all to gratify her imperious caprice.

They had not been long in this beautiful castle, when she one day presented herself in the chamber in which her husband studied his forbidden art, and there implored him to exhibit before her some of the wonders of his evil science. He resisted long; but her entreaties, tears, and wheedlings were at length too much for him and he consented.

But before beginning those astonishing transformations with which he was about to amaze her, he explained to her the awful conditions and dangers of the experiment.

Alone in this vast apartment, the walls of which were lapped, far below, by the lake whose dark waters lay waiting to swallow them, she must witness a certain series of frightful phenomena, which once commenced, he could neither abridge nor mitigate; and if throughout their ghastly succession she spoke one word, or uttered one exclamation, the castle and all that it contained would in one instant subside to the bottom of the lake, there to remain, under the servitude of a strong spell, for ages.

The dauntless curiosity of the lady having prevailed, and the oaken door of the study being locked and barred, the fatal experiments commenced.

Muttering a spell, as he stood before her, feathers sprouted thickly over him, his face became contracted and hooked, a cadaverous smell filled the air, and, with heavy winnowing wings, a gigantic vulture rose in his stead, and swept round and round the room, as if on the point of pouncing upon her.

The lady commanded herself through this trial, and instantly another began.

The bird alighted near the door, and in less than a minute changed, she saw not how, into a horribly deformed and dwarfish hag: who, with yellow skin hanging about her face and enormous eyes, swung herself on crutches toward the lady, her mouth foaming with fury, and her grimaces and contortions becoming more and more hideous every moment, till she rolled with a yell on the floor, in a horrible convulsion, at the lady's feet, and then changed into a huge serpent, with crest erect, and quivering tongue. Suddenly, as it seemed on the point of darting at her, she saw her husband in its stead, standing pale before her, and, with his finger on his lip, enforcing the continued necessity of silence. He then placed himself at his length on the floor, and began to stretch himself out and out, longer and longer, until his head nearly reached to one end of the vast room, and his feet to the other.

This horror overcame her. The ill-starred lady uttered a wild scream, whereupon the castle and all that was within it, sank in a moment to the bottom of the lake.

But, once in every seven years, by night, the Earl of Desmond and his retinue emerge, and cross the lake, in shadowy cavalcade. His white horse is shod with silver. On that one night, the earl may ride till daybreak, and it behoves him to make good use of his time; for, until the silver shoes of his steed be worn through, the spell that holds him and his beneath the lake, will retain its power.

When I (Miss Anne Baily) was a child, there was still living a man named Teigue O'Neill, who had a strange story to tell.

He was a smith, and his forge stood on the brow of the hill, overlooking the lake, on a lonely part of the road to Cahir Conlish. One bright moonlight night, he was working very late, and quite alone. The clink of his hammer, and the wavering glow reflected through the open door on the bushes at the other side of the narrow road, were the only tokens that told of life and vigil for miles around.

In one of the pauses of his work, he heard the ring of many hoofs ascending the steep road that passed his forge, and, standing in his doorway, he was just in time to see a gentleman, on a white horse, who was dressed in a fashion the like of which the smith had never seen before. This man was accompanied and followed by a mounted retinue, as strangely dressed as he.

They seemed, by the clang and clatter that announced their approach, to be riding up the hill at a hard hurry-scurry gallop; but the pace abated as they drew near, and the rider of the white horse who, from his grave and lordly air, he assumed to be a man of rank, and accustomed to command, drew bridle and came to a halt before the smith's door.

He did not speak, and all his train were silent, but he beckoned to the smith, and pointed down to one of his horse's hoofs.

Teigue stooped and raised it, and held it just long enough to see that it was shod with a silver shoe; which, in one place, he said, was worn as thin as a shilling. Instantaneously, his situation was made apparent to him by this sign, and he recoiled with a terrified prayer. The lordly rider, with a look of pain and fury, struck at him suddenly, with something that whistled in the air like a whip; and an icy streak seemed to traverse his body as if he had been cut through with a leaf of steel. But he was without scathe or scar, as he afterwards found. At the same moment he saw the whole cavalcade break into a gallop and disappear down the hill, with a momentary hurtling in the air, like the flight of a volley of cannon shot.

Here had been the earl himself. He had tried one of his accustomed stratagems to lead the smith to speak to him. For it is well known that either for the purpose of abridging or of mitigating his period of enchantment, he seeks to lead people to accost him. But what, in the event of his succeeding, would befall the person whom he had thus ensnared, no one knows.

Moll Rial's Adventure

When Miss Anne Baily was a child, Moll Rial was an old woman. She had lived all her days with the Bailys of Lough Guir; in and about whose house, as was the Irish custom of those days, were a troop of bare-footed country girls, scullery maids, or laundresses, or employed about the poultry yard, or running of errands.

Among these was Moll Rial, then a stout good-humoured lass, with little to think of, and nothing to fret about. She was once washing clothes by the process known universally in Munster as beetling. The washer stands up to her ankles in water, in which she has immersed the clothes, which she lays in that state on a great flat stone, and smacks with lusty strokes of an instrument which bears a rude resemblance to a cricket bat, only shorter, broader, and light enough to be wielded freely with one hand. Thus, they smack the dripping clothes, turning them over and over, sousing them in the water, and replacing them on the same stone, to undergo a repetition of the process, until they are thoroughly washed.

Moll Rial was plying her "beetle" at the margin of the lake, close under the old house and castle. It was between eight and nine o'clock on a fine summer morning, everything looked bright and beautiful. Though quite alone, and though she could not see even the windows of the house (hidden from her view by the irregular ascent and some interposing bushes), her loneliness was not depressing.

Standing up from her work, she saw a gentleman walking slowly down the slope toward her. He was a "grand-looking" gentleman, arrayed in a flowered silk dressing-gown, with a cap of velvet on his head; and as he stepped toward her, in his slippered feet, he showed a very handsome leg. He was smiling graciously as he approached, and drawing a ring from his finger with an air of gracious meaning, which seemed to imply that he wished to make her a present, he raised it in his fingers with a pleased look, and placed it on the flat stones beside the clothes she had been beetling so industriously.

He drew back a little, and continued to look at her with an encouraging smile, which seemed to say: "You have earned your reward; you must not be afraid to take it."

The girl fancied that this was some gentleman who had arrived, as often happened in those hospitable and haphazard times, late and unexpectedly the night before, and who was now taking a little indolent ramble before breakfast.

Moll Rial was a little shy, and more so at having been discovered by so grand a gentleman with her petticoats gathered a little high about her bare shins. She looked down, therefore, upon the water at her feet, and then she saw a ripple of blood, and then another, ring after ring, coming and going to and from her feet. She cried out the sacred name in horror, and, lifting her eyes, the courtly gentleman was gone, but the blood-rings about her feet spread with the speed of light over the surface of the lake, which for a moment glowed like one vast estuary of blood.

Here was the earl once again, and Moll Rial declared that if it had not been for that frightful transformation of the water she would have spoken to him next minute, and would thus have passed under a spell, perhaps as direful as his own.

The Banshee

So old a Munster family as the Bailys, of Lough Guir, could not fail to have their attendant banshee. Everyone attached to the family knew this well, and could cite evidences of that unearthly distinction. I heard Miss Baily relate the only experience she had personally had of that wild spiritual sympathy.

She said that, being then young, she and Miss Susan undertook a long attendance upon the sick bed of their sister, Miss Kitty, whom I have heard remembered among her contemporaries as the merriest and most entertaining of human beings. This light-hearted young lady was dying of consumption. The sad duties of such attendance being divided among many sisters, as there then were, the night watches devolved upon the two ladies I have named: I think, as being the eldest.

It is not improbable that these long and melancholy vigils, lowering the spirits and exciting the nervous system, prepared them for illusions. At all events, one night at dead of night, Miss Baily and her sister, sitting in the dying lady's room, heard such sweet and melancholy music as they had never heard before. It seemed to them like distant cathedral music. The room of the dying girl had its windows toward the yard, and the old castle stood near, and full in sight. The music was not in the house, but seemed to come from the yard, or beyond it. Miss Anne Baily took a candle, and went down the back stairs. She opened the back door, and, standing there, heard the same faint but solemn harmony, and could not tell whether it most resembled the distant music of instruments, or a choir of voices. It seemed to come through the windows of the old castle, high in the air. But when she approached the tower, the music, she thought, came from above the house, at the other side of the yard; and thus perplexed, and at last frightened, she returned.

This aerial music both she and her sister, Miss Susan Baily, avowed that they distinctly heard, and for a long time. Of the fact she was clear, and she spoke of it with great awe.

The Governess's Dream

THIS LADY, ONE MORNING, WITH a grave countenance that indicated something weighty upon her mind, told her pupils that she had, on the night before, had a very remarkable dream.

The first room you enter in the old castle, having reached the foot of the spiral stone stair, is a large hall, dim and lofty, having only a small window or two, set high in deep recesses in the wall. When I saw the castle many years ago, a portion of this capacious chamber was used as a store for the turf laid in to last the year.

Her dream placed her, alone, in this room, and there entered a grave-looking man, having something very remarkable in his countenance: which impressed her, as a fine portrait sometimes will, with a haunting sense of character and individuality.

In his hand this man carried a wand, about the length of an ordinary walking cane. He told her to observe and remember its length, and to mark well the measurements he was about to make, the result of which she was to communicate to Mr. Baily of Lough Guir.

From a certain point in the wall, with this wand, he measured along the floor, at right angles with the wall, a certain number of its lengths, which he counted aloud; and then, in the same way, from the adjoining wall he measured a certain number of its lengths, which he also counted distinctly. He then told her that at the point where these two lines met, at a depth of a certain number of feet which he also told her, treasure lay buried. And so the dream broke up, and her remarkable visitant vanished.

She took the girls with her to the old castle, where, having cut a switch to the length represented to her in her dream, she measured the distances, and ascertained, as she supposed, the point on the floor beneath which the treasure lay. The same day she related her dream to Mr. Baily. But he treated it laughingly, and took no step in consequence.

Sometime after this, she again saw, in a dream, the same remarkable-looking man, who repeated his message, and appeared displeased. But the dream was treated by Mr. Baily as before.

The same dream occurred again, and the children became so clamorous to have the castle floor explored, with pick and shovel, at the point indicated by the thrice-seen messenger, that at length Mr. Baily consented, and the floor was opened, and a trench was sunk at the spot which the governess had pointed out.

Miss Anne Baily, and nearly all the members of the family, her father included, were present at this operation. As the workmen approached the depth described in the vision, the interest and suspense of all increased; and when the iron implements met the solid resistance of a broad flagstone, which returned a cavernous sound to the stroke, the excitement of all present rose to its acme.

With some difficulty the flag was raised, and a chamber of stone work, large enough to receive a moderately-sized crock or pit, was disclosed. Alas! it was empty. But in the earth at the bottom of it, Miss Baily said, she herself saw, as every other bystander plainly did, the circular impression of a vessel: which had stood there, as the mark seemed to indicate, for a very long time.

Both the Miss Bailys were strong in their belief hereafterwards, that the treasure which they were convinced had actually been deposited there, had been removed by some more trusting and active listener than their father had proved.

This same governess remained with them to the time of her death, which occurred some years later, under the following circumstances as extraordinary as her dream.

The Earl's Hall

The good governess had a particular liking for the old castle, and when lessons were over, would take her book or her work into a large room in the ancient building, called the Earl's Hall. Here she caused a table and chair to be placed for her use, and in the chiaroscuro would so sit at her favourite occupations, with just a little ray of subdued light, admitted through one of the glassless windows above her, and falling upon her table.

The Earl's Hall is entered by a narrow-arched door, opening close to the winding stair. It is a very large and gloomy room, pretty nearly square, with a lofty vaulted ceiling, and a stone floor. Being situated high in the castle, the walls of which are immensely thick, and the windows very small and few, the silence that reigns here is like that of a subterranean cavern. You hear nothing in this solitude, except perhaps twice in a day, the twitter of a swallow in one of the small windows high in the wall.

This good lady having one day retired to her accustomed solitude, was missed from the house at her wonted hour of return. This in a country house, such as Irish houses Were in those days, excited little surprise, and no harm. But when the dinner hour came, which was then, in country houses, five o'clock, and the governess had not appeared, some of her young friends, it being not yet winter, and sufficient light remaining to guide them through the gloom of the dim ascent and passages, mounted the old stone stair to the level of the Earl's Hall, gaily calling to her as they approached.

There was no answer. On the stone floor, outside the door of the Earl's Hall, to their horror, they found her lying insensible. By the usual means she was restored to consciousness; but she continued very ill, and was conveyed to the house, where she took to her bed.

It was there and then that she related what had occurred to her. She had placed herself, as usual, at her little work table, and had been either working or reading—I forget which—for sometime, and felt in her usual health and serene spirits. Raising her eyes, and looking towards the door, she saw a horrible-looking little man enter. He was dressed in red, was very short, had a singularly dark face, and a most atrocious countenance. Having walked some steps into the room, with his eyes fixed on her, he stopped, and beckoning to her to follow, moved back toward the door. About half way, again he stopped once more and turned. She was so terrified that she sat staring at the apparition without moving or speaking. Seeing that she had not obeyed him, his face became more frightful and menacing, and as it underwent this change, he raised his hand and stamped on the floor. Gesture, look, and all, expressed diabolical fury. Through sheer extremity of terror she did rise, and, as he turned again, followed him a step or two in the direction of the door. He again stopped, and with the same mute menace, compelled her again to follow him.

She reached the narrow stone doorway of the Earl's Hall, through which he had passed; from the threshold she saw him standing a little way off, with his eyes still fixed on her. Again he signed to her, and began to move along the short passage that leads to the winding stair. But instead of following him further, she fell on the floor in a fit.

The poor lady was thoroughly persuaded that she was not long to survive this vision, and her foreboding proved true. From her bed she never rose. Fever and delirium supervened in a few days and she died. Of course it is possible that fever, already approaching, had touched her brain when she was visited by the phantom, and that it had no external existence.

Schalken the Painter

"For he is not a man as I am that we should come together; neither is there any that might lay his hand upon us both. Let him, therefore, take his rod away from me, and let not his fear terrify me."

There exists, at this moment, in good preservation a remarkable work of Schalken's. The curious management of its lights constitutes, as usual in his pieces, the chief apparent merit of the picture. I say *apparent*, for in its subject, and not in its handling, however exquisite, consists its real value. The picture represents the interior of what might be a chamber in some antique religious building; and its foreground is occupied by a female figure, in a species of white robe, part of which is arranged so as to form a veil. The dress, however, is not that of any religious order. In her hand the figure bears a lamp, by which alone her figure and face are illuminated; and her features wear such an arch smile, as well becomes a pretty woman when practising some prankish roguery; in the background, and, excepting where the dim red light of an expiring fire serves to define the form, in total shadow, stands the figure of a man dressed in the old Flemish fashion, in an attitude of alarm, his hand being placed upon the hilt of his sword, which he appears to be in the act of drawing.

There are some pictures, which impress one, I know not how, with a conviction that they represent not the mere ideal shapes and combinations which have floated through the imagination of the artist, but scenes, faces, and situations which have actually existed. There is in that strange picture, something that stamps it as the representation of a reality.

And such in truth it is, for it faithfully records a remarkable and mysterious occurrence, and perpetuates, in the face of the female figure, which occupies the most prominent place in the design, an accurate portrait of Rose Velderkaust, the niece of Gerard Douw, the first, and, I believe, the only love of Godfrey Schalken. My great grandfather knew the painter well; and from Schalken himself he learned the fearful story of the painting, and from him too he ultimately received the picture itself as a bequest. The story and the picture have become heir-looms in my family, and having described the latter, I shall, if you please, attempt to relate the tradition which has descended with the canvas.

There are few forms on which the mantle of romance hangs more ungracefully than upon that of the uncouth Schalken—the boorish but most cunning worker in oils, whose pieces delight the critics of our day almost as much as his manners disgusted the refined of his own; and yet this man, so rude, so dogged, so slovenly, in the midst of his celebrity, had in his obscure, but happier days, played the hero in a wild romance of mystery and passion.

When Schalken studied under the immortal Gerard Douw, he was a very young man; and in spite of his phlegmatic temperament, he at once fell over head and ears in love with the beautiful niece of his wealthy master. Rose Velderkaust was still younger than he, having not yet attained her seventeenth year, and, if tradition speaks truth, possessed all the soft and dimpling charms of the fair, light-haired Flemish maidens. The young painter loved honestly and fervently. His frank adoration was rewarded. He declared his love, and extracted a faltering confession in return. He was the happiest and proudest painter in all Christendom. But there was somewhat to dash his elation; he was poor and undistinguished. He dared not ask old Gerard for the hand of his sweet ward. He must first win a reputation and a competence.

There were, therefore, many dread uncertainties and cold days before him; he had to fight his way against sore odds. But he had won the heart of dear Rose Velderkaust, and that was half the battle. It is needless to say his exertions were redoubled, and his lasting celebrity proves that his industry was not unrewarded by success.

These ardent labours, and worse still, the hopes that elevated and beguiled them, were however, destined to experience a sudden interruption—of a character so strange and mysterious as to baffle all inquiry and to throw over the events themselves a shadow of preternatural horror.

Schalken had one evening outstayed all his fellow-pupils, and still pursued his work in the deserted room. As the daylight was fast falling, he laid aside his colours, and applied himself to the completion of a sketch on which he had expressed extraordinary pains. It was a religious composition, and represented the temptations of a pot-bellied Saint Anthony. The young artist, however destitute of elevation, had, nevertheless, discernment enough to be dissatisfied with his own work, and many were the patient erasures and improvements which saint and devil underwent, yet all in vain. The large, old-fashioned room was silent, and, with the exception of himself, quite emptied of its usual inmates. An hour had thus passed away, nearly two, without any improved result. Daylight had already declined, and twilight was deepening into the darkness of night. The patience of the young painter was exhausted, and he stood before his unfinished production, angry and mortified, one hand buried in the folds of his long hair, and the other holding the piece of charcoal which had so ill-performed its office, and which he now rubbed, without much regard to the sable streaks it produced, with irritable pressure upon his ample Flemish inexpressibles. "Curse the subject!" said the young man aloud; "curse the picture, the devils, the saint—"

At this moment a short, sudden sniff uttered close beside him made the artist turn sharply round, and he now, for the first time, became aware that his labours had been overlooked by a stranger. Within about a yard and half, and rather behind him, there stood the figure of an elderly man in a cloak and broad-brimmed, conical hat; in his hand, which was protected with a heavy gauntlet-shaped glove, he carried a long ebony walking-stick, surmounted with what appeared, as it glittered dimly in the twilight, to be a massive head of gold, and upon his breast, through the folds of the cloak, there shone the links of a rich chain of the same metal. The room was so obscure that nothing further of the appearance of the figure could be ascertained, and his hat threw his features into profound shadow. It would not have been easy to conjecture the age of the intruder; but a quantity of dark hair escaping from beneath this sombre hat, as well as his firm and upright carriage served to indicate that his years could not yet exceed threescore, or thereabouts. There was an air of gravity and importance about the garb of the person, and something indescribably odd, I might say awful, in the perfect, stone-like stillness of the figure, that effectually checked the testy comment which had at once risen to the lips of the irritated artist. He, therefore, as soon as he had sufficiently recovered his surprise, asked the stranger, civilly, to be seated, and desired to know if he had any message to leave for his master.

"Tell Gerard Douw," said the unknown, without altering his attitude in the smallest degree, "that Minheer Vanderhausen, of Rotterdam, desires to speak with him on tomorrow evening at this hour, and if he please, in this room, upon matters of weight; that is all."

The stranger, having finished this message, turned abruptly, and, with a quick, but silent step quitted the room, before Schalken had time to say a word in reply. The young man felt a curiosity to see in what direction the burgher of Rotterdam would turn, on quitting the studio, and for that purpose he went directly to the window which commanded the door. A lobby of considerable extent intervened between the inner door of the painter's room and the street entrance, so that Schalken occupied the post of observation before the old man could possibly have reached the street. He watched in vain, however. There was no other mode of exit. Had the queer old man vanished, or was he lurking about the recesses of the lobby for some sinister purpose? This last suggestion filled the mind of Schalken with a vague uneasiness, which was so unaccountably intense as to make him alike afraid to remain in the room alone, and reluctant to pass through the lobby. However, with an effort which appeared very disproportioned to the occasion, he summoned resolution to leave the room, and, having locked the door and thrust the key in his pocket, without looking to the right or left, he traversed the passage which had so recently, perhaps still, contained the person of his mysterious visitant, scarcely venturing to breathe till he had arrived in the open street.

"Minheer Vanderhausen!" said Gerard Douw within himself, as the appointed hour approached, "Minheer Vanderhausen, of Rotterdam! I never heard of the man till yesterday. What can he want of me? A portrait, perhaps, to be painted; or a poor relation to be apprenticed; or a collection to be valued; or—pshaw! there's no one in Rotterdam to leave me a legacy. Well, whatever the business may be, we shall soon know it all."

It was now the close of day, and again every easel, except that of Schalken, was deserted. Gerard Douw was pacing the apartment with the restless step of impatient expectation, sometimes pausing to glance over the work of one of his absent pupils, but more frequently placing himself at the window, from whence he might observe the passengers who threaded the obscure by-street in which his studio was placed.

"Said you not, Godfrey," exclaimed Douw, after a long and fruitful gaze from his post of observation, and turning to Schalken, "that the hour he appointed was about seven by the clock of the Stadhouse?"

"It had just told seven when I first saw him, sir," answered the student.

"The hour is close at hand, then," said the master, consulting a horologe as large and as round as an orange. "Minheer Vanderhausen from Rotterdam—is it not so?"

"Such was the name."

"And an elderly man, richly clad?" pursued Douw, musingly.

"As well as I might see," replied his pupil; "he could not be young, nor yet very old, neither; and his dress was rich and grave, as might become a citizen of wealth and consideration."

At this moment the sonorous boom of the Stadhouse clock told, stroke after stroke, the hour of seven; the eyes of both master and student were directed to the door; and it was not until the last peal of the bell had ceased to vibrate, that Douw exclaimed—

"So, so; we shall have his worship presently, that is, if he means to keep his hour; if not, you may wait for him, Godfrey, if you court his acquaintance. But what, after all, if it should prove but a mummery got up by Vankarp, or some such wag? I wish you had run all risks, and cudgelled the old burgomaster soundly. I'd wager a dozen of Rhenish, his worship would have unmasked, and pleaded old acquaintance in a trice."

"Here he comes, sir," said Schalken, in a low monitory tone; and instantly, upon turning towards the door, Gerard Douw observed the same figure which had, on the day before, so unexpectedly greeted his pupil Schalken.

There was something in the air of the figure which at once satisfied the painter that there was no masquerading in the case, and that he really stood in the presence of a man of worship; and so, without hesitation, he doffed his cap, and courteously saluting the stranger, requested him to be seated. The visitor waved his hand slightly, as if in acknowledgment of the courtesy, but remained standing.

"I have the honour to see Minheer Vanderhausen of Rotterdam?" said Gerard Douw.

"The same," was the laconic reply of his visitor.

"I understand your worship desires to speak with me," continued Douw, "and I am here by appointment to wait your commands."

"Is that a man of trust?" said Vanderhausen, turning towards Schalken, who stood at a little distance behind his master.

"Certainly," replied Gerard.

"Then let him take this box, and get the nearest jeweller or goldsmith to value its contents, and let him return hither with a certificate of the valuation."

At the same time, he placed a small case about nine inches square in the hands of Gerard Douw, who was as much amazed at its weight as at the strange abruptness with which it was handed to him. In accordance with the wishes of the stranger, he delivered it into the hands of Schalken, and repeating his direction, despatched him upon the mission.

Schalken disposed his precious charge securely beneath the folds of his cloak, and rapidly traversing two or three narrow streets, he stopped at a corner house, the lower part of which was then occupied by the shop of a Jewish goldsmith. He entered the shop, and calling the little Hebrew into the obscurity of its back recesses, he proceeded to lay before him Vanderhausen's casket. On being examined by the light of a lamp, it appeared entirely cased with lead, the outer surface of which was much scraped and soiled, and nearly white with age. This having been partially removed, there appeared beneath a box of some hard wood; which also they forced open and after the removal of two or three folds of linen, they discovered its contents to be a mass of golden ingots, closely packed, and, as the Jew declared, of the most perfect quality. Every ingot underwent the scrutiny of the little Jew, who seemed to feel an epicurean delight in touching and testing these morsels of the glorious metal; and each one of them was replaced in its berth with the exclamation: "*Mein Gott*, how very perfect! not one grain of alloy—beautiful, beautiful!" The task was at length finished, and the Jew certified under his hand the value of the ingots submitted to his examination, to amount to many thousand rix-dollars. With the desired document in his pocket, and the rich box of gold carefully pressed under his arm, and concealed by his cloak, he retraced his way, and entering the studio, found his master and the stranger in close conference. Schalken had no sooner left the room, in order to execute the commission he had taken in charge, than Vanderhausen addressed Gerard Douw in the following terms:—

"I cannot tarry with you tonight more than a few minutes, and so I shall shortly tell you the matter upon which I come. You visited the town of Rotterdam some four months ago, and then I saw in the church of St. Lawrence your niece, Rose Velderkaust. I desire to marry her; and if I satisfy you that I am wealthier than any husband you can dream of for her, I expect that you will forward my suit with your authority. If you approve my proposal, you must close with it here and now, for I cannot wait for calculations and delays."

Gerard Douw was hugely astonished by the nature of Minheer Vanderhausen's communication, but he did not venture to express surprise; for besides the motives supplied by prudence and politeness, the painter experienced a kind of chill and oppression like that which is said to intervene when one is placed in unconscious proximity with the object of a natural antipathy—an undefined but overpowering sensation, while standing in the presence of the eccentric stranger, which made him very unwilling to say anything which might reasonably offend him.

"I have no doubt," said Gerard, after two or three prefatory hems, "that the alliance which you propose would prove alike advantageous and honourable to my niece; but you must be aware that she has a will of her own, and may not acquiesce in what *we* may design for her advantage."

"Do not seek to deceive me, sir painter," said Vanderhausen; "you are her guardian—she is your ward—she is mine if *you* like to make her so."

The man of Rotterdam moved forward a little as he spoke, and Gerard Douw, he scarce knew why, inwardly prayed for the speedy return of Schalken.

"I desire," said the mysterious gentleman, "to place in your hands at once an evidence of my wealth, and a security for my liberal dealing with your niece. The lad will return in a minute or two with a sum in value five times the fortune which she has a right to expect from her husband. This shall lie in your hands, together with her dowry, and you may apply the united sum as suits her interest best; it shall be all exclusively hers while she lives: is that liberal?"

Douw assented, and inwardly acknowledged that fortune had been extraordinarily kind to his niece; the stranger, he thought, must be both wealthy and generous, and such an offer was not to be despised, though made by a humourist, and one of no very prepossessing presence. Rose had no very high pretensions for she had but a modest dowry, which she owed entirely to the generosity of her uncle; neither had she any right to raise exceptions on the score of birth, for her own origin was far from splendid, and as the other objections, Gerald resolved, and indeed, by the usages of the time, was warranted in resolving, not to listen to them for a moment.

"Sir" said he, addressing the stranger, "your offer is liberal, and whatever hesitation I may feel in closing with it immediately, arises solely from my not having the honour of knowing anything of your family or station. Upon these points you can, of course, satisfy me without difficulty?'

"As to my respectability," said the stranger, drily, "you must take that for granted at present; pester me with no inquiries; you can discover nothing more about me than I choose to make known. You shall have sufficient security for my respectability—my word, if you are honourable: if you are sordid, my gold."

"A testy old gentleman," thought Douw, "he must have his own way; but, all things considered, I am not justified to declining his offer. I will not pledge myself unnecessarily, however."

"You will not pledge yourself unnecessarily," said Vanderhausen, strangely uttering the very words which had just floated through the mind of his companion; "but you will do so if it is necessary, I presume; and I will show you that I consider it indispensable. If the gold I mean to leave in your hands satisfy you, and if you don't wish my proposal to be at once withdrawn, you must, before I leave this room, write your name to this engagement."

Having thus spoken, he placed a paper in the hands of the master, the contents of which expressed an engagement entered into by Gerard Douw, to give to Wilken Vanderhausen of Rotterdam, in marriage, Rose Velderkaust, and so forth, within one week of the date thereof. While the painter was employed in reading this covenant, by the light of a twinkling oil lamp in the far wall of the room, Schalken, as we have stated, entered the studio, and having delivered the box and the valuation of the Jew, into the hands of the stranger, he was about to retire, when Vanderhausen called to him to wait; and, presenting the case and the certificate to Gerard Douw, he paused in silence until he had satisfied himself, by an inspection of both, respecting the value of the pledge left in his hands. At length he said—

"Are you content?"

The painter said he would fain have another day to consider.

"Not an hour," said the suitor, apathetically.

"Well then," said Douw, with a sore effort, "I am content, it is a bargain."

"Then sign at once," said Vanderhausen, "for I am weary."

At the same time he produced a small case of writing materials, and Gerard signed the important document.

"Let this youth witness the covenant," said the old man; and Godfrey Schalken unconsciously attested the instrument which forever bereft him of his dear Rose Velderkaust.

The compact being thus completed, the strange visitor folded up the paper, and stowed it safely in an inner pocket.

"I will visit you tomorrow night at nine o'clock, at your own house, Gerard Douw, and will see the object of our contract"; and so saying Wilken Vanderhausen moved stiffly, but rapidly, out of the room.

JOSEPH SHERIDAN LE FANU

Schalken, eager to resolve his doubts, had placed himself by the window, in order to watch the street entrance; but the experiment served only to support his suspicions, for the old man did not issue from the door. This was *very* strange, odd, nay fearful. He and his master returned together, and talked but little on the way, for each had his own subjects of reflection, of anxiety, and of hope. Schalken, however, did not know the ruin which menaced his dearest projects.

Gerard Douw knew nothing of the attachment which had sprung up between his pupil and his niece; and even if he had, it is doubtful whether he would have regarded its existence as any serious obstruction to the wishes of Minheer Vanderhausen. Marriages were then and there matters of traffic and calculation; and it would have appeared as absurd in the eyes of the guardian to make a mutual attachment an essential element in a contract of the sort, as it would have been to draw up his bonds and receipts in the language of romance.

The painter, however, did not communicate to his niece the important step which he had taken in her behalf, a forebearance caused not by any anticipated opposition on her part, but solely by a ludicrous consciousness that if she were to ask him for a description of her destined bridegroom, he would be forced to confess that he had not once seen his face, and if called upon, would find it absolutely impossible to identify him. Upon the next day, Gerard Douw, after dinner, called his niece to him and having scanned her person with an air of satisfaction, he took her hand, and looking upon her pretty innocent face with a smile of kindness, he said:—

"Rose, my girl, that face of yours will make your fortune." Rose blushed and smiled. "Such faces and such tempers seldom go together, and when they do, the compound is a love charm, few heads or hearts can resist; trust me, you will soon be a bride, girl. But this is trifling, and I am pressed for time, so make ready the large room by eight o'clock tonight, and give directions for supper at nine. I expect a friend; and observe me, child, do you trick yourself out handsomely. I will not have him think us poor or sluttish."

With these words he left her, and took his way to the room in which his pupils worked.

When the evening closed in, Gerard called Schalken, who was about to take his departure to his own obscure and comfortless lodgings, and asked him to come home and sup with Rose and Vanderhausen. The invitation was, of course, accepted and Gerard Douw and his pupil soon found themselves in the handsome and, even then, antique chamber, which had been prepared for the reception of the stranger. A cheerful wood fire blazed in the hearth, a little at one side of which an old-fashioned table, which shone in the fire-light like burnished gold, was awaiting the supper, for which preparations were going forward; and ranged with exact regularity, stood the tall-backed chairs, whose ungracefulness was more than compensated by their comfort. The little party, consisting of Rose, her uncle, and the artist, awaited the arrival of the expected visitor with considerable impatience. Nine o'clock at length came, and with it a summons at the street door, which being speedily answered, was followed by a slow and emphatic tread upon the staircase; the steps moved heavily across the lobby, the door of the room in which the party we have described were assembled slowly opened, and there entered a figure which startled, almost appalled, the phlegmatic Dutchmen, and nearly made Rose scream with terror. It was the form, and arrayed in the garb of Minheer Vanderhausen; the air, the gait, the height were the same, but the features had never been seen by any of the party before. The stranger stopped at the door of the room, and displayed his form and face completely. He wore a dark-coloured cloth cloak, which was short and full, not falling quite to his knees; his legs were cased in dark purple silk stockings, and his shoes were adorned with roses of the same colour. The opening of the cloak in front showed the under-suit to consist of some very dark, perhaps sable material, and his hands were enclosed in a pair of heavy leather gloves, which ran up considerably above the wrist, in the manner of a gauntlet. In one hand he carried his walking-stick and his hat, which he had removed, and the other hung heavily by his side. A quantity of grizzled hair descended in long tresses from his head, and rested upon the plaits of a stiff ruff, which effectually concealed his neck. So far all was well; but the face!— all the flesh of the face was coloured with the bluish leaden hue, which is sometimes produced by metallic medicines, administered in excessive quantities; the eyes showed an undue proportion of muddy white, and had a certain indefinable character of insanity; the hue of the lips bearing the usual relation to that of the face, was, consequently, nearly black; and the entire character of the face was sensual, malignant, and even satanic. It was remarkable that the worshipful stranger suffered as little as possible of his flesh to appear, and that during his visit he did not once remove his gloves. Having stood for some moments at the door, Gerard Douw at length found breath and collectedness to bid

　　　　　　　　　　　　　　JOSEPH SHERIDAN LE FANU

him welcome, and with a mute inclination of the head, the stranger stepped forward into the room. There was something indescribably odd, even horrible, about all his motions, something undefinable, that was unnatural, unhuman; it was as if the limbs were guided and directed by a spirit unused to the management of bodily machinery. The stranger spoke hardly at all during his visit, which did not exceed half an hour; and the host himself could scarcely muster courage enough to utter the few necessary salutations and courtesies; and, indeed, such was the nervous terror which the presence of Vanderhausen inspired, that very little would have made all his entertainers fly in downright panic from the room. They had not so far lost all self-possession, however, as to fail to observe two strange peculiarities of their visitor. During his stay his eyelids did not once close, or, indeed, move in the slightest degree; and farther, there was a deathlike stillness in his whole person, owing to the absence of the heaving motion of the chest, caused by the process of respiration. These two peculiarities, though when told they may appear trifling, produced a very striking and unpleasant effect when seen and observed. Vanderhausen at length relieved the painter of Leyden of his inauspicious presence; and with no trifling sense of relief the little party heard the street door close after him.

"Dear uncle," said Rose, "what a frightful man! I would not see him again for the wealth of the States."

"Tush, foolish girl," said Douw, whose sensations were anything but comfortable. "A man may be as ugly as the devil, and yet, if his heart and actions are good, he is worth all the pretty-faced perfumed puppies that walk the Mall. Rose, my girl, it is very true he has not thy pretty face, but I know him to be wealthy and liberal; and were he ten times more ugly, these two virtues would be enough to counter balance all his deformity, and if not sufficient actually to alter the shape and hue of his features, at least enough to prevent one thinking them so much amiss."

"Do you know, uncle," said Rose, "when I saw him standing at the door, I could not get it out of my head that I saw the old painted wooden figure that used to frighten me so much in the Church of St. Laurence at Rotterdam."

Gerard laughed, though he could not help inwardly acknowledging the justness of the comparison. He was resolved, however, as far as he could, to check his niece's disposition to dilate upon the ugliness of her intended bridegroom, although he was not a little pleased, as well as puzzled, to observe that she appeared totally exempt from that mysterious dread of the stranger which, he could not disguise it from himself, considerably affected him, as also his pupil Godfrey Schalken.

Early on the next day there arrived, from various quarters of the town, rich presents of silks, velvets, jewellery, and so forth, for Rose; and also a packet directed to Gerard Douw, which on being opened, was found to contain a contract of marriage, formally drawn up, between Wilken Vanderhausen of the *Boom-quay*, in Rotterdam, and Rose Velderkaust of Leyden, niece to Gerard Douw, master in the art of painting, also of the same city; and containing engagements on the part of Vanderhausen to make settlements upon his bride, far more splendid than he had before led her guardian to believe likely, and which were to be secured to her use in the most unexceptionable manner possible—the money being placed in the hand of Gerard Douw himself.

I have no sentimental scenes to describe, no cruelty of guardians, no magnanimity of wards, no agonies, or transport of lovers. The record I have to make is one of sordidness, levity, and heartlessness. In less than a week after the first interview which we have just described, the contract of marriage was fulfilled, and Schalken saw the prize which he would have risked existence to secure, carried off in solemn pomp by his repulsive rival. For two or three days he absented himself from the school; he then returned and worked, if with less cheerfulness, with far more dogged resolution than before; the stimulus of love had given place to that of ambition. Months passed away, and, contrary to his expectation, and, indeed, to the direct promise of the parties, Gerard Douw heard nothing of his niece or her worshipful spouse. The interest of the money, which was to have been demanded in quarterly sums, lay unclaimed in his hands.

He began to grow extremely uneasy. Minheer Vanderhausen's direction in Rotterdam he was fully possessed of; after some irresolution he finally determined to journey thither—a trifling undertaking, and easily accomplished—and thus to satisfy himself of the safety and comfort of his ward, for whom he entertained an honest and strong affection. His search was in vain, however; no one in Rotterdam had ever heard of Minheer Vanderhausen. Gerard Douw left not a house in the *Boom-quay* untried, but all in vain. No one could give him any information whatever touching the object of his inquiry, and he was obliged to return to Leyden nothing wiser and far more anxious, than when he had left it.

On his arrival he hastened to the establishment from which Vanderhausen had hired the lumbering, though, considering the times, most luxurious vehicle, which the bridal party had employed to convey them to Rotterdam. From the driver of this machine he learned, that having proceeded by slow stages, they had late in the evening approached Rotterdam; but that before they entered the city, and while yet nearly a mile from it, a small party of men, soberly clad, and after the old fashion, with peaked beards and moustaches, standing in the centre of the road, obstructed the further progress of the carriage. The driver reined in his horses, much fearing, from the obscurity of the hour, and the loneliness, of the road, that some mischief was intended. His fears were, however, somewhat allayed by his observing that these strange men carried a large litter, of an antique shape, and which they immediately set down upon the pavement, whereupon the bridegroom, having opened the coach-door from within, descended, and having assisted his bride to do likewise, led her, weeping bitterly, and wringing her hands, to the litter, which they both entered. It was then raised by the men who surrounded it, and speedily carried towards the city, and before it had proceeded very far, the darkness concealed it from the view of the Dutch coachman. In the inside of the vehicle he found a purse, whose contents more than thrice paid the hire of the carriage and man. He saw and could tell nothing more of Minheer Vanderhausen and his beautiful lady.

This mystery was a source of profound anxiety and even grief to Gerard Douw. There was evidently fraud in the dealing of Vanderhausen with him, though for what purpose committed he could not imagine. He greatly doubted how far it was possible for a man possessing such a countenance to be anything but a villain, and everyday that passed without his hearing from or of his niece, instead of inducing him to forget his fears, on the contrary tended more and more to aggravate them. The loss of her cheerful society tended also to depress his spirits; and in order to dispel the gloom, which often crept upon his mind after his daily occupations were over, he was wont frequently to ask Schalken to accompany him home, and share his otherwise solitary supper.

One evening, the painter and his pupil were sitting by the fire, having accomplished a comfortable meal, and had yielded to the silent and delicious melancholy of digestion, when their ruminations were disturbed by a loud sound at the street door, as if occasioned by some person rushing and scrambling vehemently against it. A domestic had run without delay to ascertain the cause of the disturbance, and they heard him twice or thrice interrogate the applicant for admission, but without eliciting any other answer but a sustained reiteration of the sounds. They heard him then open the hall-door, and immediately there followed a light and rapid tread on the staircase. Schalken advanced towards the door. It opened before he reached it, and Rose rushed into the room. She looked wild, fierce and haggard with terror and exhaustion, but her dress surprised them as much as even her unexpected appearance. It consisted of a kind of white woollen wrapper, made close about the neck, and descending to the very ground. It was much deranged and travel-soiled. The poor creature had hardly entered the chamber when she fell senseless on the floor. With some difficulty they succeeded in reviving her, and on recovering her senses, she instantly exclaimed, in a tone of terror rather than mere impatience:—

"Wine! wine! quickly, or I'm lost!"

Astonished and almost scared at the strange agitation in which the call was made, they at once administered to her wishes, and she drank some wine with a haste and eagerness which surprised them. She had hardly swallowed it, when she exclaimed, with the same urgency:

"Food, for God's sake, food, at once, or I perish."

A considerable fragment of a roast joint was upon the table, and Schalken immediately began to cut some, but he was anticipated, for no sooner did she see it than she caught it, a more than mortal image of famine, and with her hands, and even with her teeth, she tore off the flesh, and swallowed it. When the paroxysm of hunger had been a little appeased, she appeared on a sudden overcome with shame, or it may have been that other more agitating thoughts overpowered and scared her, for she began to weep bitterly and to wring her hands.

"Oh, send for a minister of God," said she; "I am not safe till he comes; send for him speedily."

Gerard Douw despatched a messenger instantly, and prevailed on his niece to allow him to surrender his bed chamber to her use. He also persuaded her to retire to it at once to rest; her consent was extorted upon the condition that they would not leave her for a moment.

"Oh that the holy man were here," she said; "he can deliver me: the dead and the living can never be one: God has forbidden it."

With these mysterious words she surrendered herself to their guidance, and they proceeded to the chamber which Gerard Douw had assigned to her use.

"Do not, do not leave me for a moment," said she; "I am lost forever if you do."

Gerard Douw's chamber was approached through a spacious apartment, which they were now about to enter. He and Schalken each carried a candle, so that a sufficiency of light was cast upon all surrounding objects. They were now entering the large chamber, which as I have said, communicated with Douw's apartment, when Rose suddenly stopped, and, in a whisper which thrilled them both with horror, she said:—

"Oh, God! he is here! he is here! See, see! there he goes!"

She pointed towards the door of the inner room, and Schalken thought he saw a shadowy and ill-defined form gliding into that apartment. He drew his sword, and, raising the candle so as to throw its light with increased distinctness upon the objects in the room, he entered the chamber into which the shadow had glided. No figure was there—nothing but the furniture which belonged to the room, and yet he could not be deceived as to the fact that something had moved before them into the chamber. A sickening dread came upon him, and the cold perspiration broke out in heavy drops upon his forehead; nor was he more composed, when he heard the increased urgency and agony of entreaty, with which Rose implored them not to leave her for a moment.

"I saw him," said she; "he's here. I cannot be deceived; I know him; he's by me; he is with me; he's in the room. Then, for God's sake, as you would save me, do not stir from beside me."

They at length prevailed upon her to lie down upon the bed, where she continued to urge them to stay by her. She frequently uttered incoherent sentences, repeating, again and again, "the dead and the living cannot be one: God has forbidden it." And then again, "Rest to the wakeful—sleep to the sleep-walkers." These and such mysterious and broken sentences, she continued to utter until the clergyman arrived. Gerard Douw began to fear, naturally enough, that terror or ill-treatment, had unsettled the poor girl's intellect, and he half suspected, by the suddenness of her appearance, the unseasonableness of the hour, and above all, from the wildness and terror of her manner, that she had made her escape from some place of confinement for lunatics, and was in imminent fear of pursuit. He resolved to summon medical advice as soon as the mind of his niece had been in some measure set at rest by the offices of the clergyman whose attendance she had so earnestly desired; and until this object had been attained, he did not venture to put any questions to her, which might possibly, by reviving painful or horrible recollections, increase her agitation. The clergyman soon arrived—a man of ascetic countenance and venerable age—one whom Gerard Douw respected very much, forasmuch as he was a veteran polemic, though one perhaps more dreaded as a combatant than beloved as a Christian—of pure morality, subtle brain, and frozen heart. He entered the chamber which communicated with that in which Rose reclined and immediately on his arrival, she requested him to pray for her, as for one who lay in the hands of Satan, and who could hope for deliverance only from heaven.

That you may distinctly understand all the circumstances of the event which I am going to describe, it is necessary to state the relative position of the parties who were engaged in it. The old clergyman and Schalken were in the anteroom of which I have already spoken; Rose lay in the inner chamber, the door of which was open; and by the side of the bed, at her urgent desire, stood her guardian; a candle burned in the bedchamber, and three were lighted in the outer apartment. The old man now cleared his voice as if about to commence, but before he had time to begin, a sudden gust of air blew out the candle which served to illuminate the room in which the poor girl lay, and she, with hurried alarm, exclaimed:—

"Godfrey, bring in another candle; the darkness is unsafe."

Gerard Douw forgetting for the moment her repeated injunctions, in the immediate impulse, stepped from the bedchamber into the other, in order to supply what she desired.

"Oh God! do not go, dear uncle," shrieked the unhappy girl—and at the same time she sprung from the bed, and darted after him, in order, by her grasp, to detain him. But the warning came too late, for scarcely had he passed the threshold, and hardly had his niece had time to utter the startling exclamation, when the door which divided the two rooms closed violently after him, as if swung by a strong blast of wind. Schalken and he both rushed to the door, but their united and desperate efforts could not avail so much as to shake it. Shriek after shriek burst from the inner chamber, with all the piercing loudness of despairing terror. Schalken and Douw applied every nerve to force open the door; but all in vain. There was no sound of struggling from within, but the screams seemed to increase in loudness, and at the same time they heard the bolts of the latticed window withdrawn, and the window itself grated upon the sill as if thrown open. One *last* shriek, so long and piercing and agonized as to be scarcely human, swelled from the room, and suddenly there followed a death-like silence. A light step was heard crossing the floor, as if from the bed to the window;

JOSEPH SHERIDAN LE FANU

and almost at the same instant the door gave way, and, yielding to the pressure of the external applicants, nearly precipitated them into the room. It was empty. The window was open, and Schalken sprung to a chair and gazed out upon the street and canal below. He saw no form, but he saw, or thought he saw, the waters of the broad canal beneath settling ring after ring in heavy circles, as if a moment before disturbed by the submission of some ponderous body.

No trace of Rose was ever after found, nor was anything certain respecting her mysterious wooer discovered or even suspected—no clue whereby to trace the intricacies of the labyrinth and to arrive at its solution, presented itself. But an incident occurred, which, though it will not be received by our rational readers in lieu of evidence, produced nevertheless a strong and a lasting impression upon the mind of Schalken. Many years after the events which we have detailed, Schalken, then residing far away received an intimation of his father's death, and of his intended burial upon a fixed day in the church of Rotterdam. It was necessary that a very considerable journey should be performed by the funeral procession, which as it will be readily believed, was not very numerously attended. Schalken with difficulty arrived in Rotterdam late in the day upon which the funeral was appointed to take place. It had not then arrived. Evening closed in, and still it did not appear.

Schalken strolled down to the church; he found it open; notice of the arrival of the funeral had been given, and the vault in which the body was to be laid had been opened. The sexton, on seeing a well-dressed gentleman, whose object was to attend the expected obsequies, pacing the aisle of the church, hospitably invited him to share with him the comforts of a blazing fire, which, as was his custom in winter time upon such occasions, he had kindled in the hearth of a chamber in which he was accustomed to await the arrival of such grisly guests and which communicated, by a flight of steps, with the vault below. In this chamber, Schalken and his entertainer seated themselves; and the sexton, after some fruitless attempts to engage his guest in conversation, was obliged to apply himself to his tobacco-pipe and can, to solace his solitude. In spite of his grief and cares, the fatigues of a rapid journey of nearly forty hours gradually overcame the mind and body of Godfrey Schalken, and he sank into a deep sleep, from which he awakened by someone's shaking him gently by the shoulder. He first thought that the old sexton had called him, but *he* was no longer in the room. He roused himself, and as soon as he could clearly see what was around him, he perceived a female form, clothed in a kind of light robe of white, part of which was so disposed as to form a veil, and in her hand she carried a lamp. She was moving rather away from him, in the direction of the flight of steps which conducted towards the vaults. Schalken felt a vague alarm at the sight of this figure and at the same time an irresistible impulse to follow its guidance. He followed it towards the vaults, but when it reached the head of the stairs, he paused; the figure paused also, and, turning gently round, displayed, by the light of the lamp it carried, the face and features of his first love, Rose Velderkaust. There was nothing horrible, or even sad, in the countenance. On the contrary, it wore the same arch smile which used to enchant the artist long before in his happy days. A feeling of awe and interest, too intense to be resisted, prompted him to follow the spectre, if spectre it were. She descended the stairs—he followed—and turning to the left, through a narrow passage, she led him, to his infinite surprise, into what appeared to be an old-fashioned Dutch apartment, such as the pictures of Gerard Douw have served to immortalize. Abundance of costly antique furniture was disposed about the room, and in one corner stood a four-post bed, with heavy black cloth curtains around it; the figure frequently turned towards him with the same arch smile; and when she came to the side of the bed, she drew the curtains, and, by the light of the lamp, which she held towards its contents, she disclosed to the horror-stricken painter, sitting bolt upright in the bed, the livid and demoniac form of Vanderhausen. Schalken had hardly seen him, when he fell senseless upon the floor, where he lay until discovered, on the next morning, by persons employed in closing the passages into the vaults. He was lying in a cell of considerable size, which had not been disturbed for a long time, and he had fallen beside a large coffin, which was supported upon small pillars, a security against the attacks of vermin.

To his dying day Schalken was satisfied of the reality of the vision which he had witnessed, and he has left behind him a curious evidence of the impression which it wrought upon his fancy, in a painting executed shortly after the event I have narrated, and which is valuable as exhibiting not only the peculiarities which have made Schalken's pictures sought after, but even more so as presenting a portrait of his early love, Rose Velderkaust, whose mysterious fate must always remain matter of speculation.

The Vision of Tom Chuff

At the edge of melancholy Catstean Moor, in the north of England, with half-a-dozen ancient poplar-trees with rugged and hoary stems around, one smashed across the middle by a flash of lightning thirty summers before, and all by their great height dwarfing the abode near which they stand, there squats a rude stone house, with a thick chimney, a kitchen and bedroom on the ground-floor, and a loft, accessible by a ladder, under the shingle roof, divided into two rooms.

Its owner was a man of ill repute. Tom Chuff was his name. A shock-headed, broad-shouldered, powerful man, though somewhat short, with lowering brows and a sullen eye. He was a poacher, and hardly made an ostensible pretence of earning his bread by any honest industry. He was a drunkard. He beat his wife, and led his children a life of terror and lamentation, when he was at home. It was a blessing to his frightened little family when he absented himself, as he sometimes did, for a week or more together.

On the night I speak of he knocked at the door with his cudgel at about eight o'clock. It was winter, and the night was very dark. Had the summons been that of a bogie from the moor, the inmates of this small house could hardly have heard it with greater terror.

His wife unbarred the door in fear and haste. Her hunchbacked sister stood by the hearth, staring toward the threshold. The children cowered behind.

Tom Chuff entered with his cudgel in his hand, without speaking, and threw himself into a chair opposite the fire. He had been away two or three days. He looked haggard, and his eyes were bloodshot. They knew he had been drinking.

Tom raked and knocked the peat fire with his stick, and thrust his feet close to it. He signed towards the little dresser, and nodded to his wife, and she knew he wanted a cup, which in silence she gave him. He pulled a bottle of gin from his coat-pocket, and nearly filling the teacup, drank off the dram at a few gulps.

He usually refreshed himself with two or three drams of this kind before beating the inmates of his house. His three little children, cowering in a corner, eyed him from under a table, as Jack did the ogre in the nursery tale. His wife, Nell, standing behind a chair, which she was ready to snatch up to meet the blow of the cudgel, which might be levelled at her at any moment, never took her eyes off him; and hunchbacked Mary showed the whites of a large pair of eyes, similarly employed, as she stood against the oaken press, her dark face hardly distinguishable in the distance from the brown panel behind it.

Tom Chuff was at his third dram, and had not yet spoken a word since his entrance, and the suspense was growing dreadful, when, on a sudden, he leaned back in his rude seat, the cudgel slipped from his hand, a change and a death-like pallor came over his face.

For a while they all stared on; such was their fear of him, they dared not speak or move, lest it should prove to have been but a doze, and Tom should wake up and proceed forthwith to gratify his temper and exercise his cudgel.

In a very little time, however, things began to look so odd, that they ventured, his wife and Mary, to exchange glances full of doubt and wonder. He hung so much over the side of the chair, that if it had not been one of cyclopean clumsiness and weight, he would have borne it to the floor. A leaden tint was darkening the pallor of his face. They were becoming alarmed, and finally braving everything his wife timidly said, "Tom!" and then more sharply repeated it, and finally cried the appellative loudly, and again and again, with the terrified accompaniment, "He's dying—he's dying!" her voice rising to a scream, as she found that neither it nor her plucks and shakings of him by the shoulder had the slightest effect in recalling him from his torpor.

And now from sheer terror of a new kind the children added their shrilly piping to the talk and cries of their seniors; and if anything could have called Tom up from his lethargy, it might have been the piercing chorus that made the rude chamber of the poacher's habitation ring again. But Tom continued unmoved, deaf, and stirless.

His wife sent Mary down to the village, hardly a quarter of a mile away, to implore of the doctor, for whose family she did duty as laundress, to come down and look at her husband, who seemed to be dying.

The doctor, who was a good-natured fellow, arrived. With his hat still on, he looked at Tom, examined him, and when he found that the emetic he had brought with him, on conjecture from Mary's description, did not act, and that his lancet brought no blood, and that he felt a pulseless wrist, he shook his head, and inwardly thought:

"What the plague is the woman crying for? Could she have desired a greater blessing for her children and herself than the very thing that has happened?"

Tom, in fact, seemed quite gone. At his lips no breath was perceptible. The doctor could discover no pulse. His hands and feet were cold, and the chill was stealing up into his body.

The doctor, after a stay of twenty minutes, had buttoned up his great-coat again and pulled down his hat, and told Mrs. Chuff that there was no use in his remaining any longer, when, all of a sudden, a little rill of blood began to trickle from the lancet-cut in Tom Chuffs temple.

"That's very odd," said the doctor. "Let us wait a little."

I must describe now the sensations which Tom Chuff had experienced.

With his elbows on his knees, and his chin upon his hands, he was staring into the embers, with his gin beside him, when suddenly a swimming came in his head, he lost sight of the fire, and a sound like one stroke of a loud church bell smote his brain.

Then he heard a confused humming, and the leaden weight of his head held him backward as he sank in his chair, and consciousness quite forsook him.

When he came to himself he felt chilled, and was leaning against a huge leafless tree. The night was moonless, and when he looked up he thought he had never seen stars so large and bright, or sky so black. The stars, too, seemed to blink down with longer intervals of darkness, and fiercer and more dazzling emergence, and something, he vaguely thought, of the character of silent menace and fury.

He had a confused recollection of having come there, or rather of having been carried along, as if on men's shoulders, with a sort of rushing motion. But it was utterly indistinct; the imperfect recollection simply of a sensation. He had seen or heard nothing on his way.

He looked round. There was not a sign of a living creature near. And he began with a sense of awe to recognise the place.

The tree against which he had been leaning was one of the noble old beeches that surround at irregular intervals the churchyard of Shackleton, which spreads its green and wavy lap on the edge of the Moor of Catstean, at the opposite side of which stands the rude cottage in which he had just lost consciousness. It was six miles or more across the moor to his habitation, and the black expanse lay before him, disappearing dismally in the darkness. So that, looking straight before him, sky and land blended together in an undistinguishable and awful blank.

There was a silence quite unnatural over the place. The distant murmur of the brook, which he knew so well, was dead; not a whisper in the leaves about him; the air, earth, everything about and above was indescribably still; and he experienced that quaking of the heart that seems to portend the approach of something awful. He would have set out upon his return across the moor, had he not an undefined presentiment that he was waylaid by something he dared not pass.

The old grey church and tower of Shackleton stood like a shadow in the rear. His eye had grown accustomed to the obscurity, and he could just trace its outline. There were no comforting associations in his mind connected with it; nothing but menace and misgiving. His early training in his lawless calling was connected with this very spot. Here his father used to meet two other poachers, and bring his son, then but a boy, with him.

Under the church porch, towards morning, they used to divide the game they had taken, and take account of the sales they had made on the previous day, and make partition of the money, and drink their gin. It was here he had taken his early lessons in drinking, cursing, and lawlessness. His father's grave was hardly eight steps from the spot where he stood. In his present state of awful dejection, no scene on earth could have so helped to heighten his fear.

There was one object close by which added to his gloom. About a yard away, in rear of the tree, behind himself, and extending to his left, was an open grave, the mould and rubbish piled on the other side. At the head of this grave stood the beech-tree; its columnar stem rose like a huge monumental pillar. He knew every line and crease on its smooth surface. The initial letters of his own name, cut in its bark long ago, had spread out and wrinkled like the grotesque capitals of a fanciful engraver, and now with a sinister significance overlooked the open grave, as if answering his mental question, "Who for is t' grave cut?"

He felt still a little stunned, and there was a faint tremor in his joints that disinclined him to exert himself; and, further, he had a vague apprehension that take what direction he might, there was danger around him worse than that of staying where he was.

On a sudden the stars began to blink more fiercely, a faint wild light overspread for a minute the bleak landscape, and he saw approaching from the moor a figure at a kind of swinging trot, with now and then a zig-zag hop or two, such as men accustomed to cross such places make, to avoid the patches of slob or quag that meet them here and there. This figure resembled his father's, and like him, whistled through his finger by way of signal as he approached; but the whistle sounded not now shrilly and sharp, as in old times, but immensely far away, and seemed to sing strangely through Tom's head. From habit or from fear, in answer to the signal, Tom whistled as he used to do five-and-twenty years ago and more, although he was already chilled with an unearthly fear.

Like his father, too, the figure held up the bag that was in his left hand as he drew near, when it was his custom to call out to him what was in it. It did not reassure the watcher, you may be certain, when a shout unnaturally faint reached him, as the phantom dangled the bag in the air, and he heard with a faint distinctness the words, "Tom Chuff's soul!"

Scarcely fifty yards away from the low churchyard fence at which Tom was standing, there was a wider chasm in the peat, which there threw up a growth of reeds and bulrushes, among which, as the old poacher used to do on a sudden alarm, the approaching figure suddenly cast itself down.

From the same patch of tall reeds and rushes emerged instantaneously what he at first mistook for the same figure creeping on all-fours, but what he soon perceived to be an enormous black dog with a rough coat like a bear's, which at first sniffed about, and then started towards him in what seemed to be a sportive amble, bouncing this way and that, but as it drew near it displayed a pair of fearful eyes that glowed like live coals, and emitted from the monstrous expanse of its jaws a terrifying growl.

This beast seemed on the point of seizing him, and Tom recoiled in panic and fell into the open grave behind him. The edge which he caught as he tumbled gave way, and down he went, expecting almost at the same instant to reach the bottom. But never was such a fall! Bottomless seemed the abyss! Down, down, down, with immeasurable and still increasing speed, through utter darkness, with hair streaming straight upward, breathless, he shot with a rush of air against him, the force of which whirled up his very arms, second after second, minute after minute, through the chasm downward he flew, the icy perspiration of horror covering his body, and suddenly, as he expected to be dashed into annihilation, his descent was in an instant arrested with a tremendous shock, which, however, did not deprive him of consciousness even for a moment.

He looked about him. The place resembled a smoke-stained cavern or catacomb, the roof of which, except for a ribbed arch here and there faintly visible, was lost in darkness. From several rude passages, like the galleries of a gigantic mine, which opened from this centre chamber, was very dimly emitted a dull glow as of charcoal, which was the only light by which he could imperfectly discern the objects immediately about him.

What seemed like a projecting piece of the rock, at the corner of one of these murky entrances, moved on a sudden, and proved to be a human figure, that beckoned to him. He approached, and saw his father. He could barely recognise him, he was so monstrously altered.

"I've been looking for you, Tom. Welcome home, lad; come along to your place."

Tom's heart sank as he heard these words, which were spoken in a hollow and, he thought, derisive voice that made him tremble. But he could not help accompanying the wicked spirit, who led him into a place, in passing which he heard, as it were from within the rock, deadful cries and appeals for mercy.

"What is this?" said he.

"Never mind."

"Who are they?"

"New-comers, like yourself, lad," answered his father apathetically. "They give over that work in time, finding it is no use."

"What shall I do?" said Tom, in an agony.

"It's all one."

"But what shall I do?" reiterated Tom, quivering in every joint and nerve.

"Grin and bear it, I suppose."

"For God's sake, if ever you cared for me, as I am your own child, let me out of this!"

"There's no way out."

"If there's a way in there's a way out, and for Heaven's sake let me out of this."

But the dreadful figure made no further answer, and glided backwards by his shoulder to the rear; and others appeared in view, each with a faint red halo round it, staring on him with frightful eyes, images, all in hideous variety, of eternal fury or derision. He was growing mad, it seemed, under the stare of so many eyes, increasing in number and drawing closer every moment, and at the same time myriads and myriads of voices were calling him by his name, some far away, some near, some from one point, some from another, some from behind, close to his ears.

These cries were increased in rapidity and multitude, and mingled with laughter, with flitting blasphemies, with broken insults and mockeries, succeeded and obliterated by others, before he could half catch their meaning.

All this time, in proportion to the rapidity and urgency of these dreadful sights and sounds, the epilepsy of terror was creeping up to his brain, and with a long and dreadful scream he lost consciousness.

When he recovered his senses, he found himself in a small stone chamber, vaulted above, and with a ponderous door. A single point of light in the wall, with a strange brilliancy illuminated this cell.

Seated opposite to him was a venerable man with a snowy beard of immense length; an image of awful purity and severity. He was dressed in a coarse robe, with three large keys suspensed from his girdle. He might have filled one's idea of an ancient porter of a city gate; such spiritual cities, I should say, as John Bunyan loved to describe.

This old man's eyes were brilliant and awful, and fixed on him as they were, Tom Chuff felt himself helplessly in his power. At length he spoke:

"The command is given to let you forth for one trial more. But if you are found again drinking with the drunken, and beating your fellow-servants, you shall return through the door by which you came, and go out no more."

With these words the old man took him by the wrist and led him through the first door, and then unlocking one that stood in the cavern outside, he struck Tom Chuff sharply on the shoulder, and the door shut behind him with a sound that boomed peal after peal of thunder near and far away, and all round and above, till it rolled off gradually into silence. It was totally dark, but there was a fanning of fresh cool air that overpowered him. He felt that he was in the upper world again.

In a few minutes he began to hear voices which he knew, and first a faint point of light appeared before his eyes, and gradually he saw the flame of the candle, and, after that, the familiar faces of his wife and children, and he heard them faintly when they spoke to him, although he was as yet unable to answer.

He also saw the doctor, like an isolated figure in the dark, and heard him say:

"There, now, you have him back. He'll do, I think."

His first words, when he could speak and saw clearly all about him, and felt the blood on his neck and shirt, were:

"Wife, forgie me. I'm a changed man. Send for't sir."

Which last phrase means, "Send for the clergyman."

When the vicar came and entered the little bedroom where the scared poacher, whose soul had died within him, was lying, still sick and weak, in his bed, and with a spirit that was prostrate with terror, Tom Chuff feebly beckoned the rest from the room, and, the door being closed, the good parson heard the strange confession, and with equal amazement the man's earnest and agitated vows of amendment, and his helpless appeals to him for support and counsel.

These, of course, were kindly met; and the visits of the rector, for sometime, were frequent.

One day, when he took Tom Chuff's hand on bidding him goodbye, the sick man held it still, and said:

"Ye'r vicar o' Shackleton, sir, and if I sud dee, ye'll promise me a'e thing, as I a promised ye a many. I a said I'll never gie wife, nor barn, nor folk o' no sort, skelp nor sizzup more, and ye'll know o' me no more among the sipers. Nor never will Tom draw trigger, nor set a snare again, but in an honest way, and after that ye'll no make it a bootless bene for me, but bein', as I say, vicar o' Shackleton, and able to do as ye list, ye'll no let them bury me within twenty good yerd-wands measure o' the a'd beech trees that's round the churchyard of Shackleton."

"I see; you would have your grave, when your time really comes, a good way from the place where lay the grave you dreamed of."

"That's jest it. I'd lie at the bottom o' a marl-pit liefer! And I'd be laid in anither churchyard just to be shut o' my fear o' that, but that a' my kinsfolk is buried beyond in Shackleton, and ye'll gie me yer promise, and no break yer word."

"I do promise, certainly. I'm not likely to outlive you; but, if I should, and still be vicar of Shackleton, you shall be buried somewhere as near the middle of the churchyard as we can find space."

"That'll do."

And so content they parted.

The effect of the vision upon Tom Chuff was powerful, and promised to be lasting. With a sore effort he exchanged his life of desultory adventure and comparative idleness for one of regular industry. He gave up drinking; he was as kind as an originally surly nature would allow to his wife and family; he went to church; in fine weather they crossed the moor to Shackleton Church; the vicar said he came there to look at the scenery of his vision, and to fortify his good resolutions by the reminder.

Impressions upon the imagination, however, are but transitory, and a bad man acting under fear is not a free agent; his real character does not appear. But as the images of the imagination fade, and the action of fear abates, the essential qualities of the man reassert themselves.

So, after a time, Tom Chuff began to grow weary of his new life; he grew lazy, and people began to say that he was catching hares, and pursuing his old contraband way of life, under the rose.

He came home one hard night, with signs of the bottle in his thick speech and violent temper. Next day he was sorry, or frightened, at all events repentant, and for a week or more something of the old horror returned, and he was once more on his good behaviour. But in a little time came a relapse, and another repentance, and then a relapse again, and gradually the return of old habits and the flooding in of all his old way of life, with more violence and gloom, in proportion as the man was alarmed and exasperated by the remembrance of his despised, but terrible, warning.

With the old life returned the misery of the cottage. The smiles, which had begun to appear with the unwonted sunshine, were seen no more. Instead, returned to his poor wife's face the old pale and heartbroken look. The cottage lost its neat and cheerful air, and the melancholy of neglect was visible. Sometimes at night were overheard, by a chance passer-by, cries and sobs from that ill-omened dwelling. Tom Chuff was now often drunk, and not very often at home, except when he came in to sweep away his poor wife's earnings.

Tom had long lost sight of the honest old parson. There was shame mixed with his degradation. He had grace enough left when he saw the thin figure of "t' sir" walking along the road to turn out of his way and avoid meeting him. The clergyman shook his head, and sometimes groaned, when his name was mentioned. His horror and regret were more for the poor wife than for the relapsed sinner, for her case was pitiable indeed.

Her brother, Jack Everton, coming over from Hexley, having heard stories of all this, determined to beat Tom, for his ill-treatment of his sister, within an inch of his life. Luckily, perhaps, for all concerned, Tom happened to be away upon one of his long excursions, and poor Nell besought her brother, in extremity of terror, not to interpose between them. So he took his leave and went home muttering and sulky.

Now it happened a few months later that Nelly Chuff fell sick. She had been ailing, as heartbroken people do, for a good while. But now the end had come.

There was a coroner's inquest when she died, for the doctor had doubts as to whether a blow had not, at least, hastened her death. Nothing certain, however, came of the inquiry. Tom Chuff had left his home more than two days before his wife's death. He was absent upon his lawless business still when the coroner had held his quest.

Jack Everton came over from Hexley to attend the dismal obsequies of his sister. He was more incensed than ever with the wicked husband, who, one way or other, had hastened Nelly's death. The inquest had closed early in the day. The husband had not appeared.

An occasional companion—perhaps I ought to say accomplice—of Chuff's happened to turn up. He had left him on the borders of Westmoreland, and said he would probably be home next day. But Everton affected not to believe it. Perhaps it was to Tom Chuff, he suggested, a secret satisfaction to crown the history of his bad married life with the scandal of his absence from the funeral of his neglected and abused wife.

Everton had taken on himself the direction of the melancholy preparations. He had ordered a grave to be opened for his sister beside her mother's, in Shackleton churchyard, at the other side of the moor. For the purpose, as I have said, of marking the callous neglect of her husband, he determined that the funeral should take place that night. His brother Dick had accompanied him, and they and his sister, with Mary and the children, and a couple of the neighbours, formed the humble cortège.

Jack Everton said he would wait behind, on the chance of Tom Chuff coming in time, that he might tell him what had happened, and make him cross the moor with him to meet the funeral. His real object, I think, was to inflict upon the villain the drubbing he had so long wished to give him. Anyhow, he was resolved, by crossing the moor, to reach the churchyard in time to anticipate the arrival of the funeral, and to have a few words with the vicar, clerk, and sexton, all old friends of his, for the parish of Shackleton was the place of his birth and early recollections.

But Tom Chuff did not appear at his house that night. In surly mood, and without a shilling in his pocket, he was making his way homeward. His bottle of gin, his last investment, half emptied, with its neck protruding, as usual on such returns, was in his coat-pocket.

His way home lay across the moor of Catstean, and the point at which he best knew the passage was from the churchyard of Shackleton. He vaulted the low wall that forms its boundary, and strode across the graves, and over many a flat, half-buried tombstone, toward the side of the churchyard next Catstean Moor.

The old church of Shackleton and its tower rose, close at his right, like a black shadow against the sky. It was a moonless night, but clear. By this time he had reached the low boundary wall, at the other side, that overlooks the wide expanse of Catstean Moor. He stood by one of the huge old beech-trees, and leaned his back to its smooth trunk. Had he ever seen the sky look so black, and the stars shine out and blink so vividly? There was a deathlike silence over the scene, like the hush that precedes thunder in sultry weather. The expanse before him was lost in utter blackness. A strange quaking unnerved his heart. It was the sky and scenery of his vision! The same horror and misgiving. The same invincible fear of venturing from the spot where he stood. He would have prayed if he dared. His sinking heart demanded a restorative of some sort, and he grasped the bottle in his coat-pocket. Turning to his left, as he did so, he saw the piled-up mould of an open grave that gaped with its head close to the base of the great tree against which he was leaning.

He stood aghast. His dream was returning and slowly enveloping him. Everything he saw was weaving itself into the texture of his vision. The chill of horror stole over him.

A faint whistle came shrill and clear over the moor, and he saw a figure approaching at a swinging trot, with a zig-zag course, hopping now here and now there, as men do over a surface where one has need to choose their steps. Through the jungle of reeds and bulrushes in the foreground this figure advanced; and with the same unaccountable impulse that had coerced him in his dream, he answered the whistle of the advancing figure.

On that signal it directed its course straight toward him. It mounted the low wall, and, standing there, looked into the graveyard.

"Who med answer?" challenged the new-comer from his post of observation.

"Me," answered Tom.

"Who are you?" repeated the man upon the wall.

"Tom Chuff; and who's this grave cut for?" He answered in a savage tone, to cover the secret shudder of his panic.

"I'll tell you that, ye villain!" answered the stranger, descending from the wall, "I a' looked for you far and near, and waited long, and now you're found at last."

Not knowing what to make of the figure that advanced upon him, Tom Chuff recoiled, stumbled, and fell backward into the open grave. He caught at the sides as he fell, but without retarding his fall.

An hour later, when lights came with the coffin, the corpse of Tom Chuff was found at the bottom of the grave. He had fallen direct upon his head, and his neck was broken. His death must have been simultaneous with his fall. Thus far his dream was accomplished.

It was his brother-in-law who had crossed the moor and approached the churchyard of Shackleton, exactly in the line which the image of his father had seemed to take in his strange vision. Fortunately for Jack Everton, the sexton and clerk of Shackleton church were, unseen by him, crossing the churchyard toward the grave of Nelly Chuff, just as Tom the poacher stumbled and fell. Suspicion of direct violence would otherwise have inevitably attached to the exasperated brother. As it was, the catastrophe was followed by no legal consequences.

The good vicar kept his word, and the grave of Tom Chuff is still pointed out by the old inhabitants of Shackleton pretty nearly in the centre of the churchyard. This conscientious compliance with the entreaty of the panic-stricken man as to the place of his sepulture gave a horrible and mocking emphasis to the strange combination by which fate had defeated his precaution, and fixed the place of his death.

The story was for many a year, and we believe still is, told round many a cottage hearth, and though it appeals to what many would term superstition, it yet sounded, in the ears of a rude and simple audience, a thrilling, and let us hope, not altogether fruitless homily.

A Note About the Author

Joseph Sheridan Le Fanu (1814–1873) was an Irish writer of Gothic horror. Born in Dublin, Le Fanu was raised in a literary family. His mother, a biographer, and his father, a clergyman, encouraged his intellectual development from a young age. He began writing poetry at fifteen and went on to excel at Trinity College, Dublin, where he studied law and served as Auditor of the College Historical Society. In 1838, shortly before he was called to the bar, he began contributing ghost stories to the *Dublin University Magazine*, of which he later became editor and proprietor. He embarked on a career as a writer and journalist, using his role at the magazine as a means of publishing his own fictional work. Le Fanu made a name for himself as a pioneer of mystery and Gothic horror with such novels as *The House by the Churchyard* (1863) and *Uncle Silas* (1864). *Carmilla* (1872), a novella, is considered an early work of vampire fiction and an important influence for Bram Stoker's *Dracula* (1897).

A Note from the Publisher

Spanning many genres, from non-fiction essays to literature classics to children's books and lyric poetry, Mint Edition books showcase the master works of our time in a modern new package. The text is freshly typeset, is clean and easy to read, and features a new note about the author in each volume. Many books also include exclusive new introductory material. Every book boasts a striking new cover, which makes it as appropriate for collecting as it is for gift giving. Mint Edition books are only printed when a reader orders them, so natural resources are not wasted. We're proud that our books are never manufactured in excess and exist only in the exact quantity they need to be read and enjoyed. To learn more and view our library, go to minteditionbooks.com

bookfinity & MINT EDITIONS

Enjoy more of your favorite classics with Bookfinity,
a new search and discovery experience for readers.
With Bookfinity, you can discover more vintage
literature for your collection, find your Reader Type,
track books you've read or want to read,
and add reviews to your favorite books.
Visit www.bookfinity.com, and click on
Take the Quiz to get started.

Don't forget to follow us
@bookfinityofficial and @mint_editions